Stephen Deas

THE
MOONSTEEL
CROWN

**ANGRY
ROBOT**

ANGRY ROBOT
An imprint of Watkins Media Ltd

Unit 11, Shepperton House
89-93 Shepperton Road
London N1 3DF
UK

angryrobotbooks.com
twitter.com/angryrobotbooks
All for One and One for All

An Angry Robot paperback original, 2021

Cover by Karen Smith
Edited by Eleanor Teasdale and Paul Simpson
Maps by Kieryn Tyler
Set in Meridien

ISBN 978 0 85766 876 9
Ebook ISBN 978 0 85766 877 6

Printed and bound in the United Kingdom by TJ Books

9 8 7 6 5 4 3 2 1

MIX
Paper from
responsible sources
FSC
www.fsc.org   FSC® C013056

For Nigel, Matt, Sam, Ali, Pete, Tony & Michaela

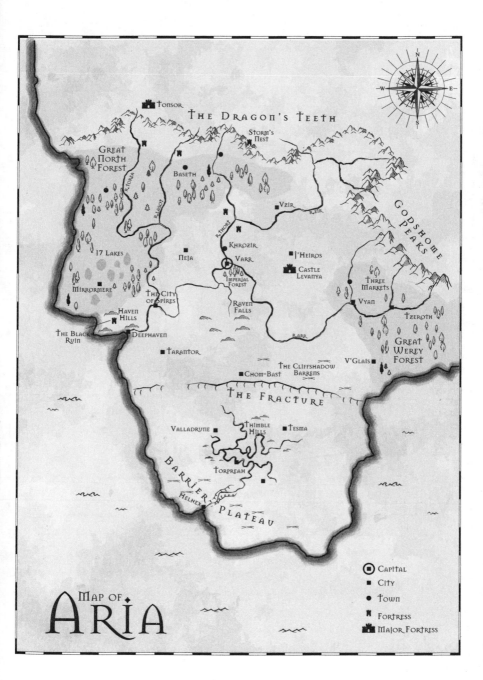

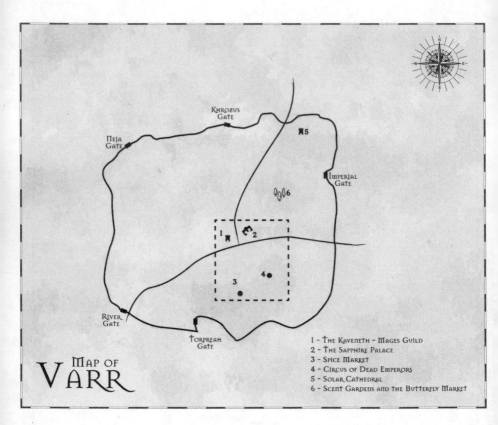

MAP OF VARR

1 – THE KAVENETH – MAGES GUILD
2 – THE SAPPHIRE PALACE
3 – SPICE MARKET
4 – CIRCUS OF DEAD EMPERORS
5 – SOLAR CATHEDRAL
6 – SCENT GARDENS AND THE BUTTERFLY MARKET

KHROZUS GATE
NEJA GATE
IMPERIAL GATE
RIVER GATE
TORPREAH GATE

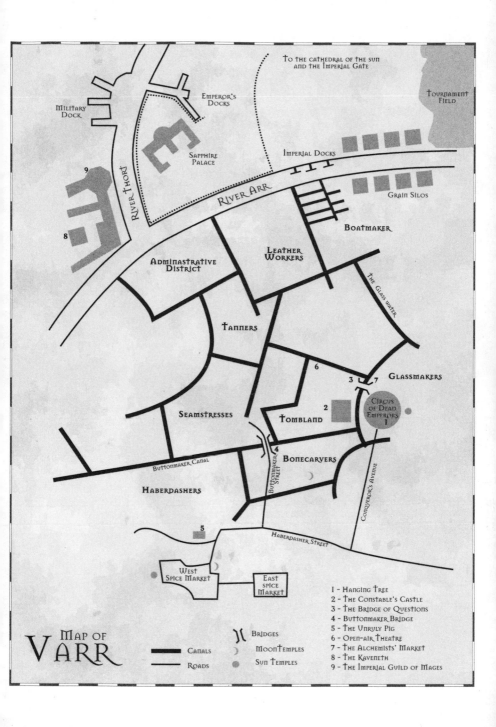

MAP OF
VARR

To the cathedral of the sun
and the Imperial Gate

MILITARY
DOCK

EMPEROR'S
DOCKS

TOURNAMENT
FIELD

RIVER THORT

SAPPHIRE
PALACE

IMPERIAL DOCKS

9

RIVER ARR

GRAIN SILOS

8

BOATMAKER

ADMINASTRATIVE
DISTRICT

LEATHER
WORKERS

THE GLASS WATER

TANNERS

6

3 7 GLASSMAKERS

2

CIRCUS
OF DEAD
EMPERORS
1

SEAMSTRESSES

TOMBLAND

BUTTONMAKER CANAL

4

BONECARVERS

BUTTONMAKER STREET

CONQUEROR'S AVENUE

HABERDASHERS

5

HABERDASHER STREET

WEST
SPICE MARKET

EAST
SPICE
MARKET

1 – HANGING TREE
2 – THE CONSTABLE'S CASTLE
3 – THE BRIDGE OF QUESTIONS
4 – BUTTONMAKER BRIDGE
5 – THE UNRULY PIG
6 – OPEN-AIR THEATRE
7 – THE ALCHEMISTS' MARKET
8 – THE KAVENETH
9 – THE IMPERIAL GUILD OF MAGES

CANALS
ROADS

BRIDGES
MOONTEMPLES
SUN TEMPLES

You can't magic away what you don't see coming.
— Sulfane

I

SETH

"Pastries! Pastries! Lovely fresh pastries!" Seth waved his tray of stale pastries left over from last night's kitchen in the Unruly Pig with increasingly forlorn hope. The Sulk had the city of Varr in its grasp like a butcher about to throttle a chicken, the air a crisp murderous cold that made Seth's lungs ache. It was the middle of the afternoon and already the shadows from the brooding cliffs of the Kaveneth reached across the tournament field. The crowd had thinned to knots and clusters huddled around bonfires, where they bought roasted nuts and cups of hot, spiced wine as an excuse to stay near the warmth. It was the same every winter: the long silent smothering of cold, the three or four months spent desperately trying not to freeze. The rich and titled fled to Tarantor or Torpreah for the winter, where everyone could get on with their intrigues, plots and occasional stabbings without the added inconvenience of frostbite. Anyone too poor to get away was hiding stashes of firewood, bracing themselves in case they had to fight to the death to defend them.

If you were poor, frankly, winter in Varr was a bit shit. *How* shit, Seth realised, was something he'd almost forgotten. Unfortunately, he looked set to be reminded.

"Pastries! Pastries! Lovely fresh pastries!" He watched, envious of the fires. For the sake of appearances, one of the Imperial family usually held out until after Midwinter before they ran for warmer climes, but this year? Midwinter was still a month away and none of the bastards had stayed, not a single one. True, there *had* been more stabbings than usual – Seth had it on good authority that the emperor's own brother had been murdered, possibly by a demon thing that walked through walls but more likely by his cousin.

He'd make up a story, he decided. Spread it around and see if he could trade it for a few bits, how the Emperor's cousin had disguised himself as a minstrel and then garrotted the prince with an enchanted lute-string, one laced with wyvern's blood to keep the moon-priestesses from divining the truth. Something like that only better, because, frankly, that was about all that the lords and ladies of the Empire mattered to people like Seth. They could do as much plotting and stabbing as they liked, but when all the plotting and stabbing happened somewhere else, it meant not as many people showed up to the winter tournaments, which meant not as many people grumbling about the cold while they bought Seth's pastries.

"Pastries! Pastries!" He was wasting his time. Anyone with sense had already fled to shiver in the comfort of their own home.

You didn't expect the *Emperor* to stay, of course. Usually it was his brother, although even Seth had to grudgingly accept that being dead was a passable excuse for Prince Halvren not showing his face. The Emperor's cousin, Prince Sharda, would have been a crowd-pleaser, if only for the frisson every time he opened his mouth in case he accidentally started a war. Actually, he'd heard rumours rumbling out of the Kaveneth that a war might be exactly what was coming. Seth had no idea why or whom the empire was planning to fight, exactly, since there really wasn't anywhere left for it to go except across the sea and the Empire didn't have much in the way of ships. Itself, probably. It had been more than three decades since the last war, after all, when Khrozus the Liberator – or Khrozus the Butcher, epithet dependent on your point of view – had seized the throne.

There was the Emperor's daughter, of course. Would people have come out to see the royal witch before she came of age or would they have stayed at home? Probably they'd have come in droves. Seth knew all too well how gawping and morbid fascination mostly got the better of common sense.

"Pastries! Get your..." *Oh, give up.*

Why? Somewhere better you could be?

Shut up. Ma Fings would always give him a scrap of floor, but that meant squeezing in with Fings' family and dealing with unwanted advances from probably at least two of Fings' sisters. The alternative was begging a corner in the kitchens at the Unruly Pig, as he usually did, where Blackhand would inevitably want something in return. It *would* be the Pig, though, because the Pig had Myla, which at least meant a chance of some intelligent conversation, at least until she was drunk. They could agree on how everyone with a title in front of their name could stab each other until they were all dead and how the world would be a better place for it, and she'd share her wine, and probably let him sleep on her floor. He had time for Myla.

Yes. Because she doesn't mind you being a parasite.

"Pastries! Get your pastries!" *Oh, fuck off.*

They'd been stale before he started. Now they were either soggy and tooth-jarringly cold or actually frozen solid. He wasn't sure which and wasn't keen to find out. His feet and his fingers weren't much better, either. His tattered boots were soaked through and starting to freeze. To add insult to injury, tantalising smells wafted from the Provisioners' Guild tent. Fresh bread and hot sausage grease and spiced wine and stewed pears. They had a fire in there too, and canvas to keep in the warmth...

"Pastries! Lovely fresh pastries...!" No one was even listening.

Wasting my time.

He looked around and spotted Fings slipping through the dwindling crowds. Put Fings in a crowd and all you had to do was stand back and watch while other people's money made its way into his pockets with a will all of its own. Fings saw him looking, waved and started to head over, and Seth was half tempted to turn and run. Fings would inevitably leave him with a handful of bits, enough to buy a hot meal; and Seth knew he ought to be grateful, except Fings would say something trite and facile and cheery and stupid while he was at it, and Seth would have to bite his own tongue not to punch him in the face, which was probably just as well, because he'd only end up doing himself an injury.

"Pastries! Pastries! Shit in a bun! Soggy crap with ice on it!" The light was fading, the air already freezing to his face. Anyone still here was desperate, broke and trying to sell something. And yet he *didn't* turn and run, because Fings *would* give him money, and right now he had nothing, and the Sulk was barely starting.

"Any of that worth eating? I'm starving." Fings sidled up and gave him a nod.

"Fresh as the day they were baked. Filled with exotic Southern spices," said Seth absently. They stood side by side, looking over the archery field, still as white and pristine as it had been in the morning.

"It wasn't Sara in the kitchen last night, was it?" Fings frowned. "Last time I had anything of hers, it was a week before I was right again."

"Don't think so."

Fings eyed the sad remains on Seth's tray and helped himself. "Nice girl, but…" he shook his head.

"I should have sold horse shit today." Seth let Fings see the miserable handful of clipped bits that were his entire worldly wealth. "At least you can burn horse shit, if you let it dry. People pay for that, you know."

"If it was Sara in the kitchen last night, you probably *were* selling horse shit." Fings offered his purse to Seth. "Help yourself."

Mostly it was clipped bits but there were a few crowns and… Seth reached in and pulled out a coin. Silver. Proper real silver. Somehow Fings, jammy bastard that he was, had landed a precious silver moon. Not an eighth or a quarter but a whole full-moon. Food for a month, that was, if you were careful.

"Yeah." Fings looked at the silver moon dubiously and wrinkled his nose. "Need to get rid of that."

"Where did you... How...?"

"You ever get the feeling there's a set of chains up there with your name on them?" Fings was looking down the river, up to the black bulk of the Kaveneth. "Some mage in the darkness, searching around, picking you out? Some guardsman on the ramparts, looking for you?" He took another pastry,

"Not really, and that's my livelihood you're eating there."

Fings snatched back his purse and his silver moon, and tossed a couple of bits to Seth. "How's the Murdering Bastard doing?"

Seth shook his head. "Badly."

"Pity."

"Really?" The Murdering Bastard's actual name was Sulfane. He'd shown up at the Unruly Pig a month ago and somehow had Blackhand wrapped around his little finger. He was, as they'd all found out, really quite good at shooting people with his bow. Just a bit... well, indiscriminate was probably about the nicest way to put it.

Fings peered across the snow. "You keep banging on how there's a war coming. Much better chance he'll get killed if he's off fighting in it rather than sitting around the Pig making *our* lives miserable." Wars were things that happened to other people, as far as Fings was concerned.

"Your wish may be granted. Blackhand wants me to forge a letter from some obscure lord no one's ever heard of that'll get your Murdering Bastard into the Emperor's Guard."

"You can do that?"

"Of course I can!"

"You going to?"

Seth caught Fings' eye. When he was quite sure he had it, he dragged it to his tray of sodden pastries and then gave Fings a baleful look. "Blackhand asked nicely. What do you think?"

What he *could* have been doing – what he *should* have been doing if his life hadn't abruptly turned into an ash-heap six months ago – was sitting in the nice warm undercroft of a nice cosy temple in front of a nice hot fire. What he *should* have been doing was putting his feet up, toasting his toes, sipping warm spiced wine and chewing the fat with other senior novices and junior priests, discussing politics, theology, and which of the fat old Lightbringers who lorded it over them was the most likely to drop dead before winter ended. He missed that. Truth be told, he missed that a lot.

"Don't read the forbidden books." What do you do? Read the forbidden books. *"Don't sneak into the forbidden crypt."* What do you do? Fuck about in the forbidden crypt. *"Definitely don't go into the forbidden catacombs."* What do you do? Not that they'd caught him on the last one.

Of course, no one had *said* that all these things were forbidden, exactly. That was the galling part. A novice was simply supposed to know by some trick of divine telepathy, and then be a good little cleric and not do them.

But you did *know. You knew perfectly well.*

All he'd ever wanted was to serve the Sun. To understand the four Divinities.

Yes, and if you'd managed to do as you were bloody well told for five minutes, maybe that's exactly what would have happened, eh? What you wanted, you cretin, was a little patience.

The end of a lifetime of dreams. There wasn't even a shred of injustice to it. Warning after warning and he hadn't stopped. Didn't even know why, not really. He just… couldn't.

"I hope you're fleecing him," said Fings.

Across the archery field, Sulfane was running from the stump of a tree. Seth watched as he vaulted onto a low platform and fired at one of the targets. He looked very determined. Dynamic. Intense. All good qualities a soldier was supposed to have, Seth supposed. He wasn't sure where being as mad as a bag of spiders fitted, whether that was good or bad or whether it simply didn't matter when you were standing in front of a thousand armoured horses bearing down on you at a gallop. Probably helped, didn't it?

"I said I hope you're fleecing him."

"Blackhand? You must be joking."

"Not Blackhand you idiot. The Murdering Bastard."

Seth shrugged. "You want him gone, I want him gone, Blackhand wants him in the guard, that's how we get rid of him." He took a deep breath and let out a weary sigh. "You know Blackhand – like a pig rooting for truffles when he thinks there's money about. Start of a new and profitable partnership he says, not that the likes of you or I will see our lives any sweeter." He pulled the tray of pastries away as Fings snaffled another one. "You and I, brother, we have the same problem. We're cowards, Fings. That's what we are."

2

MYLA

Myla crashed into the wall, felt wooden panels bend under the impact, and launched herself through the open door. Snow flew from her feet as the night air hit her. She felt the world close in, the ornamental gardens compressing into a dark tunnel, her at one end, Dinn and Arjay ahead, running down the last of the Spicers through the winter snow.

"Don't let him get away!" Wil was close behind with Brick and Dox. Somewhere, trailing at the back, was Blackhand.

The Spicers *weren't* going to get away. They were bolting for a gate which she and Dinn had tied shut ten minutes ago. It wouldn't hold for long, but it wouldn't need to.

How to end this without it getting bloody? The old skinny one wouldn't be a problem, nor the chubby one, but the other three... Two dark-skinned locals, all brawn and muscles, and a pale-skinned lad with a sword. Young, too. The sort of men who hadn't yet found themselves on the wrong end of a fight. The trouble with men like that was that they didn't understand when they were beaten. Made it hard to take them down without hurting them.

The one with the sword. Him first. If she could take him out of the fight fast, the other two might falter. He was from the south. Deephaven, maybe, like her, or possibly Torpreah, so maybe he'd be willing to talk. He was taking coin from the Spicers, that was all. She could appeal to his sense as a mercenary.

Of course, it didn't help that Blackhand kept shouting out from the back, things like *Gut them!* and *Maim the fuckers!* and *I want him skinned and his head on a fucking pike!* Didn't exactly set the best of tones for a negotiated surrender, that.

She skidded around a corner, sliding on compacted snow towards a pair of rickety shacks as the Spicers dashed between them and down the waiting alley, straight towards Dinn's tied-shut gate.

Keep Chubby and let the others go? The old skinny one would take that and be grateful. Blackhand would be livid but he wouldn't catch up in time to make a difference, and no one in their right mind argued with a sword-monk, even with a lapsed one who'd crashed out of training and drank too much.

"Look out!"

"Shit!"

The shacks were collapsing, their flimsy walls exploding outward in a cloud of snow, and then suddenly there were two shambling figures standing in Myla's path as Dinn and Arjay ran past. They stepped forward, blocking her way, and the right thing to do was to dance around them, past them, through them somehow, leave them to Wil and Dox and Brick while she stayed close to Dinn and Arjay, but there was something wrong about the way these two stood…

Dead Men.

She snatched a glance over her shoulder. More figures were emerging from the darkness around the edges of the garden. Three, four, maybe more. Like the two in front of her, they were slow and ponderous. She felt a shiver that wasn't the cold and then a blaze of hungry righteous fury.

Dead Men!

"Myla!"

Dead Men. Corpses denied the light of the sun or running water or open skies. Souls trapped in murdered bodies, bound to dead flesh until the Hungry Goddess took them for an eternity of anguish. Blasphemy and heresy, the sort that would summon a mayhem of wrathful priests and sword-monks to send the dead on their way and the living to a short, hard life in the Imperial mines, if ever they knew.

Metal glinted from their hands. Someone had given them claws. Dead Men were easy to avoid if you could run away because they weren't fast and didn't last long in sunlight; but they were hard to take down in the dark if you didn't have fire, and once they got hold of you, they didn't let go...

Fire... or blades made of Sunsteel.

Sword-monk blades, in other words.

Myla grinned and lashed out. The first cut struck a wrist, slicing through in a warm flare of light. The second skewered the nearest corpse in the face. The Sunsteel edge slid through him as though he was made of butter and snapped the tether to his soul. She glanced to the clear sky and the stars and the fat waxing moon and whispered a prayer. Fickle Lord Moon would get this one, or maybe the Ever-Shifting Mistress of the Stars would steal him.

The second Dead Man barely noticed he was missing a hand. She took him from the side, both swords in deep, setting him free. This, more than anything, was what a sword-monk was for.

"Myla!" Wil again. Behind her, Wil and Dox and Brick had scattered. Four more Dead Men were shambling around the garden, too slow to be dangerous; but down the alley, the Spicers had reached the gate. Beyond lay Spice Market Square, a flat field of trampled snow where they could scatter and run to the Longcoats, or the even the Sunguard of the temple. Dinn and Arjay were facing off against them, two on five, and the pale-skinned man had a sword, a sword against sticks and knives...

She ran faster. The snow in the alley was deep enough to crest the top of her boots, deep enough to make her clumsy and slow. The walls around her seemed blacker and taller than they had in daylight. It felt like a place to die, this alley.

No one is going to die.

Skinny crashed into the gate and bounced back with a curse and a clutch of his shoulder. "It's tied!"

"Then cut it, you moron!" Of all of them, Chubby was right to be scared. Blackhand wasn't known for his mercy. "Cut it! Khrozus! He'll kill the lot of us."

"Stop!" Myla shouted. "No one has to die here!"

"Fuck you." The pale-skinned man drew his sword. Dinn, never the brightest, swung his stick. The pale-skinned man ducked and stabbed him through the neck.

"Dinn!" Arjay leapt forward as Dinn collapsed to his knees, clutching at the blood spraying from his throat.

"I know you, don't I?" The pale-skinned swordsman ignored Arjay, leaving her to the others, and came at Myla. "What were you saying about no one dying?"

A sell-sword out of Deephaven, same as her. It wasn't only his skin, it was the way he dressed, the way he held himself, the accent to his words. He came at her cautiously, sword glinting in the moonlight. A nice weapon, which meant money, either some rich-boy idiot slumming or else Chubby had paid for someone who actually knew what they were doing. The Spicers, like Blackhand's Unrulys, mostly did their fighting by shouting and waving sticks at each other until someone backed down. Not this one though. Whoever he was, Dinn's wasn't the first life he'd ended.

Skinny was at the gate, fumbling for a knife. Arjay was wrestling with the two other Spicers and Dinn was taking his time dying and making a right scene of it. Chubby's eyes danced from her to the gate and back again. All he needed were however many precious seconds it took for Skinny to cut the rope…

"Do I *have* to kill you?" she asked the swordsman. She hadn't wanted to, running after them. But right now, Dinn's blood fresh on the snow, listening to him thrash and gurgle out his last moments, she wasn't so sure.

The swordsman caught her eye. "You're Myla."

He knew her name, did he? Then he knew what she was and he ought to be afraid. Trouble was, when she met his eye, she saw only murder.

"Jeffa says hello."

Jeffa? What the fuck did Jeffa *have to do with–*

He came at her fast, taking that moment of surprise, swinging high. Myla dodged inside the blow, expecting him to jump away to keep his distance, but he stepped in close instead and stabbed at her with a dirk hidden in his other hand. The pattern of Myla's defence shattered. She improvised a parry and crashed into him, felt the mail under his coat, smelled hints of stale beer and cinnamon as breath exploded out of them both. He staggered but stayed up; Myla felt her thighs and knees strain and then the snow betrayed her. Instinct tucked her arms and head into her body, turning the fall into a roll.

Kelm's teeth! Watch your footing! Her face was full of snow, blinding her. It was in her hair, sliding down her neck, everywhere…

"Don't let the fuckers get away!" Blackhand's shout rang through the alley. Myla scrabbled to her feet and shook off the snow, straight into a defensive form, expecting the swordsman to be on her at once… but Brick was running at him now, Brick who was all bravado and no skill just like the rest of them, Brick who was going to lose, badly and quickly…

She liked Brick.

Skinny was hacking at the rope around the gate, frozen fingers making a pig's ear of it. Arjay was on the ground, the other two Spicer thugs apparently set on kicking her to death.

She liked Arjay, too.

Right then.

She ran at the Spicers on Arjay first, flailing her swords, scattering them into Chubby and Skinny. A slash at Skinny cut his arm and sent the knife spinning out of his hand and then she whirled away as the swordsman lunged at Brick, stabbing him hard in the chest and sprawling him flat on his back.

Jeffa says hello.

What the *fuck* was Jeffa Hawat doing in Varr?

The swordsman turned to face her. A heavy leather coat hid his physique and the mail underneath, but he was strong, she knew that now, and held his blade with a loose, easy grip. He knew what he was doing.

The Dragon's Tail, then. The form came by instinct, a flick at the tip of his sword to knock it aside, anticipating his recovery, feinting, blocking the inevitable counter and then a rush. He pushed her aside and stepped sharply back but neither was enough; as she ran past, she bashed him in the head and twisted and reached low, slashing the hook of her second sword at his retreating ankle. She pulled the cut at the last. She didn't want to take his whole foot, only his enthusiasm.

The form completed. She turned, expecting to see him on the ground, but no, he was coming at her, a snarling frenzy, poise gone, hammering blow after blow, pain and indignation welded into fury. She slipped into the Wall of Seventeen Claws but his sheer savagery shattered it. A swing came in hard enough to split her to the spine. When she blocked it, the shock sent a jolt of pain through her elbow. She felt something give in her shoulder.

Speed, not your swords, will protect you. You must think only of attack, attack, attack. If you hesitate, you will fail. Sky Strikes the Earth. Begin.

A turning step forward, right sword swinging low, snapping a cut to the groin. A sweep at his ankles and then she dropped. A flick of the wrist for extra speed, an unexpected rising cut as he flailed for balance and she caught him cleanly at the wrist, severing his hand.

Dinn finally planted himself face down in the snow, red all around him, and stopped moving. Behind her, Brick was honking for air like a dying goose.

Fuck you.

A half-step forward, both swords in wild converging arcs. A moment of pure focus as the form completed into a deep stance, knee bent at a right angle, the other leg trailing behind her, swords spread wide to the stars...

The swordsman's head landed in the snow beside her. A rain of blood spattered over the alley, bright red on pristine white. Somewhere far away, Wil was shouting. She heard a shriek.

He could have told you about Jeffa.

Shit.

The head stared up at her from the snow. Eyes wide and open. She felt her old sword-mistress looking on. Bitter, mistrustful and deadly Tasahre. *Sword-monks exist to put down abominations. No hesitation, no doubt, no second chances. An ordinary man? A single look should be all it takes.*

Wil and Dox barged past, brandishing blades at the remaining Spicers, forcing them away from Arjay. Chubby was shouting at them to fight, and Skinny too, and wasn't three on three fair odds?

The other Spicers were all just staring at her.

A single look should be all it takes.

Fine. She met their eyes, one by one, and held out her swords, dripping with blood. One by one, they dropped their weapons to the snow.

Jeffa says hello.

They'd found her, then. They'd followed her all this way and they'd found her, and she'd let anger get in the way of sense again, and now someone else was dead.

I need a drink.

Dox helped Arjay to her feet. Brick was on all fours and puking but at least he wasn't vomiting blood. Wil went for Chubby. Chubby lunged and Wil grabbed his wrist, twisted, took his knife off him, and that was that. Skinny didn't even resist, too busy staring at the headless corpse and all the dark blood-soaked snow. By the time Blackhand caught up, Arjay and Dox had Skinny and the other two Spicers backed against the gate. Wil had Chubby on his knees. Blackhand took it all in, the bloody snow, Dinn with his throat ripped open, the corpse of the sell-sword and his severed head.

"Dead Men and a sell-sword, eh?" He turned to Chubby. "I hope they cost you a fortune, you unwanted dose of cock-rot." He spat, then nodded to Wil. "Take him back to the house."

"What about these three?" asked Arjay, as Dox and Wil dragged Chubby away. She wasn't standing quite right after the kicking she'd taken.

Blackhand slapped her on the shoulder, hard enough that she winced. "Two of theirs for one of mine seems fair. Pick one and gut him. The other two get to live." He headed away, Brick limping after him. The two Spicer thugs pushed Skinny forward. Skinny dropped to his knees, wailing for mercy, while the others eyed Myla. For a few long seconds, they all stared at each other. In the end, Arjay shook her head. She went to the gate, cut Dinn's rope and threw it open.

"Fuck off, the lot of you. Don't ever come back."

Arjay limped away, giving them space, and it still took half a dozen heartbeats before the first of them moved, never taking his eyes from Myla until he was at the gate. When he turned and ran and nothing bad happened, the other two followed quick enough. Arjay flashed Myla a glare, then a glance at the dead sell-sword. *Your mess. You clean it up.* She headed after Blackhand.

Alone, Myla sank against the alley wall.

Where do I run to now?

She had no idea. Didn't want to think about it.

She was still sitting there, not thinking about it, when a scream from inside the house harrowed the night. Not long after, the Unrulys came back out. Blackhand looked pleased with himself. Wil looked stony.

"...and when that pig-faced offal-bucket in Tombland comes banging on the door, tell him to piss off back to selling sheep-shit in the Dung Markets. Everyone gets the message, right? If you want a piece of the Spice Market, you deal with the Unrulys or they fucking cut your bits off! Ain't that right?" He clapped Myla on the shoulder as he passed and then walked on as though she wasn't there, stepping over the headless corpse.

"You want us to do something about Dinn?" asked Dox.

"No, leave him for the Longcoats... Of course I bloody want you to do something about him, you cretin! Drop him in the river. The other idiot, too. Myla, Wil, deal with it. Arjay, you go with them. Make sure it's done right."

Wil growled something and shot a look at Myla. She knew

exactly why he looked at her the way he did, why they all looked at her that way, a bit of fear, a bit of scorn, a bit of envy, a bit of contempt. They looked at her that way because she was a monster.

I really *need a drink.*

Arjay stretched, trying to get the kinks out of her spine. "Dinn wasn't anyone's fault, Wil." She cocked her head at Myla. *Let's go.*

Myla turned away. "Not yet. Something I need to do."

The other Dead Men hadn't wandered far. She put them down one by one. Holy work, God's work, but she took no joy from it. All she saw was the severed head of the swordsman from Deephaven, looking up at her from the snow, and all she heard was his voice.

Jeffa says hello.

Shit.

3

FİΠGS

Fings stood with Seth on the edge of the tournament field, watching the Murdering Bastard shoot stuff. If anyone had bothered to ask, he would have said that the whole business with the Spicers had started with Sulfane. The Spice Market was Fings' home: he'd grown up in its streets and he felt the ebb and flow of its tensions as though they were his blood. For the last five years, since Blackhand had come back to Varr, the Unrulys had kept Haberdashers and the Western Spice Market in line, with the usual carrot and stick of bribes and beatings, while in the Eastern Market, the Spicers had done the same. And yes, there was the blurry space between where people occasionally got a kicking, and yes, now and then things got out of hand and someone ended up dead, but on the whole it worked. On the whole, both sides had kept the peace.

Right up until the moment the Murdering Bastard had walked in.

Blackhand, naturally, claimed the Spicers had started it. Mostly, the Unrulys pretended to believe him: he *was* Black Alarand, after all, the man who'd taken down the Mage of Tombland and survived, the leader who'd seen them through bad times and made them good again, and that counted for a lot. The senior Unrulys – Wil, Arjay, Dinn, even Fings on a good day – would have followed Blackhand into a burning warehouse given half a reason. But there was another *before* that Fings still remembered, a *before* when Fings and Seth had been somewhere between boys and men, when the Mage of Tombland had had half the city underworld under the shadow of his bone-toothed whip, and Black Alarand had been his most murderous bastard lieutenant.

That was the thing: Fings had been there when the Mage of Tombland fell. He was never quite sure what Blackhand's plan had been for afterwards, but he was pretty sure that what it *hadn't* been was to flee the city for two years leaving mayhem in his wake while everyone else dropped dead like flies. Blackhand *had* come back – eventually – and settled himself in the Unruly Pig after the previous owner mysteriously left the city in an extreme hurry. He'd claimed Haberdashers and the Spice Market and generally sorted out the mess he'd made. And yes, he'd had some trouble for a while with the up-and-coming Spicers – beatings and places mysteriously catching fire and people showing up dead, that sort of thing – but eventually they'd worked it out and the world had settled into its new order. And now Sulfane was littering the place with corpses again, and Blackhand held his leash, and Fings, frankly, wanted nothing to do with it.

He felt a tug on his sleeve. A dwarfish old man with no teeth grinned up at him.

"Get lost," snapped Seth.

The old man shoved a hand into a rotten sack slung over his shoulder and pulled out a chicken's foot on a string. "Lucky charm?" He thrust it at Fings and then at Seth, and nodded at the tray of pastries. "Swap?" he said, hopefully.

"Fuck off," said Seth. The old man gave him a sour look and turned to leave. Fings stopped him.

"What do they do?" he asked.

"Do?" The old man squinted at him, full of suspicion.

Seth rolled his eyes. "Fuck's sake, Fings, don't encourage him."

"A lot of people might come and sell you something for your health or something for..." the old man pointed at Fings' crotch, "down there, if you get what I'm saying. But *these* are special, these are. *Real* special."

He eyed Fings carefully as he spoke. Seth flapped a hand at the old man's onion-breath. "Get lost, will you?"

"Used to work in the offal trade." The old man pointed down the river to the Kaveneth. "Once a week they'd send me up *there*."

Fings snapped to attention. "The Guild? No! Really?"

"No," said Seth. "*Not* really. Now fuck *off*."

The old man reached out his hand. On the back of it was a tattoo, old and faded and a bit smudged but still clear for all to see. The sign of the Guild. "Was years ago, back when the Emperor, Sun bless him, was a year on the throne and the Guild was new." The old man sidled closer to whisper in Fings' ear. "I watched them good, I did. Learned a trick or two. What do you think of *that*?"

"What *I* think is that if some mage taught you any tricks at all, you wouldn't be here trying to flog the lopped-off foot of a dead chicken to an idiot," snapped Seth. "Now would you *please* piss off! The grown-ups are trying to have a conversation."

Fings thought about this. He would have been the first to admit, if anyone had bothered to ask, that he had a bit of a thing for other people's money. No one ever *did* ask, because everyone already knew, but if there was one thing that mattered to Fings even more, it was keeping fortune on his side. Luck, if you like. With a bit of luck watching his back, he could deal with most things, because most things he could understand in a basic sort of way, and if they were sharp or angry then you ran away, and he was good at running away. Mages were different, though. You couldn't run from a mage. Mages didn't obey the rules of luck, and that made them terrifying.

He took the old man by the shoulders, led him a couple of steps away and looked him up and down. "I thought only mages could go into the Guild! I thought everyone else just dissolves into dust!"

A look of hastily-suppressed surprise flashed across the old man's face. "Y... Yes! That's right!"

"No, it isn't," called Seth. "And I can still hear you."

The old man was eagerly offering up his chicken foot, holding out his other hand for a coin or two in return. Seth came over and roughly pushed him away.

"*I've* been into the bloody Guild." He made a show of patting himself down. "Nope. Still a coherent corporeal entity, apparently. *Not* made of dust."

Fings stepped around Seth, his attention still on the old man. Poor Seth, he just didn't understand how fortune worked. "You've got a charm that protects you from *mages*?" He glanced to the ramparts of the Kaveneth. Anything that protected you from mages had to be worth *something*.

"Gods strike me down if I'm a liar," said the old man, watching him closely.

"Yes, please, gods," Seth cast his eyes to the heavens. "Any one of you, any time. At your own pace. Oh, wait, you don't listen to us mere mortals, do you? Not really."

The old man pulled another chicken foot from his satchel. He tied it to a length of fraying string and looped it around Fings' neck. "This was so I could do my work, but I don't do that no more. *This* will protect you from *all manner* of sorcery!"

Fings pulled out his purse. It *would* be a relief to have some protection...

"Fings!" Seth caught his hand. "Oh, for the love of... It's like talking to a brick fucking wall." He moved between them, pointedly blocking the old man. "They gave him a mage-charm and then what? *Forgot* to take it back? Fings, that is a chicken foot. If it had even one iota of arcane mystery invested in it, this skinny tit would *not* be selling it. It isn't even lucky, and I know that because if it *was* lucky, it would still be attached to its original fucking owner, wouldn't it? You want a lopped-off chicken's foot, I'll get you one myself. Fresh from the Teahouse kitchens. A right bloody charm-factory it is in there on poultry night."

The old man shot Seth a murderous look. He sighed theatrically. "Sulk's come early. It's a sign, isn't it? You never know when a mage might–"

"Fuck's *sake*!" Seth rounded on the old man. "Look... Alright, you win. Take a pastry and then fuck off!"

The old man helped himself to a pastry. He ate it and made a face. "Not very good, are they," he said, and then grabbed another.

Fings handed over his silver moon. The old man gaped, gaped a bit more, and then ran away.

"You... You...!" Seth seemed to be having a problem with his words.

"Brother!" Fings soothed. "Inside the Guild, day after day, week after week?" Was a shame that a man who'd once braved the Guild and risked all manner of misfortune should be reduced to selling his one and only treasure for firewood.

"You *believed* that crap?"

Fings wagged a knowing finger. "He had the mark! The mark of the Guild!"

"What, that mess on the back on the back of his hand?" Now Seth looked like he had a problem with his teeth. "He drew that himself. This morning."

"No!"

"Fings! Professional forger here. Trust me on this."

"No one would dare!" Fings shook his head. "The mages would know! Unless..." An understanding dawned on him then, proof that he was right! "Unless he had a charm that stopped them!" Yes! "See! That shows it works!"

"*What*?"

"This must be one of the most... *big*... of charms. It must be like the *king* of charms."

"The most... *big* of charms?"

Seth didn't look well. Fings pulled him close. "Besides," he whispered. "I had to get rid of that silver moon, right? It was cursed."

Seth jerked away. "Cursed? What do you mean *cursed*?"

"Was old. Still got the head of old Emperor Khrozus on it, Sun bless him, and he's dead. Been bothering me all afternoon, wandering around carrying the image of a dead man. I mean, you *know* how unlucky *that* is! And I didn't want to just toss it because, you know, silver, right? But a dead man's face carved on silver? And a *moon*, a whole *full-moon*... Something bad was *bound* to happen."

"Something bad just *did* happen!"

"Feel a bit guilty giving it to him, really."

Now Seth was clenching his jaw like something hurt. "Next time you get an unlucky coin *that's made of silver*, *I'll* look after it, alright?"

"But then–"

"Priest tricks," hissed Seth. "We know how to protect ourselves."

Fings tried a smile. "After this thing Blackhand's got going, none of us are going to go hungry this winter." He tossed some coins to Seth, because Seth was Seth, and because they'd been as good as brothers since they were eight years old, and because it was only to be expected that Seth was still a bit out of sorts from the whole business of getting thrown out of the priesthood, and anyway, a part of him was still dazzled with wonder. "A charm against mages! How about that! Maybe the Emperor has a charm like this, too, Sun bless him."

"Fings… Go away now."

"But–"

"The Emperor *is* a mage, Fings! *Why would he need one?*"

Fings spotted Sulfane heading towards them, a big fat grin all over his face.

Time to go. He turned away. "Tell the Murdering Bastard I'll be there later." Not that he *wanted* to help Sulfane, but it would be good to get away from Longcoats accidentally tripping over and impaling themselves on arrows or whatever other nonsense Blackhand was peddling these days. As he walked, he touched a finger to his new charm and wondered if it worked on Dead Men, too. There were always more Dead Men during the winter when people with nowhere else to go curled up and quietly died of the cold. Now and then you'd meet one in the dark, some fellow shambling along an alley towards you, and you wouldn't know whether it was a Dead Man or just some drunk.

But no, the Dead Men were something to do with the gods, which was why Seth knew how to make them stop. They were nothing to fear as long as you knew how to run away, and when it came to running away, Fings was a champion. Mages, on the other hand... Mages were something else, which was why swordmonks got all pissy about them, and quite right too.

He shivered, tucked his charm inside his shirt where it would be safe, and kept walking.

A couple of hours later, long after the city had slumped into darkness, he rounded the corner into Neckbreaker Yard and stopped to have a good look around. Apart from running away, the other thing he was good at was stealing things, but the trouble with being good at stealing things *and* being good at running away, he'd noticed, was that people tended to blame you for everything that went missing even when you had nothing to do with it. Example: Fings reckoned it surely should have been *obvious* that he hadn't stolen Red Kaiala's stash of silver, because it should have been *obvious* that he wasn't stupid enough to piss where he slept... and yet all he'd been hearing these last few days was how Red was going to slit him from gut to gizzard if he didn't hand it all back, which was ridiculous when he obviously didn't have it in the first place! Admittedly, he *had* borrowed a couple of old books she'd been sitting on, but those had been for Seth, and Red didn't even read, so it wasn't like she'd *needed* them, and now here she was blaming him for *everything*, just because some other stuff had gone missing about the same time. It was outrageously unjust, but Red had enough clout in the Neckbreakers for it to be a problem, so here he was, trying to make peace.

The Neckbreakers playing dice in the middle of the yard stopped when they saw him and got to their feet. They moved slow and easy, hands drifting to the hilts of their knives. They didn't do anything more because Fings wasn't stupid enough to get so close that he couldn't run, and if he ran then they wouldn't catch him, and they all knew it because they'd all grown up together.

"Necky. Toes." Fings gave them each a nod. They'd been friends, once. Still were, mostly. Him and Toes had run together. Was

Fings who'd got him his name. Fings and Toes. Made everyone laugh and so it stuck. They both owed him, little favours done over the years, not big but not nothing either. Place they'd grown up, favours were often the only currency there was, which meant people remembered and kept tally. Maybe that was why Toes and Necky weren't doing anything more than standing there.

"Red's put a quarter-moon on you, Fings," said Toes. "You should know that."

Fings touched the chicken foot hanging around his neck. Could have paid off the bounty if he'd kept that silver moon. Passed the bad luck to Red. Would that have made them square? Probably not.

"I've come to settle." Fings stooped, never taking his eyes off them, and put a purse on the ground. "It's everything I got." Everything he could spare. "You take that to Red. Tell her it's for the books and that I didn't touch her silver. If that's not enough to make things good, she can call on the Pig and put in a grievance to Blackhand. Happy to talk." Happy to talk in the safety of the Pig, at least, because the Neckbreakers paid their dues to Blackhand just like everyone else, and Red certainly *did* know better than to piss where she slept.

He left the purse and backed away. It wouldn't be enough, not even close, but maybe it would buy him the time to do whatever this job was that the Murdering Bastard said was going to make them all rich.

VARR AFTER DARK

Priest tricks. Seth watched Sulfane saunter across the filthy pressed snow of the square, idly mulling acts of petty revenge against Fings for letting a whole silver moon vanish into the gloom in the hands of a ragged old man. *Yeah. We know how to protect ourselves by reading books and discovering how things actually work and not being SUPERSTITIOUS FUCKING MORONS!*

They were just thoughts though – Fings was an idiot but Seth had known *that* for a decade and then some. They'd bailed each other out of scrapes more times than Seth could remember, and most of those times, he had to admit, it had been Fings doing the bailing. He was right about Sulfane, too. How many Longcoats had been found with arrows sticking out of them? How many had simply disappeared? Five? Six? Ten? Not that Seth wasn't as happy as the next man to see a Longcoat take a kicking, but this? This was going to come back on them, and you could bet the reprisals wouldn't fall on Blackhand, and probably not on Sulfane either

"Pastries! Get your pastries." Not that anyone cared, but he had nothing better to do, so here he was. Yelling pointless words out into the night air like a lunatic.

"Got any left? I'm famished." Sulfane caught his arm, grabbed a fistful and wolfed them down one by one. The sun touched the horizon as he did, and so Seth handed him the tray and sank to his haunches and clasped his hands and started the Twilight Prayer.

He honestly didn't know why. Habit? Must have been, because the Sunherald Martial had been abundantly clear about how the Sun wasn't listening to Seth any more. That had been right before the Sunguard had thrown Seth down the temple steps.

The only novice to meet the Sunherald Martial in the flesh. I suppose that was an achievement.

The words of the prayer circled through his head. They were pointless. *He* was pointless. Yet somehow, for reasons he couldn't fathom, he stayed where he was and let the prayer run over and over until the sun vanished behind the walls of the Kaveneth. When he stopped, he was surprised to find tears on his cheeks.

The cold, he told himself. *Must be the cold.*

"Don't know why you bother." Sulfane propped himself against a wall, picking his fingernails.

"Me neither." If his God wasn't listening, why do it? To assuage his own anguish?

Sulfane threw the last pastries away. "These are shit. Do people actually pay for them?"

Seth sighed. "Not very often." He stooped and picked them up again and pocketed them for later, because only an idiot wasted food that wasn't so rotten it had sprouted legs and was trying to escape. Sulfane, like Myla, had obviously never known what *real* hunger was like.

As if reading Seth's mind, Sulfane dragged him into the Provisioners' Guild tent and bought them both cups of hot, spiced wine. Seth nursed his, wishing it was stew, but good wine was another thing that only an idiot turned away. He savoured its heat, trying not to resent how long it had been since he'd last tasted something so good, and largely failing.

Keep an eye on Sulfane. That had been Blackhand's price for letting Seth have the leftovers from the Unruly Pig's kitchen. Could have been worse.

How long had it been? He wasn't sure. A long time.

Best not to think about it.

Sulfane bought himself another cup, and then another,

drowning his sorrows at not winning his archery tournament and steadily getting drunk. After the first few, Seth wangled a bowl of strew out of him, which was something. It was fully dark by the time they left, the night air as cold as an Autarch's marriage-bed; Sulfane was properly drunk by now, talking excited incoherent gibberish as they walked, starting and then suddenly stopping, grinning as though about to spill some dire secret and then going off on some other tack. Seth soon gave up trying to make sense of it – an odd mix of Imperial history and something about a bungled burglary, or maybe a bungled murder? With Sulfane, the latter seemed more likely.

They reached the river, the waterfront loud with hawkers shouting offers to ferry people across the water. Sulfane found them a passably sane oarsman, gave him a couple of bits, and solved the issue of unwanted nautical stories by jovially threatening to stab the man if he didn't shut up. Across the river, he made his excuses and left. *Business to attend to.*

Seth supposed this meant sticking an arrow into someone. He watched Sulfane swagger away, then took a moment to get his bearings. He didn't know *exactly* where he was, but he could see the looming bulk of the grain silos not far upriver, and the dark open space around the Sapphire Palace was almost straight across the water behind him. All he had to do was head due south until he blundered into somewhere familiar, avoiding the Longcoat Roads, whose zealous *better-safe-than-sorry* patrols kept the city safe at night for the sort of people who paid their wages by kicking the crap out of the sort of people who didn't.

They wouldn't touch a priest...

Don't. Don't even think it.

He weaved between riverside warehouses and through the unfamiliar streets of Leatherworkers. The Unrulys didn't have much to do with the Leatherworkers one way or another and no one bothered him. He veered east to avoid Tanners – avoiding Tanners was necessary if you had any sense of smell and hoped to keep it – until he reached the Deadwater and the bridges into Tombland. No one in their right mind went into Tombland at night without an invitation, so he shadowed the Avenue of Heaven's Mausoleums back towards the river until he could cross into Seamstresses, then south to Buttonmaker Street between Seamstresses and Bonecarvers. Bonecarvers made him wary because people there still remembered him as a priest, and there was bad blood between Bonecarvers and the Path of the Sun, mostly to do with bodies being lifted from the city corpse-wagons.

I just want to go home.

He heard a noise then, that quiet rustle of clothes and shambling footfalls that every novice came to recognise after a few months on the nightly hunts. A Dead Man. The creature was in the alley ahead, and in a bad state from the sound of him. Seth reached for his strips of paper and his charcoal stick, the two possessions a priest always carried. After the temple had kicked him out, he'd had Fings lift him a set from a novice in the Spice Market. It had felt oddly satisfying.

He took a few more steps down the alley until he saw the shape of the creature. It was leaning against a wall, dragging one useless leg behind it. Some poor bastard who'd frozen to death in a cellar somewhere, probably, and something had made good eating out of him too, before he'd reanimated. Dead Men weren't dangerous, not really. Yes, they could be made to be, and yes, if he stood still for long enough and didn't do anything then eventually this one would probably kill him, but you had to work at being eaten by a Dead Man, and the night patrols of priests and sword-monks made sure that there were never many about.

Then again, this was Bonecarvers. Priests didn't come here.

He used his charcoal to draw the Sigil of Peace. He didn't need to look – being able to draw the Sigil of Peace perfectly in the dark was one of the tests a novice took before they let you out on the night-patrols. The sigil carried the power of God. All he had to do was touch it to the Dead Man to sever the tie between flesh and soul. Releasing Dead Men before the Hungry Goddess found them and took their souls was holy work, the first duty of every priest.

Is this me, one day? A mindless shambling thing, dead from the cold, soul praying for the touch of a sword-monk?

And then: *Will this still even work?*

He wasn't sure. He wasn't a priest any more. The Sun no longer heard him.

The Dead Man kept shuffling towards him, pitiful and slow.

The Gods turn their backs to you. The last words he'd heard as they'd thrown him down the temple steps. Did that mean the Gods wouldn't recognise the Sigil in his hand?

You no longer exist.

Maybe it would work, maybe it wouldn't. He didn't know.

You really want to find out?

He took a step back, away from the Dead Man.

And then there's the whole business of what you found, before they threw you out.

It wasn't as if he'd forgotten.

Better to leave. Let someone else do it.

That was it.

Just until I know for sure.

Yes.

He turned back the way he'd come for a while and then turned what he hoped was west, walking blindly, not really paying attention to where he was going.

I could save souls. I could literally save souls. And now I can't.

That was what they'd taken from him.

Something he'd taken himself, apparently, was a wrong turn, because the next time he was in a place he knew, it wasn't the backstreets of Haberdashers. He'd obviously gone the wrong way entirely, because now he was on the southern fringe of Tombland, close to the Constable's Castle, far too far east and still on the wrong side of the Eastern Spice Market.

He stopped. He could keep going until Bonecarvers spat him out into the Circus of Dead Emperors and then take his chances with Conqueror's Avenue and Haberdasher Street and risk a run-in with the Longcoats. He could trace his steps back through

Bonecarvers and try again. Or he could take the short way, cut south through Spicer territory.

Shit! Fuck, fuck, shit!

The Longcoats were as inevitable as night and day. And it was a long walk back through Bonecarvers and he was cold.

The Spicers, then. Wasn't Blackhand hitting them tonight? With a bit of luck, they'd be hiding or licking their wounds; and for a while it looked like he was right – the back-streets of the Eastern Spice Market were deserted – but then he turned a corner and almost walked into two of them coming the other way. And, of course, they recognised him as soon as they saw him, and he ran, and they chased after him and caught him before the first corner, a flying tackle that sent him sprawling into dirty packed snow, scraping the side of his face across a wall as he fell. He staggered up, feeling the sting and burn on his cheek, and then they were on him, spinning him round and punching him in the face until he went down and felt something very old sigh inside him, and curled up into a ball.

Just let it happen. It's not like you don't deserve it.

A boot caught him in the face. He tasted blood. As the next kick landed, he let himself drift away. They'd kick him until they were bored, and then they'd go away and he'd limp home, because that was how it always was, how it had been for as long as he could remember outside the years he'd spent serving the Path of the Sun.

Plague take you. Me. All of us.

Maybe this time they'd go all the way. Maybe this would be the one that killed him. If it was, he honestly couldn't find the energy to care. He supposed he ought to but really, all things considered, perhaps it was for the best? Anyway, there wasn't much he could do about it. Wasn't it odd, though, the way the mind worked? Here he was, possibly about to die, busy remembering with vivid clarity the taste of a peach and the fevered tension of crossing the river as a young novice.

"Stick him," said a voice. "Stick him and let's go!"

So that's it. I'm going to die. In an alley in the dead of night. For nothing.

Can't say you didn't see it coming, right?

He wasn't properly conscious. He vaguely heard some shouting. The knife never came; and then someone was lifting him up, hauling him roughly to his feet.

"Khrozus' blood! Seth?"

Seth tried to open his eyes. One refused outright but he managed the other. Brick was looking at him, bristling with a pity that hurt almost more than his ribs, although his ribs would doubtless take the prize come tomorrow. He wondered briefly what had happened to the two Spicers and found he didn't care.

İ

İΠTERLUDE

Seth grew up near the north walls of the city and the road to Khrozir. He knew that because he saw the steady parade of men and wagons full of stone as both were being built. Mostly, though, his impressions of that part of his life were of cold and hunger and beatings from boys and girls who were all bigger than him, and of learning to survive by becoming sneaky and devious and unseen, and, when he *was* seen, meek and servile.

At some point – later, he could never quite remember how it had happened – he was adopted by a gang calling themselves the Bigs. The Bigs treated him with the usual scorn and contempt but at least the beatings stopped. They used him as a distraction while they stole things – small crying child, lost and scared – or else as a lookout, until Seth hit on the ruse of being stricken by a divine vision. A God-struck child, it turned out, was a wonderful diversion, right up until he did it once too often and got caught. The other Bigs abandoned him, melting into the crowds while the Longcoats took him to their watch-house and a serious-faced man told him he'd likely spend the rest of his life in the Imperial Mines.

The threat was an empty one – only grown men were sent to the mines – but child-Seth didn't know any better; what he *did* know was that no one was going save him and no one was going to rescue him. Surrounded by these grizzled men with their clubs and stern words and hostile faces, his fear turned. Something snapped. He was…

Angry.

The Longcoats held him for a day and Seth told them everything. He even made up a few things. Rage, he discovered, was cold and vast, indomitable and fierce. And it worked. The Longcoats went out and rounded up the Bigs and let him go.

I'd keep out of sight a while, they said as they pushed him back onto the streets. *Some of your friends are still out there. Maybe get out of the city.* One of the Longcoats gave him a hunk of old dry bread and two precious biscuits, and that was that. Seth didn't ask where he was supposed to go. He walked out and kept going and never looked back.

The river, when he reached it, seemed impossibly vast. His legs and his feet ached from walking and he didn't have any money, so he sat and ate his biscuits and watched the armada of little boats going back and forth. It was summer and the air was hot, and he wasn't hungry and he wasn't cold. He was lost, but being lost didn't scare him. Being lost meant that no one could find him to hurt him.

He'd never been to the river before. But he could see the other city on the far side and understood that this barrier was his escape, that it was a wall between him and his past, that if he could somehow cross it then no one would ever find him, or come after him, and that he'd be safe. He joined a clutch of people scrambling onto a raft and asked if he could go too, but they pushed him away. Someone told him he'd need a half-bit to pay the boatman. A half-bit would buy a loaf of bread and wasn't to be sniffed at, but he knew boys who came home sometimes with halves and quarters they'd found dropped in the markets, so he walked along the river and scrabbled in the dirt on his hands and knees until a heavy hand hauled him to his feet. The hand was attached to a giant with a big grey beard, the biggest Longcoat Seth had ever seen, with a heavy leather coat and cap and a big rounded stick hanging by a loop from his belt and an angry face demanding to know whether he was a thief.

Seth explained that he needed to cross the river. He'd had a half-bit to pay the boatman, he said, but he'd lost it.

Is that where you live? asked the giant. Seth wasn't sure about lying to giants, even if they were Longcoats, but he nodded because that seemed to be what was wanted. An odd expression crossed the giant's face then. He put Seth down and gave him two coins.

Find your way home, lad, he said.

Crossing the river had felt like crossing into another world. He revelled in the strange streets and the unfamiliar smells. The houses and the shops and even the people seemed different and alien. He walked and walked until he couldn't walk anymore, until it was getting dark and his bread and biscuits were gone. He was hungry by now and didn't know what to do or where to go, but the summer nights were warm in Varr and he still had the second coin the Longcoat giant had given him and so he still wasn't scared, only tired.

He found himself in a busy square full of exotic stalls selling sacks of weird seeds and leaves and brightly coloured powders. On the far side was a grand old building that had a lot of steps leading up to gaping arches painted in bright and gaudy yellow. It seemed to call him, warm and welcoming, and so he went and sat on the steps and wondered where he should go next; and he was just thinking that maybe he'd curl up and go to sleep right there on those steps when another boy came and sat beside him. The boy had had two peaches.

"Not seen you around here before," said the boy with the peaches, and bit into one, the juices running down his chin.

Seth shook his head. He nodded at the building behind them. "What is this place?"

"Temple of the Sun," sniffed the boy with the peaches, as though it really wasn't anything important. "You got a name?"

"Course."

"What is it?"

There was the name his mother and his brothers and sisters called him, but that boy was gone. He needed something new.

"Seth." he said.

"I'm Fings," said the boy with the peaches. He pointed across the square to where another boy was stealing a cabbage off the back of a cart. "That's my brother, Levvi." He offered Seth his second peach. "This is the Spice Market. Best place in the whole wide world."

Years later, on the day Seth took his robes on what they guessed was his fourteenth birthday, Fings walked with him up those same steps. By then, they were as good as family. Seth never knew whether anyone ever looked for him, whether his real family were even still alive. He didn't care. He never knew what happened to the Bigs, either, but he still felt an anxious twinge whenever he crossed the rivers into the Military Quarter, never quite rid of the fear that they might come after him, even that time he'd gone with all the other novices to see the Emperor and realised why there were no old priests in Varr, not a single one.

5

MOONSTEEL

Myla wrapped the dead sell-sword's head in his own cloak while Dox and Arjay stripped the corpse of anything they could sell. Once they were done, Arjay shouldered the sell-sword's body and Dox took Dinn. They skirted the open space of the Spice Market and made their way through the narrow streets and alleys of Haberdashers to the bridge over the Westthreads canal. They walked in silence, Wil scouting ahead to make sure they didn't stumble into any Longcoats.

At the bridge, Arjay dropped the sell-sword off the side, cracking the ice over the frozen canal. Then she and Dox clambered down to the water's edge, bashing at the ice with their sticks to break it further, pushing and poking at the body until the sluggish current sucked it under and took it away. They did the same for Dinn. Wil kept watch.

"Seriously?" Myla asked.

"Be months before this all thaws," Arjay said. "By then he won't be anything but bones. No one's going to know."

It seemed so abrupt. "But Dinn—"

"Dinn said his prayers at dawn and dusk, but he was more Moon than Sun. It's what he would have wanted."

Wil nodded to the hole in the ice. "Toss him in."

Myla didn't know anything about him, this man she'd killed. Tossing him into the water would give him to the Moon. Was that what *he* would have wanted?

Did she care? He'd tried to kill her.

The Moon had a lot of followers in Varr, but this man had come here from Deephaven, like her. In Deephaven, almost everyone sent their prayers to the Sun.

Shouldn't have killed him. I needed him to talk.

No chance of that now.

She stood on the bridge over the hole in the ice, holding the head in its wrapping of coarse thick wool, unwilling to let it go. A body was too big but the head on its own? Could she smuggle him onto a corpse wagon without the Longcoats knowing? Let the priests take him to the fire-pits and send him on his way to the Sun? It was the head that mattered.

I need a drink.

"Oh, for Kelm's sake!" Arjay snatched the bundle, shook the head free of its cloak and let it fall. It splashed into the black water and sank. Wil and Dox had already gone.

"Go back to Deephaven," Arjay said, not harshly, more like a disappointed mother. "You don't belong here."

Arjay turned and trudged away through the snow and Myla followed, keeping her distance, which was fine, because keeping her distance meant no one was close enough to her to get hurt, which was why she'd come to Varr in the first place.

Not that running had done her any good, by the looks of things. She supposed she shouldn't be surprised that the Hawat brothers hadn't believed she was dead and had coming looking for her. Not even much of a surprise that it was Jeffa who'd found her.

At the Teahouse, the Unrulys had gathered, the whole inner circle, Blackhand with his back to the fire, Fings and Wil and Arjay and Dox and Topher and Brick, all of them talking at once, an angry cacophony of voices. They stopped as she came in.

"One more to go," grumbled Blackhand. "Where the fuck is Sulfane?"

"*Business* to attend to." Seth sat hunched into himself looking like a building had fallen on him. One side of his face was so swollen it had almost swallowed his eye. Beside him was a half-empty bottle of wine. Myla snatched it and took a long deep swallow.

"Khrozus, what happened to *you*?"

Seth swatted the question away. He set his one good eye on Blackhand and nodded towards the stairs, then swiped the bottle back from Myla.

"Found him on the street," chuckled Brick. "Kissing Spicer boot." They all laughed, all except Seth and Fings.

"Murdering Bastard probably slipped upstairs," Fings bristled. "Helping himself to another free one with Lula, like he helps himself to everything." He glared at Blackhand.

"Manners, boy." Blackhand sounded mild but Fings jerked like he'd been slapped. Seth forced himself up and hobbled closer, bent over like it hurt to stand straight.

"We had a good chat though, me and Sulfane. All the way back from the contest." His one good eye was firmly on Blackhand. "Something about a barge from the City of Spires filled with silver? The *Emperor's* silver. He was drunk. You want to think about that, or shall I be the one to tell him to keep his fucking mouth shut?"

Seth held Blackhand's eye.

"Go and rest," Myla said. "You can use my room. I'll take the floor."

"He got us a score," Blackhand said. "Fings and him are going to–"

"I don't want to know." Seth shook his head. "Tell him his letter will be ready when he gets back." He limped towards the stairs. No one offered to help. Blackhand leveled a hard stare at his back. Always liked to push his luck with Blackhand, did Seth. Always liked to push his luck with everyone, from what Myla could see.

"Do it right and there's a room here for you as long as you want it," said Blackhand. "If you can find some manners."

"Arrogant prick," muttered Wil after Seth had gone. Myla crossed the floor and helped herself to another bottle of wine, necking it as Blackhand grinned and emptied a bag onto the floor; a couple of rings, a night-black pendant and… was that a severed hand?

"The Spicers are done." Blackhand picked up the hand and

tossed it at Fings, a warning to mind his tongue maybe, or maybe he was simply too pleased with himself to care. "They're finished."

Fings dropped the hand in disgust. "You know this ain't over. We might be sweet in Haberdashers but that was the Spice Market. Longcoats there... They're taking Spicer coin, not yours, and you already got them frothing mad what with half of them tripping over their own feet and accidentally impaling themselves on arrows."

"Two," snapped Blackhand. "Two of them."

"Two?" Fings was almost shouting. "Might be there's only two the Murdering Bastard was too stupid to make disappear after he stuck them, but how many have gone missing? What, and they all just upped and left the city in the middle of the Sulk? The wanker in charge over there might be a knob who thinks he's practically related to the Emperor but he's not *stupid*. And now this?" He poked the severed hand with his toe and shook his head, as if trying to shake a wasp out of his hair.

Myla took another swig of wine. The beginnings of a buzz, just enough to blunt the edge. She'd never seen Fings so animated. Never seen him go up against Blackhand, either.

Blackhand grimaced. "It's done. We were never there."

"Well that's very nice to hear but who's he going to believe? You or the man with a stump for an arm?"

Now Blackhand laughed. "He's not going to be *talking*."

"Really? Why's that?"

"Why'd you *think*?"

Myla frowned. They'd carried the bodies of Dinn and the sellsword and dumped them, but not Chubby. And Blackhand had stayed behind...

What did you do?

Fings threw up his hands. "Can't take a piss without tripping over some bloke with an arrow sticking out of him these days."

"Fings! It's not—"

"It's not going to come back on us? It *is*. You *know* that. It's going to be like Tombland all over! You got to—"

Blackhand jumped up and took two quick steps towards Fings...

...and there were her hands, on the hilts of her swords. Faster than anyone could blink, but they all saw it.

Instinct.

Blackhand stared at her. An odd look. Shock and... yes, a moment of fear. He bared his teeth and held her eye as she forced herself to let her hands fall to her sides. "Anyone comes after us, Myla can just lop off another head, right?"

"She did *what*?"

Wil grinned and drew a finger across his throat. "*Schnick, schnick* and done. Clean off."

"A bloke with no head now, is it?" Fings spat. "What we calling that? A shaving accident? Kelm's teeth!"

Wil shrugged. "He killed Dinn. Can't say he didn't have it coming."

"Bodyguard," Arjay spoke quietly. "Outsider. He chose his fate."
Jeffa says hello.

"It was an accident," said Myla.

Fings gawped. "You chopped his head off by *accident?*" He stopped, frowned hard, then picked up the pendant Blackhand had tossed onto the floor. "Where'd this come from?"

"Sell-sword Myla killed," said Wil. "He was wearing it."

Fings peered some more and then tossed it to her. It was a black, smooth metal and icy cold. Myla thought she saw something silver shimmer across its surface... no, *inside* the metal itself. She ran her fingers over it and felt engraved lines. She turned it, trying to make them catch the light, but they refused.

"What is it?" asked Blackhand.

"Moonsteel," she said.

Fings clutched at his throat and turned in a full circle, his other hand raised to the heavens. "Kelm's Teeth? Really? You know where that shit comes from, right? Mages, that's where! You can't have that in here!" He started nervously fondling what looked like a chicken's foot on a string hanging around his neck.

Wil went very still. "Tombland?"

A moment of unease swept through them, even Blackhand,

until Myla tossed the pendant to him. It wasn't hers, after all. "Moonsteel is a divine metal. This came from the moon-priestesses of the City of Spires, not from any mage. It's probably just an ornament. Worth gold if it's something more."

Blackhand tossed it back. "You killed him. You keep it." He clapped his hands. "Arjay, Dox, you need to lie low a while. Fings: crack of dawn tomorrow, you and Sulfane are out of here."

"I'm not going out the city with that murdering–"

"Yes, you are. Like Seth said, there's a barge coming up-river stacked with silver. Sulfane knows where and when but he needs a man who can slip in and out without anyone seeing. That's you. Wil, you go with him. Keep everyone in line and make sure Sulfane holds his tongue." He bared his teeth at Fings. "Myla, too. Best you're out of the city a while, I reckon."

Best I am, she thought, although her attention was with the glinting moon, shining out from the depths of the pendant between her fingers, like a tiny eye peering at her.

6

ΠEEDS MUST AS THE DEVİL DRİVES

The Murdering Bastard, as far as Fings was concerned, was a smouldering lump of foul-tempered trouble who was going to get all of them killed. He'd walked into the Unruly Pig a month ago and disappeared into a room with Blackhand. The arrangement was simple: he wanted a letter forged, Seth was the best forger in the Southern half of the city, and, for the time being at least, Seth belonged to Blackhand. Blackhand, in return, wanted something done about the Spice Market Longcoats who were protecting the Spicers. No one had said anything about treasure barges – even if they had, Fings wouldn't have believed it. Blackhand was always going on about hidden treasures when he wanted something done, and they always turned out to be ten parts trouble and no parts actual treasure.

Now the Murdering Bastard wanted a burglar as well as a forger, did he? Fings wasn't at all sure how he felt about that. Helping Sulfane was, he reckoned, a bad idea even in principle, and probably much worse in reality because murdering bastards were… well… murdering bastards, and while he could outrun almost anyone, he couldn't outrun an arrow.

On the other hand…

Out of the city.

He'd never done that. Not once. Not one single step. Yes, he'd gone as far as the new southern gatehouse to see Levvi on his way to Deephaven a few years back, scampering up someone's cart to gawp like a little boy and then climbing up onto a roof tall enough to look past the walls. He still remembered that like it was yesterday, staring at the wide road outside the city bursting with wagons and people and a menagerie of animals long after Levvi was out of sight, the summer air hot and dry, thick with noise and rich with the smells of animals and people...

It was as close as he'd ever been.

The thought jangled inside him. He felt the pull of it. Varr wasn't safe – he'd seen what had happened to Seth. And the way Seth was these days, trying to pick fights with Blackhand, of all people... Seth was changing, and not for the better. And then there was the business with Red. Wouldn't hurt to disappear for a few days. A purse filled with the Emperor's silver wouldn't hurt, either, assuming he didn't end up with an arrow sticking out of him.

All that, but most of all it was coming up five years since Levvi had left, and sooner or later, maybe after this winter was over, Fings was going to have to go look for him.

He stayed in the Pig that night instead of going home, watching Myla get drunk in a corner on her own and mulling it all over. The next morning, Brick and Dox and Arjay went out for dawn prayers at the temple in Spice Market Square and came back with word that the Longcoats in the Eastern Market were buzzing like a hive of angry hornets, out in force and looking to crack Unruly skulls. They'd put word out to any other Longcoat chapters willing to listen, too.

"We got prices on our heads, lads," said Brick. For Fings, that was what did it.

He found Myla in the stables. Myla, who had a horse and those fancy swords and came from more money than the rest of them put together, probably even more than Blackhand, and who took it all so much for granted that she didn't seem to even notice. He stood in the doorway, wary of crossing the threshold. Not that there was anything *wrong* with the stables, it was just that crossing a threshold, any threshold, was a choice you couldn't take back, so best to stop a moment and think about the luck of a place before you did. *This* place had Myla in it, and Fings couldn't decide whether Myla was a lucky charm or a walking curse. Definitely one or the other, though.

"You hear what Brick said?" he asked, staying carefully just outside.

Myla nodded. Not that the Longcoats would bother *her*, even if they'd worked out by now that she was one of Blackhand's.

"Got some things to sort before we go," he said

Myla wrinkled her nose. "You want me to come with you?" She was brushing her horse. Fings had no idea what to do with horses. As far as he was concerned, they were big and dangerous and didn't belong inside a crowded city. A lot of the time he reckoned that the people who *owned* horses didn't belong in cities either.

Sulfane had a horse.

"Well…" His business was *his* business, not hers and no business of anyone else, so no, not really, and he wasn't all that bothered about the Longcoats either because he knew how to avoid them, but how did you say all that to someone who lopped off heads and then casually claimed it was an accident?

"I don't want to spend the morning with Sulfane," Myla added, which he had to admit seemed reasonable. "And the rest of them hate me."

"No they don't." *Dislike* was more the size of it. It wasn't personal, it was just… Myla didn't belong, that was the thing. Everyone knew it, like everyone knew she was only passing through, that she wouldn't stay, that Blackhand only let her hang around and treated her like she was something special because she didn't ask for much and because those swords of hers were frankly terrifying even when they stayed strapped across her back.

"It might help if you didn't chop people's heads off," he added, and then mentally kicked himself. *Idiot.*

"I didn't mean to."

"Yeah... About that."

He stopped. *Don't ask.*

Myla was looking at him, expectant.

No, Don't! "How does a beheading happen... by accident?" *Oh, for pity's sake.* Yeah, one day his mouth was going to get him stabbed, but sometimes the stupid thing just had a will of its own...

"Habit," she said.

"*Habit*? That's even *worse*!"

Myla shot him a fierce look. Fings took a step back and checked over his shoulder for a clear exit – now that was a *proper* habit, one with sense to it, not like lopping off heads.

"Um?"

"You follow the sequence of the forms. It's instinct. I just... I didn't *want* to kill him. I wanted to talk to him. I think..." She trailed off.

Fings eyed her. Killing someone because you forgot not to wasn't exactly encouraging; but he knew remorse when he saw it, which at least made her better than Sulfane, although possibly in the same way that getting an apology after being stabbed was better than being laughed at after being stabbed, an argument that, to Fings' mind, overlooked the principal issue of a lot of bleeding.

"You scare them," he said. "Wil and Blackhand. The others follow. You know?"

"I *scare* them?"

She seemed surprised, which Fings found bewildering: how could she *not* understand? "You know what Blackhand calls you when you're not around? 'Death with tits'."

"*Excuse* me?"

"Have *you* ever heard him say that?"

"No!"

Now she's angry. Great job, Fings. Great job. Maybe you should just leave. He forced a grin. "You know why?"

"Because it's degrading and rude?"

That made him actually laugh. "Blackhand? Oh, yes, because

Blackhand's always so polite to the rest of us, right? No, because you *scare* him. You could take him apart, him and Wil and half the Unrulys put together, and he knows it." Fings had a sneaking idea that Sulfane could probably beat the crap out of Blackhand too, so maybe it wasn't such a bad thing that Myla was coming with them, which got him to wondering whether he should try and stay on her good side, at least until this treasure thing was done. Not that he much wanted to, but needs must as the devil drives, as Ma Fings liked to say. Lesser of two evils, et cetera, et cetera. Full of useful old sayings, Ma Fings, and wasn't that why he'd come out here to the stables in the first place?

"Anyway," he said, almost sure he was going to regret it. "I've got to go. Come along if you want. Just don't… chop anyone up, alright?"

Myla nodded. She snatched up a skin of what Fings hoped was water but which was probably wine, and followed as he led the way out into the backside of Haberdashers, a tangled warren of yards and alleys where the Longcoats wouldn't be watching, the sort of place you had to grow up in to know your way around.

"The thing is…" he started, and then hesitated, because he'd tried this in the early days with Sulfane and the Murdering Bastard had laughed in his face. "This whole business with the Spicers: it *is* going to come back on us. You saw what happened to Seth? And it's happened before."

"Blackhand had a man at his mercy last night, mutilated him and then killed him. Badly."

"Yeah… That's Sulfane bringing out the worst in him, though." It wasn't and he knew it: ten years ago, Black Alarand's name had hung like a murderous shadow over the Spice Market.

Myla took a swig from her skin and offered it. Fings hesitated and then accepted, because why not? Wine, and not the watered crap Blackhand would have given him, either. He took another swig and handed it back. He wasn't surprised but… sword-monks were supposed to live off rainwater and their own ineffable smugness, weren't they?

They crossed into Seamstresses side by side as far as Buttonmaker Street. Fings thought for a moment and then headed on into Bonecarvers. It was daylight and Myla looked dangerous enough for them to be left alone, and there wouldn't be any Longcoats in Bonecarvers.

"Keep your eyes open here," he muttered, "and don't come this way at night."

"Dead Men?"

"And worse."

"I'm not afraid of Dead Men."

"Me neither, but I still don't want to hang out with their friends." He puffed his cheeks. "I don't know, maybe those swords you got would work. Seth says they're special?"

"Sunsteel."

"You *really* a sword-monk?" Didn't seem likely, a sword-monk washing up at the Unruly Pig. But they already had a failed priest, so why not?

"I might have been, if I hadn't left. I trained with them for years."

"Seth says you must be the real thing because of them swords. Says they don't give the swords until you give yourself to the Path. Until you're ready."

"I got mine early. I... did something unexpected."

"Must have been quite a big something."

"I suppose it was."

Myla didn't say any more and Fings didn't push. Some places it was best not to tread.

"You know Seth better than anyone," she said a while later.

"We're brothers. Sort of." Fings shrugged.

"He's... not like the rest of you."

He knew what she meant. Seth orbited the Unrulys because Fings was there and because he had nowhere else to go, but it wasn't his calling.

"How long was he a priest?"

"He was never a *proper* priest, only a novice."

"I was never a *proper* sword-monk. Still...?"

"A long time." He tried to count the years in his head. There was the crypt. The business in Tombland. Blackhand coming back and taking the Pig. Levvi leaving... "Nine winters? Ten? Something like that. Can't even step inside a temple now, poor bastard. Broke him, that did." The old Seth had had meaning and purpose. Faith. Now...?

"He's denied the Light?"

"Yeah, that's the one."

"What did he *do*?"

"Ask him yourself if you really want to know." It wasn't something he fancied explaining, wasn't sure he even knew the answer, not really; fortunately they were coming out of the warren of Bonecarvers, which meant either cutting through Tombland and the Alchemists' Market on the western edge of Glassmakers – something Fings wasn't going to do even in daylight – or crossing the Circus of Dead Emperors where Longcoats would be keeping watch for cutpurses and pickpockets.

"Keep your head down." He eased into the crowded space of the circus, scanning for familiar faces. It was hard on account of the Hanging Tree in the middle of it all, a weird thing with branches that sprang from one another all at right angles, some dropping straight back into the ground and sinking more roots until the overall impression was of the leftover skeleton of some vast and absurdly complicated burned-out barn. A Tree of Anvor, Seth called it, brimming with history, not least of which was being the centrepiece for Varr's old tradition of hanging the condemned rather than burning them.

Over to his left, on the other side of the Shattered Bridge and the Kingswater, rose the grey stone walls of the abandoned Constable's Castle, decked with turrets, and with smoke coming out of one of its chimneys, so not quite as abandoned as everyone liked to think. *Castle* was a bit much, too – it was more of a large and well-fortified house – but to reach the Constable's Castle these days meant crossing through the Alchemists' Market and the Bridge of Questions into Tombland, and Fings wasn't going anywhere near Tombland unless he absolutely had to.

He looked around. Longcoats this far from the Spice Market probably wouldn't know an Unruly if they saw one, although you could never be sure and Myla did stick out like a sore thumb... Except it turned out that Longcoats were the least of his worries: today, the Circus was full of Imperial soldiers, head to toe in dark red leathers and with spears and short stabbing swords. They were stationed in pairs, flanking the statues of the old dead rulers of the Empire. They weren't *doing* anything, just standing there, making everyone uneasy.

Well... a few dead Spicers was hardly going to catch the Emperor's eye, so whatever this was, it wasn't anything to do with the Pig. There was an *air*, though. A tension Fings didn't like. He pulled two feathers from a pocket, stuck one between his teeth and pressed the other into Myla's hand.

"Suck on this."

"Not that kind of girl, Fings."

"I'm not–" He flushed bright red, grabbed her wrist and pulled her into the crowd. "Khrozus! The feather." Which Myla had obviously understood right from the start – except when he looked back, she was twirling her feather between her fingers and looking confused, like *Suck on this* was somehow unclear?

Suck on a feather and don't ever stray, unfriendly eyes won't ever look your way.

Fings tugged her towards the statue of the Talsin, the last of the Torpreahn emperors, the one whose head Khrozus had paraded through the city...

Should have sucked on a feather. Probably still be alive.

...Straight past the two imperial soldiers standing there, who didn't pay the slightest bit of attention...

Of course not. Got a feather.

...through the bustle at the end of Weavers' Way and into the first alley.

Got a feather, feather, feather...

He looked back. No one had come after them. He pocketed his

feather and snatched the other from Myla. She looked at him like he was mad.

"Suck on a feather in times of need and no one who means harm will pay any heed. *Everyone* knows that!"

"You're saying that sucking on a feather... makes you... invisible?"

Fings stared at her like she was daft. "*Invisible*? What am I? A mage? Course not. Just... people don't look at you." Hard to notice, was more like it.

Myla was still looking at him like he was mad. Fings shook his head and walked away. "You're not like the rest of us, either." The words came out huffy, but that was what you got for making life unnecessarily difficult.

"I... did something." And there it was, that regret, same as when Seth talked about being a priest.

"That why you left Deephaven?" *Don't ask.*

"Yes."

"Chop someone up, did you?" *Fings! For Kelm's sake!* "Sorry. Not my business."

Myla sighed. "I should probably leave Varr."

Fings sniffed. *I don't want to know.*

He *did* want to know.

No! No, I don't!

"You do stick out a bit," he said. Varr was home to all sorts now the old Torpreahn emperors were gone and the Empire had someone on the throne who at least *looked* like they didn't come from somewhere else, but none of that really helped if you were the only person in the whole entire world who carried the weapons of a sword-monk but didn't wear their robes.

They turned the corner into Locusteater yard and there was Toes, leaning against a door. As he saw Fings, he snatched for his knife, and then he saw Myla, and stopped and threw a glance towards another door like he didn't know what to do, and that was the exact moment Fings' day turned to shit, because behind that door and up some stairs lived Ma Fings and Fings' four sisters.

İNTERLUDE

"In the beginning came the four divinities, the Gods of the Sun and the Moon, the Goddesses of the Stars and the Earth. The Sun clothed himself in light and declared: *Behold! I am the strongest and the brightest!* The Moon stole his brother's light and danced behind his sister and declared: *Behold, I am the fickle and ever-changing, the sorcerer, the thief who cannot be caught!* The Stars broke into a thousand lights and declared: *Behold, I am everywhere! I am knowledge and understanding!*

"But the Earth covered herself not with light but with trees and flowers and birds and beasts and declared: *Behold! I am life!* And the Sun and the Moon saw what the Earth had done and were envious, and so created peoples of their own to live upon their sister among her birds and beasts. The children of the Moon were of quicksilver and water: fickle and arrogant half-gods, sorcerers and immortal, each imbued with a fragment of their creator, which is why the Moon no longer shines as bright as the Sun, for a part of him lies within each of his children. The Sun, jealous of his own light, created men and women with no such spark, but to us gave instead the gift of bearing new life.

"And the children of the Sun prospered and multiplied, and spread across the Earth, and became masters of bird and beast, tree and flower. Seeing this, the Earth grew angry and covered herself in snow, and cast the Black Moon into the sky to blot out the Sun and all its warmth, and the children of the Sun became cold and hungry. Many perished, until the half-god sorcerers of the Moon took them into their enchanted spires and gave them protection. Thus began the Shining World, the Second Age, ruled by the immortal mages, masters of the eight elements, of earth and fire and water and ice and metal and air and light and dark. In time, from among these magi, rose two brothers greater than the rest, and so began the War of Mages, and the Shining World was destroyed, and the Earth gaped wide and swallowed the King in Silver and his brother both, but such mages could not easily be destroyed, even by a Goddess. With his final breath, the King in Silver smote his brother such a blow that the very substance of the Earth splintered and broke apart, and the Black Moon fell from the sky and was shattered, and so ended the Second Age, and the third began, and the children of the Moon passed from this world, and always since have the children of the Sun have sent no souls to the Hungry Goddess of the Earth, for they know..."

The ringing of the Twilight bells drowned whatever else Lightbringer Otti had been about to say, and Seth was out the door in a pack of novices, fleeing and taking with them a collective sense of relief that the next lesson with Otti wasn't until Moonday, which was three whole days away. Seth went to the Hall of Light for Twilight Prayers, ate, performed his evening duties, and helped some of the other novices, mostly for something to do. Later, back in his bed, he listened to their breathing. Once he was sure the others were asleep, he slipped back to the Hall of Light. This late, the hall was empty.

Almost empty. Fings stepped out from his hiding place behind a statue of the hero Kelm, sucking on a feather like he didn't have a care in the world.

"Did you get everything?" Seth asked.

Fings grinned and showed a coil of rope and a plank of wood. "It'll be *easy*."

It wasn't whether it would be *easy*, it was whether they'd be caught. If they were caught then they'd be thrown out, which probably didn't mean much to Fings, but mattered a whole lot to Seth. "I need to see what's down there." Seth wasn't supposed to know that *down there* even existed. But Fings didn't need to know that.

Behind the altar to the Sun, covered by a frayed old rug, was a door in the floor. When Seth had found it and asked Lightbringer Otti what it was for, Sunbright Jakeda had taken him aside after Twilight Prayers and told him he'd learn the answer once he was a Lightbringer. Which had been good enough until a book he wasn't supposed to have read claimed that the Temple to the Sun in Spice Market Square had a crypt. A crypt was an unholy place where dead bodies were kept away from the light of the Sun and the Moon and the Stars, so that *couldn't* be right.

And yet here it was, a door in the floor.

Seth pulled back the rug. Fings tied his rope around his plank. A few nights ago – their first attempt – Fings had opened the door and found a shaft that dropped thirty feet straight down before opening into a space that neither of them could see.

"You want me to go?" Fings asked, tying a foot-loop into the other end of the rope.

"No." Fings probably wouldn't even understand what he was looking at. "I'll tug when I need you to pull me up." Fings could shin up and down ropes like he was some sort of spider but Seth had never learned the trick of it.

He found a mangy scrap of fur being pressed into his hands. "Keeps ghosts at bay," Fings said.

"There's no such thing as ghosts, Fings."

"Huh. Says you. Works on Dead Men too."

Seth almost laughed. Dead Men in a temple to the Sun? He pulled open the trapdoor and Fings lowered him down. Half an hour later, Fings pulled him out again.

"Well?"

Seth shook his head. "Just an empty room full of dust. Anyone come by?"

"No."

Fings pestered him with more questions and Seth brushed them away, saying it was all nothing and boring and promising more when they weren't skulking around in the dark in places they weren't supposed to be. Eventually, Fings sloped away – Seth had no idea how Fings got in and out of the temple without anyone ever knowing, but he seemed to largely come and go as he pleased – and Seth went back to his cell.

He didn't sleep, though.

He couldn't say what he'd *expected* to find. Probably, if he was honest, the empty room full of dust he'd told Fings was down there. Certainly not six skeletons, each wearing old rotted robes and chained down to stone slabs. Yes, *chained*. Five of the slabs had the same three words carved into them.

Iconoclast.
Apostate.
Heretic.

No names. Nothing to identify the bodies; but the sixth slab had been different. It was obviously older from the way the engravings had worn, and the way the rotten cloth of the skeleton's robe was nothing but rags. That one had carried another word.

Sivingathm

Weeks later, when he couldn't find what *Sivingathm* meant, or even what language it was, he asked Lightbringer Otti. He immediately knew he'd made a mistake from the way the Otti's face froze.

"Where did you hear that name?"

"Some of the other novices were talking," Seth said. "I overheard it. I don't know who said it."

"Forget it."

Seth nodded and promised that he would, and it never seemed to occur to the old Lightbringer that he'd already given Seth the answer he needed.

Sivingathm was someone's name.

7

RED

"Toes?" Fings wasn't liking this. Not at all. He felt the tension like a cord tying them together.

"Fings." Toes eased the knife back into his belt and moved away from his perch, wary, hands held wide so Fings could see them. "It's not... it's not what I wanted." Another glance to the door. Fings followed his eyes.

"Toes... What's she done?"

"It... It wasn't enough, Fings." Toes bolted then, and Fings found himself split clean in two, one half desperate to give chase, the other half desperate to run away while he still could. He didn't know what to do. His family were in there, the only thing that really mattered.

"His name is Toes?" asked Myla, dubiously. Fings ignored her. Red was here. To leave a warning? Or had she come to cut a throat and teach him a lesson?

No. She wouldn't. It hasn't gone that bad. Not yet.

Sulfane murdering Longcoats. Seth beaten almost to death, lucky to be alive, Myla lopping off heads... Maybe it *had* gone that bad. Maybe the whole world had gone bad...

"I suppose you know someone called Legs, too? Or Knees?"

Myla, apparently, had decided to be unhelpful. "Actually–"

"Fings!" Red strode out, pushing Yona ahead of her, Fings' youngest sister. Red shoved Yona to the ground and put a foot on her, keeping her down. "Get him, boys."

It took Fings a moment to see the two men who'd slipped into the yard behind him, cutting him off. Krato and Hik, all beefy arms and empty heads. Red must have had them lurking in wait somewhere. Crafty. But then Red always did have a streak of cunning. He closed his eyes and waited for what came next.

What came next was a grunt and a shriek; when he looked, Hik was rolling in the dirt clutching his privates and Krato had both hands to his throat, eyes bulging and gulping for air like a fish out of water. There was a long slow scrape of steel. Myla drawing one of those nightmare swords of hers.

"Come near me again and I'll kill you," she said.

"Who the fuck is this?" Red pushed down, grinding Yona into the cobbles.

"She's with Blackhand," said Fings. "And so am I, and I left you more than them books were worth so I don't owe you nothing, so you'd better let her go, Red. I don't want us fighting."

"You took my silver."

"I didn't touch your silver. I took your books. That was all."

"I *know* you took my silver."

"I *didn't*!"

Krato had just about worked out how to breathe again but he didn't seem keen on going anywhere near Myla. Hik looked like he was staying down for a while. Toes came out of the house. As he did, Red took her foot off Yona's back, pulled her to her feet and had a knife to her throat, all faster than Fings could think.

"You pay what you owe, Fings, or *I* take something from *you*."

Fings caught the blur of a movement from Myla, a look on her face he didn't recognise, an incandescent anger as her arm whipped to her side, like she was remembering something else. "No!" He lunged, trying to catch Myla's hand, seeing the knife there. "Don't!"

He caught her wrist before she let it fly.

"No," he said again. "No, no, no! We don't... we don't..."

He was almost in tears. Red was looking at him, half

contemptuous, half angry, half puzzled. Fings ignored her, grabbing Myla.

"These were friends, once. Red and me, we go way back. And Toes. And Krato, even if he *is* a complete knob."

Myla looked like she simply didn't understand.

"We don't... We don't *do* this to each other." He turned back to Red and caught Yona's eye. "Sis all right? Ma? They hurt you?"

Yona gave a little shake of her head. Red still had the knife at her throat.

"Put her down, Red. You don't want to do this."

"Try me."

She wouldn't. "I didn't take your silver, Red."

"I don't believe you."

She won't. "I gave you all I got!"

"Wasn't enough."

"I ain't got what you want!" Myla was edging around the yard now, keeping an eye on Krato and Hik while she watched Red and Toes.

"Someone has to pay, Fings. That's the way. You know it."

Another scrape of steel as Myla drew her second sword. "I don't know you and I don't know your dispute, but you cut that girl and I'll spread you across this yard." Which was pretty much how Fings felt about it, although he didn't quite see why Myla would feel the same.

"I'll do a job for you," he offered. "You name it, I'll get it. Whatever makes us even."

"You pay me what you owe me. Here and now." Red glanced at Myla. "Her being here says you're good for it."

Fings found he was shaking. "I don't–"

"How much?" asked Myla.

Red grinned. "Five full-moons."

Despite everything, Fings couldn't help a surge of outrage, because yes, maybe he *had* had a quick look at Red's stash that night when he'd taken those books, and it wasn't *that* much.

Myla tossed a purse. It clattered to the cobbles at Red's feet. "I've got four. I'll buy the debt."

"I said five."

"Consider that sword-monks can smell lies. Consider that you can walk away from here with four silver moons. Consider the alternatives."

Fings saw Red twitch. Toes went to the purse and opened it, looked inside, and nodded. He could hardly have made it more obvious how he wanted Red to take what was being offered.

Red let Yona go.

"Are we good, Red?" Fings asked.

Red gave him a long hard look, then walked over, spat on her hand and offered it. Fings spat on his own. They shook, and Fings reckoned she meant it, if only because coming after him for a second time probably looked more trouble than it was worth.

"Cross me again, Fings, and I'm going to hurt you."

"I ain't crossing anyone, Red."

But she had her back to him already, shooing her Neckbreakers ahead of her, keeping away from Myla and those swords. Toes spared him a glance, a sort of sorry sad little look like he was a bit ashamed, and then they were gone. Fings ran to Yona and hugged her and took her back inside and made sure everyone was alright, and told them all he was going away for a while but that he'd be back soon, and gave them all the money he had left, which wasn't very much but would last while he was gone. It took a bit of a while, all in all.

Myla was still there when he came back out, on her haunches, back against a wall, staring into nothing, holding her wineskin in one hand. It was empty, he saw.

"Sorry," he said, although *sorry* was nowhere near enough.

"Sure. We're all about to be rich, remember?" Myla smiled but she didn't mean it, or the words either. She didn't believe in Sulfane's treasure barge.

"I mean I'm sorry about… grabbing at you."

She gave him an odd look and then, weirdly, started to laugh.

"I thought you might hit… you know…" But he hadn't. That was the thing. He hadn't been frightened for Yona at all.

Myla spun, fast and sharp. He caught the flash of a blade in her hand again and then the knife arrowed across the yard, as fast and deadly as one of Sulfane's arrows, and stuck quivering in a wooden shutter.

"No, you didn't," said Myla. "But I'm glad you stopped me."

Her thanking *him* made no sense that he could see. He mumbled something about paying her back one day, and meant it too, but she didn't seem interested. And then, for some reason, he wanted to confess, and it was all right there on the tip of his tongue, how the truth was that he *had* taken Red's silver. He hadn't *meant* to, knew he *shouldn't*, he'd just wanted the books for Seth; but the silver had been there, right in front of him, begging to slip into his pockets. And so that was what had happened, and it was all so stupid, because you didn't piss in your own yard. Everyone knew that.

He bit the confession back. Couldn't. He was too ashamed, and Myla would only ask the obvious question: *why?*

An accident? Habit? Instinct?

He wasn't sure he wanted to know.

8

WİПTERSCAPE

South of Varr sprawled a forest as old as time, protected by Imperial edict as an exclusive preserve for royal sport. Myla knew this because Seth had told her. Then he'd told her how the luckless poor would venture there in winter, desperate enough come the last weeks of the Sulk to brave the cold and the Emperor's guards and the monsters that lived there in search of firewood. She studied it as she rode out of the city's South Gate. It looked large and wild and like it might be a good place to hide. She'd fought monsters and she wasn't afraid of them.

She wasn't afraid of Jeffa Hawat, either, but she *was* afraid of what it meant that he was in Varr.

They followed the road around the walls to the south bank of the Arr and took a ferry across the water a few miles downriver. The land here didn't look so promising – fields and farms as far as the eye could see, all connected by a network of canals that joined everything to the two great rivers, the Arr and the Thort. She'd seen it all on her flight from Deephaven, too, but it had been summer then. City girl that she was, she'd imagined the land around Varr as a deserted snow-covered wasteland through winter, miraculously blooming to life in spring as though people and plants burst fully formed from the ground, even though they obviously didn't. She couldn't imagine anyone living in a wilderness of so much snow; yet here they were, and if anyone had told her, back in Varr in front of a nice warm fire, how many would be out and freezing in the middle of the Sulk, she'd have thought them mad. She was the daughter of a merchant and knew perfectly well that barges plied the rivers all year round, but knowing and seeing were very different things. There must have been hundreds, pushing their way against the current towards the capital, so loaded they looked ready to sink, or else drifting easy on the long journey back to the City of Spires, to Deephaven and the sea.

Jeffa says hello. Well, Jeffa wouldn't find her in a hurry, not while she was out here. Question was, what to do next? Where to go?

There were other alternatives, of course. She could let him find her. Or *she* could find *him*.

And then what? Kill him? And exactly what would that solve? Exactly nothing, that's what.

Wil and Sulfane were sullen as sulking children from the moment they left the city gates, but Fings walked beside her with a face permanently full of wonder, gradually asking more and more questions like an over-excited child. She was grateful for that because she knew the river and how it worked, and it gave her something to think about that wasn't Jeffa Hawat, and so she answered him as best she could. She explained that the road beside the water always stank of shit through summer on account of all the animals pulling barges and how the Emperors hadn't liked the smell, which was why there was a second road half a mile inland. She pointed out how the up-river traffic stayed by the north bank while the downriver traffic stayed out in the middle, explained how the barges heading downriver from Varr didn't need to be towed because of the current. She told him how the north bank of the river had been dredged and excavated and shaped while the far bank was untamed, how the little specks he could see on the far side of the water were tiny rafts where men caught fish using diving birds. She even tried explaining how it had all come to be this way because of the iron mines and forges around the Fenris capital of Neja, halfway to the City of Spires. All the way from Varr she talked, and Fings listened, and she shared her wine with him - painstakingly refilled at every opportunity - and in truth it was a joy to see the world at work, to remember the lessons she'd had as a child and actually see them unfolding in the landscape in front of her.

Then there were the waystations. She knew they were there, of course, and had heard the stories, but her trip up the river in summer had been in secrecy and hiding. She'd expected something like the Unruly Pig, but the first waystation was more like an entire village, two huge halls and two dozen outbuildings, barns and stables for a hundred animals, a score of men and women working even with the snow two feet thick all around and drifts as high as a house. After that first night, there was another every half a day, close enough that each morning as they set out, they could already see the smoke rising from the next, visible for miles over flat fields of snow tinged pink in the dawn. Even now, on the edge of winter, the stations were a hive of noise and motion, of chatter and smoke, as though the cold and the snow didn't make a jot of difference.

If Jeffa was in Varr, looking for her, it didn't *have* to mean that anyone else knew she wasn't dead, did it? Maybe the rest of them still thought she'd died in the fire, like they were supposed to?

But life was never that easy.

She watched Wil and Sulfane sitting in their corner, terse and broody and nursing their food, neither with much to say. If it wasn't for Fings, she would have been the same, preoccupied with whether she should simply keep going to the City of Spires or strike north for Neja or south for Tarantor or even Torpreah, or whether it was better to return to Varr and take what was coming, or even go to Deephaven and look for a ship across the sea. But Fings... Watching him lifted her spirits. He was like a child in a world full of wonders, bantering with the staff and the crews of the barges and anyone who would talk, dazzled by the sheer number of people, rich and poor all mingled together.

She kept coming back to thinking about how he'd stopped her in Locusteater Yard. She could have killed that woman. She could have killed all of them, and he knew it, and it would have solved all his problems, and yet he'd stopped her, willing to take the chance that he could make it right. And yes, she was happy enough not to have more blood on her hands, but it was more than that. There was a courage in Fings. A loyalty and a deep sense of right and wrong. Did any of the others see it? Seth probably, yes, but the rest of them? No. What they saw, they mistook for weakness.

Fine. She'd see this one through. Do whatever it was that Blackhand wanted them to do, get them safely back to Varr, and then she'd leave. Take a barge to the City of Spires, maybe. Jeffa wouldn't expect that.

Still wouldn't solve anything.

Inevitably, she saw the look in Fings' eye, the temptation to lift a purse. Whatever his code, other people's money wasn't a part of it, but they'd both been there when Blackhand had given his last orders. A glare at Wil. *No fighting.* Then her and Sulfane. *No bodies.* Then Fings. *No stealing.* And she'd almost seen Fings thinking about that in his head, turning it into *No getting caught*, which would be fine because he *almost never* got caught...

She caught his eye and beckoned him over.

"Don't," she said.

"Don't what?"

She raised a warning finger. "You know what."

"Maybe on the way back?" The way he grinned at her was like a child begging for a treat. She shook her head, which made him sigh and sit beside her and sulk for a bit, and then rant about how easy it would be to slip away with so many people passing through, how he could *smell* the money, how a few days in a place like this and he could repay his debt to her. She listened and tried to sound stern when she said no, but it was hard not to smile.

"You can pay me back when we've done this thing for Sulfane," she told him, when he went on again about how she'd squared things for him with Red. It wasn't the money, though. She'd stood up for his sister, and that turned out to count for something. It left her with a warm feeling.

On the second day, she walked and led her horse, and Fings walked beside her and told her about Ma Fings and his sisters and how he meant to get them all away from this one day, get them set up somewhere nice where they didn't have to worry about food and staying warm, maybe go to Deephaven and find his brother Levvi after all these years. In the evening, she bought a bottle of wine and nursed it, watching Fings make friends everywhere he went. It was hard not to envy him.

"Come and dance," he said, when they were both half-drunk, but she shook her head.

Jeffa says hello.

She drank some more.

The third day passed in much the same way. In the evening, they stabled their horses and hurried into the warmth. Fings pestered her for the umpteenth time about the money he owed and she gave him the same answer: that he could pay her back for Red whenever he had the money and not to worry about it. Someone started with the inevitable pipe, and a fiddle joined in, and Myla watched Fings dance – a bit like a spider having a seizure but you had to admire his enthusiasm – and drank another bottle of wine, and decided *fuck it*, and so they danced together, and it was wonderful because Fings didn't want anything from her, or from anyone at all, except to share his joy at the world and his sense of freedom, and yes, that little voice still rattled around in the back of her head about Jeffa, what was she going to do, where was she going to go, how Sulfane might be planning to stab them all in their sleep the moment he had what he wanted, but it was a *small* voice now, and so she stayed awake with Fings and they talked and danced and relished the warmth until they were both yawning, and then settled into a corner of the commons, and Fings fell asleep with his head on her shoulder and–

And it was suddenly dark, and the air was full of snoring, and Sulfane was prodding her in the ribs, and her head hurt, and it seemed like she'd barely closed her eyes.

"What the...?"

"Time to get to work."

She nudged Fings. When they slipped outside, the cold was bitter and Wil was already shivering. Fings yawned and tutted at them for leaving footprints everywhere like idiots, then fished out a scrap of fur on a string from the sackcloth bag he carried with him everywhere, and offered it to Myla.

"You'll want this," he said. "Stop anyone from hearing you." He reached into the bag again, pulled out his chicken's foot charm and looped it round his neck, then his trusty feather.

Myla blinked. Her head was cloudy. Too much wine, not enough sleep, and the cold had dismally sharp edges and everything hurt.

"Barge is here," whispered Sulfane. He glanced at the sky, to where clouds covered the moon.

"What day is it?" Fings fished another charm from his bag, a piece of carved bone on a thread.

"Moonday," said Wil.

Fings nodded and looped the charm around his wrist. "Don't suppose we can wait a couple of days?" he muttered. "Sundays are best for burglaries because the next day is Towerday and Towerdays are best for hiding."

Sulfane rolled his eyes.

"No," said Wil.

"Could be worse. As long as we're away plenty before dawn." Fings made a helpless face. "Once it's Abyssday, frankly the best thing is to stay in bed. Worse than Magedays." He tutted and shook his head. He was doing it deliberately, Myla decided, getting under Sulfane's skin.

"Just shut up and get on with it!"

She had to hide a smirk. Apparently, it was working, too. *Clever? Probably not…*

Fings slipped a last silver charm around his neck. "Fickle Lord Moon. Have to get on the right side of him. Get it wrong and Moondays are worse than Magedays. Get it right… Get it right and you can get away with almost anything on a Moonday. God of thieves, the Moon." He grinned and spread out his hands and walked in a slow circle, mumbling some prayer Myla didn't recognise.

Sulfane let out a growl between gritted teeth. "When you're *quite* done."

They skirted the waystation to the river. There were a dozen barges moored at the jetties but only one of them had a pair of sentries huddled around a lantern. Myla couldn't see the colours they wore, not at night, but one, at least, was clearly a soldier.

"Silly buggers might as well have hung up a sign," muttered Fings. "*Stuff worth stealing! Come and get it!*"

"Two men came ashore," said Sulfane. "No others."

"Who are we robbing?" Myla asked. The outline of the soldier's armour had her thinking Imperial Guard. She remembered what Seth said. *The Emperor's silver.*

The other sentry moved to the edge of the barge to take a piss. He was wearing a robe. Fings hissed.

"Is that a mage?"

"Don't be daft!" Sulfane sounded very sure. "Some clown trying to make you *think* he's a mage to put the fear of the Sun into dumb cocks like you, more likely."

"Who, *exactly*, are we robbing?" asked Myla again. She shook her head, trying to clear out the wool and the cobwebs. Too much wine and not enough sleep. Stupid...

"Yeah, what *am* I lifting?" asked Fings.

"The Emperor, that's who you're robbing." Sulfane grinned. "And what you're lifting, Fings, is a wooden box. Square. About the size of your forearm along each side and a few fingers deep. Plain, not engraved. Don't open it, because if you do, we're fucked. Anything else, you keep as much as you can carry." He bared his teeth a little more, like wolf about to make a kill. "There's silver on that barge, my friends. Bags and bags of it. Enough to pay a king's ransom, *if* you can get it. So. *Can* you?"

9

THE TREASURE BARGE

If you can get it? Fings bristled. Of course he could bloody get it! He was the best burglar in Varr, maybe the whole Empire! He had his charms and his feather. He liked that the two mugs on the barge had a lantern, too, because it meant they couldn't see for shit more than ten feet into the darkness around them. Either they were stupid or they had no idea what they were doing.

Sulfane clapped him on the shoulder and turned back to the barge. "I'll deal with the sentries. You slip inside, get the box and whatever else you can carry, we all vanish into the night." He hesitated. "There's more soldiers inside. Should be asleep by now."

Fings nodded. He knew how to be quiet.

"Like I said, there should be a fortune in silver, but you come out and you haven't got that box, you go back in and you get it. Clear?"

Fings nodded, the words "silver" and "fortune" slipping through him like a slug of Myla's brandy. The Murdering Bastard's plan had more murdering than it needed, but the rest seemed reasonable, insofar as it left Fings to make it up as he went.

"Nah," he said.

"What?"

"Well… It's a Moonday."

"So?"

"So I don't want you screwing this up." The slipping in and out didn't look too bad but the unnecessary murdering felt vaguely insulting – more chance they'd raise the alarm than if Sulfane just did nothing at all, probably. "What if you miss?"

Sulfane's expression was like someone had taken a whole summer of thunderstorms and stuffed them into one face. "I don't miss."

"Anyone can miss on a Moonday. And one of them is a mage."

"No, he isn't."

"What if he *is*?"

"Then he'll be a dead mage. You can't magic away what you don't see coming."

"You want to shoot them, wait two days. Sunday. Great day for sticking arrows in people, a Sunday. You want this done now, on a Moonday, we do it the way I say."

Sulfane looked like maybe he was happy to stand and argue about this all night, which would have suited Fings just fine, but then Wil put a nervous hand on Sulfane's shoulder.

"He's a knob sometimes, but he's the best there is. He ain't ever let us down. Let him do it his way."

Fings held Sulfane's eye until the Murdering Bastard looked away. He wasn't so sure about the *vanish into the night* part of this plan either – all very well in the city, but out here? Out here, sooner or later, they'd be in the middle of a field full of snow in broad daylight with a handy trail of footprints behind them.

Worry about that once your pockets are stuffed with silver, eh?

"I need Myla's knapsack and your cloak," he said. The knapsack because he needed something to carry whatever he looted, and Myla's was oiled leather and so whatever he put inside would stay mostly dry. Sulfane's cloak because it was thick and warm and he was about to get very, very cold.

Myla gave him her knapsack and rubbed her eyes and winced. Sulfane grudgingly handed over his cloak. Fings put the cloak and some bits from his bag into the knapsack, took out his Thief's Candle, lit it, and then started to strip. Wil looked at him like he was a lunatic.

"What you *doing*? It's freezing!"

"You be waiting with all this when I come back, or the first place I'm going is inside in front of a fire, don't matter what else is happening." Fings gave his clothes to Wil. Standing in the snow, his feet were already screaming and it was only going to get worse.

He passed the candle to... almost to Wil as well, but at the last moment chose Myla instead. "Keep that. Don't let it go out until I get back. If it *does* go out then you need to get away quick. Don't wait." Hard to get a real proper Thief's Candle on account of all the stuff that went into them that he didn't want to know about: fat harvested from executed murderers and the fingers of dead babies and all sorts. Expensive but they worked, that was the thing.

Cold, cold, cold! He padded towards the river. The two sentries had done the obvious thing, set themselves up beside the little plank bridge to the waystation jetties. You couldn't cross from the jetty without walking straight through their circle of light, and no one in their right mind would be in the river on a night like this. At least, that was their thinking, so that was exactly what Fings was going to do. From there...

I'm sure we'll think of something. Get aboard first.

If the air was cold, the river was a thousand times worse. A thin film of ice crusted the bank where there wasn't much current. The shock of it ran up his leg as soon as he touched it. His toes went numb. Cold like this could kill you in minutes. He'd seen it happen.

Murdering Bastard better be right about that silver. Fings slid into the water and tried not to scream as everything clenched against the ice. He forced his arms and legs to move, quiet and steady, no splashing, all silky smooth and dragging Myla's knapsack in his wake. He'd learned to swim almost as soon as he'd learned to run, learned the hard way in the canals and rivers of Varr.

Frozen in the winter, shit and dead things in the summer. Certainly teaches you to swim with your mouth shut...

He came around the riverward side of the barge, out of sight, pulled himself aboard, opened the knapsack, threw the cloak onto the deck and shuffled his feet. No wet footprints, in case one of the sentries came around this side. Not that that looked likely...

Shivering violently, he wrapped himself in Sulfane's cloak as soon as his feet were dry and crept through the darkness to the stern and the door that led inside.

Be warm in there, at least. He was counting on that.

The might-be mage was standing twenty feet away with his back turned. Fings put his feather between his teeth and sucked at it and touched the charm around his neck. Chances were good they wouldn't see him even if they looked right at him, not with their night eyes blinded by that lantern. He pressed his ear against the door and turned the handle, slow and quiet. When he'd turned it enough, he pulled it open a crack. The air inside was warm and fragrant, the stale smell of too many men in too small a room for too long a time. He had a quick argue with himself over whether to go in slow and quiet or whether to do it quick, but quick meant getting out of the cold, and he was freezing. At the first lull in the breeze, he darted inside.

No one stirred. No shouts from the sentries.

See. No need for any murdering. He hoped Sulfane had been watching.

The air inside was dark and stifling, loaded with snores but Sun be praised it was *warm*. Fings stood like a statue, feeling his skin tingle and waiting to see if anything moved. If they did, all he could do was run, but *this* was why he was burning his precious Thief's Candle, this bit of luck he needed right here.

A tiny window at the bows gave a little light. His eyes started to adjust...

Oh... Crap.

There were men sleeping on the floor. He'd expected that but they were *everywhere*, maybe twenty of them. He whispered a silent prayer to the Moon as he took in the room. One cabin running from front to back of the barge. Sulfane's box, whatever it was, had to be here. Somewhere. Buried among all these sleeping bodies.

Shit.

Just find it and get out.

Yeah, and the silver...

He waited. No one stirred.

Right, then.

Fings had grown up in tiny rooms with their floors packed by sleeping bodies. He took his time, careful, delicate steps, so precise that the air hardly felt his presence. Ghostlike in a circle round the cabin, slow as the sun crossing the sky, fingers questing, feeling out every corner and nook, all the way from back to front and back again...

No box. No silver. Only a room of snoring soldiers.

Crap! Now what?

The obvious thing – the *sensible* thing – would be to slip out and tell Sulfane that his box wasn't here. Trouble with that was the Murdering Bastard wouldn't believe him. People would start having accidents with arrows and having their heads lopped off and all that malarkey, and it *was* a long way to have come...

What have I missed?

He'd been everywhere. High, low, every corner...

He sighed. There was a lower deck. Of *course* there was, there *had* to be. With an entrance helpfully hidden under a floor covered in sleeping bodies

He flexed his fingers. So it was going to be *difficult*, was it?

Yeah. But I'm Fings, greatest burglar in the empire.

He pulled a tarnished bronze ring with a crudely carved face from Myla's bag and kissed it. *Kiss the face of the king in the dark and fortune will be yours until dawn.* That's what the witch-woman who'd sold it to him had said. The Thief's Candle ought to be enough on its own but it never hurt to be sure. He eased back around the room on his hands and knees, on his belly, feeling the floor around each sleeping body, gently curling up as though he was just another sleeper any time one of the guards shifted.

It all took time. He must have been there well past an hour by now. Slow and steady was the key to this sort of thing but his candle would only burn so long. Sooner or later, the moon would set and he'd lose his luck. One of the soldiers would wake and need a piss or something, and that would be that.

His fingertips found a notch in the floor wider than the gaps between the planks. The ends and edges of a trapdoor. With slow patience, he squeezed himself between two of the sleeping guards. Born and raised in a crowded space full of brothers and sisters and cousins, he'd learned long ago how this worked, how to carve his own tiny space with nudges and knees and elbows. The sleeping soldiers grumbled and muttered and moved over and dropped right back into sleep again, never awake enough to realise that Fings was Fings...

Best burglar in the empire. Best burglar in the whole Sun-blessed world!

He nudged and poked and waited until the trapdoor was clear, then gave it a few minutes and then a few minutes more to be sure. Once he went down to the lower deck, he didn't have a clear escape.

Patience. It's all patience.

He eased the trapdoor open and glided to the lower deck. No one else was there. And he could *feel* how close he was to that moment when he'd hold whatever loot was waiting for him for the first time. Always the best part...

Like the one above, the lower deck was a single open space that ran from bow to stern. *Un*like the one above, there were a lot of chests. A *lot* of chests.

There's always a chest. With a lock. Always one of those, too.

Except there wasn't. He opened the first. Inside were soft cloth bags full of...

He froze at the faint clink of coins.

Money.

MONEY!

He didn't know how many chests there were all together, but more on each side of the room than he had fingers. He went from one to the next to the next. They were all full of it. He felt giddy. There wasn't this much treasure in the whole of Varr! The Murdering Bastard might even be worth all the trouble he'd caused after all.

Oh, Fings, you've got it made now, lad, if you can just get out of here…

One bag. That's all he'd ever need. One bag and he could live like a king. One bag and he could take Ma Fings and all his sisters and they'd always be warm in winter and never be hungry, and maybe he could take a boat to Deephaven and find Levvi and tell him he could come home again, that everything was fixed…

Up in the bows, he found a stand, something like a chair with some sort of metal cloth draped over it. He ran his fingers over its surface. A mail coat. Too heavy and noisy to think about moving.

Pity.

He sighed. But what was this? A sword in a scabbard, lying next to the armour. Did he *want* a sword? Not really. Maybe for Myla? She seemed to like them.

Too big, too loud, too heavy, too clumsy.

His hands moved on. Another chest, smaller than the others. Inside it was a small pouch holding three rings. Under the pouch was a sheaf of papers. Under *that* was…

He eased it out. A plain square wooden box, exactly like the Murdering Bastard had said.

The rings and the papers went into the knapsack. The box…

Gold? Gems? Something so precious it's worth more than all this silver? Sulfane had known it was here. Stood to reason it was the most precious thing.

He risked a gentle shake but there was no clink from inside.

Time to go. He could almost feel the edge of his luck, close to all used up: the Thief's Candle in Myla's hand, burning to a stub, the moon drooping towards the horizon. He pushed the box into the knapsack and stuffed in as many bags of money as he could manage. *The tighter you pack them, the less they rattle, right?* Shame to leave so much behind but he needed his arms for not drowning. Patience and not being greedy. That's what made for a good burglar.

Right. Like when you didn't steal Red's silver but actually you did?
Shut up.

He hoisted himself back among the sleeping guards, pulled the knapsack up behind him, closed the hatch, and tiptoed his way to the door. He pressed his ear to it and couldn't hear anything. How to slip past the sentries on the deck on his way out had been something to wonder about; but as he eased himself into the slightly brighter darkness of the outside and strained his eyes to find them, he saw he needn't have bothered. They were gone. Both of them. No trace.

The Murdering Bastard up to his tricks again, was it?

You could go back and grab another couple of bags of money.

He pushed the thought away. That was the thing about luck. Didn't matter how many charms and talismans you carried, what mantras and prayers you said, if you took the piss then luck would leave you swinging from a rope. He ran a silent dance of carefully planted feet, off the barge and down the jetty and to the shore, and ducked into the first convenient shadows for a bit of a think about what came next.

The snow, that was the thing. He knew exactly how to vanish in Varr, but out here? And this wasn't some two-bit spice merchant they were burgling. He was used to *that*, people who'd get angry and hire a few men for a few days or maybe throw some money at the Longcoats, but all you had to do was lie low for a couple of weeks until they gave up because it simply wasn't worth it. This? A barge and two dozen armed men and a mage and half the Imperial Treasury in silver? *This* was stealing from Someone Who Mattered. People Who Mattered had long arms and held grudges. Known for it, they were.

But you knew that before you came. You just didn't want to think about it.

The Murdering Bastard had to have some sort of plan, didn't he? If he didn't, Wil was good for this sort of thing. And Myla, too, probably the cleverest person he knew except for Seth. So yeah. Maybe they'd be alright. Either way, time to merge into the night and be away with a fortune in his pocket.

Worry about tomorrow when it comes.

There was *one* thing though, before he went back to Wil and Myla, one little thing he just had to do, even if he knew he shouldn't. Because in the end, he just couldn't bring himself to trust Sulfane, not even a little.

He opened the box.

Inside it was a plain band of black metal about the size to be nice and loose around someone's neck. A torc?

There was writing etched on the inside.

He peered closer.

A tiny glimmer of silver light flickered, deep inside.

Moonsteel.

Oh. Oh, fuck!

10

PRİEST OF AΠ AΠGRY GOD

Even this late, the Teahouse was usually full of noise. Blackhand would be moving among raucous clusters of merchants and hangers-on, passing out free drinks and eliciting delicious titbits of information for Fings or Wil or one of the others. Sara and the other girls would be perched on knees while Myla sat in a corner and glowered. It was a point of hot dispute between her and Blackhand that she wasn't allowed her swords inside the Pig while Wil strutted openly with his knives. Fings reckoned that was because Wil laughed and joked and smiled and looked friendly as a puppy until you got on the wrong side of him, while Myla generally looked as though she was contemplating the most satisfying way to cut you up; but the real truth was that Blackhand and Wil went back a dozen years and more, while Myla simply didn't belong.

Like me.

So why do I stay?

Because it's safe.

Is it? Is it really?

That was the thing. Was Blackhand's protection really worth anything? Hadn't stopped him being almost kicked to death by those Spicers. He might be a failed priest but he could still read and write in three different languages and he knew more about history and theology than most Lightbringers. Sure, living under

Blackhand's wing was safer than living on the streets, but it wasn't the only option, was it?

A nice cushy job as a clerk to some spice merchant. Adding numbers, writing letters, counting sacks and barrels?

Seth turned his eye back to the papers in front of him. Sulfane's letter. Seth wasn't sure he had an opinion on Sulfane one way or the other. Didn't have many opinions at all, these days, except that if there was a reckoning coming then they deserved it, every one of them.

Ah well. Myla was letting him have her room while she was away; and since the alternative was going back to Ma Fings or sheltering in his secret place under a few planks propped against a wall – and he was just waiting for the night when they were all stolen for firewood – almost anything was preferable. The warmth of the Pig hugged him close.

He cleared the papers and headed for bed. Inevitably he'd wake at dawn and say his prayers, no matter how much he didn't want to. And then, no matter how bruised he was, no matter how hard it was to get to his feet, he'd stumble to the kitchens and bag up any leftover pastries from the night before, eat the ones too damaged to sell, go out to the square to read one of his precious, books for a while, fall asleep until mid-morning, wake up stiff as a stone and half frozen, spend the next ten hours being abused, kicked and ignored, eat most of what he had to sell, and end the day looking at two or three half-bits in his pocket. He'd wonder whose life he was leading and who had the one that should have been his, and then he'd drag himself back to the Teahouse for the evening and do it all again.

Time to turn in.

He lay down and closed his eyes. He wondered, as he wondered every night, how long he had before the others came back. The longer they were gone, the longer he had a bed.

He did promise you a room.

And what's that worth, a promise from Black Alarand?

Not much.

Soon, he was dreaming. In his dreams, he drifted high into the sky, over mountain tops laid in neat little rows like pastries on a tray. Above him burned a bright red star with many names. The Baleful Eye, The Revealer, The Exposer of Truth, The Bane of the False and the Corrupt, The Unraveller of Mysteries.

The Emperor is dead, it said.

He'd seen an Imperial Messenger tear through the Square today. They wore black, always, but this one had been wrapped in grey shrouds of death. He remembered wondering whose death the messenger was carrying; now, in his dream, he knew as surely as he knew the stains and scars on his fingers.

The Emperor. The Emperor is dead.

Blankets of cloud wrapped him, warm against the winter air. A pinprick of light appeared below, a pyre, piled high and burning fierce. Black shadows flickered around it, melted into formless shapes by dark furs heaped around their shoulders. Seth flew closer. One of the figures abruptly threw off his furs and looked up. The face that looked up at him was half ruined, one side a mass of scars like it had been burned or ravaged by the pox, one eye white and blind.

And then it was gone, and it was only a dream.

Never steal what you can't fence.
– Seth

11

ΠΟΤ HOW THIS WAS SUPPOSED TO GO

Fings gave Myla his candle and slipped away towards the river bank. Wil and Sulfane watched the sentries on the barge for any sign of trouble. Myla yawned and rubbed her temples and wondered what they were supposed to do if Fings got caught. Fight everyone at the waystation? Because that's what it would come to.

She'd washed up in the Unruly Pig in the middle of summer, drawn by the Spice Market and a distant half-memory of hearing its name in Deephaven. She'd paid for a room and called herself Myla, her old childhood nickname, a shortened *my lady*. The silver she'd brought with her from Deephaven had been running low and so she'd been looking for a merchant who'd take her on as a clerk or an agent or even as an apprentice, someone who wouldn't ask too many questions and whose business took them far away but not across the sea. For all these things, the Spice Markets of Varr seemed perfect, so she'd asked around, looking for traders who liked to flirt on the edges of respectability. She kept hearing the same name as a place to go: the Unruly Pig, known for its freedom from pickpockets, for the quality and variety of its entertainments, and because Blackhand, so they said, could arrange almost anything you could imagine, for a suitable price.

An evening in the Pig was all it took for her to understand that half the clientele were thugs and thieves like Wil and Fings, urban bandits who behaved themselves under Blackhand's leash because the Teahouse was warm, because the food was often free and – pastries aside – usually good, and because tongues loosened with liquor and narcotic spices sometimes let slip things they shouldn't. For a while, after Blackhand approached her, it felt like she'd found a home. But she hadn't. She understood that now. All she'd found was a place where she could stop running for a while.

Jeffa says hello.

Everyone in Deephaven thought she was dead. Her own sister. The Hawat brothers. All of them. That was how it was supposed to be. That was how it was supposed to end.

"If they catch him, we have to let Fings hang," she said, looking at Wil. "Don't we."

Wil didn't say anything. She supposed he was ignoring her; but then she caught his face and she saw she was wrong. He was thinking the same: that there was nothing they could do and that he didn't like it.

"Best burglar in Varr," he said at last. "Fings don't ever get caught."

She almost asked why Blackhand had sent her and Wil then, if all they could do was watch. But the answer was obvious. Wil was here to keep an eye on Fings and Sulfane, to stop either of them getting ideas Blackhand wouldn't like. And *she* was here because Blackhand wasn't sure that Wil could handle Sulfane on his own.

Sulfane nodded to the woods on the other side of the road. "There's a stream. It's frozen over but there's water running underneath. Follow it into the trees. I'll get the horses from the stables. I'll take them and go ahead and lay some false tracks. I'll wait for you where we can split off."

As he headed away, Myla almost called after him to ask what was to stop the rest of them slipping off some other way and leaving him in the lurch, but the answer was obvious.

Because I'll hunt you until I find you and then I'll kill you.

"Did you know, before we got here?" she asked Wil, after Sulfane had gone.

"Know what?"

"The enemies we're making." The cold was seeping into her, despite her coat. Wil didn't answer but his face said no, he hadn't.

"It is what it is," he said.

She watched the moon, marking time by its track, slowly sinking into herself under the weight of the night. The white-gold moon. Some people still called it that because in legends there had been two moons, the Moon of White Gold – the God who made his own path through the sky – and the Black Moon that blotted out the sun. It was a story, that was all, a myth of the time when half-gods walked the world.

Black Moon come, round and round. Black Moon come; all fall down. She smiled, savouring the memories of childhood that came with the rhyme, and then the smile fell away, as one memory inevitably led to another.

The moon slipped towards the horizon. Myla stamped her feet and blew on her hands. Fings' candle burned steadily down. The sentries on the barge talked and stretched and yawned. She squatted, back against a wall. Her head drooped and she closed her eyes. When she opened them again, the candle was little more than a stub.

Shit.

The mage went to the front of the barge to take a piss. The soldier followed and did the same. It was odd the way men did that; and then, as if it was what he'd been waiting for all along, a shadow skipped through the circle of lamplight on the deck; a minute later, Fings was standing in front of her, stark naked under Sulfane's cloak in the freezing cold, and the night stayed quiet and there were no shouts of alarm.

"Did you…?" Wil was eager to go.

"Yeah, yeah. In the bag." He thrust the knapsack into Myla's hands and she almost dropped it, surprised by the weight. Fings grabbed his clothes off Wil and started to dress, shivering and shaking. "Silver. Stacks of it. More than we could carry, all of us together. Enough to buy a castle! Where's the Murdering Bastard?"

"You find that box he was after?"

"Yeah." Fings nodded, but Myla heard a wariness in his voice. She wondered: was now the time to run? Make her own way off into the night? In a way, wouldn't that be helping? Laying another false trail?

She didn't know. Her head hurt. She couldn't think.

You were going to see this one through, remember?

They found Sulfane's stream, the snow trampled, the ice broken underneath. Myla followed Fings. She wanted to ask about the barge and what had been inside.

If Jeffa found me in Varr, he'll find me anywhere.

The woods were still and muffled by snow so even a whisper sounded loud. She could barely see where she was going. Wading up to her knees through freezing water with no moon and the trees closing overhead, her feet were soon numb while the rest of her was slick with sweat at the effort.

If he knows you're alive, it doesn't matter where you go. You know that.

She did. And it couldn't stand. Something would have to be done.

Like what?

She didn't know how long they'd been going when Sulfane stepped out from the trees behind them; she turned, hand reaching for one of her knives, half expecting to see him with a dozen waiting men all ready to put the three of them in the ground, but it was only him and their two horses, standing patient and silent in the dark.

"Did you get it?"

Myla handed him the knapsack. Sulfane tore into it as though his life hung in the balance, yanking at the wooden box until it was free. He ran his hands over it and grinned and then grabbed Fings.

"Did you open this?"

"No!"

"What's inside?" asked Wil.

"None of your business."

"Blackhand know about this?"

"Come dawn, I go my way and you go yours. You want to ask him when you get back to Varr, I'm not going to stop you." Sulfane pulled a fistful of something like sand or salt from a pouch at his belt and sprinkled it in a circle around himself. He flicked the catch on the box and eased it open. A soft light came from inside, so faint that even in the woods under a moonless sky, Myla barely saw it.

"I thought you said not to open it," grumbled Fings.

Sulfane snapped the box closed, stuffed it into a satchel and slung it over his shoulder. "I said for *you* not to open it."

Fings didn't answer, but as they left the stream and headed into the woods, Myla saw how he kept grabbing at the chicken's foot around his neck.

Sulfane led them through trees packed tight enough that snow appeared only in patches and sprinkles underfoot. Fings and Wil danced between them, Myla following behind, leading her horse. Before long, she saw the dim glow of a lantern bobbing ahead. Sulfane stopped, looped his horse's reins around the trunk of a tree and strung his bow. "I'll deal with this," he said. "My business, not yours, so you just stay quiet and don't let them know you're here." A dozen steps into the darkness and Myla lost sight of him.

She sidled up to stand beside Fings. "You looked," she murmured. "Didn't you."

Fings stared straight ahead.

"You opened it." She put a hand on Fings' shoulder. He jerked away.

"So? So did the Murdering Bastard."

"*He* used a circle of salt and iron to keep sorcery out. Or in."

Fings hissed and started after Sulfane. "He's a got a–"

"Don't." Myla grabbed his arm. Fings shook her off.

"You think it's an accident, other people creeping around these woods at the dead of night?"

"Of course it isn't."

The lantern turned suddenly brighter. Fings shook his head and headed towards it.

"Fings!" Myla followed; but by the time she caught up, Fings had stopped and had pressed a finger to his lips.

She looked back for Wil, but he hadn't followed. Ahead, she could see three other figures around the lamplight, and Sulfane talking like he knew them. The lantern was on the ground. The man nearest stood beside it while two others held back a pace to either side, where the light made it almost impossible to make out anything about them. There could easily have been more and neither she nor Sulfane would know.

The words were quiet but she picked up the gist.

You got it?

Yes.

"See!" hissed Fings.

Sulfane took the box from his satchel and set it on the ground.

You come alone?

Yes.

Your thief?

Sulfane drew a thumb across his throat.

"*Bastard*," hissed Fings. He took a step forward. Myla yanked him back.

"If he was planning on murdering us, why have us hold? Why tell them he's alone?"

Sulfane stepped away from the box like he was expecting something in return, and that was when one of the men standing behind the lantern shot him; but Sulfane must have seen it coming because he was already diving away, and the bolt only caught him in the arm. He staggered but didn't fall, then ran, and the three men gave chase.

"Wil!" Myla broke cover towards Sulfane. One man swore and turned, trying to head her off, but now their own light picked them out and made them easy to see. As he ran at her, she slipped a knife from her belt and threw it. He lurched sideways and the knife missed, and then Myla was on him with her two swords. He parried her first strike, but missed the backswing that severed his hamstrings as she ran past. She didn't even break stride as he screamed.

The man chasing after Sulfane caught and tackled him. They wrestled and then broke apart and staggered up. The man drove a knife into Sulfane's side, doubling him over, and then he must have heard her coming because he whirled and saw her and froze. Sulfane took him from behind with a knife of his own. He stabbed it into the man's neck and then into his chest and again and again and again, six, seven, eight times, and it was all Myla could do not to stop and stare…

"Behind…"

She turned and saw the last of the three men walking towards her, apparently not armed or in any great hurry. She sprang into guard. "Stop where you–"

"Die," he said, and something hit her in the chest, a deep impact on her breastbone that threw her back and knocked the air out of her, as though he'd hit her with a hammer, as though she'd been kicked by a horse.

He pointed at Sulfane.

"Die."

Sulfane held the man he'd stabbed like a shield. The man spasmed and arched with such violence that Myla heard his bones snap; and then he seemed to shrivel into himself as though crushed by some invisible hand. Sulfane threw him aside and snatched his bow off the ground but he was never going to be quick enough.

The mage pointed again.

"D–"

The word turned into a gurgle as Fings appeared from the darkness behind him and hit him round the head with a log. The mage staggered, and then Sulfane's first arrow caught him in the throat and a second hit him in the chest. With the third, he went down. Fings backed away in a hurry as Sulfane stumbled closer and stabbed the dying mage until he stopped moving. Myla lay in the snow and watched it all happen, helpless, trying to remember how to breathe, trying to understand the weight she felt on her chest, and then Fings was beside her, offering her his hand, pulling her up.

Sulfane staggered to his feet. "More?" There was an animal snarl to him. He had a crossbow bolt still buried in his arm and his face was a mask of pain. "Eh? Pox-ridden fucks! Any more of you?"

Myla clutched at Fings, still struggling to breathe.

"Where'd he get you?" he asked. "How bad?"

She managed a couple of gasps.

Sulfane sagged against a tree. "There were three. Where's the other one?"

Fings shrugged. "Myla got him."

"We're all in... deep... shit..."

"Who were those people?"

"What... What happened?" Wil panted, finally catching up.

"Fucked if I know..." Sulfane's face glistened with sweat. His breathing was fast and shallow.

Liar, Myla wanted to say, but she couldn't. She looked at Fings, but Fings was looking at Wil.

"Myla first," was all he said.

"No... point," growled Sulfane. "Was a mage. Used a death word. You can't... You can't save her."

Was *that* what this was? She'd seen the man point, heard him say the word, but she'd seen him do it to the dying man Sulfane had shoved in the way of the second strike, and what he'd done to her hadn't been anything like *that*. Except... she was slowly finding that she could still breathe after all, and it reminded her of the time Sword-mistress Tasahre had kicked her full in the chest all those years ago and knocked all the air out of her lungs. She'd thought she was dying *that* time, too.

She started to laugh, which hurt like being crushed under a falling building, but she couldn't help herself. She wiggled a hand under her cloak and touched the Moonsteel pendant from the Deephaven sell-sword and yes, it was warm. Almost hot.

"Just… winded…"

By the time she could move again, Wil had Sulfane on his back, cajoling Fings to help. There was a lot of snarling and swearing as they pulled the bolt out of Sulfane's arm. The knife wound in his side looked worse. Not deep in the belly, which would have meant slitting his throat as a mercy, but a long and ragged slash nonetheless, and a lot of blood. By the time Wil and Fings were done, Sulfane was drifting in and out of consciousness. Wil slung him over the back of his horse and Myla tethered it to her own. They went back to the lantern and found Sulfane's box and, a little way away, two horses, their reins looped around the stump of a tree. They looked for the third man, the one she'd crippled. When they didn't find him, there wasn't much to do except keep going and hope Sulfane didn't die, Fings muttering *See*, and *Murdering Bastard*, and *Didn't I say*, and *Told you so* under his breath until Wil told him to please shut the fuck up.

At dawn, they took Sulfane off his horse to have a better look at him. Fings stitched the wound closed – badly, probably – but there wasn't much else to be done except get him somewhere safe and hope he lasted. Wil took Sulfane's horse and rode ahead, trying to work out where they were, leaving her and Fings to keep watch; and Myla wondered whether he was thinking the same as she was, that maybe they might do better to leave Sulfane behind, him and that box and whatever was in it. Leave it all out here in the snow and walk away.

"That wasn't some random bunch of blokes who happened to be wandering the same woods as us in the middle of the night," Fings muttered. It was about the sixth or seventh time he'd said that to her. "You saw that, right? You *did* see that?"

"I saw, Fings."

"We didn't steal it for *him*. We stole it for *them*."

"I know." Sulfane was still breathing and still unconscious. Myla took the pouch of powder from his belt and tasted it. Salt and powdered iron, just as she'd thought. She sprinkled a circle on the ground as Sulfane had done, took the box, stepped inside, and opened it.

Fings watched her.

"Don't reckon we should have done this," he said.

Inside the box, wrapped in black velvet, lay a circlet of Moonsteel, and Myla reckoned Fings was right. And yet they had, and there it was, the Moonsteel Crown of the Empire.

It crossed her mind then that maybe she'd a made a mistake running out to help Sulfane when she could have stayed quiet and still and let everything play out without her. Let Sulfane be killed, let those men, whoever they were, take what they wanted. Sulfane had said he was alone, after all, and she still had their sacks of silver. But she hadn't, and in the end neither had Fings. Instinct, pure and simple.

She closed the box and tossed Fings a bitter smile.

"You know what this is."

Fings nodded. "Yeah."

"I saw the Emperor when he came to Deephaven, years ago," Myla said. "He was wearing this. Never takes it off, is what I heard, even when he sleeps."

Fings snorted. "Well he ain't wearing it now."

"No." And then, since Fings didn't seem to quite grasp just how big a storm of shit Sulfane had walked them into, she added: "You realise you saved Sulfane's life back there?"

"Eh?"

"That mage. He was about a second away from turning him inside out."

"No! What?"

Myla smiled as sweetly as she could, packing the Emperor's crown back into its box, quietly enjoying the look of despairing horror as it settled across Fings' face.

"Fuck. *Fuck!*"

12

THE ΠOVICE

Seth woke sodden and shivering, drenched in his own sweat despite the cold dawn air. He couldn't move. Or rather, he *could* move but he didn't *want* to move, on account of everything still hurting like a bath of broken glass from getting beaten half to death that night before everyone left to do whatever it was that was making Blackhand as nervous as Fings on a Mageday. He didn't *want* to move because he was warm and cosy in a proper bed in a room with a proper roof where you couldn't see the sky through the cracks, while the air outside was cold and the world was cruel.

He turned his head and saw sigils glowing among the papers strewn across the floor. Suddenly he was awake. Very, very awake, but when he looked again, they were gone.

He'd had the same dream for three nights in a row now: The Baleful Eye – the one-eyed god with the ruined face – and a place full of archways covered in sigils. Three nights in a row made it a sending, which explained having to remind himself who and where he was before his body felt his own again. Priests were no strangers to sendings... Except he *wasn't* a priest, not anymore, and they hadn't simply expelled him from the temple, they'd cut him off from the light, which meant that as far as the gods were concerned, he didn't exist. So why would he get a sending?

A suggestion to repent?

But he'd have run back to the temple and grovelled for forgiveness at the first hint that *that* might ever have been enough. If repentance was the message, it wasn't *him* that needed the sendings.

They'd started on the night he'd almost died. Maybe the Spicers had kicked something loose. Maybe he was going mad.

Seth, the mad hermit of the Spice Market? Sounded about right.

He dragged himself out from under his pile of blankets. The air in Myla's room was cold but the heat of the Pig's hearths and kitchens kept it from freezing. If Blackhand kept his word and gave him a room in exchange for Sulfane's letter, it would be the attic cupboard with the hole in the wall where he couldn't stand straight without thumping his head and where sometimes it *did* freeze in there. Still, when the alternative was sleeping on the streets and fighting to the death over scraps of firewood...

There *was* another spare room, of course. Sulfane's room, across the corridor, lying empty while he was gone. Myla was coming back, but Sulfane was supposed to fuck off to the Imperial Guard, wasn't that the plan?

Shows up out of nothing and Blackhand treats him like fucking royalty while I slave my arse off for him, and all I get is a closet?

Him and Myla. The pair of them.

Thoughts like that never came to anything good.

Still...

He looked over his scattered papers. None of the Unrulys had any idea how hard it was to make a good forgery. It wasn't the words – those were easy – but the handwriting, the seals, the coats of arms, the making it look and sound authentic. You wanted to mimic something? First, get your hands on a sample...

Outside the shutters, a pink pre-dawn light struggled through a murky sky. Seth slipped out, down steep wooden stairs that creaked with every step, into the main hall of the Teahouse and out while the rest of Blackhand's guests still slept. The Pig was quiet this early, only the kitchen girls already up, but the days were short this close to Midwinter, and the sooner this was done, the better.

A sending was a sending. Something was coming and he had a duty to tell the Dawncaller or one of his Sunbrights. They wouldn't want to hear it but what could they do? Excommunicate him a bit more? If they didn't want to know, that wasn't his problem.

Do your duty.

Something dreadful lurked behind that thought, a hope he was desperately trying to squash, the absurd notion that they might listen to him and think *Oh! A sending! It must be a sign!* and forgive him and take him back...

They wouldn't. He knew that, but there it was anyway. Stupid pointless going-to-fuck-you-up hope.

The doors to the Temple of the Sun in Spice Market Square were open wide when he arrived, latecomers for the dawn ceremony hurrying up the steps to be lost inside. Spice merchants, mostly, with their retinues of servants and hangers-on. Folk with money, because if you were poor like Seth then you went to the small hall around the back where the rich and glorious didn't have to see you. Lightbringer Otti was always at the top of the steps round the front, though, giving out blessings, and Otti was someone who might listen long enough to actually pay attention.

Seth stood at the foot of the steps, summoning his courage. Snatches of conversation wafted past him.

"...harvest around Tzeroth was good this year..."

"...A copper off the grain tax, do you think?" "Not if there's war afoot..."

He scanned the columns for Otti but didn't see him. What he *did* see were two pale-skinned sell-swords dressed like they were from Deephaven talking to a skinny old clerk from the Spice Merchants' Association. After what had gone down with the Spicers, Seth reckoned maybe Blackhand might want to know about that.

The three of them moved inside. Seth started up the steps, still looking for Lightbringer Otti.

"...Srendi claims she saw one of the Taiytakei across the river yesterday..."

"...They say the Princess Royal has been seen at the palace."

"I heard the same." "I heard she came into the city in secret two nights ago..."

A flash of yellow robes among the columns around the door. Seth faltered. It wasn't Otti at the top of the steps today but Otti's old apprentice, Lightbringer Suaresh.

Once upon a time, Seth would have walked on up, performed the three rites of supplication and honouring, then confronted Suaresh. But that novice was gone, and one of the Sunguard was watching, and maybe they recognised his face or maybe it was just that he was ragged and dirty and had no place here, but did it even matter? Lightbringer Suaresh wouldn't listen. Seth and Suaresh had been novices together. Chalk and cheese. Goodygoody, never-ask-questions, thick-as-a-plank Suaresh, and Seth, the brilliant maverick, always three steps ahead of the others and yet always in trouble. Or that's how it had seemed to Seth, at least.

Lightbringer Suaresh despised him.

The Sunguard started down the steps towards him. Slow, no hurry, as though nothing was wrong, but he was definitely coming Seth's way.

Maybe best to come back another day.

No! Go up there.

Maybe this evening at Twilight. Or tomorrow. Keep coming back until he found Lightbringer Otti doing the blessings of entry. That was probably best, wasn't it?

Face him!

Worst came to the worst, he could ask Myla for help when she came back. No question they'd let *her* inside...

Face. Him!

He turned away.

Useless pathetic coward.

Turned out the priests were right: his soul *was* corrupt. It was rotten with fear and trembling with despair; and all the courage and strength he'd thought was his? It wasn't. They'd taken it from him, along with everything else.

13

BRİDGES AΠD GOBLİΠS

Far to the north of Varr sat a range of mountains: a wild place, unexplored, uninhabited and separating the northern extents of the Empire from unknown lands beyond. There, snowflakes settled on raw jagged spikes of stone, piled on top of one another, squashed each other flat and ganged into glaciers. The glaciers inched their way south until they melted into thousands of tiny streams that cascaded and carved their way through the north of the empire, merging into frothing white torrents. One by one, they came together as they ran south, joining into the great water highways of the northern empire to be carved into the web of canals and channels and water meadows that fed half the world. They soaked into the earth, siphoned through root, stem and branch into seeds and fruit, and were plucked and harvested and shipped to Varr and Deephaven in sacks and barrels. Those that survived made their way to the mighty river Arr in a hundred man-carved channels where they were carried away to the sea.

"And *I* say we leave it here," said Myla.

"We can't *do* that!" Wil was having none of it.

The whole snow thing was quite poetic, Fings thought, although he had no idea what a glacier was or how the whole "river of ice" thing could possibly work. He was doing a lot of that sort of thinking at the moment, partly because it was all fresh in his head from talking to Myla these last few days, but mostly because he was bored of listening to the other three argue. What he could see for himself was that wherever these channels came making their merry way out of the fields and forests north of the river, the road to Varr spanned them on bridges made from the colossal trunks of ancient trees. What with being covered in snow and more dropping in a steady fall from the sky and with the water all frozen and buried and everything white in a sea of yet more white, lurking under one of those bridges made for a fine place to hide.

Which was just as well, really.

"Goblins," he repeated, not that anyone was listening. As he was sure he'd known right from the start, burgling the barge had been one thing; getting away with it was turning out to be another. The sun had risen. Moonday had turned into Abyssday, and, certain as eggs were eggs, everything had gone to shit, which was the way Abyssdays were wont to be. So here they were, hiding huddled under an invisible bridge, shivering and listening to the occasional thud of horses above. There were a *lot* of soldiers about.

"Goblins." He tried again. "We can't leave it *here* because of goblins. They love to live under bridges."

"Oh, shut up!" Disappointingly, Sulfane hadn't died yet; in fact, Fings was starting to worry that Sulfane might not die at all, although he clearly wasn't quite with it, which at least mostly kept him quiet.

"But–"

"Fings!" Myla shot him a glare. Fings sighed. Myla, apparently having been hit on the head while he wasn't looking, wanted to bury everything in the snow and pretend none of this had ever happened, which was obviously daft. Wil, more pragmatic, reckoned on burying it and coming back later; and Fings could *sort* of see the point of that, insofar as the alarm had very clearly been raised. They'd obviously stirred up a right hornets' nest, and there were soldiers everywhere, probably mages too, since the stuff they'd stolen was hardly inconspicuous and possibly gave off all manner of sorcerous auras... and so yes, fine, getting back to Varr and the Pig without getting caught and hanged was maybe going to take a good dash of luck... All of *that*, he had to concede, was right... but luck was something you could *make*, if you knew what you were doing, whereas he knew with absolute certainty that if they left everything behind, no matter how carefully hidden, it would all be gone before anyone came back.

"Goblins *do* live under bridges," he said. "Everyone knows that. There's probably goblins right here, right now, watching and listening. We leave all this behind, they're going to find it and swipe it." Timing, that was the thing. If they could wait it out and go through the city gates on the next Moonday, Fings reckoned he could make all the luck they'd need. Had to be a Moonday, though, and then it would be down to whether the Moonsteel thingy inside the box *wanted* to be found.

"Fuck's sake! *What* goblins?" Sulfane was in clearly in a lot of pain, so it wasn't *all* bad.

"*The* goblins! *Everyone* knows about *goblins*!" Fings looked to Myla in case she felt like seeing sense, but mostly she was looking at him like there was no such thing as goblins and he was just making shit up to be difficult.

"So what do *you* suggest?" Wil was clearly out of sorts as well. Fings wasn't sure whether that was because Wil had reached the fight in the woods too late to be useful, or because if he *had* reached it in time, he would have found himself completely out of his depth and knew it. "We need to get Sulfane back to the Pig! He might die!"

Fings didn't see a problem with that but decided not to say so. He nodded to the bags of silver instead. "We take him to a waystation. Pay someone to look after him. Take the rest back to the Pig. Come back later and get him when he's better." He smiled, a little bit smug at finding a way to keep the loot *and* get the Murdering Bastard out of his hair.

"Pay with what? A fistful of freshly minted silver? You think no one will–"

"I don't think either of you understand what we've done," snapped Myla. "This isn't some–"

More hoofbeats on the road above shut her up. Fings stuck his feather in his mouth and danced in a circle, whispering a little rhyme to the air to keep them hidden. What he *really* wanted was to be on the other side of the river, but the moment he said so, Wil would ask how they were supposed to get there and Fings didn't have an answer for that. They hadn't found a handy boat lying around, trying to swim the Arr in winter was ridiculous and no one had admitted to being able to fly. So here they were.

The hoofbeats thundered across the bridge overhead and receded. They didn't slow. Fings stopped his dance. Riders came by every few minutes now, mostly in ones and twos but sometimes in sixes and dozens, some going one way, some going the other, and he was the *only* one sucking on a feather and dancing in little circles.

At least it was snowing.

"Look!" He braced himself to try again. "It's just... not *here*!" He couldn't even *start* to make sense of why Sulfane seemed to be going along with burying everything given the trouble he'd gone to, stealing it in the first place.

"Could we... protect ourselves from these goblins somehow?" Myla offered a patronising smile.

"Tricky buggers, goblins." Fings made a show of thinking hard. "There *are* ways. Trouble is, they're not exactly reliable."

"Fuck's sake!" croaked Sulfane. "There's no such thing!"

"Are too."

"You ever *seen* one? What do they look like?"

Fings bristled. "They look like... like *goblins*!" Even without goblins, it was so *wrong*, leaving so much money unguarded out here in the middle of nowhere. Wrong in the way that burying a corpse was wrong. Deeply, heretically, all kinds of wrong. Wrong, wrong, *wrong*!

"Goblins aren't real, Fings," said Wil.

Fings clutched at his chicken's foot and made himself take a few deep breaths. "The thing is," he said, slow and careful so they couldn't possibly pretend not to hear, "*apart* from goblins, is that one of you pillocks is going to come back and dig it up without telling the rest of us." He stared firmly at Sulfane.

"I say we just throw it all in the river." said Myla.

Fings spluttered.

"*She* won't." Sulfane grunted and bared his teeth at Myla. "And the rest of you wouldn't have the first idea how to shift what's in that box even if you knew what it was. And no, we're not throwing it in the fucking river. None of you have *any* idea what that's worth."

Fings wasn't so sure about any of that. That fancy Bithwar woman in Bonecarvers, for a start, she could move almost *anything*. And Blackhand had friends all over the city. Well, not exactly *friends*, but people who could get things done that you wouldn't believe, provided there was money in it...

Wil kept looking at Myla and Sulfane, and Fings could see what he was thinking. *I'm going to open it. I'm going to see what all the fuss is about.*

Sulfane grimaced. He was seeing it too. And then his face changed as some great dollop of understanding arrived. He turned and looked at Fings.

"You *did* open it, didn't you?" he said. "Back at the barge. *That's* why they're already out looking." He tried to lurch to his feet and then collapsed back into the snow, his face a mask of pain.

"Did not." Fings stuck out his jaw. *Hurts, does it? Good.*

"Yes, you *did*. You fucking *dick!* What did I tell you? Don't open the fucking box!"

"*You* opened it!" snapped Fings.

"*I* took precautions, you prat! See, every time someone opens that box, a mage in Varr knows where it is. A very powerful mage, and a very dangerous mage. She won't come looking herself, not out here, but oh, look! Now the roads are crawling with soldiers and we're fucked!" He bared his teeth. "You take it to Varr and open it *there*. See what happens *then*." He shook his head. "She'll be on you like a case of the pox."

Salt and iron. Fings fiddled with the charm around his neck

and concentrated very hard on his boots, careful not to catch Myla's eye.

"*I* opened it," said Myla. They all looked at her. Sulfane's face said he wanted to kill something but Myla wasn't having it. "I took the same precautions you did, so you can get off your throne of righteous pissiness. We all looked. We all know it's the Emperor's crown in there." Which wasn't quite true, because this was the first Wil was hearing of it, but never mind. "This isn't something we want any part of. So I say we leave it here." She looked tired, kept rubbing her eyes. "Take the money if you must, but leave the crown. When we get to Varr, we send a message to someone. Tell them where to find it."

"What? We give it *back*?" Wil looked like he was struggling with something difficult. Fings reached for the chicken's foot around his neck. *Best pretend I didn't hear that.*

"And the people who sent us here to steal it?" Sulfane laughed. "You think they'll be happy about that?"

"The people who sent *you* to steal it, you mean? The ones who already tried to kill you?"

Fings gave Sulfane a long, thoughtful look. "One of them got away," he said, because sometimes he couldn't help himself, even when he knew he shouldn't say anything. "And *you* told them you'd gotten rid of us. So, if you die... Aren't the rest of us all in the clear?" He did his best not to sound too hopeful. "All very grateful to you, of course..."

"If I die, you're all fucked," hissed Sulfane. "So be glad it ain't happening."

Myla was shaking her head. "Fings, the one who got away knows Sulfane wasn't alone. We don't get out of this so easily."

Wil took a deep breath. "Alright. We bury it." He looked up at the bridge. "We bury it and we get Sulfane back to the Pig. We get a moon-priestess to fix him up, and Blackhand makes the final decision. He's the boss."

"And this?" Fings dropped a bag of silver in the snow and stared at it. "Because you'll need one of these if it's a moon-priestess you

want!" Even if Myla was right about the crown thing, the silver...
That was warmth and food and safety and shelter for his family,
that was.

"It stays," said Myla, in a growly sort of way suggestive of
unpleasant sword-related consequences for anyone who cared to
disagree.

Fings turned away. "So that's it then, is it? Every man for
himself? Just... leave it here and see what happens?" They could
pretend all they liked but none of them could *really* be happy with
this. One of them *would* come back, because that was what *always*
happened.

In his pocket were the rings he'd taken. He'd be keeping those.
What the rest of them don't know, and all that.

"What about these?" He pulled out the papers he'd looted.
Sulfane was past caring and Wil only shrugged, but Myla, *she* was
about to say something, of course she bloody was, and Fings could
see right away that he wasn't going to like it. He fingered the bone
charm stitched into the bottom of his pockets, the one that was
supposed to turn his tongue to silver, metaphorically speaking, and
put on his best gap-toothed grin. "How about we take them for
Seth?" He offered her the papers, flashing a quick glance at Sulfane.
"Maybe find out what that bastard has got us into?" The papers felt
soft, like a baby's skin. They smelled of a spice he didn't recognise.

"No. If anyone recognises them, they're as dangerous as that
crown."

Fings rubbed the bone charm in his pocket some more. "But
it's not like they're obvious, is it? I mean, anyone sees a crown,
they're going to be all, *Holy shit, that's a crown!* But this is just bits
of parchment. People carry that sort of thing all the time, right?"

"Fings! No!"

"I was thinking, you see... If you want to give it back, you're
going to need to get someone important to actually pay attention.
This might be how you do it. You know, show them you're the
real thing and not just some chancer." Not that Fings had any
intention of giving anything back to anyone.

Myla gave him a hard look, then sighed and snatched the papers off him and shoved them inside her coat. "Fine."

"We'll take some of the silver, too," said Wil. "Not much, but Fings is right – we'll need it if we want a priestess."

They sat and waited for a bit after that, miserable and with nothing to say, listening to the silence of the falling snow punctuated now and then by another pair of soldiers galloping overhead. When there hadn't any soldiers for a while, Wil prodded Fings. "Go with Sulfane. I'll keep watch on the road while Myla buries it."

Fings looked at him as though he was mad. "Me? *I* ain't going anywhere on my own with that murdering bastard!"

"Yes," said Wil, "you are."

"Oh, wait, you think *I'm* the one who's going to come back and dig all this up while the rest of you aren't looking?"

The way the other three of them looked at him then, it was almost hurtful.

14
THE VALUE OF APPRECiATiOn

Seth took his forged letter and sat in the commons by a window. The light in Myla's room was atrocious and he wanted to see whether the inks looked right in daylight, not that Blackhand would notice or care. Probably no one else would either, but Seth considered himself a craftsman. A week had passed since he'd taken his beating from the Spicers and he still wasn't right. He supposed he should probably go and see Fings' weird herbalist friend, or Fings' weird hedge-witch friend, or another of Fings' weird friends, the only trouble being that he didn't have any money.

The letter was perfect. He hobbled to the kitchens. Blackhand liked to loiter there in the morning. *Plenty of knives handy.* His own words.

"Well?"

"Sell-swords in the Spice Market," said Seth. "Looked like they were from Deephaven. They were talking to a Guildsman, the old skinny one who works ledgers at the Merchant House." By now, he'd followed them and knew where they were staying.

Blackhand rolled his eyes. "Holed up in Tombland with the remnants of the Spicers. Brick and Topher are keeping an eye. Anything else? Something actually useful?"

Seth held up Sulfane's letter. When Blackhand reached for it, Seth snatched it back. "Let's talk about that room you promised."

Blackhand smirked, then realised Seth wasn't joking. "Oh, like that, is it? Right." He drew out the word as his face scrunched up in exaggerated thought. "No more favours, eh? Alright, I suppose I can agree with you on that. Although… What month is it, Seth?"

"I just need–"

"The Light and the Dark, isn't it?" Blackhand nodded sagely. "The Light and the Dark. Hard to believe Midwinter is still weeks away. Sulk's going to be long and hard this year. People already freezing to death on the streets and we're hardly even started." He put on a frown of deep thought. "You came here… what was it? Month of Lightning? Just before the Solstice of Flames if I remember right."

"Blackhand! I only need–"

"Lightning, Answering Prayers, Learned Discourse, Reincarnation, Contemplation, Light and the Dark… have I missed any?" They both knew he hadn't. "Six months. Call it five, let's be generous. Five months of pastries from my kitchens, food from my tables whenever the fancy takes you, a roof over your head… anything else I should mention?"

"The favours I've done in return?" *A dozen, at least.*

Blackhand acted like he hadn't heard. "And now you want me to give up a room for a bit of scribbling on a piece of parchment? Any idea how much that would cost me? No, course you don't, because you don't ever pay for fucking *anything*."

"I bloody do," growled Seth.

"Oh yeah? Pay for the inks, did you? Or the parchment? *Any* of it?" Blackhand took a quick step forward and snatched the letter out of Seth's hand. "No more favours, is it? Right then. If that's the way you want it. You want a room, you fucking pay for it."

Wait, what? "Hey!" Seth hurried after him. "You said–"

Blackhand plucked a coin out of his pocket and flicked it at Seth. "No more favours, so here's for your time and trouble. Now fuck off."

Seth stared after him, then bent to pick up the coin. A quarter-moon. A furious tirade of words made it to the back of his mouth and then got somehow stuck and wouldn't come out. He sighed and turned away.

Coward.

The pastries left from last night were sitting by the kitchen window as usual. He gathered them into a basket and turned to go, and there were Dox and Arjay, standing in his way. Dox smacked the basket out of his hand, scattering pastries across the floor. As if they hadn't fully made their point, Arjay stamped on the nearest. Seth stared at the smeared mess.

"Feel better for that, do you?" he asked.

Dox shoved him. "You heard the boss. You don't take nothing from us no more." Beside him, Arjay shrugged. A *what-were-you-thinking* sort of shrug. He shuffled out of the kitchen. What *was* he thinking?

Oh, I don't know. That for once in his life, that greedy scabrous leech would show a shred of decency? That he might keep his word?

Out in Haberdashers, he headed for the Spice Market, more from habit than anything else.

Remember what it was like?

What what *was like?*

Respect.

He *did* remember, that was half the trouble. He remembered walking with Fings and Levvi to the temple in Spice Market Square. He remembered stripping naked on the steps, him and all the other novices. He remembered feeling small and stupid at how skinny and scrawny he was and how everyone was probably looking at him and sniggering... and then Dawncaller Jannesh coming out in her yellow and gold with the senior priests all following in a line, how she stood in front of each new novice and touched them on the top of the head before giving them their new robe. He remembered her standing in front of him, small and radiant as the sun itself, the power of her presence, its calm strength. He remembered how he felt as her hand brushed his brow, that overpowering sense of arrival, of belonging to something, of a brotherhood, of a place that was sure.

Let the light come in. And he had, and for a while it had been beautiful. And then, somehow, he'd taken a wrong turn, and now here he was. In the darkness with no light at all.

He stopped. Across the square was the temple he'd called home for the best years of his life.

You did this to yourself. Not them. You.

It wasn't as though they hadn't warned him. When Lightbringer Sharimiana had caught him with the book he shouldn't have been reading, she'd lectured him for an entire afternoon. When he'd asked Dawncaller Jannesh about the catacombs, she'd given him a week of silent penance... but he couldn't help himself. *Why was there a crypt? Why were there bones?* No one buried their dead, not ever. Corpses went to the fire, to the water, to the open skies if there was no other choice. To the Sun or the Moon or the Stars but never under the ground. To be buried was to be chased for eternity by the Hungry Goddess, to be devoured if she caught you.

Iconoclast. Apostate. Heretic...

From across the square, Lightbringer Suaresh was heading towards him. That had to be a sign, didn't it? Seth was getting a sending, and sendings were rare and they mattered. Whether Suaresh liked it or not, he'd have to tell whoever was Dawncaller now. They'd have to listen, and they'd see the truth, that it *was* a sending, which meant the light hadn't abandoned him, so maybe, just maybe... he could go back?

Suaresh saw him and stopped. Seth almost broke into a run. *Just talk to him. Don't ask for anything. Show them how sorry you are...*

He faltered. Suaresh was pointing at him, and now two of the temple Sunguard were hurrying over. When they reached Seth, they didn't even give him a chance to speak, simply smashed him to the ground and held him there, pinioned.

Seth cried out: "Brother! Brother! Please! I have to talk to Lightbringer Otti! There are sendings! Brother Lightbringer! I have sendings! I have a–"

The words collapsed into a gasp as a boot crushed his head into the ground. Now, finally, Suaresh came close.

"Lightbringer Otti has passed to the light," said Suaresh. "*You* did that to him."

He lifted his robe then, and pissed over Seth's head, then walked away, the Sunguard at his heels. Seth stayed where he was, sitting on the stones of the square. The spectacle of a beggar being pissed on by a priest had drawn a small crowd, children mostly, pointing and laughing, a few adults looking on in revulsion.

Laugh all you like.

One of the children threw a stone. It hit him in the chest, and then Seth was on his feet because he'd seen this happen before, seen a beggar stoned to death by laughing children while passersby cheered them on. Running only ever made it worse, so he walked right at them, daring them. Sure enough, they scattered to let him through. Another stone hit him as he passed, on the back this time. He walked behind a stall and then made a quick dash between brightly coloured awnings and into a narrow alley. He turned and growled.

Come at me now, fuckers.

No one came.

He left the market behind him and walked through Seamstresses and Bonecarvers, blank and without much idea where he was going until he washed up at the Circus of Dead Emperors. Stationed around the ring of statues were a company of Imperial Guard. On another day, he might have tried to sell them pastries, enthusiastically vocalised his support for his beloved Emperor, and pumped them for news; but today he was empty-handed, and the soldiers were dour-looking and wore grey shrouds of mourning.

The Emperor is dead. He already knew it. He'd seen the courier, black and scarred with grey. He'd felt it in his sendings.

Still…

He walked to the nearest of the soldiers and wrapped his voice around the most educated-but-slightly-foreign priestly accent he could muster. "I am… ah… a priest of the Holy Order of the–"

The soldier shoved him aside, although as shoves went, he was gentle about it. "Clear the way."

"What?"

The soldier nodded up the Avenue of Swords. "I said clear the way, priest! Her Highness the Princess-Regent approaches."

Sure enough, armoured soldiers were riding towards the Circus, scattering the crowd. Seth scurried out of the way to watch.

Hold on, what? Princess-Regent?

Two dozen riders entered the circus, their heavy armour decked out in red and white and with all the fancy plumes and sashes you could imagine. A tall man rode in their midst, head to toe in black Moonsteel plate, and a girl beside him in black Moonsteel mail. The man had a helm covering his face but the girl didn't. On her head was the gold Circlet of the Moon.

Well there's a first. He'd never seen a Princess-Regent before. Never seen a Princess-anything, for that matter.

Princess-*Regent*, though?

He looked at the girl with the crown and stifled a giggle, imagining all the Lightbringers and the Sunbrights and the Dawncallers working themselves into apoplexy. A moon-worshipper, a sorceress and even if you put all that aside, *definitely* a penis short of acceptable… With a bit of luck, a few might explode from sheer outrage.

The riders reached the great Hanging Tree and stopped. The man and the girl dismounted, which only went to point how short she was, and how young.

Too young.

Pretty though.

Pretty doesn't stop knives.

Who else? The emperor's cousin? Everyone hates him.

The Overlord of Varr, obviously!

Everyone hates him *even more!* Just ask Myla. Although the Overlord *was* the only one of Emperor Khrozus' generals canny enough to have survived the last twenty years. The Torpreahns had had deep pockets when it came to the vengeful murder of anyone and everyone who might stand between them and getting back their throne, and yet they'd never managed to touch him. And not for want of trying, by all accounts.

Obvious choice, when you put it that way…

Dead before Midwinter?

Maybe not if Overlord Kyra plans to marry her.

Isn't he her uncle?

And?

And old enough to be her grandfather?

And?

Fuck's sake.

The sun-priests had never liked the late Emperor. They'd hated Khrozus before him, but *that* they'd brought on themselves when they'd lined up behind the Torpreahn degenerate, Talsin. Big mistake. That was why there were no old priests in Varr...

He giggled, and then felt oddly guilty. Was that what he wanted for the people who'd been his friends, his tutors, the people who'd shown him kindness when he'd been a homeless frightened boy, who'd given him food and shelter and then, later, knowledge. Did he wish them dead? Did he hope for them to be butchered by a mad king? It was the sort of question that demanded an honest answer, and so Seth looked hard and discovered that no, no he didn't, not even Lightbringer Suaresh. He wanted their respect, yes. He wanted an apology. He wanted them to see that they were wrong and that he was right. He wanted to watch them weep at their foolishness, but they had to stay alive for that, so no, he didn't want them dead.

Blackhand, though...

He watched the Princess-Regent walk into the maze of the Hanging Tree, heading for its heart.

Good luck, girl. Fuck knows you're going to need it.

He turned away then, hiding his grin from the grey-clad soldiers, crossed the Circus of Dead Emperors and made his way through Glassmakers until he reached the Bridge of Questions and the entrance to Tombland. It wasn't long before someone caught his arm.

"I want to talk to what's left of the Spicers," he said. "Tell whoever wants to know that I can give them the Teahouse on Threadneedle Street."

Now was the time. Fings and Myla were away, were going to be away for days. Wil, too, not that Seth much cared one way or the other. He'd find a way to make sure Brick was out of the Pig when it mattered, Maybe Dox and Arjay too, even if they *were* arseholes. The rest could just take their chances.

Blackhand, though?

Blackhand could fuck off and die in a fire.

15

TAKEΠ

Myla watched Fings and Sulfane climb back to the road then Sulfane lever himself onto his horse, struggling against the pain, and ride away, Fings walking beside him, grumbling to himself. The falling snow was getting thicker and they were quickly out of sight, lost in a haze of white. Her head throbbed. Mostly, she just wanted to curl up under the bridge near her horse and fall asleep. The last thing this overflowing pisspot of a day needed was a hangover.

"And you?" she asked, looking at Wil. "Are you really going to keep watch on the road while I do all the work?"

Wil shook his head. Of course he wasn't. He didn't trust her, not *that* much.

She pointed down the gully where the frozen water cut its way to the river Arr. "There are some trees down there. You can't see them now through the snow but they're there. We'll do it where no one can see us from the road."

He liked that.

"Wil... We should walk away. We still could. We shouldn't have done this. No good will come of it."

That, not so much.

Ah well. I tried.

She carried the box with the Emperor's crown while Wil carried the bags of silver. They trudged to the trees and in among them, to where the ground was hardly touched by the snow, then doubled back, trying not to leave a trail that led straight from the bridge. Myla picked a place where the snow looked deep. She scooped a handful and pressed it to her face, holding it there until the burn of the cold was unbearable, trying to wake herself up, and then they buried the crown in its box, took a little of the silver for themselves – the money she'd given up to save Fings' sister really had been all she'd had – and then buried the rest and did what they could to cover it up. The falling snow would finish the job, given time. She marked the spot with a stick planted in the ground so they'd be able to find it again, and then they went back the way they'd come, retracing their steps. From the trees, Myla looked back. The bridge was invisible through the falling snow but their tracks were obvious.

"Should have let Fings do it," she muttered.

Wil snorted. "Not if you want it still to be there when you come back."

She let Wil mount her horse behind her. They followed the gully and the frozen river to the banks of the Arr, and then Myla meandered through snowdrifts and a field until they were back in sight of the road, waiting to blend with the first traffic of the day from the waystations.

"You think it was clever sending Fings and Sulfane together?"

Wil made a sour face. "Best of a bad set of choices."

A lonely horseman galloped along the road, almost lost through the falling snow, and then came the first cluster of wagons. Myla joined them, dropping in a little way behind, keeping her distance, almost but not quite out of sight. The snow was getting heavier, making it hard to see more than blurred shapes on the road.

Jeffa says hello.

She should head the other way. Leave Wil and Fings and Sulfane and Blackhand with the consequences of what they'd done. Get away from Varr, pretend to be dead again, follow the instinct that said *Turn back and run away* and start another new life somewhere on the other side of the world. It was what she'd done in Deephaven. She had her swords and her horse and now enough fresh coin in her satchel that she wouldn't have to offer herself to another man like Blackhand in exchange for room and board. Not for a while, at least.

Down the long road to the City of Spires. Start new. Why not?

Because sword-monks don't run. Sword-monks don't turn their backs.

But that was exactly what she *had* done in Deephaven. She wasn't a *real* sword-monk. Not even close.

She was still trying to work it out when Fings came shambling out of the snow at the roadside, leading Sulfane's horse and wrapped in Sulfane's cloak, waving them down. She stopped, and Wil asked what Fings was doing here, why wasn't he on his way to Varr and where was Sulfane, and Fings huffed and shook his head and then it all came out of him in one long tirade: how Sulfane had left the road, how Fings had been sure he was doubling back and so had followed – carefully, of course – only to find Sulfane waiting for him.

"I *told* you he was going to take it all for himself." Fings threw his hands in the air in exasperation. "I knew it! And there was nowhere to go, nowhere to hide or nothing! And then the strangest thing!" Fings touched the chicken's foot around his neck. "He draws back the bow and I'm thinking this is it, I'm dead, but then his arm gives, the one where he got shot, and the arrow goes flying off sideways! I know I can outrun him so I just go, but then I look back and he's fallen over in the snow and he isn't moving... I think he's dead!"

"Dead?" Myla sniffed the air. Something about Fings smelled odd.

"Yeah. Stone cold. I mean, no, he wasn't, not really, not when I left him the first time, right? Because I thought maybe it was a trick so gave him a bit of a prod. You know, expecting him to lurch up all grabby and stabby, but he didn't move, not even a little bit. But he *was* still breathing."

"The first time?" asked Myla.

Wil looked him over. "You're wearing his cloak."

"Took his horse too," Fings agreed. "Came looking for you lot to get some help, only I couldn't find you in all this bloody snow. So I went back and he was still there..."

"Only this time he was dead?" asked Myla.

"Yeah. So I thought I might as well grab everything worth the hassle of shifting. I mean... no point just *leaving* it there, right? Didn't get all of it though because some other lot showed up. Horsemen. Luckily, I saw them before they saw me, so I buggered off."

"Horsemen?" Shit. "Who?"

"Didn't stop to ask. Didn't seem the wise choice."

Myla closed her eyes and offered a quick prayer to the Sun. *See. Should have kept going the other way...*

"So... You took all his stuff and left him." Wil was struggling.

Fings shrugged. "Yeah. Course. I mean... he was dead, right? And there were these other riders. What else was I supposed to do?"

It made no sense. Sulfane luring Fings away? Maybe. Turning on them? If Fings had come back with a story of a struggle and him stabbing Sulfane because he didn't have any other choice, she probably would have believed him. Wil surely would. But just dropping dead?

"He was hurt, Fings," she snapped, "but he wasn't about to die."

"He just keeled over!"

"Fings!" She looked straight at him. "Did you kill Sulfane?"

"No!" He couldn't meet her eye, though. Myla got off her horse and slowly went to Fings and touched his face and made him look at her.

"Sword-monks can smell lies, Fings. Remember? Now try telling me what *really* happened."

Fings slumped a bit, and then suddenly maybe he *didn't* run away when Sulfane tried to shoot him and his arm gave out, maybe he'd been carrying a stick with him, a nice branch, the same branch he'd used to lamp the mage last night. Kept it on account of how lucky it must be. How maybe he'd whacked Sulfane with it and knocked him down.

"He wasn't dead though! He *wasn't!* And then it's like I said. I went looking for you lot. Couldn't find you so I went back. And then there were these riders and–"

"Show me."

It took a while, long enough for Myla to think Fings was leading them a dance, but he got them back to the place in the end, marked by streaks of fresh blood in the snow. No Sulfane, though, dead or alive. At this, Fings looked truly bewildered. They dismounted and searched as best they could, and Fings pointed out the furrow through the snow where someone had been dragged away, and then Myla found more horse tracks, at least four riders and maybe twice that number. *That* part of the story, then, was true.

She looked to Wil, uncertain. "Do we follow?"

Wil shook his head. "Soldiers," he said. "Has to be. No one else about."

"We didn't *see* any…" Not that that meant much if they were scouring the countryside. With the snow coming down like it was, you could ride up pretty close someone before they spotted you, if you were quiet enough about it.

"You *sure* he was dead when you left him?" asked Wil, and Myla knew what he was thinking: *Because if he's not, we're fucked.*

iii

İnTERLUDE

Dawncaller Jannesh knew Seth had been down in the crypt. Seth had no idea how and she never said, but she did. There was a... a wariness, that was it, after he'd discovered the bones of Sivingathm, whoever Sivingathm was, and so Seth became the perfect student. He listened and was attentive to every word. He read everything they let him read and waited for the wariness to go away. Months passed, then years. Seth and the novices around him outgrew the last trappings of childhood and became men. He still slipped out of the temple, now and then, but if the Lightbringers ever knew, they showed no sign. No one ever caught him.

Three years after Seth took his novice robe, when it was obvious that he was the brightest of them by far, Dawncaller Jannesh sent him across the river to the cathedral with its library, the biggest outside of Torpreah. He learned a new history there, one that went back further than the honest-but-weak Emperor Talsin and the civil war, the wicked usurper Khrozus and his sorcerous, Moon-loving son, Emperor Ashahn. They taught him about the first emperors, how the light of the Sun had been brought to this land from another. He learned the volumes of stories of the Shining Age. He listened and watched, looked at the world around him and understood why some people looked different and why that mattered even though everyone said it didn't. Most of all, he saw that even here in this great cathedral that held all the knowledge of the world, their stories were wrong. He found his thoughts snagging on every hole and inconsistency. Like the half-god brothers whose war had shattered the world, the Black Moon and the King in Silver; yet other books referred to *all* half-gods as Silver Kings, and the story he'd been taught as a novice was that the Black Moon had been hurled into the sky by the Hungry Goddess to punish the Children of the Sun, and was nothing to do with half-gods at all.

He found names. Isul Aeiha. His old friend, Sivingathm, but they all led to nothing.

"It's like an apple," he said to Fings one day. "They hold it and they show it to you and say *This is an apple. See the apple.* Back in Spice Market Square, that was all it ever was. See the apple but you can't touch or taste it. Over here, they peel it a little. That's what they're giving me, Fings. A bit of peel and telling me it's an apple. But I know there's more. I can *see* it, even while they're pretending it isn't there. The flesh under the peel. And what about the rest? The seeds? The core? I don't think *they* even *know*!"

He was cautious in the cathedral at first, probing at the edges of their stories with his questions. He was good at tricking them with words and so every now and then they yielded an answer. But he never got to the flesh of the fruit and soon realised that he never would, not that way, and by then they were watching him again, and so he went back to being the model novice they wanted.

A book went missing from the Sunherald's personal collection, from a place where only the Sunbrights and the Dawncallers could go. Seth had been in the temple hall when it happened with about a hundred witnesses but they questioned him anyway. A sword-monk listened to his answers, sniffing for lies. Sivingathm and the Spice Market crypt weren't forgotten.

Another year passed and Seth did as he was told and took care never to put a foot wrong. By the time he found what he was looking for, two Sunbrights and a Dawncaller had told him he wasn't well-suited to being a priest and perhaps should find another calling. He'd seen other novices, far less capable than he was, elevated to Lightbringer, and knew that this was their way of nudging him towards the door. But Seth knew better: this *was* his calling, the only calling he'd ever have, and to honour that calling meant finding the truth, and so he took what he'd discovered and added it to the foolhardy bravery of a young man who thought he finally understood the world, and slipped out one night and met Fings, and together they snuck into the back yard of the chapel near the Circus of Dead Emperors, just on the edge of Glassmakers.

"You sure about this?" Fings was cautious these days. Seth put that down to Levvi having been gone so long and Fings having to look after the family all on his own.

"I'm sure," said Seth. "This is it."

They crept past the stables, past the incinerators for cremating anyone rich enough to avoid the body wagons and the mass pyres that burned every day all around the city. Behind all that was an overgrown garden, very green and surrounded by crumbling stone walls, and an iron gate with an old lock. A place forbidden to novices – to anyone, as far as Seth knew – but no lock could resist Fings for long.

Fings wrinkled his nose. "Ain't this where they bring Dead Men?"

It was, but only after a priest or a sword-monk had set them free. What came to the incinerators were the empty vessels of flesh and bone.

"There's a treasure down there," said Seth quietly. He wasn't sure if that was true in any way Fings would understand. What there *was*, was knowledge. A truth that even the Lightbringers and Sunbrights didn't know, maybe even the Dawncallers.

Fings twitched and fiddled idly with the collection of charms around his neck. He poked at the old lock on the iron gate and shook his head. "Rusted solid." Instead, he shinned up the wall like he was a squirrel and tossed a rope from the other side. Even then, Seth barely managed to haul himself over to where a squat stone building stood through long grass and thickets of thorns, invisible from the gate. Someone had sealed it off, but then all the old priests had either fled after the city fell in the civil war or else Khrozus had killed them. Drowned them, to be precise, so their souls would go to the Moon and not the Sun, vindictive bastard that he was.

Did anyone alive even know this was still here?

The entrance was hidden behind a tangle of briars. The place looked utterly forgotten and Seth had to hack a way through. There wasn't a door, only a gap in the stone. Inside...

There it was. A round hole in the ground, lined with stone like the shaft of a well. An entrance to something. Catacombs, if you believed one story, the Underworld itself if you believed another.

Fings lit a lantern. "You want to go down *there*?"

"Treasure, Fings." Seth half-expected a pit filled with the skeletons of the unburned dead, or else something like the crypt under the temple in Spice Market Square, or, worst of all, nothing. Instead, the hole was an entrance to a wider shaft, neat and circular and set with a spiral of narrow white stone steps.

"Wait a minute..." Fings shuttered his lantern. "What the holy Sun...!"

Seth saw it too, now his eyes were adjusting to the gloom. The whole shaft was aglow with a dim and gentle silver light.

*Moon*light?

He ran back outside and looked up. A fat crescent, almost a half-moon.

He ran back and looked down the shaft.

The light was the same.

This. *This*. The truth behind all the stories. The *real* truth.

"That ain't right. That's mage-work, that is." Fings was twitching, shifting from one foot to the other and back in agitation.

"No." Not sorcery. Something else.

"We should go back."

"No one's been down here since before you and I were born."

"Yeah. Got to be a reason why this place is all locked up and forgotten, don't you think?"

"But that's why we're here, Fings."

Fings shook his head. "I ain't going down there and nor should you."

"Why?"

But Fings wouldn't budge and so Seth went on his own. The walls were a smooth white stone, seamless and curved and with a quality of workmanship beyond even the great temples of Varr. There was no damage, no cracks, no sign at all to say how old they were. Old, though. Older than the city above.

Deep, too. He made his way down the curve of the stair until the entrance was a tiny black hole far above. He had Fings' lantern but the glow from the stone itself was enough, the silver light of the half-moon in the sky above. Now and then, side-tunnels opened into the stair, some vanishing into darkness, some aglow and reaching out as far as Seth could see, others ending in carved arches ringed in sigils that he didn't understand.

What is this place?

A better question might have been: why was it hidden? He had no idea, but each new tunnel was another question begging for an answer.

The walls abruptly fell away as the stairs brought him into a vast round chamber. A dozen tunnels led off into the gloom while in the floor, in the centre of the spiralling steps, a hole opened into another vault some twenty feet below. For all Seth's mutterings about treasure, he had no rope, no ladder, so all he could do was lie at the edge and shine Fings' expensive lantern down to see what he could see.

What he saw were skeletons. Three of them, lying together in the middle of the floor. Two wore mail that glinted a deep yellowy-brown, too dark for gold. Brass, if Seth had to guess, although how it had stayed untarnished for so long was a mystery. The floor was a mosaic, detailed and intricate, but the light was too dim for Seth to make it out. When he leaned right into the hole, he saw at least one other passage leading away, its secrets clasped tight in darkness.

There were more sigils written around the entrance to this

second vault. Seth didn't know what they meant so he took out
his paper strips and his charcoal, the tools he used for setting Dead
Men to rest, and copied them as best he could. As he did, he knew
he wasn't alone. There was something else down here. Something
not quite dead.

Back in the hole, the skeletons were only bones. The brass mail
had disappeared.

He'd imagined it?

Maybe...

The trip back was a blur. Seth told Fings what he'd seen and
then talked and talked about what it could mean, not that he had
much idea. They'd come back with ropes, the two of them. They'd
take whatever was there and they'd be rich, although the real
treasure was something far more precious than gold. That night,
asleep in his cell, Seth dreamed of a vault of white stone ringed by
archways leading to nowhere, each covered in sigils.

Three days later, the Sunguard threw him down the cathedral
steps. Seth never did go back to the vault. Whenever he managed
to take a breath from not starving to bring it up, Fings changed
the subject, and Seth was too busy surviving to go back alone –
or at least, that was what he told himself. Eventually, he stopped
asking. He knew well enough what Fings wasn't saying. The place
carried a curse, and it had dropped on Seth, and Fings didn't want
any part of it.

He *could* have gone back alone, of course. No reason not to.
Apart from the fact that by then, he knew just a little bit more
about what was down there, and it scared him shitless.

16

THE RIVER GATES

Time was, the city of Varr hadn't had any walls. Hadn't had them because it hadn't needed them. When Khrozus had stormed out from Deephaven and launched his lightning march on the capital, Emperor Talsin's generals had dug earth ramparts and erected wooden barricades and set their armies to defend them. Fings knew the story because when he was small, the old man who might have been his mum's uncle or might have just been some old man who liked to hang around, used to tell it every chance he got, how he'd taken the Emperor's coin and been a soldier. He'd sit and smoke his pipe and talk about how the city had plunged into a bitter unnatural cold on the night that Khrozus came, and never mind that it was Midsummer. How thousands had shivered right in the middle of the Solstice of Flames while the two great rivers froze, something they almost never did even in the depths of the Sulk. How at the crack of dawn, Khrozus had charged his infamous cavalry, horses shod with spikes for the ice, right past the barricades, the Usurper at their head, past the ten thousand men waiting to fight them, right up the frozen river to the heart of the city. How he'd seized the Kaveneth and the Imperial Palace with hardly a drop of blood being shed, and how a stroke of bad luck had led the fleeing Emperor Talsin straight onto Khrozus' sword. By the end of the first day of what everyone had said would be a six-month siege, old Khrozus had Talsin's head parading through the city on a stick, and that was that. According to the old man, Khrozus had ordered the walls built that very day, before he'd even crowned himself and sat on Talsin's throne, and half Talsin's army had put down their spears and set to work building without so much as blinking, because coin was coin, and who cared whose head was on it, as long as their own was still attached to their body?

Fings wasn't sure how much of that he believed. Seemed more likely that some idiot had forgotten to shut a gate somewhere, that that was how old Khrozus the Clever had got in. Probably all the stuff about sorcerous cold and freezing rivers was guff to make it sound better. What he *did* know was that the walls had taken years to build, echoing through the city from end to end and still going on long after Khrozus had met the wrong end of a knife. Fings even remembered some of it himself – people flocking into the city for the new Emperor Ashahn's coin; and even though the southern walls had been long finished by then, Ma Fings still liked to remind them all how she'd watched them go up, how everything around them had been cleared, slums and huts flattened and burned, trees cut down, the ground levelled, how she'd suddenly had to find a new place to live, as if the whole affair had been designed specifically for her personal inconvenience. Khrozus had even bent the Great Torpreah Road, tearing up the last fifty miles and letting the land grow wild, building a new road that ran under the walls before reaching the one vast gatehouse through which all traffic to the south had to pass.

And then – and in Ma Fings' opinion they could all send thanks to the Sun for this – someone had accidentally spilled some poison on a knife and Khrozus had accidentally stabbed himself with it several times before getting so confused about what was going on that he'd jammed it into his own eye socket. According to Ma Fings, this sort of accident happened all the time to Imperial families, and in this case just as well, because Khrozus had been all set to raise a range of mountains around the city and change the course of the rivers and the Great West Road and all manner of things that even Fings was fairly sure Emperors couldn't actually do. Fortunately, Khrozus' successor, Emperor Ashahn – Sun bless him – either wasn't as batshit paranoid as his father or didn't have as many spare sorcerers kicking around; no new mountain ranges had sprung up, and the Great West Road ran as it always had, along the north bank of the Arr and straight to the River Gate.

Fings sat behind Myla on the back of her horse and chomped on an apple, one of a bag pilfered from a waystation a couple of days back while Myla wasn't looking, thinking about all those stories Ma Fings used to tell. Wil was a little way behind. They were close to the walls and the air smelled of home, a sweet waft of shit and piss and beer and rot. He hadn't noticed it before, but coming back to it was like opening the front door to your own house and finding a warm fire already blazing in the hearth.

Almost home.

He'd done everything he could think to stack the scales of fortune in their favour. He'd sucked on feathers and left signs in the snow to distract evil spirits from following them. He'd walked half the way back to Varr with a coin under his tongue. In the evenings at the waystations, he hadn't stolen *any*thing – well, *almost*, apart from his bag of apples. He'd done everything he knew to keep their luck sweet and now here they were, spitting distance from the walls and nothing bad had happened. Even the weather was helping, a steady fall of snow that morning after they'd lifted the loot, then clear, now coming down again. Much worse and the guards on the gates wouldn't be able to see their own hands in front of their faces. Even Sulfane getting shot and stabbed had worked out in the end, as long he really *was* dead.

I just whacked him one! That's all!

Sulfane really *hadn't* been dead when Fings left him, and he really *had* gone away to look for the others and then come back to find riders dragging Sulfane out of the snow, and Sulfane hadn't been moving, so dead it was. Myla didn't believe him, of course. She thought he'd killed the Murdering Bastard himself. Smarted a bit, that did, but Wil had seen it for what it was: a situation where there was nothing to be done, and like Wil had said, Fings obviously wasn't making it up about the riders, so what else could they do? And so all that was left of Sulfane was a bloodstain in the snow and some vaguely unpleasant memories, and that was the end of the matter, and, frankly, good riddance.

The riders. Yeah. He'd seen them right enough. They hadn't been soldiers. He'd decided not to mention that part, but it bothered him. If they weren't soldiers, who else had been out there, freezing their nuts off in the snow? Friends of the mage he'd smacked round the head with his log?

He finished his apple and started another. Apples were lucky, and there was never any harm in having one or two to tip the scales of fortune. Close to home, soldiers up on the walls, him with rings in his pockets stolen from the Emperor himself, now wasn't a time for inviting fate to take a shit on them.

The rings were another thing he'd decided not to mention since it would only cause trouble. Wil would get cross about not leaving them behind, Blackhand would demand a cut, and Myla would probably start banging on about giving them back, like *that* was ever going to happen.

He sucked on his feather as they rode past a line of soldiers, too miserable in the falling snow to be paying any attention. Then more came up behind them, six fast riders. *These* Fings recognised: a red field with five white towers emblazoned on their shields, crossed with a grey sash of mourning. Soldiers from the City of Spires, which made them the Emperor's men.

At the gates, Longcoats were stopping every wagon.

"Weapons," said Myla quietly, although Fings thought he detected a tiny hint of I-told-you-so. "They're looking for weapons."

"Weapons?"

"Those sashes. Someone's dead. If it's the Emperor, they'll be worried about a Torpreahn revolt."

Fings felt an uncomfortable squirm in his guts. No *if* about it, not really, not when they'd just lifted the Emperor's crown from a river-barge and buried it in the snow. Myla had to know that, too. He sighed. Ma Fings would definitely have words to say about him getting mixed up in stuff like this. Maybe Myla was right about giving it all back. Well, *some* of it, at least...

Whoa! Steady there!

He reached for another apple. Never hurt to make sure. "If the Emperor's dead, who does that leave in charge of things?" Not that he cared but maybe he should. Whoever it was, they'd probably be wanting their crown.

"The Overlord will crown the Emperor's son and declare himself regent, most likely." Myla spat. "Deephaven won't stomach that. Nor will the Torpreahns. He won't last."

They reached the gatehouse and followed the soldiers from the City of Spires into a dark tunnel, walls and ceiling lined with slits and holes of death, then out into an open space almost the size of Spice Market Square. A stream of wagons followed behind until the gates closed. The place was crawling with Longcoats and even Imperial Guard, all with their grey sashes of mourning. The sashes put Fings on edge. Went without saying that death was unlucky, and so he sucked on his feather some more as they looked over every wagon, every crate and box and barrel.

Maybe Myla was right. Whatever they were looking for, the Longcoats apparently didn't care about a couple of riders from Deephaven. The inner gates opened, Myla rode into the city, and it was like something he'd held clenched inside him for days finally relaxed.

Home.

"You want to wait for Wil?" he asked. It seemed only fair, but the snow was getting worse and he was too cold to muster much enthusiasm. His stomach ached. Bloody hard work keeping all that bad luck away.

"He knows where to go."

The streets past the gates were nearly empty, white and still when they should have been crowded, the city drowning under the falling snow. Dull grey pennants hung from every other door as though the whole place had come down with the plague. They crossed the river on one of the bigger ferries and made their way to Spice Market

Square and stopped at Blackhand's warehouse – not *overtly* his, of course, because if it was *that* obvious then the Spicers would have burned it down months ago – but this was where they were meant to wait while Wil went ahead to fetch Blackhand. What was *supposed* to happen was that they'd offload whatever they were carrying before going back to the Pig, Sulfane would get his share and his letter, and Blackhand would pay them each their cut... Except the warehouse was shuttered and locked, Sulfane was dead, there wasn't any loot, and Wil was somewhere behind them.

In his head, Fings counted off the days since the barge and decided it was Mageday. He didn't like Magedays at the best of times, but in *this* weather?

Magedays? Best thing is to stay in bed.

"I'm going to... go a different way," he said, not even quite sure why but happy to be guided by instinct when it came to these things. "Something don't feel right."

He jumped off Myla's horse and jogged through the streets and alleys, losing sight of her in the falling snow almost at once. Bloody weather didn't make using the backstreets and alleys easy and he had to check three times whether he was in the right place before he reached Threadneedle Street. He walked on past the Pig and ducked into Nightveil Alley. The snow had the whole city muffled to silence and there was almost no one about. The doors to the Pig were shut, even though it was barely twilight, and Blackhand almost *never* closed the doors. Perhaps for his own death, but even that struck Fings as unlikely.

Could be the weather?

Could be.

He watched as Myla loomed down the middle of Threadneedle Street on the back of her horse, the road all to herself. He watched as she stopped in front of the Pig, hesitated a moment, then dismounted. As she went to the door, the sense of something bad about to happen almost pushed him out of the shadows, running across the street to warn her, *Don't go inside!*

Almost. Not quite though.

17

BLUE ROBES

Myla had met the Emperor, once… well, had been at the same place at the same time, at least. She'd necked a bottle of very expensive wine, got into an argument with someone she didn't know about how the Emperor was cursed – it had been a year since Empress Whatever-Her-Name-Was had died (not Empress Arianne, Sun bless her, but the one after) – punched someone she *did* know in the face when he'd mistaken her backside for a place to rest his hand, stolen another bottle of wine, almost ended up in bed with a rather handsome footman, and finished the evening crawling home. It hadn't been, as Mistress Tasahre had acidly noted, very sword-monk-like.

She remembered his crown. Black Moonsteel. It was one of a pair, brought from old Anvor by the first emperor. One of black Moonsteel, the other of yellow gold. Well, golden Sunsteel actually, but they looked much the same.

The Moon for the king, the Sun for the prince who shall follow him. That was how the old saying went.

She stopped. They were crossing the middle of Spice Market Square and she realised she couldn't actually see any of the buildings any more.

Curse this snow.

Fings shifted behind her. He was still hiding something about what had happened between him and Sulfane. Three days and she hadn't winkled it out of him; then again, she still couldn't decide whether "goblins" were something he'd made up as an excuse not to leave three bags of silver buried under a bridge, or if he truly believed everything he'd said. She wasn't sure *he* knew, either.

She picked a path and trotted on until the outline of the Sun Temple loomed out of the snow. Why was the Emperor's crown stashed on a barge and not sitting on his head? The answer was in the pennants hanging from every other door, in the grey sashes worn by the imperial soldiers.

I need a drink. Blackhand had a good cellar, if you knew where to look.

No. You need to think.

She knew what Sulfane had been after, now it was too late to do anything about it. The Moonsteel Crown was the symbol of the Emperor's authority, the gold circlet the symbol of continuity, the mark of his successor. The stories she'd heard back in Deephaven said the twin crowns were linked, that whoever wore one could read the thoughts of the other. Was that why Sulfane had been so particular about not opening the box. Was that what his salt and iron were for?

Was *that* why someone wanted them?

What bothered her more and more, though, was that he'd known exactly where and when to find it. He'd known before they left Varr.

I should have kept going for the City of Spires.

Yes. Concentrate on her own problems. Leave Varr and all this mess behind her – yet she couldn't. Someone had known the Emperor was going to die, weeks before she and Fings and Wil had left Deephaven. Sulfane had taken them straight to the barge. He'd come with salt and iron. He'd opened that box and known exactly what he expected to see. The men in the woods. The mage who'd tried to kill her. They'd all known.

But how?

It was bloody obvious, wasn't it? The Emperor had been

murdered. It had been planned months in advance and Sulfane and that mage were both a part of it.

She shivered. Fings and Wil wouldn't have the first idea what they'd done. Even Blackhand probably wouldn't understand. They'd blundered into the middle of something far too vast for any of them to comprehend.

She stopped again, close to the edge of Spice Market Square, and felt Fings shift behind her.

"I'm going to... go a different way," he said, and slid off the back of her horse. "Something don't feel right." He slipped away. Myla wasn't about to argue. *Not right* seemed like something of an understatement.

Have we started a war?

Should she care? One emperor was like the next. Silver moons were silver moons, no matter whose head was on the back of them; but she remembered Deephaven. She was too young to have lived through the siege but it was ground into the collective memory of the city, the brutality of it.

Yes. She *should* care. Someone had told Sulfane to what to steal and where to find it. Sulfane had found himself a band of thieves to do it, and now here they were in the middle of something. He'd made her a part of it. He'd made her complicit and now he was dead, and someone in Varr had the power and money to have a mage in their pocket and was probably wondering where their stolen crown had gone. They'd start looking, and they'd start by looking for Sulfane.

It's a coup.

The Emperor's oldest son was six years old, his second son a year younger. The Emperor's brother was dead, barely cold in the ground. No one had seen the Emperor's sorceress daughter for months...

I really do *need a drink.*

She reached the Unruly Pig. The doors were closed but the fires were burning inside, soft light spilling from the windows onto the broad mess of snow that was Threadneedle Street. She could hear the merry chatter of merchants talking shop.

Something don't feel right. Fings was right. It didn't.

She looked around but there was nothing else to see through the silence of the falling snow.

One by one they fall, the weak, the strong, the tall... A rhyme for children but it had a truth to it. If someone was trying to assassinate their way to the throne, then Sulfane had put the Unrulys square in the middle, and now he was dead. And there was another thing: Fings had taken her back to where Sulfane had collapsed but there wasn't a body. Yes, there were a lot of horse tracks and it looked like someone had carried him away, and she couldn't think of a better explanation than Wil putting it down to soldiers, but the whole business had a bad smell to it. There was something Fings wasn't telling them. She didn't have a true sword-monk's sense for lies, but she had the beginnings of it. She'd seen Sulfane's wounds. Yes, they might have ended in him dropping dead if he'd turned feverish, but not *that* quickly.

Maybe Fings hit him harder than he thought? Maybe the cold took him?

And then bunch of soldiers had shown up and made off with the body? A bit convenient, wasn't it? True, there *had* been soldiers scouring the roads, looking for whoever robbed their barge. True, she'd seen their tracks, but still...

I should have followed them. I should have seen for myself.

The Pig sounded quieter than usual. Stifled, perhaps, by the falling snow. She still wasn't sure why she'd come back, but here she was. Duty? Because Blackhand had to understand what Sulfane had done? Frankly, after she told him, the only sensible thing left was to make friends with a fine vintage and then run, long and far, not to the City of Spires but to the edge of the empire and beyond.

Maybe burn down the Pig, like she'd burned that barge in Deephaven? Make Jeffa think she'd gone up in flames again?

Hardly going to fall for the same trick twice, is he? Didn't even fall for it the first time, by the looks of things.

She pushed open the doors and crossed from a doomed world

of morbid shadow into a bright festival of life and colour. The Pig's warmth burst over her. People turned to look. It was like waking from a deep dream.

Light of the mind and strength of the limb and warmth of the heart and courage of the soul. She ran the sword-monk mantra through her head, steadying her thoughts as she scanned the crowd. Mostly they were the usual, regulars and Unrulys. She spotted the three spice merchants who'd been rooming upstairs before she left and who were either hatching some crooked deal or else Blackhand was hatching one at their expense. A slender man she didn't recognise was idly passing his hand back and forth through the flame of a candle. A couple of Bonecarvers were sitting by the windows. Two men in striking blue robes were heading for the door, the only ones who weren't sitting down, and then her eye caught Blackhand, standing in the far corner of the room, leaning against the wall...

His fingers flicked a sign at her: *Danger! Danger!* She followed his gaze...

The men in blue weren't heading for the door. They were heading for *her*.

Blue?

Oh, crap!

Mages. How could she be so slow?

"You're Myla." It wasn't a question; but then like Fings had said before they left, how many people carried a pair of sword-monk blades except actual sword-monks?

Light of the mind and strength of the limb and warmth of the heart and courage of the soul. Myla nodded. Her hands stayed where they were but they were thinking very hard about those swords now, how fast she could reach them. Whether she could be faster than a mage with a Death-Word.

Unlikely.

"I am Vashali. Guild Mage. One of the Emperor's sorcerers, Sun bless him." He gave her a moment for that to sink in, presumably in case she'd been living under a rock for the last decade and hadn't already worked it out.

Light of the mind and strength of the limb... The *dead* Emperor's sorcerers, she reminded herself.

Vashali looked pointedly to her swords, presumably an acknowledgement of who and what she was, and how he knew perfectly well that the immediate instinct of a sword-monk confronted by a mage was generally to stab first and ask questions later, and maybe could she not?

"This is my apprentice." He waved his hand at the other mage, a slight gesture as if wafting away a bad smell, and then a blurred image appeared in the air between them. An archer, unrecognisable, standing across a river, poised ready to shoot. "You know this man."

Again, it wasn't a question. She felt a pressure on the edges of her mind. The memory of the Emperor's crown in her hand flickered in her head. She pushed it away. *Warmth of the heart and courage of the soul...*

"You carry the weapons of a sword-monk. Is that really what you are?"

"I am... in training to be one." *Light of the mind and strength of the limb...*

"I see," said the mage.

Warmth of the heart and courage of the soul... She felt a pressure fighting through the mantra. He was testing her, skimming the surface of her thoughts. "I don't recognise him." Which was true enough because the image was terrible. "But I think I may know who you mean." Presumably Sulfane.

"Be truthful, please," said the mage. "Sword-monk or not, it will go better for you."

"I believe you." *Strength of the limb,* "But I don't understand." In this, at least, she meant every word. *Warmth of the heart...*

"You do not need to. We are looking for him. He was here. Where did he go?"

"Downriver," she said, almost without thinking, as though the words had been sucked out of her. "He went downriver." *Light of the mind...*

"And you were with him?"

"Yes." *Damnation!*

"Why?"

"I needed to be out of the city for a few days." *Strength of the limb...*

"Why?"

"Someone attacked me. I hurt him. He has friends. I preferred for the confrontation not to escalate." He wouldn't have any trouble reading the truth behind *that*, at least.

Warmth of the heart... The pressure was growing, strengthening with every word.

"This man. Where is he?"

"The man I hurt?" *Courage of the soul...*

"The archer."

"I don't know." *Strength of the limb...*

"Where did he go?"

"There were four of us. Sulfane went ahead..." *Light of the mind...*

"Sulfane?"

Courage of the soul... Shit! "That's the name he gave. He left after the first night. I haven't seen him since." The lie felt like hands inside her skull, slowly crushing her. The mage stared and Myla stared back, running the mantra over and over, still wondering if she could put a sword into each of them faster than they could rip through her thoughts and freeze her where she stood, and what would happen if she did.

Did she *want* to?

The pressure faded as the mage Vashali reached for the string around her neck and pulled the Moonsteel pendant from under her shirt, an invasion that would have cost him his hand at the very least if she'd been a *real* sword-monk. His eyes flickered, a moment of puzzlement and wonder.

"Where did you get this?"

Light of the mind and strength of the limb... "A thief offered it to me. He didn't know what it was. He didn't know its value."

The mage let the pendant go. "All Moonsteel is property of the Guild," he said.

"The priestesses of the City of Spires who make it may disagree with you." *Light of the fucking mind and strength of the fucking limb and why are you fucking arguing about something so fucking unimportant? Let them see you don't want a fight!* "Claim it if you want." She held the pendant out.

The mage took it and looked it over and then tossed it back. The pressure on the edges of her mind was a dull thing now, faint and subtle. "There's history here but no power. Do with it as you wish. If you hear word of this man Sulfane, please bring it to the Guild."

They moved around her, one either side. She heard the door open, felt a rush of cold air, felt a blast of snow sting her skin and then subside.

Light of the mind and strength of the limb...

She stared at the pendant long after the mages were gone, the mantra repeating of its own volition. She didn't move, maybe didn't even blink as the Teahouse noise of the Unruly Pig slowly began to rise again, until Blackhand came and took her arm. He had his priorities right, at least, pressing a cup of wine into her hands before he started with the questions. She could have kissed him for that.

"What the fuck happened? Where are the others?"

Myla took a deep swallow. "Fings is close. Somewhere outside. Wil isn't far behind."

"Sulfane?"

"Dead. Do you know what we've done?"

She looked at him sharply, caught his eye before he could look away and held it, daring him to lie. He didn't say anything, but gave a taut little nod. As close to an admission as she was likely to get.

"Did you know before we left?"

Blackhand pursed his lips. Myla shook his hand off her arm. For a fleeting moment, she thought about taking his head. Right here in front of everybody. Bastard had known all along. He deserved it.

"What the fuck are you getting us into?" She snatched the bottle from his hand. "Did you... Did you send those men to kill us?"

"What?" Blackhand's surprise looked real. "What men?"

"There was a mage waiting for us." Myla bared her teeth. "Sulfane killed him. Now there are more. Do you know what that means?"

Blackhand shrugged it off. "A few days and they'll move on. Weather it out, girl."

"Weather it *out*?" Myla pushed him away. "The Emperor is *dead*, and we stole–"

He was quick, give him that, stepping up close and pushing her back against a wall and clamping a hand over her face. "Mind your mouth!"

She let him feel the knife pressed against his ribs. He stepped away.

"Weather it out?" she hissed. "*That's* your plan?"

Blackhand glowered, throwing glances all around. Everyone in the Pig was watching. "We'll talk. When the others get back."

"I'd tell you the only way from under this is to run, but I know you won't."

"If that's what you need to do, I'll see you get your share before you go."

"My *share*?" She sounded shrill. "My share of *what*?"

"Keep your voice down!"

She kept the bottle. On her way to the stairs, she passed Seth dozing near the fire. She reached into her coat, pulled out Fings' crumpled papers from the barge and gently put them in his hands.

"You're the scholar," she muttered. "See what's here and then burn them when you're done. If you need a floor tonight, knock before you come in."

Fuck all this shit. Fuck Blackhand and fuck Jeffa. She had money again, and so tonight was for drinking. Tomorrow, she'd worry about the rest.

18

SİGİLS

Seth, cold and bone-tired, watched Myla head upstairs. Seeing her set off an odd burst of feelings. Pride and envy and pity, mostly, which made no sense until he realised that a part of him admired her. Pity and pride for her faith in a god who would inevitably let her down, envy for a courage he could never match. When it hit him, that odd understanding, he almost went after her and told her what was coming; but leaving the kitchens meant risking Blackhand seeing him, and he was rather hoping to keep a low profile tonight.

The door into the alleys of Haberdashers opened. Fings stumbled through, bringing in a swirl of snow. He shivered as he saw Seth. "Is it safe?" He had his feather between his teeth and looked ready to run right back out if he had to. Seth raised an eyebrow.

"Still alive, then."

"Yeah, about that… Did I just see two mages?"

"They talked to Myla. She held them off. You should be happy – they're after Sulfane. Been here three nights on the trot now, looking for anyone who knows him." He slowly shook his head. "Mages in the Pig. Fings, what have you done?"

Fings screwed up his face and made some weird gesture with his hands. "I can't stay here. Not if there's mages!"

"Relax. They left." Seth looked to the window and the snow falling outside. It would be waist-deep in the alleys by now and it wasn't showing any sign of letting up. Of course, he *could* mention that there might not be a Pig to come back to tomorrow...

Fucking Spicers. He'd really fucked things up this time. Was only supposed to be Blackhand that got hurt. Done and dusted before Fings and Myla and Wil and Sulfane ever came back, but oh no, they had to have that fucker from Deephaven with them, him with his hard-on for Myla's head on a pole.

Fings shook his head. "Even so."

"Look, I'm glad you're back, and I'm glad you didn't irritate Sulfane into killing you, but where is he? Because if there are mages looking for him, someone had best make sure they don't find him."

"Yeah. Not much chance of that. He's dead."

"Go on."

Fings dragged him into one of the empty backrooms Blackhand used for his more private guests. They sat by the fire and Fings told him the story. It had the usual Fings quirks: vague and full of exaggeration, a tall tale about a crown and piles of silver and a mage and Sulfane dead, his corpse taken by the Emperor's soldiers and all the loot left hidden outside the city... and of course everything that went wrong was Sulfane's fault, and all the loot had probably been stolen by goblins by now, and it was all a waste of time. Eventually, Fings ran out of words and the warmth of the fire started making his head droop. Seth fetched a blanket and left him snoring in a chair, and set about having a look at the crumpled pages Myla had pushed in his face.

They were parchments, absurdly fine and very old. The writing was in three different languages in three different hands and written at three different times. The most recent script consisted of a few banal notes in a well-educated hand, albeit with an old-fashioned and pompous flourish. Pretty but with nothing interesting to say: the writer clearly didn't know what he was looking at. The oldest script was one he couldn't read but he knew what it was because he'd seen it before: the sigils from that night with Fings in the catacombs, etched around the dead-end archways and the entrance to the second vault...

He spread the sheets out across the table and very quietly swore: the third was a religious script. From the fading of the inks, he reckoned it dated to somewhere around the civil war. The paragraphs were carefully written, detailed and startling. He was looking at a translation, or at least a partial one. Someone, some forty years ago, shortly before Khrozus had been marching on Varr, had gone down to the catacombs and worked out what those sigils meant.

Sigils for commanding and containing the dead.

Right there in front of him.

He felt a chill shiver through him. A pair of Guild Mages didn't come down from the Kaveneth for a few stolen sacks of silver. And what was a crown when it came down to it? A bit of metal you could melt down and turn into an expensive pisspot, that's what.

Was *this* what they'd been were after?

Six pages barely scratched the surface. There had to be more...

Out in the commons, he heard new voices. Wil and Blackhand. Seth hurriedly stuffed the pages away as they came in. Blackhand shook Fings awake and gave a Seth a look.

"What you doing here?"

"Waiting for Sulfane."

"Well he's dead, so you can piss off unless you fancy paying for room and board like every other fucker." Blackhand hauled Fings off his chair and took him upstairs, presumably so they could argue about how much shit they were in and whose fault it was. When they were done, Fings would come back to the kitchens and go back to sleep, and Seth would wait a while and then wake him up, and then put a candle in a window, and they'd go to the pantry and disappear into the tunnels, and then the Spicers would come, and that would be that.

Blackhand had it coming, right?

Right?

He spread the pages back out across the table and there it was, a tiny pang of guilt. Not for Blackhand, not even for Wil or Dox or

Arjay or any of the others who might get their throats cut tonight, but for what he was about to do to Myla.

She barely notices you exist.

Nevertheless, there it was.

She can look after herself. She'll be fine.

Yeah. Like *that* was going to work.

He turned back to the pages. Only one way to know whether the translation was right: he'd have to go back to the catacombs, like he'd always said he would. Except he was scared. Night after night, the dreams or sendings or whatever they were said the same, *Go back, go back!* And he ignored them because the thought of going back terrified him enough to turn his bones to jelly.

And now this. A chance like this would never come again. And what did he have to lose? The priests had given him a life and then they'd taken it back. If he had any real family, he had no idea who they were and no desire to find out. Blackhand treated him like shit scraped off the street. For all the work he'd done, for all he'd given of himself, he had exactly nothing to show for it.

He lit another candle. The Pig was done. Myla, Blackhand, all of them…

He'd get Fings out. Make sure he was safe. Brick wasn't here, and he felt good about that. But why Myla? Why, of all of the people he was about to betray, did he feel guilty about *her*?

She'd be the right person to have down the catacombs. Her and those swords.

She wouldn't come. If she knew what he wanted to do, she'd stop him. She might even kill him, if that was what it took.

How do you know if you don't ask?

Because there's nothing more self-righteous than a sword-monk.

But that's not what she is.

She follows the Path. She has faith.

And you don't?

No.

Liar.

He heard the way the others talked when Myla wasn't around.

She was an outsider like he was. She didn't belong, like he didn't belong.

We're nothing like each other. She had a horse and money and those swords.

Still...

No. Different levels of the mountain.

Really? That shit again?

The Empire, Seth had long ago decided, was like a mountain. At the bottom were the beggars and the homeless. People like him. Above, were those who could scrape enough money to afford food and warmth, people who got by – people like Fings. Then those with a trade and some tools; and then above that, everything was equally unreachable and thus all the same, whether it was the Emperor or the merchants bringing spices and teas into Spice Market Square, like the mountain disappeared into a layer of cloud. Above the cloud were the Sunbrights and the Dawncallers and anyone with money, all in crisp, clear sunlight and knowing exactly where they stood; and the cloud was still there below them, but they couldn't see through it to all the people who kept the mountain standing, and so they forgot that those people even existed. That was the part of the mountain where Myla had been born. Above the cloud. It was where Seth wanted to be. Where he *deserved* to be.

See. Nothing remotely alike.

Liked her bed while she wasn't here though, didn't you? Apparently, his conscience didn't give a shit about clever social metaphors.

Fuck off.

You realise I'm you. It's actually yourself *you're telling to fuck off. I'm going to help you out here: you feel guilty because she still has faith, and so do you, and that makes her your sister whether you like it or not.*

Still fuck off.

Oh, deal with it!

The voices from upstairs were getting heated. Fings banging on about Sulfane, Blackhand having none of it. Seth took a deep breath. He had to go back to where it all went wrong. Back to the white room under the earth. He had to get past how bone-cracking scared he was; because the thought of being under the city in the dark again filled him with... Well, not dread because he was already full of *that* from what he was about to do, letting the Spicers though the tunnel, one half of him expecting to be murdered for his trouble, the other half expecting Blackhand to somehow already know, to walk in all sad and disappointed and beat him to death in a slow, casual rage. No, he was past dread. Utter pants-shitting terror sounded more like it. He tried to remember ever being this scared before.

It wasn't like this before. The first time you went.

No. He hadn't been afraid back then. Not one little bit. The priests had done this to him.

No. Not them. What happened after.

No. Not that either. You're scared because what if you're wrong?

He rubbed his eyes and yawned. The sigils in the catacombs were the same as the sigils in front of him. He was certain.

...Alone in a place he shouldn't be. A cold place deep within the earth. A vaulted circular hall surrounded by archways that should have been doors but led only into blank raw stone...

He jerked.

What the fuck was that?

The image of a somewhere else had been there for an instant, no more, but it left him with a sense of disconnection, that it was Fings and the Unruly Pig and the fire in the hearth that were the vision and not reality...

Get a grip.

The Spicers were out there, waiting. No going back. He went to the pantry and moved the sacks of flour. He opened the door to the tunnel. Once they were outside, he'd let Fings lead the way through Haberdashers and Seamstresses and around Bonecarvers and the Circus of Dead Emperors. Fings had a knack for knowing which way trouble lay and picking a different path, exactly the way Seth didn't. It seemed hardly fair: how Fings made his living put danger in his path at every possible opportunity, yet he slipped through it like water through a dying man's fingers. And Seth had done everything right, hadn't he? Worked hard, learned to read and write and do his numbers, found his way into a respectable way of life...

One thing. I did one *thing wrong.*

It wasn't *one* thing. He knew that.

He looked at the sigils on the papers once more and then stuffed them in his shirt. Couldn't let Fings see them. He'd lose his shit.

No. No going back, not even if he wanted to.

19

CHAOS AПD FİRE

It felt to Myla as though she'd hardly closed her eyes before there was a knocking on the door, and then Fings and Seth were coming in without a word of invitation.

It was still the middle of the night, and she was tired and her head was full of wool from the empty bottle of wine beside the bed.

"Fuck's sake," she growled: "What do you want?"

"To thank you for letting me sleep here while you were gone," said Seth. "Nice to get a window."

"Thank me in the morning." Myla turned back to her pillow.

"No. You need to wake up and you need to listen." Seth crossed the room, carrying a candle. "Those mages. I know what happened out there. If they get hold of Fings or Wil, they won't hold back, not like they did with you. They'll get it all, and then this place is dead. You know that, right?"

"Go. Away."

"Wil knows where you hid the stuff!" hissed Fings.

"Seth! Fings! Fuck! Off!"

"No! We got to talk about it *now*!"

Myla took a deep breath and yawned and sat up and tried to shake the cobwebs out of her head. They were looking at her like a pair of anxious children.

"Me and Fings are splitting," said Seth. "Those swords of

yours might have fooled them but they won't be nice twice. You know that, so why are you still here?"

The question hung between them. Seth was right. Jeffa being in Varr and now this? She ought to go south to Torpreah or east to Tzeroth or west to Neja or the City of Spires. Just get out. Shouldn't have come back here at all, not really.

"Myla?"

She rubbed at her temples and yawned again, trying to make the world come properly into focus. "I've got nowhere else to go," she said, which felt like it barely scratched the surface.

"I have," said Seth.

In the flickering light of the candle, she caught a look on his face that she couldn't unravel. Not fear, exactly. An odd mix of purpose and dread.

"You do?" Fings sounded surprised.

"Fings and I know a place they'll never think to look."

"Oh no we don't!" said Fings, apparently catching on to something he didn't like. "No, you bloody don't."

"Where else, Fings?"

"I ain't going *there*."

"*I* don't want to go there either!" There was a hunger in him, though. She saw it. He was lying.

"Yes you do!"

"Where's *there*?" asked Myla stifling yet another yawn. "And tell me again why this can't wait until morning?"

"Don't mind him. There's things worse than mages."

You didn't have to know Fings all that long to know what he thought about mages. She couldn't imagine what he thought was worse. Actual demons? "I'm not going anywhere," she said. "In the morning, I'm going to talk to Wil and Blackhand. We're going to give back what we stole, and that'll be the end of it. In the morning. When it's light." And then she was going to leave. "Now let me sleep." She lay back and closed her eyes.

"Give it back?" Fings sounded shrill.

"Fings! Go away!"

Seth let out a little sigh. "That's not really the—"

"Who you going to give it to? Eh?"

"I don't know, whoever should have it." In the gloom, Fings was almost invisible. "Fings, you're still here. Would you *please* both fuck off!"

Seth put the candle on the windowsill. "And exactly who *is* that, do you think? Who should have it? Overlord Kyra, the Butcher of Deephaven? Are you going to give it to *him*?"

"Seth..."

"Or were you thinking further south? One of Talsin's heirs?"

"Seth!"

"Khrozus didn't get them all, you know. Or how about across the river to the Kaveneth? Give it to the Guild? Save them the trouble of hunting for it?"

"Seth, I *will* kill you if you don't let me go back to sleep."

"Or maybe you were planning on walking into the palace to find our new regent and hand it over? Oh, didn't you hear? We have a child witch-queen now. Here's daddy's crown, sorry for the fuss? You think you could get even close?"

Myla sat up despite herself. "They put the Emperor's *daughter* on the throne?"

"Or she put herself. Myla, do you *really* think anyone is going to be all understanding and forgiveness? And do you think no one else will try to stop you? You think there aren't two sides to this, maybe more, and all of them want what you and Wil left hidden in the snow? I'm sorry to be here in the middle of the night, but we need to leave, right now, before those mages come back, or someone even worse." Seth crouched beside her bed. "I know you come from a different world than the likes of me and Fings. I had a glimpse of that world once. But that's your past, not your here and now. You think those swords will protect you? They won't. You think you can undo what you've done? You can't. We're all fucked. It's run and hide, or stay and swing. It really is that simple."

"Maybe Blackhand has a way out." Did she believe that? No.

No, Seth was right. Made you wonder what had happened to him, someone as clever as him living the way he did.

She took a deep breath. Her head was still swimming.

"What do you suggest?"

He was watching her. "Like I said, I know a place no one will look."

"No, no, no." Fings wrung his hands in agitation.

"I'm listening," Myla said.

"I'm not," said Fings. "I'm going home. I've got a family. What about them? What about Wil?"

"What about him?" asked Seth. "He'll stand by Blackhand to the end. Like he did when we lost Sand and Rev. You remember that, right?"

"I'm going to talk to him." Fings marched to the door, then stopped and turned on Seth. "Don't go back there. Please."

"*Me*? No one's looking for *me*, Fings. *I* didn't steal the Emperor's fucking crown."

"I didn't know what it *was*, did I?" Fings stood in the half-open door, waved his hands around, a helpless gesture, and then was gone.

Seth followed as far as the doorway. "It's not far," he said.

"What about Blackhand?"

"You really owe that prick anything?"

Blackhand had known what Sulfane was stealing and hadn't thought to mention it. No, Myla reckoned she didn't owe Blackhand anything at all. But then, that wasn't really the point.

"I'll give you a minute." Seth left his candle in her window and closed the door behind him. Myla sat in the gloom, head in her hands. *What do I do now?*

She knew the answer. Jeffa Hawat knew she was still alive. He was hardly likely to have kept that to himself. That was the truth of it. Half a year since she'd left, all the trouble she'd taken to get away, a whole new life carved out for herself… Yet there it was. Sooner or later, she'd have to face who she was and what she'd done.

Did she like what she'd become, here in Varr? Not really.

She dressed and put on her swords. Seth was waiting outside in the corridor.

"The kitchens. There's a tunnel out from one of the pantries. Leads to that warehouse he uses. Blackhand thinks I don't know but–"

"A tunnel?"

"You think they haven't got someone out there, watching for Wil? Or you, if you leave?"

"Seth… I know you're right. Almost everything you say is right. But… I'm not coming. I have to fix this, otherwise… I think I'm done with running from my mistakes. At some point, you have to stop, don't you? You have to stand and face who you are and what you've done?"

Seth looked at her like she was mad. "And you think *this* is the right time for that?"

"Is there *ever* a right time?"

"Myself, I might have picked something smaller." Seth took a deep breath, held it, then let out a long sigh. "Got to do what you got to do. You ever been to the City of Spires?"

"I passed through on the way from Deephaven." Hard not to, the way it straddled the river.

"You saw the five towers?"

Myla smiled. "They're difficult to miss."

"Too tall to be real?"

She'd seen them from the river. The five spires in a ring around the city's heart. She'd looked at them and tried to make sense of what she was seeing. *Too tall* was hardly the start of it.

"White stone with an inner light of its own that makes them shine at night? That's what I heard. Never been, so I don't know if it's true."

"White, yes. But I passed through at midday so I couldn't say about the light."

"The Torpreahns think they were the first, that Torpreah is the jewel of the empire, but another people lived here long before they ever crossed the sea. Crowns, Emperors, none of it matters.

Food. Shelter. Staying alive… but the rest?" He shook his head. "Don't do this. Save it for something important."

"I think I've been saying that to myself for too long already."

Seth nodded. "Then goodbye. You deserve better than Blackhand." He reached out a hand as if to touch her, then changed his mind. "We both did."

He padded away down the corridor. Myla watched until he turned the corner to the stairs, then went back into her room. The candle was still in the window. She blew it out and sat against the wall in darkness, wide awake now, thinking of everything that had brought her to this moment. Her life in Deephaven. The Temple of the Sun and the sword-monks who'd trained her to fight. Sword-mistress Tasahre with the scar on her neck that no one would ever explain, but which whispers said was because of a boy. Lucius and Soraya, her brother and her sister. Jeffa and Sarwatta Hawat, and everything that had gone between them, the soaring hopes that had turned so bitter. Fleeing in the night. Burning the barge to make everyone think she was dead. Taking what she could from the wreckage of her ruined family and leaving her sister to pick up the pieces. The river to Varr. All coming to this.

When she closed her eyes, she saw that night in Deephaven, although it wasn't what *really* happened because she hadn't been there, because if she *had* been there then she would have stopped it. Soraya slipping out because she was in love. Truth was, Myla had been a little bit in love with him too, and Soraya knew it, and that was why she went, to steal a march on her little sister.

If I'd had the grace to stand aside…

She saw Sarwatta looking up at her from the floor where she'd left him. He was laughing at her because he knew. *You tell yourself you did this for her but you didn't. You did it for yourself. You did this out of spite.*

A scrape on the floor outside her door snapped her back. The room around her was dark, the black night outside her window filled with falling snow. She watched, perfectly still, as the door cracked open and the figure of a man eased into her room.

Someone she didn't know, bringing with him a scent of cloves and sulphur...

A flame flickered into life in his palm. Myla took two quick steps and had a knife at his neck before he even knew she was there. She kicked the door closed.

"Stay very still."

Cloves and Sulphur froze, hands outstretched. She'd taken his light to be a tiny lantern, but there was only a flame, burning bright over the palm of his hand.

A mage.

Shit. Her fingers tightened on her knife. In the black and white world of the sword-monks who'd taught her, mages were the enemy. They were also very, very dangerous. She'd seen that much for herself.

Take his head! Do it NOW!

She stepped back and shifted into guard, swords drawn. The mage did the same, except that in each palm he held a tiny globe of fire. He brought one palm to his lips and blew on it. A streak of flame leapt across the room and bloomed into life like a candle, except there was no wick or tallow, only air. He blew again, until four flames floated in a circle around them.

"I'm here to talk," he said.

"And for that you creep into my room in the dead of night without so much as knocking?" She couldn't see much of him, despite the flames, but she could see some. Enough to recognize that he was neither particularly tall, nor particularly short, nor particularly anything. Enough to recognize that he wasn't wearing the robes of a Guild Mage.

"The Guild are watching. I am obliged to be discreet."

"Show me your face." Something about him felt familiar. Something about the way he held himself.

The fire in his hand bloomed a little brighter. He drew his hands apart, letting them light his features, and then she knew: he was man she'd seen earlier that evening, the stranger playing with a candle flame, idly looking on as the two Guild Mages had questioned her...

A mage but not a part of the Guild? What did that leave? *An abomination* is what Tasahre would have said, but she would have said that about Guild Mages too, and what would Tasahre say about *her*? Probably an abomination as well, these days. A sword-monk who'd turned her back on her training.

Khrozus but she was tired. "What do you want?" How far would she get running from someone who could throw fire from his hands? Probably not far.

"My name is Orien," he said. "I am apprenticed to Mistress Novashi, fire-sorceress to the Princess-Regent." He made a sour face at her swords. "I don't suppose you could put those away, could you?"

"No."

The mage Orien steepled his hands, tiny flickers licking from each fingertip. She saw his face clearly now, golden in the light of his fire. He was young, skinny, with big honest eyes. "My mistress would appreciate your... cooperation."

"Then your mistress can come and talk to me herself. I recommend coming in daylight and not like a thief."

"My mistress has the ear of our Princess-Regent, who happens to owe both Lady Novashi and the Sorcerer Royal a great deal. I'm sure all three would love to come in person for tea and a chat, but they're a little busy right now. You know how it is: plots against the throne, uprisings in Tzeroth, religious warfare in Deephaven, the Torpreahns mustering armies, whispers stirring beyond the Dragon's Teeth of white skinned-men with blood-red eyes who wield sorcery as freely as other men piss in the snow, that sort of thing. Never a dull moment. So, it falls to the likes of you and me to–"

"Just tell me what you came to say and then get out."

He smiled, then. It would have been a nice smile, she thought, if it hadn't come creeping like a cockroach into her room in the middle of the night.

"You tricked Vashali, but he could have forced his way into you. Your swords fooled him but he *will* come back. I want the same thing they do, and for the same reason. Unlike the Guild, my mistress is more... flexible. I want you to take me to the man they're looking for. Before the Guild find him. And they *will* find him."

"I can't help you."

The mage splayed his fingers. Little darts of fire shot into the air. "I think you can."

"Ah." Myla smiled. "Threats. Finally." She took a step back, ready to spring, but Orien lowered his hands.

"I'm not your enemy. I might be the best friend you can have."

"Go away, wizard. My answer to you is the same as it was to the others. And not being my enemy doesn't make you my–"

A muffled crash sounded from the kitchens below. *Too early for the kitchen girls to be up.* Myla bared her teeth. "Not my enemy? Really?"

Panic flashed over the mage, his silky poise gone in an instant. "Shit! The Guild must–"

A sudden movement brought the tip of Myla's sword to the skin of his neck. "Sword-monks can smell lies, mage. You know that, don't you? How many are there?"

"I don't know!" he squeaked. "I don't know anything! I came alone, I swear!"

Fuck's sake! Trouble was, she believed him. She stayed very still, eyes on the mage, ears straining...

Creeping footsteps in the hall outside. Someone trying to be silent and not making a good job of it. A creak of leather, the whisper of cloth scraping along the wall. The door to her room started to ease open...

If I'm still here tomorrow, I'm fitting a fucking latch. Myla yanked it open. A naked blade gleamed in the gloom. She grabbed the wrist holding it and pulled, hauling a very surprised man into the room and throwing him at the mage. As they crashed together, she slammed the door shut in a second man's face, kicked the first in the knee as he tried to find his balance, swept his legs out from under him and then her foot was on his neck, crushing his throat, her other sword pointing straight in the mage's face. The mage's eyes had gone like saucers.

Running feet outside. Then a voice yelling: "Here! She's up here! She's not dead! He didn't do it!"

She looked to the mage, ready to gut him. "*What* didn't you do?"

"I... I... I..." The mage was shaking with fear, about the last thing she'd expect from a sorcerer who could possibly turn her inside out with the snap of his fingers. "I don't know! I don't know who these people are!"

"Kill me in my sleep?" she asked. "Was that it?"

"No! I... I... I don't know what's happening!" The mage looked as though he was trying to push his way backwards through the wall. Myla risked a proper look at the man on the floor and realised she knew him. Knew his face, anyway. He wasn't a mage or a Guild Man or anything of the sort. He was a Spicer.

"Oh for... Really? Tonight?" Spicers in the Teahouse? "You couldn't have waited until tomorrow, or come *last* night? It *had* to be tonight?" She stamped the prostrate Spicer, knocking the air out of him, gave the mage a look – if that's what he really was, because the way he was shaking like a cornered squirrel was starting to give her some strong doubts on that score – and ran out into the hall, yelling and banging on doors. "Spicers! Spicers in the Pig!" Where were Wil and Dox and Arjay and Brick and all the rest? "Spicers in the Pig! Up! Up!"

Three men lurked at the top of the stairs. Myla growled and whirled to meet them. The hall was narrow enough they'd have to come at her one at a time. They were a gang of thugs while *she* was a sword-monk. She'd cut them to ribbons if they tried it.

"Leave," she said, "before I kill you."

The Spicer at the front backed away, pushing into the two men behind him. At her back, another door opened. One of the girls. Lula? Sara?

"Get Blackhand! Go upstairs and get everyone up." She'd hold them here, at the top of the stairs to the commons. And she *would* hold them, because none of them would dare try her, she could already see that in their eyes.

She walked towards them, slowly at first, then faster, closing the gap. The Spicers started to edge away. As soon they did, she charged. They turned and fled, two of them tripping over each other, falling and tumbling down the steps. She stamped them down as she leapt past and slammed into the back of the last, knocking him flying and then leaping and landing on him at the foot of the stairs. She heard his ribs crack, heard his shriek as all the air flew out of him and then she was free and in open space and...

Shit.

There were more here, waiting. Spread calmly across the commons as though they were expecting her, and they weren't Spicers, not these. They had short swords for stabbing and cutting and carried themselves like...

Like Deephaven mercenaries.

"Hello, Shirish."

The Spicer with the broken ribs groaned. She heard the scrape of him moving on the floor, a whimper with every breath. And what she *ought* to do, what she *wanted* to do, was whirl and bury the point of a sword in his back while he was still down and helpless.

No. No more killing. Not unless she had to.

"Hello, Jeffa."

"You know how hard it was to find you, once I realised you weren't dead? And then, just as I had you, you disappeared. I was starting to worry. I thought maybe you'd moved on from Varr. Should I call you Shirish? Or should I call you Myla now?"

A growl from the stairs and then running feet. One of the Spicers she'd knocked down, back up and coming at her. She turned and shifted sideways and swung low, lacerating the air with a zigzag whirl of blades and then shoving him on as he skittered helplessly past. She felt the tip of one sword bite. The Spicer howled and fell and slid to stop at the feet of the men spread out in front of her.

She waited for them to come, blades held high. "You want to take me? Try it." The other Spicer was getting to his feet behind her. From the sounds of things, there were more upstairs. Even without them, Jeffa had too many sell-swords for her to fight all at once. "You and me, Jeffa." She might get two or three before they cut her down. No more than that. She feinted at the closest mercenary, testing his reaction. He shied away, batting at her blade, but he didn't look like he was about to panic. Wary, but they weren't afraid of her.

Jeffa then. Single him out. "Working for the Spicers, Jeffa? That's a bit of a step down, isn't it?" *Cut off the head and the body dies...*

"Common interests, Shirish." There he was. In the middle, standing back, ready to watch while others did his dirty work.

Of course.

"I was thinking of giving up. Maybe I was wrong. Maybe you really *were* dead. Then I heard whisper of some demon-bitch with sword-monk blades in Varr. After that..." He shook his head. "Give yourself up, Shirish. There's a messenger already on the way back to Deephaven. Once my brother knows you're still alive... Well, you know what that's going to mean for your brother and your sister. You could spare *them*, at least."

"Touch either of them and I will kill you all!"

Jeffa nodded. On cue, the sell-swords advanced, moving to flank her, cutting her off from a dash to the kitchens or to the windows. They edged in slowly, all of them at once until the circles of their blades were about to overlap.

"This won't be gentle, Shirish. You took the head off one of these boys. I should tell my brother to be thankful it was only his balls you had from him in Deephaven."

Back up the stairs. She could hold them in the hall where they could only come at her one at a time...

Another step closer...

Into one of the rooms. Lock the door...

Flame flared behind her, a bright and dazzling light that flew from the top of stairs into the middle of the room. She caught a flash-frame glimpse of Jeffa's face, glaring gleeful murder...

Go!

She turned and bolted. A Spicer loomed right in front of her, knife half-raised. She slashed and took his hand. The second cut was flying at his neck as she heard him scream...

No!

She twisted the blow, hitting him with the flat, knocking him out of the way as she ran past, taking the steps three at a time. Jeffa yelled something but she didn't hear what. A dart of fire shot past her, and then another. The mage Orien, grinning like an idiot.

"Ha-*ha*!"

She looked back, half hoping to see Jeffa's mercenaries wrapped in flames and screaming, but no. The mage was throwing sparks, nothing more. It had startled them, bought her a few seconds, but that was all. She barged past him. He'd have to look after himself, and if he couldn't then he was an idiot; and somehow there were two more Spicers in the hall where there weren't supposed to be any, all startled panic as she barrelled into them in a whirl of edges. One blade connected with something hard, the other with something soft. A Spicer howled. She punched one in the face, smashing his nose and his teeth and knocking him down, kicked the other through a door, and then she was through, and somehow neither had stuck a knife in her. She whirled back and stared at Orien.

"Where the fuck did *they* come from?"

A crash from the stairs at the other end of the hall, the ones leading to the upper floor where Blackhand lived, then shouts. A bundle of figures came hurtling down, two silhouettes being chased by what looked like almost a dozen. She heard Blackhand shouting *Kill these fuckers*, and Wil too, but the silhouettes were Dox and Arjay. They saw her and stopped and turned to face the Spicers coming from above.

So that was it, was it? The three of them, trapped in this hall.

Changed things, though, if Dox and Arjay had her back...

The Spicers coming down the stairs crashed into Dox and Arjay, all shouts and knives and clubs. Arjay screamed. Dox bellowed her name, full of rage and panic. Myla let out a whoop and charged, hoping to send the Spicers running, and it might even have worked, except the hall between the rooms up here was too narrow for her to get past Dox. The Spicers backed away and then stopped, Blackhand held between them, yelling and cursing and trying to break loose and generally getting in the way, but with a knife to his throat, and where were the *fuck* were the rest of Wil's men?

"Give me the bitch with the swords and the rest of you can go." The Deephaven sell-swords were cresting the stairs from below, Jeffa still carefully at the rear where she couldn't reach him. "Don't and I'll gut every last one of you!"

Dox was bent over Arjay. Myla stood over them both, a sword pointed each way down the hall, the Spicers holding their ground at one end, Jeffa and his sell-swords advancing from the other.

"Give it up, Shirish. I meant what I said. I'll kill everyone else here if you don't."

Myla nudged Dox. "Get her away. Out a window. Carry her if you have to." She turned to the mage, who was doing some edging of his own, mostly looking for a way out. "Wizard, this is where you *do* something."

"Like what?"

"Like make their heads explode!" Arjay was on her feet, leaning on Dox.

"Last chance, Shirish!"

"No one can do *that*!"

"*Burn* them, then!"

"I…" He stood looking at her, helpless and pathetic. Jeffa, slow and calm as you like, nudged one of his sell-swords and unshouldered a crossbow. He set about cocking it.

"I don't want to kill you, Shirish. I just want to take you back. Doesn't matter to me how broken you are."

"And what your brother has in mind isn't worse than bleeding out right here?"

Jeffa sniffed. "Not up to me, Shirish."

Myla looked at Dox and Arjay.

I'm sorry.

She sprang for the nearest door and crashed through, snatched the chamber pot from under the bed and smashed it into the window, shattering wooden struts and fragile glass. Twice more, knocking away as much of the debris as she could, and then the mage was in the doorway, running like a scalded rabbit, and the first Deephaven sell-sword was right behind him. She hurled the pot at both of them, not bothered who she hit. The mage lunged forward and crashed to the floor while the sell-sword shied back. Myla slammed the door shut and held it as the mage picked himself up.

"Kelm's teeth! Can't you do *any*thing?"

The door shuddered as someone rammed into it.

"The window! Go!"

The door shook again, almost knocking her off her feet. The mage looked at her as though she was mad, then looked around the room as though hoping to find some other way out that he hadn't noticed. Myla levelled a sword at him.

"Now!"

The door heaved for a third time. Three men on the other side, pushing her back and she didn't have the strength to hold them. The mage danced to the window and hovered there, paralysed for a moment. He started to climb out, trying gingerly to pick his way around the broken glass. The door heaved yet again, and in a moment...

Myla let the door go and bolted for the window. She gave the mage a good hard kick, sending him flying out of the Pig, spun to face the onrushing mercenaries, screamed and slashed the air in front of their faces, bought herself a moment of hesitation, and turned and dove head first after the mage, twisting and spinning in the air, landing hard in an explosion of waist-deep snow, sprawling on her backside and dropping both her swords. More snow showered around her, into her face and mouth, a shocking cold. Pain lanced through her ankles and her knees, but not enough to matter. She pushed herself upright, floundering in the snow, grabbing for her swords, slicing her hand on broken glass...

Shouts from above. They were at the window. Just for a moment, she thought she might go back, march in through the front door of the Pig and take Jeffa from behind while his men were all in the wrong place, then take as many of the rest as she could before they cut her down...

No.

The mage was groaning in a crumpled heap a few feet away. Jeffa was at the window, fumbling with his crossbow. She snatched her swords and ran, forcing herself through the snow into the darkness of Nightveil Alley, then stopped and looked back.

Orien floundered in her wake. No one was coming after her from the Pig.

One thing to be surrounded by hired swords. A whole other one coming after me in a dark alley, eh, Jeffa?

"Wait!"

Myla ducked into the shadows of a doorway, let the mage limp right past her, then stepped out and pressed a sword to his back.

"Your mistress has the ear of the Princess-Regent? What is she? The palace lamp-lighter?"

He bristled at that, despite her steel. When he turned and dusted himself down, there was blood on his face and on his clothes, mixed with snow. From his hands where he'd cut himself on the broken glass of the shattered window.

"Is *any* of what you told me true?"

Orien's face twisted with some old bitterness. "Every word."

She watched him carefully and sniffed the air, then gestured back at the Teahouse. The mage bit his lip and shook his head. *Nothing to do with me.*

Did she believe him? Yes. She did.

"The man the Guild are looking for..." *Khrozus, am I really doing this?* "What do they want from him. The truth. All of it. Right now."

"He took something. They want it back and... They think he had something to do with the Emperor's murder."

"And what's all that to you?"

"The thing he took... It needs to go back where it belongs."

"And that's it? He gives it back and gets to walk away?"

"If he gives it to my mistress, yes."

Another sigh. *Apparently, I am.* "If I tell him what you said. If he believes you... *If* he believes you... How does he find you?"

iv

INTERLUDE

The two of them lay on the temple roof, staring at the stars. Fings had brought a pipe and a little bag of Haze he'd swiped from the market. There was a pleasant buzz inside Seth's head. A month had passed since his visit to the crypt under the temple in Spice Market Square.

"I found this place," said Fings. "Near the south gate. It's like a walled village in the middle of Claymakers, only it's some old wall that's half tumbled down and doesn't have any way in or out. You have to use a ladder or a rope, but on the *inside*... There's this witch-woman who does the best charms in the city, and she says there's a shaft right in the middle of their patch that just goes straight down into the ground. Stairs and everything. Said it was a bad place."

"*Is* there?"

Fings shook his head. "I went to have a look, but if there ever *was* something there, some mutton-head built a shack on it." He passed the pipe to Seth. "Probably just some story. Or maybe an old well. You know where there has to be another crypt, though? Tombland."

Seth reckoned Fings was probably right about that. Only problem being that the city canals made Tombland into an island, the bridges were all watched, and the Mage of Tombland had a bee in his bonnet about priests in general and Sun-priests in particular.

He sniggered and took a drag on the pipe and passed it back to Fings. "The mage," he said, and then had a go at what he hoped was a spooky ghostly sort of noise.

"The mage," Fings had a go too, and then they were both making ghost noises until they had to stop because they were both laughing too much.

"You hear the story about the Lightbringer and the two sword-monks who tried to go after him?" asked Seth, when he'd recovered.

Fings chuckled. "Went in and never came out." Which was the story everyone told, but Seth knew better.

"Not so. Way they tell it here, people were pelting them with rubbish and tipping piss-pots on their heads the moment they crossed the first bridge. Like everyone already knew they were coming and why. The Lightbringer isn't having it, right? Says to keep going, so they do. Next thing you know, there's a crowd of people blocking the way and refusing to move. The sword-monks tell the Lightbringer he should turn back, but this Lightbringer is from Torpreah, see. He's come all this way to put a warlock in the ground and so he won't back down. Tells the sword-monks to cut down anyone who stands in his way. The sword-monks draw their swords but still the crowd doesn't move. By now there are hundreds. The streets and alleys all around them are packed. They're trapped.

"One sword-monk sheathes her swords, like she won't do it. The other picks out some big fellow and tells him to move aside. When he doesn't, the monk kicks him. Down he goes. The sword-monk says she'll kill him if he doesn't get out of the way. When he still won't move, she puts a sword to the back of his neck like she's going to do it. Right then, an arrow comes out of nowhere and skewers the Lightbringer in the mouth. Kills him dead as a stone, just like that.

"Of course, the sword-monks completely lose their shit, but the crowd is already parting for some little old man carrying a bow. He's frail and wizened and clearly can't manage to even draw the thing, but he walks right up to the sword-monks and falls on his knees and points at the dead Lightbringer and says: *It was me. I did that. I accept my punishment.*"

Fings took a long suck on the pipe and blew a mangled effort at a smoke ring. "It wasn't him, right?"

"Course it wasn't, and everyone knew it, but he still said it. The monks knew he wasn't the one, but what else could they do? They brought him back and had a trial and he never wavered in his story and so they hanged him, but not before they cut him off from the light."

"They what?"

"No fire or daylight or running water to take his soul. They brought him up to this roof, right here, and laid him out for the wind and the stars to take him to the Mistress of Many Places."

"What? When they all *knew* he didn't do it?"

"Well... It was that or go off murdering the whole of Tombland, I suppose. Only, the next morning, the body had gone. No one ever knew where, or what happened to it. Word started going about that the mage had disguised himself as the wind and taken him back, but what *I* think is that one of the sword-monks brought him down and quietly sent him to the fire-pits on the back of one of the corpse wagons."

"Why would they do that?"

Seth shrugged. "To send him to the light. Because he asked for forgiveness."

Three weeks later, Fings found a way into Tombland. Blackhand, who'd been one of the Mage's lieutenants for as long as Seth could remember, had been invited to the old Constable's Castle to celebrate the summer Solstice, and Fings had persuaded Blackhand that he and Seth would be useful eyes in a place like that. So they went, the two of them and Blackhand and Wil and Wil's two big brothers, Sand and Rev, and while Blackhand and the Mage were eating and talking, Fings and Seth took it in turns slipping off looking for secret passages and tunnels and the like, until two of the Mage's bodyguards suddenly stabbed the Mage of Tombland in the back, and Sand and Rev and Blackhand and Wil all suddenly had knives, and before either Fings or Seth had a chance to catch a breath, the Mage and all his inner circle were dead, and then Sand and Rev stabbed the two bodyguards who'd turned on the mage, six times each and all in the gut, and left them to bleed out while Blackhand went back to his feast.

"Because they were traitors," Blackhand said later when Wil asked him why he'd murdered the bodyguards. "And that's what happens to traitors."

Wil found Sand the next morning, in the middle of Spice Market Square, crows swarming over him, an expression of terror on what was left of his face. Three days after that, Rev hanged himself. No one knew why, but before that day was done, Wil and Blackhand had left Varr, and it was two whole years before they came back.

If there was a crypt, Seth never found it.

20

A MATTER OF FAMILY

A man had to have his priorities. Fings had grown up with Ma Fings and all his sisters, and his big brother Levvi who'd looked after them. It wasn't easy to feed seven hungry mouths and Levvi had never quite managed, which was why Fings had taken to helping. Tooth-pulling was what he told them. He really had pulled a few rotten teeth, too, knew how to do it and everything, not that there was any coin in it.

He reckoned Ma Fings knew all along that he was picking pockets and cutting purses and lifting pies and loaves and whatever else he could get away with. The two had an understanding, never given voice: she never asked, and Fings never said anything, because Ma Fings sure as shit hadn't raised a thief for a son, but if Fings stopped thieving then they'd all starve, because Levvi simply couldn't feed them all on his own.

After Blackhand and Wil took over the Teahouse on Threadneedle Street, after they came back from wherever they'd gone after they'd murdered the Mage of Tombland, Fings had fallen in with them again. As far as his sisters were concerned, he ran errands for the rich merchant folk who like to drink at the Unruly Pig, but the truth was that he was Blackhand's pet burglar. Little things, mostly, but then one day Blackhand had sent him north of the river to swipe some old seal or other, the sort of job that needed time and watching and thinking and working out how to do it, not the usual slip in, stay quiet, do the lift, slip out. Took a few days but he'd got it done, no fuss, no problems. Blackhand got what he wanted, and Fings hadn't said a word about the fifty silver moons he'd lifted at the same time, all of which he'd taken home and was enough to keep his family from starving for two full winters, even without what Levvi brought back.

Was supposed to be a secret, that stash, something only him and Ma Fings knew, yet somehow Levvi must have found out because that was the only way Fings could explain why, a couple of months later, Levvi had decided he was leaving. Two years, he reckoned. Off to Deephaven where silver and gold fell out of the sky and landed in the pockets of any young man with energy and ambition. He'd make his fortune and then come back, and they'd all live like kings and never have to work again.

That was what he'd said.

Ma Fings hadn't liked it, not so soon after losing her first granddaughter to the pox, but she'd let him go. Fings had walked Levvi to the city gates. They'd hugged and slapped each other on the back, and Fings had told him to go and get rich and look after himself and come back like he'd promised, and Levvi had said yes, he'd do all those things, but it was down to Fings to keep their four sisters from going hungry while he was gone. And Fings had promised that he would, thinking of those fifty silver moons hidden under the floor back home.

Two years turned into three, and then four. The silver had slowly gone and Levvi hadn't come back. His sisters still talked about how he was probably out there on some Taiytakei ship, sailing between the worlds and getting richer by the minute. He'd come home this winter or the next and shower them in silver. The same, every year. They never gave up hope.

Ma Fings didn't talk about Levvi anymore. But out there, hidden under a bridge and buried in the snow, was exactly the fortune Levvi had been looking for. Which was largely what Fings was thinking about as Seth led him through the tunnels from the Pig in the middle of the night.

Using the tunnels made sense, Fings reckoned, what with mages everywhere, but the tunnels only got them into the back alleys of Haberdashers where the snow was up to his knees and now and then they had to turn back because it had drifted deep enough to swallow a man whole. He and Seth took it in turns to forge a path, Seth muttering about Myla staying behind, Fings not listening because his head was full of silver and what it meant, and how they all had to get out of Varr on account of mages in the Teahouse, and on a Mageday, too, and it didn't *stop* being Mageday until sunrise, and Magedays were days to trust your instincts when those instincts were telling you something wasn't right, and right now they were screaming.

They crossed the Circus of Dead Emperors and skirted the edge of Glassmakers. Fings stopped a couple of streets short of Locusteater Yard.

"Wait here a bit," he said, because you could never be too careful on a Mageday. "Just... I got a feeling, is all. Won't be long."

He pushed on to Locusteater Yard alone and spotted them at once: two men pressed into the shelter of a doorway on the far side, wrapped in thick coats, bored and cold and up to no good, because no one on honest business was outside on a night like this. He hunkered down and watched until he was sure they weren't anyone he knew, which meant they weren't Red's Neckbreakers. Maybe they were looking for someone else, then, but Fings hadn't stayed alive this long by taking that sort of chance.

Could just turn and go.

He slipped around to Big Hole Alley, sinking to his waist in snow that had been piling up all winter because no one ever came this way. He dug into the drift until he reached a pair of loose boards, pulled them back and wriggled into the cellars of Fat Sazl's gin-house, fumbling through the dark, the fumes making him light-headed until he found the ladder up to the tiny yard where Sazl took his deliveries.

The yard was empty. Fings pulled himself out onto the trampled snow, blew on his hands to try and get some warmth back into his fingers, then scampered up the wall, scaling the warped wooden frame from one tiny window to the next until he reached the third storey and the attic room where he and Levvi and all his sisters had been raised. There was no glass in the windows, hadn't ever been any of *that*, but they were shuttered and hung with a blanket to keep in the warmth. He poked his knife through the crack in the shutters, lifting the latch that kept them closed, folded them back, pushed the blanket aside and swung his legs through, feeling with his feet for the floor...

A hand grabbed his foot and yanked, and then pushed hard. Fings yelped as he almost pitched off the wall.

"It's me!" he hissed.

Ma Fings helped him in. "Idiot boy! What you doing coming through the window in the middle of the night?"

He waited until everyone was awake to answer; and it took a lot of whispering and saying the same things over and over and being on the wrong end of a lot of angry prodding, but in the end he had them all listening and told them the way it had to be: there was trouble at the Teahouse. Blackhand had upset some Very Bad People, and so it would be best if they took themselves away for a bit, maybe downriver for a few days to stay at one of the waystations there, preferably right now even though it was the middle of the night and cold enough to freeze the sun, and also maybe to use the secret way out and not go through Locusteater Yard. All of which went down like a turd at a tea party, even when he showed them a handful of fresh silver moons that was probably enough to keep them fed and sheltered for a month.

"On a night like this?"

"In the middle of the Sulk?"

"Who's going to look after this place?"

"Be full of Neckbreakers or something before we're gone a day! We'll never get it back."

Five yammering voices telling him he was an idiot, but there was only ever one voice he needed to convince. He waited out the torrent until Ma Fings decided he'd suffered enough.

"Two of us need to talk," she said, and after that it was the two of them whispering alone as Fings told her what needed to be done and why. Ma Fings wasn't stupid. She knew what he was, deep down, and what he did to keep them from starving.

"Won't be for long," he said, when she finally nodded.

"Was always coming, a day like this," she said.

Fings didn't know what to say.

"This once. Then it stops."

And that was that. After tonight, she wouldn't take a single coin unless she knew it came from honest hard work.

"Maybe we should all go to Deephaven," he said. "Look for Levvi. See how he's doing, you know?"

"Maybe you're right. Maybe we should." He could see what she was thinking, though. *Levvi isn't coming back. He's gone.*

A shout from outside broke the tension. In the yard, three men were facing off against...

Oh, crap! Really?

By the time he'd bolted down three flights of steps and reached the yard, one man was pulling himself on his belly with a leg flopping useless and leaving a trail of blood in the snow, a second had apparently had the sense to run like buggery, and the third was cowering against a wall, whimpering, eyes fixed on the bloody point of Myla's sword pointing at his face. Myla was shaking. Whether it was anger or simply the cold, Fings couldn't tell, but she certainly wasn't dressed to be out and about on a night like this.

"Myla! What you doing *here*? I thought you was staying in–"

"Spicers," she said.

The man against the wall...? Yeah... Up close, Fings reckoned she had the right of it. He was a Spicer, and a long way from home.

"They took the Pig." She shuddered, and maybe it was anger *and* the cold. "They got Blackhand and Wil. Dox and Arjay got out, I think. Arjay was hurt. The others... I don't know." She shook herself. "I couldn't think of anywhere else to go."

Fings blinked, trying to make sense of it. "What?"

"They got into the Pig, Fings! Spicers. They've taken it. It's all gone."

First mages, now this? And all of it down to the Murdering Bastard. *His* fault.

See! Didn't I say? Almost a shame he was dead and couldn't be stabbed some more.

"But–"

"Someone let them in." Myla leaned closer to the Spicer pinned against the wall. "The man from Deephaven with the swords and the money. Jeffa. Is it just me he wants or is there something else?"

The Spicer shuddered. "I don't know! I don't know anything about it. All I knew was–"

"What 'man from Deephaven'?" asked Fings, then realised he had a more pressing question: "And why are you *here*? This ain't nowhere near Blackhand's turf!" Made sense for the Spicers to go after Blackhand if it was revenge they wanted, but it didn't make much sense that they'd come after *him*...

Unless they knew about the barge. But how could they?

The Spicer stared at Myla's sword. Couldn't take his eyes off it so there wasn't much room for him to be more scared than he already was, but he gave it a go.

"Someone inside the Pig let you in," said Myla. "You tell me who, you get to walk away. You don't, I leave you a cripple."

Fings blinked. "Maybe they just–"

"Fings! They knew my room and came straight to it. Someone told them. The doors to the commons were still barred from the inside. Someone let them in through the back." Her hand tightened on her sword. "Who *was* it?"

The Spicer cringed. "I don't know! I don't know anything about it!"

"The tunnels..." Fings almost bit off his own lip, trying not to squeak. He didn't much like the idea of someone selling them to the Spicers, though he supposed you had to expect that sort of thing now and then; but what he *particularly* didn't like was how Seth had said to leave through the tunnels on account of mages watching the Pig, and how Seth had put a candle on the sill of Myla's window and left it there, and how that was exactly the sort of thing you did as a sign for someone outside. A sort of *Come in now* message, or maybe *This is where to find the mad woman with the crazy swords if you're that daft you want to give it a go.*

Myla was looking at him. "Tunnels?"

"Yeah..." Couldn't be right, though. Not with how Seth had tried to get Myla to come with. "Yeah, there's a tunnel..."

Seth, you idiot. What have you done?

He rounded on the Spicer, flailing for something else for Myla to think about. "I ain't her and I ain't Blackhand and I had nothing to do with all this crap between you and him. So, what's with the three of you all the way out here on Neckbreaker streets on a night like this? How'd you even know where I live, eh?"

He felt a stone inside him then, deep, dark and heavy. Red. Had to be. Payback for stealing her silver, even if she'd got most of it back...

"The sell-swords said to watch Locusteater Yard." The Spicer was doing a good job of trying to press himself through the wall at his back.

"Sell-swords? What sell-swords?" That was the trouble with the world these days. You did what you could to put something right and people still came after you. They never stopped. Just kept coming and coming until they put you in the dirt or ground you into dust.

"I don't know! They just showed up!"

"Just *showed up*, eh?" Took and took and took until there was nothing left. Like they had from Levvi, who'd worked every waking hour over in Tanners until his fingers were raw, until his hands had sores that never healed, until he couldn't take another day of it and left for Deephaven to make his fortune and never came back. "You came after my *family*? Is *that* it?"

"I don't–" started Myla.

Fings stabbed the Spicer in the neck. He didn't even notice he'd done it until he had the knife in his hand, blood all over it, blood all over the Spicer too, running out of him and into the snow, his bug-eyes gawping up like Fings was some sort of dread-horror Dead Man.

"Fings!"

Fings stared at his bloody knife in bewilderment. *What did I just do?* He didn't feel bad. Didn't feel much of anything at all, except maybe a bit surprised.

The Spicer gargled blood and spat out some mangled words that a part of Fings reckoned were probably choice and uncomplimentary thoughts on his parentage. The rest of him didn't really know what was going on, even as he stabbed the Spicer a second time, and then something hit his wrist and the knife flew out of his hand.

"Fings! Fuck!" Myla was staring at him like he'd gone mad.

"What?" He looked at his hand, not quite sure why his wrist hurt or why he'd dropped the knife, marvelling at the blood. Not his blood. Spicer blood.

"I think he was here for me, not for you, that's what. I'd rather hoped to ask him some questions."

The Spicer gargled and swore in wet, blood-spattered clots and scrabbled at the wall, and then there was some sort of blurry movement from Myla and he slumped and fell silent.

"Did you just… Did you just *murder* him?"

Myla's look was all daggers and edges. It sunk in, then. What she'd done was give the Spicer mercy, that was all. *He* was the murderer. He stared at the corpse, not quite understanding why he'd done what he'd done. He'd never stabbed anyone before. He and Seth were the ones who ended up curled on the ground getting kicked, not the ones who did the kicking. Didn't have it in them.

Or so he thought.

Myla wiped her sword in the snow. It left a dark streak. What had she said about the man she'd killed that night before they'd left Varr? An accident? Habit? Instinct? Rubbish, that was. People killed because they were killers.

He picked up his knife.

So... I'm a killer.

"The third one got away," said Myla. "We should go."

"I don't... I don't know why I did that."

"Yes, you do. Now get your family. We need to leave."

He reckoned she was probably right about that.

21

THE VOİCES OF THE DEAD

Seth swore under his breath. For all the layers he'd thrown on, his feet were numb and his fingers burned. He was cold and bored and alone, and Fings had been gone for ages. He blew on his hands and paced up and down, the snow crunching under his feet, the freezing air sucking the last warmth out of him. He was restless and thinking of Myla and wishing his conscience would shut up: what was done was done, and that was the end of it.

Still, he found that he hoped she'd managed to get away.

What if she killed them all?

That wouldn't be so bad either, unless one of the Spicers had survived and Blackhand discovered how they'd gotten into the Pig. But no. He'd seen the Deephaven soldiers. There were limits to what even a full sword-monk could handle, and Myla was far from being that.

You sold her. Worse than you sold the rest of them.

I tried to get her to come away! He didn't understand why she'd refused.

You put a candle in the window to show them where she was.

At least the Spicers had had a fight on their hands. He hoped it was a good one, if only so that when the stories were told of Blackhand's end, they'd be about Myla and not about him. They'd be about the woman with the swords who'd stuck to who she was. They'd be about her courage and how she'd fought, how she'd made the Spicers pay, not about the shit-stain of a traitor who'd stabbed Blackhand in the back. Not that Blackhand didn't have a fair share of treachery under his own belt. Just ask anyone in Tombland.

You really are a dirty piece of work,

A shout broke the night. Not close, but not far away either.

He should go to the catacombs. Stay there until all this was over. Hardly anyone knew they were there. Certainly not Blackhand or Wil or any of the rest of them. And the people who *did* know... none of them ever actually went inside.

So why don't you?

I'm working up to it.

Coward.

He should take the papers Myla had given him. The unexpected chance she'd brought to reignite his life into something worthwhile...

And there she was again. Myla...

Fuck.

He oozed out of his hiding place and crept after Fings. As he did, he heard more shouts, a shrill scream, and then someone came bolting out from Locusteater Yard and ran straight past him, not bothering to even look, face like he was about to shit himself.

Fings?

Seth crept to the passage that led into the yard.

Oh.

His heart stopped for a second.

Oh, fuck.

Myla.

A second Spicer was lying in the snow. She had a third backed against a wall.

Fuck, fuck, FUCK!

Weren't you were thinking just now how good it would be if she put up a fight? Aren't you pleased?

Oh, fuck off!

He swallowed hard. So this was it. He was as good as dead. In a way, it was a relief.

No! No, it isn't!

He watched as Fings came running out and stood with Myla, asking questions, the Spicer, terrified, answering. So far, no one had seen him.

So get away, you knob! While you still can!

His legs wouldn't move. *Maybe she left before it happened?*

Didn't look that way from how she was jabbing her sword at the Spicer she had backed against the wall.

She doesn't know it was you, *though.*

But Blackhand would.

Then Fings stabbed the Spicer in the neck. Seth gawped, not quite sure whether his eyes were playing tricks. Fings did it again, and then Myla's sword flicked out and it was over.

Alright…

Fings went back inside. Myla stayed out in the yard, pacing through the snow, fast and tense like she was working her way up from a simmering righteous wrath to full-on incandescence. Seth tried again, telling himself to run, but his legs stubbornly weren't getting the message. Myla dropped to a crouch by the dead Spicer and helped herself to his coat, and then Fings came back out and had his whole family with him, all of them still throwing on their clothes and in a mighty hurry, which told Seth all he needed to know: they were running, and they were doing it right now, because something had happened that meant they couldn't wait…

The Spicers took the Pig!

So… Blackhand was dead? So why was Myla here?

What the fuck happened?

He didn't know. And he *needed* to know.

She's right there. Go and ask.

Oh fuck right off!

Seth skittered out of the passage and into the street beyond and pressed himself into the deepest darkest shadows he could find. He watched as Myla headed for the river, plunging through the snow with Fings' family in her wake. He saw Fings head off to where they'd parted, heard him call out a few times, then watched him come trotting back, muttering and shaking his head, following Myla towards the river.

… A cold place deep within the earth. Archways that should be doors, but led only into blank raw stone…

Seth closed his eyes.

…The presence of something. Flickers of shadow in the corners. He turned to look but there was nothing…

He waited.

…except sigils, carved into the floor, the walls, the arches, the ceiling, every surface. Sigils that made no sense…

Only… only maybe now they *did* make sense…

As soon as he was sure that Fings wasn't coming back, Seth scurried into Locusteater Yard. One Spicer was propped against a wall, slumped, a dark smear of blood across the snow where he'd dragged himself. He wasn't moving. The other lay flat on his back, covered in blood from where Fings had stabbed him. They were both dead, so that was something, at least. Seth crouched by the body and pulled Myla's papers out from inside his coat. He wasn't sure why, but the doubts and the fear and the uncertainty were gone. He knew exactly what he was doing.

He didn't have paper of his own, or a quill or any ink, but he had a knife. He pricked the ball of his thumb and squeezed, then daubed a little blood onto the dead Spicer's face and copied the first of Myla's sigils. He stepped back, tense, waiting. He wasn't sure for what. Some flash of light or surge of power? *Something*, though…

A breath of wind rustled the snow. The dead man twitched. Seth jumped back, falling over himself in his haste. He stared at the corpse. It lay quite still.

"Who are you? *What* are you?"

Dead lips moved. Words rasped into the bitter night. A name…

"Why are you here?"

On the look-out for the bitch with the swords, the Dead Man said.

"Looks like you found her," Seth said.

The Dead Man stayed silent.

On the night after that first visit to the under-city, he'd dreamed of the vault of archways. When he'd awoken, he'd felt a sense of strength and of bright all-consuming purpose. Hunger and lust and passion. Not a desire of the flesh but something deeper, a desire of the soul. Now, he felt it again.

I'm talking to a Dead Man.

Crouched over this corpse he'd brought to life, he knew at last why the priests had cast him out. Down in the catacombs, he'd found something and brought it out. It was inside him, and all the priests and the masters and tutors he'd lived in awe of, they saw it and they were afraid.

They were terrified.

In the alley, kneeling beside the cooling corpse of a man he'd never known, he felt that sense of purpose again, hot and hard and glittering like diamond. The corner of his lip curled into a snarl. Here were the answers he'd been looking for. Here was the truth they'd tried to hide, but he'd found it anyway.

And now... Now...

He didn't know. Somehow, the whole bit about Myla maybe gutting him like a fish if she ever found out what he'd done was rather spoiling the moment.

Seth let out a long battered sigh. "Go on then. What did she ask you and what did you tell her?"

You can't run from what you're carrying on your own back.
— Myla

22

THE MORNING AFTER

The waterfront never slept, not even during the Sulk. Fings found a barge heading downriver for the City of Spires and saw his sisters aboard. There was some haggling, and then Myla fished silver out of her purse and Ma Fings didn't lift a finger to stop her, even though Fings knew she had a dozen pristine silver moons stuffed under her skirts. He might have said something if he wasn't too busy feeling messed up about the Spicer he'd stabbed, and worrying about Seth, and whether the last brother he had left was a traitor, and how long it would be before Myla started asking difficult questions.

Ma Fings looked him up and down one last time before she got on the barge. She shot a glance at Myla. "You'll stick with that one, if you've got any sense."

"Bye, Ma." He was as tired as a dog and frozen to the bone and unsure what she meant. He watched as the barge edged out into the water, and it felt wrong, not being with them. They had money and it wasn't going to be for long and it was the best way to keep them safe, but still… he couldn't help thinking about Levvi and how he'd never come back.

Myla touched his arm. "I need to find somewhere warm." She was shivering under her stolen bloodstained coat. The snow had stopped and sky was clearing but that only made the cold bite harder. "And so do you."

"I should have gone with them," Fings said. He wasn't sure why he hadn't. "Spicers will be watching everywhere now." Didn't even have anywhere to stay...

"The place Seth was talking about? You know it?"

"I know it but I ain't going there. And nor should you." He didn't know what he'd say if Myla pressed for more. Certainly not how there were places under the city with the skeletons of ancient corpses strewn about, all reeking of sorcery and witchcraft and the like. She *didn't* ask, though, so they stood by the river, oblivious to the brink-of-chaos frenzy of the docks around them, watching the barge with Ma Fings and his sisters until it rounded Talsin's Bend and vanished out of sight.

"I'll find us a room then," Myla said, which wasn't as daft as it sounded, not here on the docks where it was completely normal for people to show up at any hour you pleased, thrown up by the river and dressed like anything you could imagine.

"Yeah."

He didn't move until Myla pulled him away. By then, she had the shivers so bad she couldn't stop herself. Hard to say how late it was. Halfway between dawn and midnight? Something like that.

"The coat," he said. Couldn't be going into the sort of place Myla would choose wearing that. From the size of the bloodstain, it was obvious someone had died. When she shrugged it off, she was dressed like she'd left the Pig in a hurry, which she probably had. One of her hands was wrapped in a crude bandage. All that thinking on the Spicer he'd killed, and watching his family vanish down the river, he'd forgotten what had brought it all on.

Myla sat him down in some place he didn't recognise. A room full of warm air but she was still shivering. She asked for blankets. When they came, she draped one of them around his shoulders and then huddled, pulling the rest tight around herself. Fings stared across the room at the idle scatter of yawning boatmen, quiet and well dressed, not the usual riffraff. A boy put a bowl of hot stew on the table in front of him. For a bit, Fings stared at that instead. By the looks of it, it was made of something better than rotting vegetables and miscellaneous gristle, which was more than he'd ever have spent out of his own purse.

"Why'd you stab that Spicer?"

His eyes drifted to Myla, a new place to stare. This seemed to annoy her. She snapped her fingers.

"Fings! Talking to you!"

He shook himself. "You could have frozen to death, you know," he said. "Going out in the Sulk dressed like that. People do."

Myla batted the air, irritably. "Why'd you stab that Spicer?"

"Your colour's coming back," he said. "So that's good. You looked like a Dead Man when we came in."

Myla shrank into her blankets. "You nearly killed him."

"You what?"

"The Spicer."

"You mean I didn't?" Not that that made things any better. He'd *meant* to. Not killing the Spicer simply made him incompetent as well as a murderer.

There are worse things to be bad at than stabbing people, you know.

They'd left him there. Him and the one Myla had crippled. Lying out in the snow in the middle of the night, too weak to move. Likely as not, the crippled one was dead by now as well, taken by the cold. Fings tried to feel bad about that and found he couldn't.

"I don't know," he said. "I just… That was my family. They ain't got no one else to defend them."

All down to him now Levvi was gone.

"I still think it was me they were after."

Fings shrugged and shook his head. "Why?" Couldn't think what else to say.

Myla let out a long, exhausted sigh. "When I was in Deephaven, I trained at the temple every day. The sword-monks had been there for nearly ten years by then. Everyone was afraid of them but they'd take you on if they thought you had a future. They were serious about what they did and expected the same from their students. Put a toe out of line and they'd beat you down, but you knew how bad it *really* was from how hard the lash came. My teacher was one of the gentle ones. It was... I think she understood, sometimes, when people made mistakes. She'd punish us the same as the others, but you could tell when her heart wasn't really in it."

Myla reached across the table, took his hand and squeezed it. "I don't know what she'd say about what you did. It wasn't right. But..." She let go. "I have a sister in Deephaven. Soraya. The head of our family after our parents left for Torpreah to be close to the Autarch. Very pious, they were. Soraya, too." She made a wry face. "Anyway, there was a young man, handsome and rich and everything you could want. One of the old families, money dripping out of their ears, not like us upstart new-bloods. He was out of reach but my sister set her sights on him anyway. She knew how to catch a man's eye. She turned his head and for a while it seemed like they were going to be married."

She took another deep breath and let out a shiver, like she was finally getting rid of some weight she'd carried for far too long. "I don't know exactly why I tried to steal him. I loved my sister. I told myself it was to test him; and there *was* some truth to that, but... I was also very jealous. It wasn't even *him* I wanted. I just wanted..." She shivered again. "She was my big sister. She was the first-born, the one who was going to inherit our name and everything we had. I just wanted... to not always be in the shadows, I suppose.

"He wasn't shy. It didn't bother him at all that he was courting my sister, he would have had me without thinking. Almost came to it, too, but somehow that made it wrong, the ease of it. I mean, it was wrong however you look at it, but it showed me what sort of man he was. Showed me what sort of husband he might be, too. When I changed my mind, he wasn't inclined to agree. Called me names and wouldn't let go, so I punched him in the nose and left, and that was that. It wasn't the first time I hit someone in anger."

"I stabbed that man in the neck," said Fings. Seemed like opening a man's throat carried a tad more weight than merely giving someone a fat lip.

"Yes. Well." Myla made a sour face. "That was not the end, you see. My sister's fiancé had a different version of that night. Told all his friends how he'd had me, how I'd cried out for more. Told everyone else how I'd begged for him, how he'd had to throw me out of his bed. When my sister heard, she went to him the next night and she *didn't* punch him. In the morning, he threw her out and laughed in her face, told her she was crazy for imagining any of it had ever been real. And I know that's how it would have ended sooner or later, even if I hadn't done what I did, because that was how he was. But the way he treated her and then laid it all at *my* door... The last time I saw my sister, she was screaming in my face. She had such a strength, in her way, and he broke her."

Myla turned away, staring towards the fire, eyes shining, then looked back and forced a smile across the pain. "I gave him a few days and then went back. I called him out right in front of his friends. I slapped him and insulted him until he drew a blade, and then took his knife from him and stuck it in his balls. That's why I had to run. Why I came to Varr. I fled onto a barge and then set it on fire. I was sort of hoping everyone would think I was dead, but last night, his brother was there in the Pig. It's me he's after, not the rest of you." She drained her bowl. "We do crazy things for family, Fings. And I'm not particularly sorry, and I still think he deserved it. So, go ahead and lash yourself for what you did, but know that if it was me swinging the rope, my heart wouldn't really be in it." She stood and rested a hand on his shoulder. "And now I'm going to get some sleep, and you should do the same."

Fings watched her go. Nice to know why she was really here in Varr, he supposed, not that he much cared. Sort of nice that she was trying to make him feel better about what he'd done, but sort of missed the point, too: he didn't feel *bad* about what he'd done. Sending Ma Fings and his sisters off on their little errand? He felt bad about *that*. Not knowing whether Seth had wandered off out of sheer boredom or whether something had happened to him? He felt bad about that, too. But the Spicer? Mostly what he felt was confused by how easy it had been. Mostly, he didn't *feel* anything.

Ah well. Myla telling her story hadn't been for *him*, anyway. She'd told it because she needed it out of her. Which was fine. He could live with that.

He shrugged and ate his stew.

23

COUNCIL DAY

Fings had once explained to Myla how getting around the city worked in Varr: there were roads the Longcoats walked – the Longcoat Roads – and roads they didn't. The Longcoats kept their roads safe and free from shit, snow, Dead Men and robbers. If you looked like you had money, they doffed their caps and called you sir and madam. If you didn't, they mostly decided you were probably a robber and served up a civic-minded beating and spot of mild mugging. In winter, Fings told her – it had been late summer at the time, the air stifling hot – the Longcoats *did* generally keep their roads open when the snows came; but while they were *supposed* to load the snow onto wagons and cart it out the city, it was a whole lot easier to shovel it into the nearest alley, where it would pile up all through the Sulk until half the back-streets of Varr were clogged with three feet of packed ice and no one could get anywhere.

They left the docks at midday and took a Longcoat Road back to the Spice Market. Myla kept her blankets wrapped around her; whenever they passed Longcoats clearing snow, she let them see her swords and that was always enough. They reached the Unruly Pig and she pushed on the door. Fings hung back, ready to run, not happy at the idea of coming back until someone else could tell him it was safe. Myla, on the other hand, was quietly looking forward to a few Spicers maybe still loitering about the place, figuring she could practise sword-forms on them until they felt ready to answer some questions. All in all, it had been a thoroughly shitty night.

The Teahouse commons looked as though a storm had passed through: tables turned over, chairs smashed, porcelain shattered, wooden plates and bowls and goblets scattered all across the floor. In the kitchen, pans were bent and strewn about, urns smashed, while everything in the pantry had been looted or spoiled and ruined. Myla rummaged through the wreckage until she found a bottle they'd somehow missed. She cracked it open and took a long swallow.

"Spicers did this?" Fings asked. She nodded.

Upstairs was more of the same: everything gone that could be carried away, everything else smashed or torn. They found the remains of a fire in Blackhand's study, all his papers destroyed. There wasn't much blood.

Fings went to the hearth and reached into a gap behind the chimney. He pulled out a small lock-box.

"What's that?" Myla offered him her bottle but he waved her away, too busy rubbing his hands in anticipation.

"Blackhand's stash! They missed it!"

"You know where he keeps the key?"

"Key?" Fings was already fiddling with a tiny leather roll of lock-picks. "You think Blackhand tells me where he keeps *that*?" He chuckled gleefully. "But ain't no lock ever made to keep old Fings out for long."

He squatted beside the bed and carefully placed three crude wooden effigies. Myla squinted, trying to see what they were. She took another swig of wine. She was starting to feel it now, that little buzz that made the world a better place.

"Spirit-watchers," said Fings. "Keep people away while I'm working. Embarrassing when you're in the middle of it and someone comes. Raises difficult questions." Fings frowned. "Not that Blackhand's going to show while I'm at it, I suppose."

There was a note on the desk. Myla picked it up. She read it, then quietly put down her half-empty bottle.

So much for that.

Fings was looking all disappointed. He'd opened the box only to find it empty. "Crafty bugger! You'd have thought…" He must have seen the look on her face. "What?"

She waved the note at Fings. "*To Fings and Shirish: bring what you buried in the snow. Tombland. One week. If you don't, both your families die.*" The writing was neat and clipped. An educated hand. She wondered idly whether Seth would be able to tell any more…

Fings' eyes bulged. "How…? Who's Shirish?"

Myla put a hand on his shoulder. "Me. I'm Shirish."

"No." He pushed her away. "How…? No! No one else knew. No way the Spicers–"

"Blackhand."

"Yeah, but Blackhand would never–"

"Fings! The Spicers came for revenge. Look around you. There's no blood. They didn't *kill* Blackhand, they *took* him. You think he wouldn't squawk about some big stash hidden outside the city if that's what it took to stay alive?" There was Jeffa, too, but Jeffa wanted *her*, nothing else. Or would that still be true, if he knew about the crown? *Did* he know? Someone clearly did, and the same someone knew her real name, so who else could it be? "We have to go back and get it."

"But…" Fings flailed desperately.

"They took Wil, and he helped me bury it! He knows where it is!"

"But… We can't just… We can't just *give* it away! I mean… it's probably not even *there* anymore, and even if it–"

"Goblins? Really?"

Fings met her gaze, all wide-eyed and earnest. "Yeah! Goblins!"

Myla sighed.

"No! We can't! All that silver… No! We just… No!"

"Fings!"

He was staring at her like she was deranged, fumbling with the chicken's foot around his neck, absently making signs against bad luck. Myla tried again.

"This could work out. We give the Spicers what they want and they give us Wil and Blackhand. Then we run to the Guild and tell them where to look! *We* keep the silver and the Spicers take the blame for what we did!" Jeffa too, but Jeffa wasn't Fings' problem. And of course, it wasn't the *crown* that Jeffa wanted. It was her.

But still...

"But–"

"Fings! This could solve everything!" Her mind was racing. Jeffa. Jeffa in chains in the Kaveneth! Yes! "Fings, it *has* to go back where it belongs."

"No!"

"If it doesn't, we're going to have started a war!"

"No!"

"Fings! They are threating my family. They're threatening *your* family." Fings' family, who were safely hidden away. Unlike hers.

"Yeah, but–"

"I'm not asking. I'm saying how it's going to be.

That earned her a look of utter outrage. "You can't just... Was *me* that snuck onto that barge and lifted it. You can't–"

"Fings!"

"You *can't!* We *all* did it, right? You, me and Wil."

"And Sulfane."

"Yeah, but he's dead so he doesn't count."

"And the Spicers have Wil! He *knows* where it's hidden! If they get it out of him, we get nothing! *You* get nothing!"

Fings shook his head. "He wouldn't."

"You want to chance it?"

"What... What if there was another way?"

"What, you mean because they came here after *me*, last night? You want to trade *me* for–"

"No!" Fings' face was like she'd suggested he sell his own sisters, but surely that was exactly what Jeffa had in mind. "What I *mean* is... Couldn't we rescue him or something?"

Truth was, she might have tried it that way for someone else.

No. Make the trade. Get the millstone of that stolen crown off our backs and put in on Jeffa instead. It'll be a trap, of course, but you'll fight your way out of it, and then you'll set the Guild on him and cut and run. "I'm sorry, Fings. If it's only you and me, I don't see how. Maybe we can keep the silver. But not the rest."

They went back downstairs and out to the stables, and that was where they found Wil. The Spicers had cut him up pretty badly before they'd finished him off.

"Fuck," she said.

Fings looked like he was going to be sick.

"At least he can't tell them where to look." She crouched beside the body and screwed up her face. They'd tortured him, by the looks of it. "Unless he already did."

She frowned then, peering at what looked like crude symbols cut into Wil's cheeks, one on each side. Some sort of squiggle with a line through it and a circle over the top.

"That mean anything to you?"

Fings shook his head, although from the way his eyes went wide, she thought it probably did.

"Fings?"

He shook his head again. "Tombland," he said. "It means they're in Tombland."

Well, the note already said that, didn't it? She closed Wil's eyes and got up. Poor bastard. Not that she'd ever much liked him, but it looked like he'd gone out slow and messy, and that wasn't something she'd wish on anyone.

Her thoughts flashed to Sarwatta Hawat.

Alright. *Almost* anyone.

Her horse had gone, of course. Fings seemed relieved, not that it was going to stop her from doing what needed to be done. If anything, after all the snow, taking a barge down the river would be quicker.

"You did the right thing," she said, "getting your family away."

They looked each other up and down.

"So?" she asked.

"So?"

"You coming?"

Fings stared at his feet. "No. Got to find out what happened to Seth. Suppose I'll look for where the Spicers are keeping Blackhand, too. See what's to be done. Besides, you're the one who knows where to look, right?"

Myla cocked her head, surprised he'd leave her to do this on her own, but he looked like he meant it. She put a hand on his shoulder. Fings looked at it there as though it was some sort of unexpected growth, then nodded. Touching, how it didn't seem to worry him how she might simply take everything and run.

"I'll bring it back and I'll find you. And then we'll decide, alright?"

He kept looking at her after she let go, and then he pulled loose the leather thong around his neck and offered it. Hanging off the end was his half-rotten chicken's foot.

"Keeps mages away," he said.

She put it on to please him, trying not to gag at the smell. "Just... Stay safe until I get back. Six days, give or take." When he nodded and there was nothing more to say, she left and started on the long walk back to the river; and she'd half hoped he'd come with her at least as far as the docks, maybe lead the way through the maze of alleys and yards and slums that made up Tanners and Seamstresses and Bonecarvers... but he didn't, and the alleys were all blocked with snow anyway, and so she took the Longcoat Roads because there really wasn't any other choice.

The Guild probably had people watching for her. Jeffa too. They'd all be watching the Pig, and she was hardly inconspicuous.

So they'd both be following her, then.

Good. Setting them against one another was looking like her only way out.

She crossed the Circus of Dead Emperors and stopped for a bit, pausing by the frozen fountain and the Hanging Tree. It was a decent plan, trading the barge loot for Blackhand and then setting the Guild loose. Jeffa and his sell-swords and the Spicers all taken by mages, Blackhand back in the Unruly Pig, all of them rich thanks to the sacks of silver Fings had lifted... If you were an

Unruly, that probably all looked pretty good, but the more she thought about it, the more she saw that it wouldn't set her free, not really. Even if it got Jeffa off her back, there'd be someone else soon enough, because now that Sarwatta Hawat knew she was alive, he wouldn't ever let it go. And if the Guild *did* take Jeffa and the Spicers, so what? Jeffa would fall over himself to tell them who she was. She'd be back to having to run again, this time with a horde of angry mages at her back.

I could kill him. Find him and kill him.

And then what? Kill all his sell-swords, too? And all the Spicers? Was that who she was? A killer? And even if she did, even if she did all that, then what? Sarwatta wouldn't just come after *her*, he'd go after Lucius and Soraya and everyone who carried her name.

Fact was, there *wasn't* a way out. Not for her.

She reached the river docks and took a ferry to the North shore. Upriver, massive grain silos lined the water. Downstream lay the snow-covered sprawl of the Imperial Palace and its grounds, then the churning waters where the river Thort roared down from the mountains in the north to merge with the Arr, then the low cliff and the black brooding buttresses of the Kaveneth, the Imperial Fortress.

I could take the silver and run...

But run where? Something Tasahre used to say: *You can't run from what you're carrying on your own back.* That's what this was. Besides, she was a sword-monk, or at least something close. Sword-monks didn't run.

Stalls set out along the Imperial docks offered scribes and runners, all ready and waiting to take messages from Important People and hurry them to other Important People, passing on whatever Important News couldn't wait.

Was there another way out of this? A real way? A way to make it look like Jeffa was the one behind what they'd done? Because that was what it came down to, in the end. Either they got her and she died – quick or slow depending on how she let them take her –

or she took them all down at once. Not just Jeffa, not just him and his brother, but all of them, the whole family, their fortune, their dozens of ships, their hundreds of hired swords, their generations of history. All of it at once...

She sat in front of the young scribe and wondered why he was giving her such a strange look, until she realised that she was laughing and crying both at once. The idea was preposterous, of course, never going to work, and she wasn't going to run because that wasn't who she was; and so in the end, they *were* going to catch her, and all she was doing was delaying the inevitable, and so the least she could do was go out with her head held high.

"I have a message for the palace," she said.

V

İΠTERLUDE

They sat on the cathedral steps, Seth in his novice robes, Fings looking like he'd rather be almost anywhere else. It was late summer, a warm balmy evening, and Radiant Square was teeming with the rich and privileged gathering for the Twilight Prayer. It was exactly the sort of place, Seth thought, where Fings would want to be: purses everywhere and every one of them full of silver. Even the servants here were richer than anyone Seth knew.

"Still no word of Blackhand?" he asked. "Wil?"

"I heard they went east. Tzeroth, maybe."

"You think they'll ever come back?"

Fings shook his head. He hadn't been the same since the business in Tombland, and then what happened to Sand and Rev. Months later and he was still festooned in lucky charms, most of them meant to keep sorcery at bay. It *was* uncanny though, Seth had to give him that, and Sand and Rev and Wil and Fings had been tight.

"Shouldn't mess with mages," Fings said.

"*We* didn't. It was Blackhand. What happened to Sand and Rev is on him."

All the years they'd known each other, been almost like brothers, and Fings had always been the one who led the way. Not anymore. Tombland had knocked that out of him.

"Still…"

"How's Levvi?"

"Got himself work in Tanners." Fings shook his head. "Way he's going, he'll be a Longcoat before long."

Seth couldn't help a smile. "Can you imagine it?"

"That's the bloody trouble, I *can* imagine it. When's the last time you saw him? He's changed. He's not who he was. It's all... After what happened with Fiya..."

Fings' big sister was going to have a baby. Ma Fings was a walking thundercloud, although Seth thought he caught a tiny hint of glee at the idea of being a grandmother, now and then. Whoever the father was, Fiya wasn't saying, probably because Levvi and Fings had both sworn to murder whoever had done it. Levvi, for some reason, had taken it hard.

The steps were crowded with worshippers heading into the cathedral. The sun was close to setting. Seth got to his feet. "I have to go. You ready?"

Fings didn't move. "I don't know about this."

"It's going to be easy. His Highness Prince Halvren is in there. The Emperor's brother! The Sunherald himself is going to lead prayer tonight and every Lightbringer, Sunbright and Dawncaller in the quarter is going to be there."

"Yeah," grumbled Fings, "and every sword-monk, too."

"And all the Sunguard, and every last one of them is going to be in the Lighthall. They've even got us novices there too, and we *never* get to sit through Twilight Prayer with the upstanding lords and ladies of court. Outside the Lighthall, this place is going to be quiet as a mausoleum."

Fings gave him a hard look.

"Fine, fine, bad analogy. My point is that no one's going to see you."

"The Gods will."

Seth pressed a solar charm into Fings' hand. "The Gods will be firmly paying attention to their heralds. But if it helps, take this. It's a blessing."

Fings considered this for a moment and then nodded.

"You know what to do?"

Not that there was any chance Fings had forgotten. He could probably find his way to the Sunherald's rooms blindfolded. Seth handed him a scrap of paper with one word written on it.

Heresies.

"It has to be this one. I've seen it in his library but there's fifty books and they all look the same. Black leather, word etched in silver. Just this on the front, nothing else."

"What's it mean?"

"It means stuff you're not supposed to say. It was written by a Dawncaller back in the days of the first emperors. A long time ago. Once the Sunherald calls the Twilight, you're going have about six hands before prayers are over. It'll be a long one tonight."

Fings shrugged. "Be in and out in three, probably."

They went their separate ways, Fings to steal a book that novices and even Lightbringers were forbidden to read, Seth to take his place in the great cathedral. He was purposely a little late and trod on a toe or two, enough to earn a glare from a couple of nearby Lightbringers without getting himself into any real trouble. Enough so they'd remember seeing him there. The Lighthall fell quiet. In front of a prince he despised, the first Sunherald of Varr called them to pray for the Sun to return and for tomorrow to see a new dawn. Seth, who'd heard it all before, quietly closed his eyes and dozed.

The Sunherald discovered he'd been burgled almost as soon as the Twilight Prayer was over. There was the expected ruckus, the Sunguard searching the cathedral, all the novices standing outside their cells while sword-monks turned them over, no one allowed out, that sort of thing. No one got much sleep. At sunrise, the Dawncallers cast their divinations to search for whatever had gone missing and declared that it was no longer in the cathedral. Everyone decided without anyone actually saying it that the Prince or someone in his entourage must have done it, because that was the sort of thing a son of the usurper would do. By the end of that day, the outrage seemed almost forgotten.

A twelvenight later, it was Seth's turn to run errands for the temple kitchen. He crossed the river to where Fings was waiting. Fings handed over the book, wrapped in sackcloth. And there it was. Sivingathm's *Heresies*.

"Got a bad feeling about this," said Fings, but Fings had bad feelings about almost everything these days. Seth just about remembered to thank him and then scurried away, bought himself a room for the night and started to read. All through the night, every page and every word, until by the end, he knew why Dawncaller Sivingathm had been buried as an apostate. It was right there in the pages he'd written, the absurd heretical claim that the sigil every novice learned to quiet the Dead Men wasn't a sigil of the Sun at all, but of the Hungry Goddess, and that every time they used it, they damned a soul to eternal agony.

He thought about that and wondered why any priest would ever think such a thing? And as he wondered, it struck him that Dawncaller Sivingathm had started as a sword-monk, and that sword-monks never learned the sigils. When it came to Dead Men, they used their Sunsteel blades.

24

BROTHERS

Fings watched Myla head off towards the docks, then went carefully round the Pig again in case he'd missed anything. Most of the blood was around the bottom of the stairs where Myla had cut down at least one of the Spicers. He found the broken window where she'd jumped down to Threadneedle Street, and another where someone else had escaped into the alleys of Haberdashers. He couldn't see any trace of anyone else. Dox, Arjay, Brick, Topher, all the boys and girls who worked the kitchens and the commons, none of them.

The silence made his skin crawl so he went outside, thinking maybe he should have gone with Myla just to get out of the city. Blackhand and Wil were lost. The rest of the Unrulys had scattered. Myla, Seth, his family, everyone he knew.

But no. He'd already lost one brother. He was damned if he was going to lose another, no matter what Seth had done. So he walked to the edge of Bonecarvers and squatted for a bit under Samir's Folly, an absurdly ornate bridge across the Bonewater that no one ever used. It was a good place to sit and mull things over, a quiet place where no one would bother him. He felt the weight of it, of being the only one left.

Think!

He eventually found Seth in almost the last place he expected: out in the Spice Market with his tray of leftover pastries, all a bit mangled on account of the hurry in which he'd lifted them from the kitchen last night, but otherwise carrying on as though nothing had happened. People were back on the streets and the afternoon sun even carried a bit of warmth. You could almost believe the Sulk hadn't started if you ignored the great drifts of snow blocking every alley.

"What happened to *you*?" Fings asked. Seeing Seth felt like a stone lifted off his chest. "I thought a Dead Man got you or something! Where did you go?"

"I left," said Seth.

"I know you bloody *left*! What happened?"

"I got cold and then Myla showed up."

Fings eyed him. "You two got a problem?"

"Only that she was littering dead Spicers about the place. Seemed best to stay out of her way."

Something about Seth wasn't right. There could be plenty of reasons for that, Fings supposed. Starting, of course, with how Seth was maybe the one who'd sold them out to the Spicers in the first place.

"Did you go back to...?"

"No." Seth stared at his feet, almost like he was ashamed.

"*Did* you?"

"*No!*"

They wandered aimlessly through the market for a bit, enjoying the smells and the banter while Seth tried to sell his pastries, and Fings lifted the occasional purse and tried to work out what he should do and where everybody was and how to find Blackhand and get him back, but most of all how to ask Seth about the whole business with the tunnel and that candle in Myla's window; and then suddenly they were by the steps to the Market Square Temple.

"You remember that night?" Seth asked, although it was never meant as a question, since how could either of them forget? "Behind the incinerators round the back of–"

"Course I do."

"There are other ways down, right?"

Fings gave a grunt, not much liking where this was going.

"I need to go back, Fings."

Right. "No, you don't."

"I know why you say that, but I do. Would you help me? If I asked?"

Fings reached for the charm around his neck, almost panicked when he didn't find it, and then remembered he'd given it to Myla. "It's all just tunnels full of riffraff with no place else to take shelter from the cold. Muggers and murderers, the lot of them." *A bit like Tombland.* Which, most likely, was where the Spicers were holding Blackhand.

"Not *all*," said Seth.

"No, not *all*." Fings sighed. "Look, this is why you got... This is why what happened... *happened.*"

Seth gripped his arm. "I'd go on my own except I can't because the only way I know is through that fucking temple, and if I go anywhere close, the Sunguard aren't just going to give me a kicking, they're going kill me!" He let go. "That and I'm fucking terrified. But I *have* to go back, do you understand?"

"Not really."

"Fings! You and me... we're brothers, right?"

"Yeah," said Fings miserably. *And I already lost one of those.*

"I *have* to go back! Look at me, Fings! How much worse can it get? What have I got to lose? Nothing!"

You've got me, thought Fings, but he could see how that wasn't going to make Seth change his mind. "Personally, I quite like being not dead."

"You don't have to come inside. Just show me the way."

"There's other stuff needs sorting first."

"Like what?"

Fings led Seth away from the temple and set about telling him everything that had happened at the Pig last night after they left, the Spicers in Locusteater Yard, about going back to the Pig that morning with Myla to find Blackhand gone and Wil cut to ribbons, about Myla heading out to bring back the treasure she'd buried –

not that it would be there, of course, because of the goblins. How the two of them were probably all that was left of the Unrulys. He watched Seth carefully as he spilled out Myla's story, how someone had let the Spicers in, how the Spicers had been with some Deephaven mercenaries looking for her, how they'd known exactly where to find her. He told it as he'd heard it and watched as he did; and there it was, the nervous twitch of the head that was Seth's tell.

It was *you.*

Seth. His brother in everything but blood. He had to ask. *Had* to. He thought about dancing around the edges of the question, seeing what Seth would say, but hearing a lie about a thing like that... Fings reckoned it might just break something between them that couldn't be fixed, so he just came out and asked.

"Was you, wasn't it? That's why we went out the tunnel. You left it open for them. They were waiting."

Seth looked away.

"Why?"

When he didn't answer, Fings grabbed him and shook him.

"Why? Seth! Why, why, why, why...?"

"Because Blackhand's a fucking shitstain, that's why!" Seth shoved Fings away. "Because he deserved it! Because he had it coming! Because he's a leech and a parasite who sucks the life out of everyone he touches. Because..." Seth clenched his fists. "Tombland, Fings! You remember? You remember Sand and Rev? And now this? We're all going get stabbed or hanged, and it's all his fault and he doesn't give a *shit*!"

Fings stood very still, waiting until Seth ran out of breath. Didn't much like Seth bringing up Tombland, not with what he'd seen carved into Wil's skin back in the stables.

"Blackhand... Let's say he *did* have it coming, what with the whole Sulfane thing, which I'm not saying he did, mind. What about Wil? You didn't see what they did to him. Did *he* have it coming?"

"Blackhand's fucking lapdog? If what happened to Sand and Rev didn't knock the scales off his eyes–"

"Dox? Arjay? Brick?"

"Brick wasn't there."

"Dox and Arjay were. Myla says Arjay got hurt."

Seth didn't have an answer.

"And Myla? The candle in the window? That's what that was, right? You were telling them where to find her."

"I tried to get her *out*!" Seth clenched his fists. "I tried to make her come *with* us!"

"Yeah, but she didn't." Fings made an unhappy face. "There were Spicers in Locusteater's last night. Looking for her."

"Fuck!"

"Yeah. Fuck. Got to say, Myla wasn't too happy about it all. That why you scarpered last night when you saw her?"

Seth stared at his feet.

"Doesn't seem to have worked out it was you, for what that's worth. At least, not yet."

"You going to tell her?"

Was he? Couldn't say he wasn't tempted. Couldn't say Seth didn't deserve it.

He shook his head. "Can't see as that does anyone any good, does it? Anyway, she's gone. Got any sense, she won't be coming back. If she does..." He shrugged. "Best you tell her yourself."

"And have my head chopped off?"

"If that's what she decides. But she won't, because she's not like that, and because by then you're going to have done what it takes to put this right." Fings took a deep breath. "We're going to see a witch, and *then*, if we *have* to, I'll take you where you want to go and we can see about lifting all that cursed treasure you reckon is down there, and *then* we're going to see what's to be done about Blackhand and the Spicers. But *first*, we're going to look for Dox and Arjay, and *then* we're going to that fancy woman in Bonecarvers that Blackhand's tight with, and you're going to get her to help us."

It seemed simple, laying it out like that. Seth would help him find Blackhand. Blackhand would find a way to deal with this lot from Deephaven was who were after Myla. If and when she came back – empty-handed, of course, because of the goblins – Seth would make his apologies and Myla would let it go. Blackhand would never know, and everything would be back the way it was before the Murdering Bastard had shown up and thrown everything into chaos. Yeah… All in all, Fings was starting to feel pleased with himself. They only had to find where the Spicers were hiding and sneak Blackhand out, and how could that be harder than stealing an emperor's crown from under the nose of two dozen Imperial Guard?

"You want *me* to help you rescue *Blackhand*?" Seth looked at him like he was poison.

"Yeah. Yeah, I do."

"Fings… I'm sorry about Myla and I'm glad she got away. I'm sorry if anyone else got hurt. But Blackhand?" He leaned close and looked Fings hard in the eye. "Letting the Spicers gut him was sort of the point. You get that, right?"

"Yeah but–"

"He does nothing but use people up! You, me, Wil, all of us!"

"Yeah but–"

"*No!*"

"What about Wil?"

"What about him? You want me to be sorry he's dead? Well I'm not. Blackhand started this war, not me. What happens when you find Dox and Arjay? You going to tell *them* it was me who let the Spicers into the Pig?"

Fings couldn't look him in the eye. "Course not."

"No, because they'll kill me. Like Blackhand will kill me. Like–"

"No!" Fings stamped his foot. "I'm *not* going to tell, alright? You're my brother!"

"But I'm not, am I? I'm not your fucking brother! I'm just some stray you picked up off the street!"

Fings felt his face burn. He had to look away. Somehow, hearing Seth say something like that, that was worse than what he'd done last night.

"Shit." Seth sounded exhausted. "Fine. I'll help you with the Bithwar woman, at least. But don't tell me Blackhand wouldn't murder the lot of us if that was what it took to save his own skin."

Fings stared at Seth aghast. Seth stared right back, until Fings had to look away again. They were family, the Unrulys. Maybe not Seth because Seth had always somehow stood apart, but the rest of them, him and Blackhand and Wil and Dox and all of them.

Family. That was how it was supposed to be. Blackhand even said as much.

25

THE FANCY WOMAN OF BONECARVERS

Half the city had heard of Tarran Bithwar's father. Seth thought perhaps he'd even met the man once, a long time ago, that maybe he'd come to the Pig, back in the day. Tegran Bithwar was the merchant-adventurer who'd travelled the Empire seeking treasures and curios, fucking, drinking and swinging his sword as he went until he'd grown fat and rich and settled in Varr to start a family... and also a successful business buying and selling the same curios as before, but letting other people have all the adventurous fun of death-traps and old plagues and murderous bandits and suchlike.

That was the story, but Seth happened to know that most of it was rubbish. The *real* Tegran Bithwar had always been a thief and a fence whose success was due to the right mix of discretion, caution and ruthless opportunism. Old Bithwar lived across the river in the Palace Quarter now, doing the same as he'd always done, but for people with longer names and more impressive titles – which made him exactly the right sort of person to ask, in a purely hypothetical sort of way, what the bloody Khrozus an honest thief was supposed to do with a Moonsteel crown that just happened to have fallen in his lap.

There was no chance that either Seth or Fings was going to get

anywhere close to a man like Tegran Bithwar, of course, but that
was alright because his second daughter was busy carrying on the
family business in Bonecarvers, and Tarran Bithwar definitely
had come to the Pig a couple of times, sailing in like she was
some sort of royalty with a couple of burly men always following
around. It said something that Blackhand let her get away with
that in his own yard.

They found her in the street outside her shop, shovelling snow,
mixed in with a small crowd of locals all doing much the same.
Like priests, the Longcoats stayed out of Bonecarvers.

"Fings!" She smiled brightly as she saw them. "And... Seth, is
it?" She nodded at the snow, thigh-deep in places where it hadn't
yet been cleared. "Here to help?"

Seth forced a smile. Fings shrugged and then nodded.
"Glassmakers is all snowed in. Tanners don't look much better."

From what Seth had seen of Bonecarvers, even the alleys
here were being cleared, the snow carried to the frozen canals in
handcarts and dumped there in huge packed mounds.

"They've both got their problems at the moment. Are you here
about Blackhand?"

Fings said yes, they were. "That and I got something needs
looking at."

"I'll have my manservant brew up one of Blackhand's special teas."
She whistled, and then beckoned as one of the men digging snow
stopped and looked up. Tarran thrust her shovel at Seth, who took it
without thinking. "Feel free to dig. When you're done, come inside."

Seth looked at the shovel. Fings was the one asking a favour,
not him, so why was *he* the one holding it? He wondered what
would happen if he simply walked off and sold it.

"Have a look at these," Fings said, pressing a pouch into her hand.

Tarran gave him an obscure look that could have meant anything.
"I'll have my man call when the tea's ready," she said, and went back
into her shop, her man at her heels. Seth handed Fings the shovel.

Half an hour later, the manservant came back out, ushered
them inside and brought a pot of something which smelled like

a mixture of Spice Market Square and the Pig's stables. Tarran offered Seth a thimble-like cup. She poured the tea herself.

"I'm certainly interested to know where you got these." She looked at Fings.

"Er…" Fings glanced desperately at Seth. "Can't… really say."

Tarran nodded like she heard this all the time. "Especially since one is an Imperial signet ring belonging to the late Emperor, Sun bless him, and the other has a symbol engraved on the inside that no one is ever supposed to see."

"It does?"

"I hear the Spicers took Blackhand."

Fings looked to Seth again. Maybe he'd been hoping Seth would do the talking, but Seth didn't want to be here, and so he sipped his tea and made some appreciative noises like it was very nice, even if it mostly smelled of stale horse, and kept his mouth shut.

"You can have this one back." Tarran tossed the signet ring into Fings' lap. "My advice? Hold on to it for a few years and try again. Right now, a ring from an Emperor who died mysteriously only a week ago is more trouble than it's worth. If you need to shift it, melt it down and sell it to a goldsmith. But this…" She held up the second ring, which, as far as Seth could see, was a plain silver band. "This has a much more interesting story, although I'll have to go across the river. If you can wait a few weeks, I might sell for this for quite a pretty pile."

Fings shook his head and started to his feet.

"You've got four days," said Seth. "Otherwise we go somewhere else."

Tarran snorted. "Where?"

"We'll melt it, same as the other one." Seth having never seen whatever ring it was Tarran was holding or even known it existed until a minute ago, there didn't seem much point in trying to sound clever.

"You *really* don't want to do that." Tarran pursed her lips. "It's what? A half-moon of silver? At best? I'll give you that right now if that's what you want, but I might get you a dozen gold Emperors, given time. Tell you what: leave it with me. I'll take it over the river and we'll see what we can do. Come back in four days and I'll give you my best price."

Seth shook his head. "It stays with us." Whatever *it* was.

"What do you mean *a symbol that no one is supposed to see*?" asked Fings.

Seth tried not to twitch. Let Fings get it into his head that something was cursed or unlucky and he'd throw it into the nearest canal, even if it was solid gold. Tarran probably knew that, too...

"It goes back to the war and Lord Kyra Levanya." Tarran settled back into her chair. "Overlord of Varr now, but a general for Khrozus back then. After the war, he disappeared for a year and everyone thought he was dead."

"I know the story." Seth cocked a glance to Fings, who almost certainly didn't. "Khrozus takes the throne, he and the Levanya have some falling out, the Levanya vanishes and then two years later he's suddenly back, Overlord of Varr, in charge of the Imperial armies, Khrozus' right-hand, everything. Khrozus' son even married one of his relatives. His niece? The Sad Empress, the one who got murdered on the road by what just might have been a band of sword-monks in disguise."

Tarran nodded. "Yes. But *before* he came back to Varr, Kyra Levanya popped up at a place you've never heard of called Valladrune. It's down south, not far from Torpreah, and the reason you've never heard of it is because Kyra destroyed it. He burned it to the ground, killed every man, woman and child, salted the earth for miles in all directions; you name it, he did it. Khrozus declared that Valladrune had never existed, that the twelfth House of the Empire had never existed either, that there were eleven royal Houses and that that was all there had *ever* been. The Torpreahns squealed, but they'd just lost a war and were too busy shitting themselves to do much about it... this being the same noble Lord Kyra as nailed Emperor Talsin's twelve-year-old grandson alive to the gates of Deephaven to keep the loyalist army from assaulting them."

The same Lord Kyra that Seth had seen in the Circus of Dead Emperors. The same Lord Kyra who now sat behind the throne, telling his puppet regent what to do?

Tarran held the ring up to the light. "The symbol here is the symbol of the Empire's twelfth House, back when it had one. A winged serpent rampant wearing a solar halo wrapped around a sword. After the trouble Khrozus went through to obliterate their memory, I imagine it's a collector's item. You know, I can't even remember what they were called." She scratched her head and tossed the ring back to Fings. "Come back in four days and I'll have a price. Now tell me about Blackhand."

Fings told it all again, same as he'd told it to Seth except the part about the Spicers being let into the Pig by Seth, and then the whole business about some knob from Deephaven who was after Myla. Tarran listened with such blank attention that Seth couldn't tell how much she already knew.

"I'll get you some more tea," she said when Fings was done, and left.

"I don't really see how that helped," said Seth after a bit. Hard to read someone like Tarran Bithwar.

"You have to *ask* her!" glared Fings.

"*You* ask her."

Tarran returned with fresh tea and refilled their cups. "Is there anything else?"

"You heard anything?" asked Fings. "About Blackhand? Like, where they've got him?"

Tarran shook her head.

"But you *do* still know people in Tombland, right?" asked Seth.

A twitch. Only a flicker but she couldn't quite hide it. Fear? Irritation? "Not since the Mage disappeared." She hadn't liked the question, though. Seth nodded, then tipped back his head and squeezed his eyes tight shut.

"Have you ever had cause to visit our glorious Sunherald's private suite?"

"I have. Why?"

"You've seen that set of bronze mail he has?"

"Bronze? I thought it was brass."

Seth grinned. "Very good. You *have* seen it. I always wondered how much work it was to keep clean."

Tarran cocked him an eye. "Where are you going with this?"

"Turns out it's no effort at all because it doesn't tarnish."

"Then it's not brass."

"Ah, but it *is* brass. It's brass that doesn't tarnish. How much would you say that was worth, a suit of enchanted never-aging armour?"

Tarran gave a thin smile. "A lot more than even I could muster, I should think."

"I know where it came from." Seth smiled back. "You find out where the Spicers are holding Blackhand, I'll tell you where to look."

They watched each other and then Tarran gave a little nod. *Deal.*

Ten minutes later, Seth and Fings were walking out of Bonecarvers, across Seamstresses and back towards the Spice Market.

"What was that about brass and mage-working and the Sunherald?" asked Fings.

"Whetting an appetite. Getting you what you wanted."

"Where's it from then?"

"Where do you think?" He waited for Fings to look and then pointed down at the ground.

"Seriously?"

"I've done my bit. Now you do yours." And never mind that the way he'd tantalised Tarran Bithwar had pretty much forced Fings to keep up his end of their bargain. "Also…" because it had been nagging at him ever since Tarran had described the symbol carved on its inside. "Can I have a look at that ring, then?"

Fings passed it to him. Seth held up to the light and there it was. A winged serpent rampant wearing a solar halo and coiled around a sword.

"You know where we've seen that before, don't you?"

Fings nodded. Of course he did. Tombland, years ago, on another, much bigger ring, one that happened to live on the Mage of Tombland's finger.

Fings looked nervously around them and made a sign against evil spirits. "Thing is... that's the same as someone carved into Wil's face, after they left him in the stables."

"What? Fuck!"

"Yeah."

"*Fuck*! You don't think the Mage is back, do you?" Which was dumb, and Seth knew it the moment the words came out, but some things... some things you didn't easily forget.

Fings shuddered. Seth patted him on the shoulder.

"He's dead, Fings. Long dead. We both saw it." The words didn't seem to ease Fings. They didn't ease Seth all that much either, if he was honest.

They crossed the market through the crowds and all its wonderful smells. Opposite the Temple of the Sun stood the Temple of the Moon, smaller in recognition of its place in the order of things, but still grand. Fings squeezed between two wooden tables loaded with a hundred varieties of dried leaves, past piles of sacks filled with southern exotica, and into a narrow alley that ran past the temple into a derelict scatter of ramshackle houses and old stone buildings, half crumbled and fallen and propped up with newer wooden walls, empty windows covered in thick hides, a rookery of tiny streets where the Longcoats never came. Seth drew a deep breath. These stinking crowded pits where people went in and sometimes never came out and no one ever knew why? This was the Varr that had birthed him. As much as he tried to get away, this was their home, him and Fings both.

They crossed a bridge – no more than a plank of wood – over one of the narrow canals that littered the city. Fings led the way through another warren of streets and alleys and then stopped, their progress barred by an odd wall, no blocks or bricks but honed from solid white stone. A rusty iron bar lay discarded in the dirt. Fings picked it up.

"They only let you in if you know the knock," he said. "And you got to be careful who you tell, right?" He hefted the bar over his shoulder and struck the wall twice. The stone made an odd ringing sound. Fings paused, struck it twice more, then put the bar back where he'd found it. Seth ran a hand over the white stone. It was as smooth as polished metal and there were no cracks or seams, as though it had been moulded from a single solid whole. The top was smooth and rounded but uneven. As though it had been... melted?

"This place doesn't glow in the dark, does it?" It looked, he thought, a lot like the white stone of the catacombs.

A head popped up over the wall, took one look at Fings and vanished again. A moment later, a rope ladder came over. Fings grinned and climbed, and Seth followed. From the top, he saw that the white stone ran in a perfect circle several hundred feet across, as though it was the base of some vast but long-fallen tower, its ruin long ago carted away.

A tower of white stone.

Like the towers of the City of Spires?

A ring of wooden huts, heavily draped in furs and skins, nestled against the inside wall. The ground between them was thick with snow.

"I never knew this place was here..." murmured Seth.

"You should come in the summer," said Fings cheerily. "Pigs and chickens roaming all over. Bit like one of them waystations on the river. Best let me do the talking. They don't much like strangers."

Fings followed the inside of the wall until he reached a shack with a collection of bones strung over the door.

"Probably best you stay outside."

Seth rolled his eyes. He could see *exactly* what was on the other side of the door. Here, if you believed in that sort of thing, was a witch who crafted charms; this was a place where fortune was made, luck stolen, chance betrayed – everything you needed to pick the pockets of fate and cut destiny's purse. *If* you believed in that sort of thing.

"Are you shitting me?" As far as Seth was concerned, what he was *actually* seeing was a collection of rubbish literally picked off some garbage heap. Inside would be more of the same, and some old crone in a rocking chair, all cracking joints and clicking bones.

Fings gave him a look that could have set fire to something, went inside and closed the door behind him. Which was probably for the best. As long as Fings didn't end up trading that ring for a bag of dried pig entrails or something equally stupid.

Seth decided he didn't want to know.

It started to snow again. The sun was low. They were running out of daylight. Was that a good thing? He wasn't sure.

Fings emerged with two strings of bones round his neck, a luridly coloured feather between his teeth, and holding a black bag made of something like velvet and containing – as he proudly displayed – a gaudy collection of feathers and bones strung together by two strands of tendon. He gave the feather to Seth and then removed a string of bones and put it around Seth's neck. Then he pointed to the middle of the stone ring. Out in the snow, right in the centre, stood a single solitary wooden hut.

"Way in is down there."

"Down there?"

"Told you years ago," he said with a grin. "Some mutton-head built a house on it."

26

THE RIVER

Myla watched the snow fall on the deck of the barge, shivering under her thick coat. What if everything she was trying to do somehow actually worked? What if the Guild got their crown and dealt with the Spicers and Jeffa while they were at it? What if Sarwatta magically gave up and no one was after her? What then? Was the rest of her life running around frightening people, chopping off heads now and then as Blackhand's hired thug? Was that what she wanted?

No.

Then what?

Wil and Blackhand went back a decade or more. Same with Fings. Six months ago, when she'd come to Varr, she'd have cooked in the kitchens and served at tables as long as it came with a roof over her head and a chance to stop running, but she'd been trained as a sword-monk and raised as a merchant's daughter. She was educated, she could fight, and she knew enough to get a good price for anything that crossed her path. She could work the Spice Market. Set up a proper business. Turn the Pig into the heart of something that spanned the Empire, if Blackhand would let her...

He wouldn't, though. This feud between him and the Spicers, she'd seen how he'd gone out of his way to make it grow, like it was the fight he wanted, not the victory at the end but the struggle that came before. Blackhand was one of those men who'd always be fighting until someone put him down.

Maybe that was the answer she was looking for? Let Blackhand fall. Take over the Pig. Turn into a spice merchant?

Did that sound so bad?

The barge sailed on, riding the current of the river for hour after hour. The snow fell in steady silence, everything white except the river itself, until the sun sank and the steersman eased them to the shore. Gangs of men were shovelling snow, clearing the paths from the jetties to the stables and the barn-like waystation house. She walked past soldiers in the red and white of the City of Spires: the Emperor's men, cold and bored. With her swords hidden, they ignored her. Around a couple of fires, traders from the river shivered and blew into their hands and shared cups of hot, spiced wine around an impromptu market, buying and selling a little of whatever they were shipping. A single barrel of this, a few sacks of that, a chest of the other, all skimmed from their cargoes. She passed them slowly, remembering the faces in case one day she needed someone who might not be picky about provenance as long as the price was right.

Orien and the Guild were looking for Sulfane. Not for her or Fings or Wil, only Sulfane. Why? Orien obviously knew that Sulfane had been a part of stealing the crown and so presumably the Guild knew it too, but they would have destroyed her on the spot and picked over the pieces at their leisure if they really thought she knew where to find him.

Unless… they didn't *want* him found?

Sulfane hadn't stolen that crown for himself. Someone had set him on that path. Who?

And then Orien. Why creep into her room in the dead of night and risk having his throat cut? Why not barge in with a band of soldiers at his back? Come to that, how *had* he got into the Pig that night?

Because he was with Jeffa?

No. His fear had been real, and she did have at least a little of the sword-monk gift for smelling lies.

Why don't you just ask him?

She kicked at the snow in frustration. Orien was a mage, and not a very good one. Beyond that, best assume everything was a deception. There was no *forgive and forget* here, no *too busy with other matters*, not after what she and Fings and Sulfane had done. No, a mage was a mage was a mage. They were all the same, Guild or not, and the three of them would rot in the deepest darkest cell the Kaveneth had to offer.

There had been a mage in the woods that night.

She paid for a private room and tried to sleep but her mind refused. She'd told Fings she was coming back. She'd also told him they'd decide between them what to do next.

Why not just run?

That question again? Run where? Back to Deephaven? To Lucius, and put him in *more* danger? The sad truth was that Fings and Seth and Blackhand were the only friends she had, possibly the only friends she'd *ever* had, outside of her family.

Put it that *way and I should just walk out into the river and drown.* Except that was just another way of running.

Sulfane had known about the barge. He'd known the Emperor was going to die. He must have known where and when and maybe even who and how. Was *that* why the mages were hunting him?

Sulfane was in the middle of it...

And Orien was a mage too...

It was just a piece of Moonsteel...

And right before Midwinter...

In her dreams, she was six years old and the city was celebrating. Emperor Ashahn had an heir, a daughter born on the first morning after Midwinter's night, an auspicious time symbolizing light and strength and justice and wisdom. Somehow, the Unruly Pig was in Deephaven too, and she was with Blackhand and Fings and Wil, and even Lucius and Soraya were there, and others she'd once thought of as friends, all brimming with joy, toasting the health of the new Princess. They were all so happy, but *she* knew better. She knew it was a terrible lie, that the Emperor's heir had been born in the depths of night, the last night of the old year when the Sun was gone and the fickle Moon ruled alone for a few final hours, the time of chaos when all the omens were reversed. Light and strength? No, the true omens were of sorcery and a terrible endless darkness.

Black Moon! Black Moon!

She shouted and screamed and pulled at them but all they did was turn and smile and beg her to join the rapture.

And then suddenly she was awake, and it was dark, and it had all been a dream.

The second day on the barge passed much the same as the first. This time, as the light failed and they pulled in to the shore at the next waystation, a cloaked and hooded figure was waiting for her. He followed her inside and sat down across the table, all shrouded in shadow as if that somehow made him dangerous and mysterious.

"I got your message," he said "I came alone."

So here it was. Her last chance to decide which way this was going to go. And yes, she could probably reach across the table to stab him if she had to, probably without anyone else seeing, at least not straight away. But she could have stabbed him last time, too, which would have been a lot easier.

"Hello, Orien," she said.

27

THE UΠDERWORLD

I made a dead man talk. The thought echoed through Seth's head. It wouldn't leave him alone. Never mind Blackhand, never mind the Spicers, never mind Fings or Myla or any of the rest. *I made a dead man talk.*

After Locusteater Yard, he'd wandered in a trance, oblivious until the cold finally got to him. He didn't remember sleeping, exactly, only dreams of ice and mountains, of falling, of bottomless gaping holes deep in the belly of the earth, of a room of archways and faces; but more than anything, of dead lips moving, of blurred words struggling for freedom from a dead mouth.

I made a dead man talk. Either that, or he was going mad.

Myla's papers had six sigils explained precisely. The words echoed the words he'd seen in Sivingathm's *Heresies*: the sigils came from the Hungry Goddess, not from the Sun. They were her words of power.

He looked around, spotted a pile of firewood, helped himself to a good solid-looking branch when no one was looking, then leaned on it as though it was a crutch. He followed Fings through the snow to the centre of this ruin of white stone, this ruin that made him think of Myla, of the last conversation they'd had about the towers in the City of Spires. Had there been a spire here, too, and all that remained was this stump?

Fings reached the hut. He pushed open the door, gentle, as

though he half-expected the whole place to come down on him at any moment. Hard to believe this shell of old rotten wood barely holding itself upright hid an entrance to the under-city, and yet there it was: ancient stairs spiralling down into the earth, the stonework in perfect order, as though the Emperor's architect had laid it only the day before.

White stone. Seamless. No joins, no cracks, as if the whole thing had been shaped from a single monolith.

"Let's not do this," pleaded Fings. "Wasn't anything but bad luck the last time."

"What are they going to do?" Seth made a face. "Excommunicate me some more?"

"What if there's something there?"

"Like what?"

"What if there's an accident? What if you die down there? What if they catch you and give you to the Hungry Goddess?"

"They wouldn't do that." Seth was reasonably sure. *Reasonably* sure. "Look, all we're going to do is have a quick poke around for anything valuable we can sell to that Bithwar woman, alright?"

"No we're not. We're going down there because you've got some daft idea there's something hidden that your priests don't want anyone to know."

Seth reckoned he couldn't really argue with that. "Maybe there *is* something down here. If so, it'd be worth a few silvers, eh?"

"And you think no one else already thought of that?"

"I'm sure they have, but there are places down there that I can go that most other people can't."

"Yeah." Fings shook his head. "That's what bothers me."

"Fings! We had a deal."

"For me to show you the way in, not for me to help you kill yourself! Well. There it is. Off you go."

Seth grabbed Fings' shirt. "I'm not going to fucking kill myself! Don't you understand? There *is* something down there that the Path are trying to hide! It's why they threw me out! It's..." He shoved Myla's papers into Fings' hands. "Look! Look at them!

These are the keys, Fings! The fucking keys! It's the same writing as I saw in that room!"

"Worth something, are they?" Fings stared at the papers as though they'd stabbed him.

"To the right person? Priceless."

"Bloody Murdering Bastard and that bloody barge." Fings turned away from the door and the shaft and its little hut, muttering to himself.

"Fings!"

"Fine!" He turned back. "Fine, I'll show you how to get back to that place we went before, but you ain't going in there on your own." He pulled a pair of tallow candles from his bag and offered one up. "Best I can do. And we ain't going into any place where I don't see a fast way out, neither."

Seth counted the steps down and lost track. Somewhere past two hundred, the stair eased smoothly into a large open space, exactly like the vault under the incinerators on the Circus of Dead Emperors.

...He stood alone in a place he shouldn't be, somewhere deep within the earth...

For a moment he felt a flash of hunger mixed with utter panic.

...Hands held out before him. Sigils glowing in each palm...

"There's lots of tunnels come out of here," said Fings "You could get lost if you're not careful. Most of them don't go anywhere much." The sound of Fings' voice pushed back at the visions. Seth took a hold of his panic.

"So you *have* been down here before!"

"Only this far." Fings shuddered. "Talked to others, though. Goes all over the city, this place."

"And you can get to the vault under the Circus of Dead Emperors?"

"What, the cursed one that got you kicked out of being a priest, you mean?"

Seth gritted his teeth. Tempting to finally tell Fings that it wasn't where they'd gone that had done it, it was what Seth had found and brought back.

I made a dead man talk.

"Yes. That one. Like you promised."

"You said there was just bones. Don't see how some old bones are going to help us find Blackhand."

"There are symbols carved into the walls." Blackhand could still go fuck himself. "I never really figured out what they were or what they did, but now I have. If I'm right, I can trade that knowledge." *Or the knowledge I've already got, because an unscrupulous man who can make the dead spill their secrets might make a shitload selling that particular little talent.*

He kept that bit to himself, figuring Fings probably didn't want to hear. Besides, when it came down to it, that wasn't who he was. Not really.

Was it?

"Fine. This way." Fings obviously thought all this a very long way from *fine*, but he led the way anyway, into one of the tunnels. By Seth's estimate, they'd largely gone southwest from the Spice Market to reach the under-city entrance, and so it should have been a good hour to walk to the incinerators by the Circus of Dead Emperors; but they'd been going less than half that time when the tunnel opened into another vault.

Fings stopped, hands on hips. "Here. This the one?"

"You sure?"

But Fings was right: the same staircase, and with the hole in the middle leading to a second vault below. Seth peered over the edge, and there they were: three skeletons sprawled over a mosaic floor.

"I don't suppose you brought any rope." Fings sounded hopeful. "Because I didn't, and I don't know how else you're going to get down."

Seth emptied his bag: a lantern and plenty of rope, borrowed from Blackhand's stores.

"You had that all the time?"

Seth tied the rope around his stolen branch and fitted the branch across the hole. "Can you climb that?"

"I can but I ain't going to. I ain't going down *there* and nor are you!"

"Yes, Fings, I am."

"What if something happens? What if some… *thing* shows up? What if you need to run? How you going to get out?"

"You'll be standing here, ready to haul me up."

"But–"

"I'm a priest, Fings. There's nothing here to fear. It'll be like the crypt in the temple. You remember that? Just a lot of dust."

"I wish we'd never done that."

"But we did, and here we are."

The lantern went first, and now Seth could see into the chamber properly. A circular room, shaped as half a sphere. Fragments of wood and china scattered against the walls. Three skeletons lying on the floor. A mosaic, half lost to age, and three archways spaced around the walls, all facing onto blank white stone, sigils running around each edge. The archways were the mystery, the sigils his key to solving them.

Observe the form, observe the detail, divine the purpose. Old words from one of his tutors, hoping against all the evidence that Seth's class would start to see the deeper meaning behind the texts and artworks they studied. Well, maybe he shouldn't have hoped quite so hard, because that was exactly what Seth had done, and no one had much liked the consequences.

"Ready?"

Fings swore. He touched all his charms one by one and then stuck a feather between his teeth and lowered Seth into the vault.

The floor was dry, pieces of wood crumbling to dust in Seth's fingers, the remains of chairs and tables. Shards of broken china, once decorated with intricate patterns, now reduced to such a web of cracks that there was nothing to say what the pictures had once been. Stabbing knives made of bronze and wood, the wood again falling apart under Seth's touch, the bronze so rotten with verdigris that he had to break one in two to see the gleam of metal underneath.

On impulse, he pulled off his boots to feel the mosaic floor against the soles of his feet. He ran his fingertips over the bones of the three skeletons, feeling their age. The skeleton in front of him was damaged. A chipped rib. A knife in the heart, or a sword, or something similar. When Seth examined the second, he saw the same.

"What you doing?" Fings didn't sound happy. Seth ignored him. These skeletons weren't Dead Men, not after all this time. Just bones.

He went to the third skeleton. Lying in the shadows at the edge of the room, near the bones of its outstretched hand, was a long-bladed bronze dagger. This blade was sharp and clear, no sign of age, no trace of verdigris.

Should be enough to keep that Bithwar woman happy. Seth stuffed the dagger into his bag. *So, one of them stabs the other two and then dies moments later?* He frowned. Where was the sense in that...?

The skeleton beside him sat up. Seth swore and staggered back, almost tripping, pulling paper strips and charcoal from his coat. He scrawled the sigil every novice learned for stilling the Dead Men and lunged, slamming the paper against the skeleton's skull. The skeleton crashed back and fell to pieces.

"Seth!" Fings peered down from the lip of the hole above. He couldn't have seen what just happened though, or he'd be screaming bloody murder about how they needed to leave.

Seth took a deep breath. "Tripped over a skeleton, that's all," he said. "It's fine. Just spooked myself."

Alright. So not *just bones. So maybe don't touch them.*

He watched the other two skeletons and scrawled two more sigils, just in case. When they didn't show any sign of moving, he turned his attention to the archways. He was missing something. The sigils on Myla's pages were only a fragment. Somewhere out there was a text far greater than the six meagre sheets she'd given him.

Where's the rest?

Still on that barge? Somewhere else?

Who wrote them?

The script being a religious one suggested it was a priest or a sword-monk...

Why would a sword-monk or a priest write about the sigils of the Hungry Goddess?

Why not? Sivingathm did.

Yeah, and look how that worked out for him.

Fine. But does it matter?

The sigils from Myla's papers were all to do with the dead. The ones around the arches were different.

Something to do with barriers? Doorways?

"Be dark outside soon," called Fings. Seth had almost forgotten he was there.

...He held his hands out before him. Sigils glowed in each palm...

He picked up his lantern and looked again at the three skeletons on the floor.

Not just bones...

I made a dead man speak.

Presumably that didn't work on skeletons. In Seth's experience, talking generally needed lips and a tongue and lungs and so forth.

Which leaves five others...

And only a complete idiot would simply draw them out and slap them onto a handy nearby skeleton to see what happened, right?

He drew one on himself instead. If the notes on Myla's papers were right, it should let him see...

SNAP

...Same chamber, same arches, same sigils, same mosaic on the floor, but now two of the three dead men wore brass mail armour and were sitting around a table in animated conversation. He knew they were dead because their flesh was translucent, and he could see their bones and the tiny flickering glories of light inside their skulls that he knew, without knowing how, were their souls. They were playing a game with a board and carved pieces; and then one of them looked up and stared straight into him, and the walls began to melt and twist and squirm, and the glowing silver light turned black and suffocating, and he fled, blind with mindless terror, bolted this way and that, racing ever faster, screaming...

SNAP

The three skeletons lay on the floor as before. Seth stared at them while his heart pounded, as he tried to grasp what he'd seen.

The dead. That's what. The lost souls of the unburned dead. Burn the body and the spirit was guided by the fire, to join the glory of the Sun and be born again. Sink a corpse in water and Fickle Lord Moon would take them to much the same end. Leave bodies lying under a clear open sky until nightfall and the Lady of the Stars would claim the fallen. Hide them from the Sun and the Moon and the Stars – leave them in a forgotten chamber buried under the ground being a very good example – and they wandered lost until the Hungry Goddess swallowed them into the darkness and oblivion at the heart of the earth.

The dead souls he'd seen were these, he understood. Two, not three, because he'd already set one of them loose.

Left for centuries and the Hungry Goddess hasn't devoured them? Is that possible? The Lightbringers taught their novices that the unburned dead had days at best.

Still... Let's not try that one again, eh?

"You nearly done?" called Fings.

"Nearly." He couldn't keep a slight squeak out of his voice. Instinct demanded he set them free. Strike them with the Sign of the Sun. Except... *was* it the sign of the Sun? Sivingathm's *Heresies* said not...

What, then? Carry out their bones and take them to one of the corpse wagons?

He tried to imagine Fings' face hearing *that* idea... But a priest's duty, above all else, was to release the spirits of the dead so they would be free. In service of that duty, the Path carried bodies, every day, in snow and rain and sun, to the incinerators and the fire-pits. So why not? One of those incinerators was almost right over his head, wasn't it?

While he was thinking on it, he pulled another strip of paper, drew the sigil he'd used in Locusteater Yard, and put it onto one of the skulls. He could still do the right thing after this stupid experiment didn't work. He'd show himself for a fool and then he'd find a way out of here and–

He felt the faintest breath of air tickle at the hairs on his wrist.

You do *remember why you got kicked out of the temple?*

Shut up.

He looked up to see whether Fings was watching, but he wasn't. Just as well…

How the fuck is a skeleton supposed to talk, anyway? Clack its teeth at you? One chomp for yes, two for no?

He felt a breeze on his arm from the mouth of the skull. A faint, whistling whisper brushed his ears. A groan echoed around the chamber.

Shit! He shone the light up at the hole in the roof. Waved it about a bit.

"Fings?" What if Fings left him here? He'd be trapped. The way out was right above him, the rope hanging and waiting. But he couldn't climb it.

Anyone else, they'd just shin right up. Even the kitchen girls from the Pig could do it. Not you, though.

Another rustle of air. Seth almost jumped out of his skin.

You know this is going to end badly.

Didn't everything?

You could have done something with your life.

Still could, couldn't he?

"Fings!"

Even if he *could* climb the rope, he probably didn't have enough oil in his lamp to reach the exit. Even if he did, he'd probably get lost trying to find his way out. Could he remember which tunnel would take him back the way they'd come?

I made a dead man speak. That had to be worth something, didn't it? It was something he could sell. Maybe not to someone like Blackhand, but there had to be a way… He should stop now. Stop with what he had and make something of it. He could show Fings and Myla and…

Oh, you could, could you?

They could use it on Sulfane! Find out who'd set them up...

Know where to look for his corpse, do you? Also, if you'd paid attention back when we thought we were growing up to be a Servant of the Light and not some piece of human detritus, you'd know this only works on the unburned dead. Sulfane will be ash by now, if they didn't just toss him in the river, so—

The skull clicked and hissed and turned to look at him. Seth screamed.

Take the sigil off it, you moron!

He couldn't move.

Unless your idea of a fun afterlife is listening to yourself say "I told you so" all the fucking time, TAKE THAT SHADOW-DAMNED SIGIL OFF!

Shut up! "Is this place Kheredesh?" he asked, his voice thin and wavering. That's what Sivingathm had called it. Kheredesh. Last bastion of the Shining Age of the God-Father Seturakah, Splinterer of Worlds. Whatever all *that* meant.

Seturakah. The Black Moon?

Take. The sigil. Off!

Everything the Path had taught him before they broke his heart and cast him out told him to leave. A good novice would go straight to the nearest temple. A good novice would have left already... No, a *good* novice would never have come here in the first place...

He snatched the sigil off the skull and slapped a second in its place to set it to rest. The skeleton fell to pieces.

Now... was that so hard?

"Fings!"

Don't visit the Forbidden Crypt, they said. So what do you do? Don't read the Forbidden Books, they said. So what do you do?

Shut up!

Don't delve into the Forbidden Tunnels, they said. So what do you do?

Shut up! "FINGS!"

Don't mess about with the weird sigil-things that you don't understand, they said... well, actually they didn't, but anyone with an ounce of common sense—

Shut up shut up shut UP! What he *ought* to do was leave and run straight to the nearest stock of firewood, pile this chamber high and burn it to ash.

He wasn't a good novice. They'd told him so.

"Can we go yet?"

Fings was peering down at him. Seth didn't think he'd ever been so pleased to see another human face in his whole entire life.

28

FİRE AПD İCE

"You came alone?" Myla asked.

From under his hood, Orien beamed. "Me and a spare horse. Just as you asked."

Myla didn't smile back. She'd already picked out the two men watching her. The woman she'd been when she fled Deephaven wouldn't have noticed, but six months of living in the Unruly Pig had taught her to know when she was being watched. So: two men dressed to be inconspicuous but carrying hidden weapons, sitting at a table not too far away, nursing their drinks and flicking glances her and Orien just a little too often. They hadn't been on the barge that brought her down the river, so they must have followed along the road from Varr. Either that or they'd followed Orien.

"Where's your friend the archer?" asked Orien.

Myla watched her two stalkers out of the corner of her eye as she smiled. Orien thought he was here to meet Sulfane.

"He's not coming," she said.

Orien twitched. He didn't like that.

"He's not coming because he's dead." She scanned the room. Her instinct was to believe the mage had done as she'd asked and that it was only him and a spare horse waiting to meet her, but instinct wasn't always right.

What would I do? Play along until I saw the crown for myself and

*then have my heavily armed friends show up, and how convenient that
someone already dug a hole in the snow just the right size for dumping a
body?* The mage didn't seem the type for a spot of casual murder,
but she'd been wrong about that sort of thing before.

"So... Why am I here?" he asked.

"Why, exactly, are you looking for Sulfane?" *Or would I wait
until we next stopped for the night?* She thought not. Easier to hide
the well-armed friends, but too much risk of something going
wrong. "You said he took something. What did he take?"

Orien shook his head. "Sulfane?"

"Yes." Myla gave him a hard look. "You crept into my room in
the middle of the night, asking about him. Remember? The man
you were hoping to meet?"

"That's his name?"

"Kelm's Teeth! None of you even knew his name?"

"What I know is that the Guild are looking for him. Whoever
he is, they think you know him. And you *do*, too. It would please
my mistress to get to him first." Out of the corner of her eye, Myla
watched the men who were spying on her. They'd picked up a friend.

"That's it? That's all you know? That the Guild are looking for
someone?"

Orien shrugged. "And that he took something and we want it
back."

"We?"

"Those of us whose loyalty is to the Princess-Regent and the
throne."

"I see. And what did he take?"

"I can't tell you."

"Not much use then, are you?"

A flicker of annoyance crossed Orien's face. "Nor are you, if he's
dead. Look, what I *can* tell you is that the Emperor was murdered
only days ago, that it was assassination by sorcery, not by blade,
that the Guild are running around like they have ants all over them
about certain... *items* that have gone missing, that the Sorcerer
Royal is behaving very strangely, and that as a result, my mistress

is of the opinion that the Guild are not entirely to be trusted. Also, if you help *me*, the Guild will have no reason to come back and question *you* again. It might be in your best interests."

"Might it, indeed?" Myla tried not to laugh. "I don't know anything about the death of the Emperor. What I *do* know is that Sulfane came to the Pig a couple of months back wanting a letter forged to get him into the Imperial Guard, and a thief to help him steal something." She shrugged. "None of us knew what he was after until we had it in our hands. But–"

"You were *there*?"

Well. That *was stupid of you…*

Myla sighed and waved for another couple of beers. As she did, the third man sitting with her two shadows got up and headed out. "Yes."

"Then…" He leaned forward, wide-eyed and excited.

"Careful! Eyes on us."

He jerked back as though stung, and looked around.

"Khrozus!" Myla grabbed his hand and squeezed it, reaching out with her other hand to cup his face and coax him close like she might a lover, mostly to stop him from gawping. "You're really shit at this, you know!" She didn't dare flick a look to the two men watching them and this *so* wasn't the place to have this conversation, but apparently Orien's take on subterfuge and subtlety was that they were things for other people. "I think they followed one of us from Varr. No, *don't* look! Now–"

They were only inches apart, and then suddenly there weren't any inches left because Orien was kissing her. Myla squeezed his hand hard enough to feel his fingers crack. The mage squeaked and pulled back, but only a little before she stopped him.

"What the fuck was that?" she hissed.

"I… I thought…" He looked so crestfallen… Khrozus, he really *did* think…

She let go and slumped and tipped her head back to stare, eyes closed, at the ceiling.

I really need another drink.

On the other hand, sometimes you had to work with what you were given. She beckoned him back close and whispered in his ear. "Sulfane stole the Emperor's crown. *You* said it needs to go back where it belongs. *I* think that's open to interpretation. So if I take you to it, what exactly will you do with it?" She held him in place, one hand locked around his wrist, the other cupping the back of his head. Just two lovers, sharing a moment. "Also, if you do what you just did again without asking, I'll hurt you."

"I... What will I *do* with it? Give it back, of course!"

"To whom?"

"To the Princess-Regent!"

"She's not *really* going to sit on the throne. We both know that."

"You're wrong."

"She's not even of age!"

"Yes, but she *will* be in another two weeks."

"Midwinter."

"Exactly!"

"Give me one good reason not to leave it all buried in the snow."

"Because if you don't, there will likely be a war."

"Why?"

"It's a symbol. You know how it works, don't you? With the twin crowns? The one you stole belongs to the heir. If she doesn't give it to him, it looks like she's usurping his power. If she tries to avoid that by giving him her own crown, it looks like she's abdicating and that Overlord Kyra is the true regent. You think Torpreah will accept that? Helhex? Tzeroth? Deephaven? Tarantor, even? The Butcher of Deephaven as regent means war. Is that what you want?"

"She's a fifteen year-old girl and the Butcher is her uncle. You think Torpreah and Deephaven won't see through *that*? You're telling me *she's* going to keep the empire together?"

"Her Highness may be a fifteen year-old girl, Sun bless her," Orien pulled back and looked Myla in the eye, a bright ferocity surging through his words, "but she could rip every secret out of your head and kill you with a thought! Give her a chance, she *will* hold the throne."

"How very reassuring." Orien's eyes blazed, a flicker of real fire in them. Myla let him go. "Khrozus," she smirked. "Are you in love?"

"No!" He was blushing, though. "You'd have to meet her to understand."

"I would, would I?"

"It's not the Torpreahns we should be worrying about. Just… Please. If you know where it is… Just take me to it and let me take it back."

"And you'll make it all go away like it never happened?"

"For you? Yes!"

He wants to prove himself to his mistress, does he? I suppose I can work with that. Sulfane surely hadn't been stealing the crown only to give it straight back to the people it belonged to in the first place, and whoever *had* sent him on his way to that barge, *they* weren't getting it, not after the double-cross in the woods. "You'll forgive me if I need a bit more than your word on that. Khrozus' blood, I barely know who you *are*!"

"Money, is it?" He looked almost sad.

"No, but I may need your help."

"For what?"

She waved a boy over and had him refill their cups. "Right now? Act drunk and lovestruck." She leaned towards him again and twirled a finger in her hair and smiled and watched him with big eyes, the way Soraya had watched Sarwatta Hawat. Soraya had always been good at that, that expression of rapt intensity that inevitably reeled in whoever she wanted. Myla could see it working on Orien right now, even though he knew she was faking it.

I learned from the best, she thought, and then *He* does *know this is all fake, right?*

"Why were you waiting for me that night?"

"I was following the Guild."

"But they weren't after me, they were after Sulfane. If they actually knew what he'd done, they would have been more forceful. I think they were looking for him because they thought he could lead them to someone else. Who?"

Orien didn't have any answers to that, not really, but she let him talk to kill the time, shooting a glance now and then at their two shadows to make sure they were still watching. Someone who didn't want the late Emperor's daughter to sit as regent, which could have been almost anyone from the Path of the Sun through the Torpreahns and their allies to the Butcher of Deephaven himself. The mage had a lot to say, though, and dropped a lot of names. Myla had the idea she was supposed to be impressed.

"Maybe someone stole it simply so they could give it back?" She smiled sweetly. "The Guild, or some noble house trying to curry favour? Be the hero of the hour? Could even be some mage no one's ever heard of? Or maybe your princess who can kill people with a thought wasn't ever supposed to get the crown in the first place. Maybe *she's* the one who stole it."

She half expected him to bristle and sulk at that, but he only laughed. "There are two crowns, you know that. The Moonsteel Crown for the Emperor, the Sunsteel Crown for his heir. The Emperor gave her the Sunsteel Crown years ago. She's not supposed to sit as regent. He wanted her to sit as Empress. But he'd probably have to have consolidated his power for another decade or two to get away with *that* idea."

He kissed her again, a soft touch that didn't go away. Myla grabbed his hand and held it tight, about to crush his fingers, but their two shadows were watching – they weren't even hiding it now. "Did you not…"

…And the air was warm and made her skin tingle, and she was a little tipsy and it *had* been a long time and he *was* quite handsome, and there was a pleasant buzz in her head and…

…And she was back in Deephaven, and he was Sarwatta, hands all over her…

She reached around the back of his head, pulled him hard

against her, forehead to forehead, broke the kiss, looked him in the eye and kicked him in the shin. Hard.

"I warned you, mage. Next time, I draw blood."

The third man had come back to join her two shadows. He stood beside them, bent over, whispering something in their ears. He looked like he wasn't staying. For a moment, none of them were watching her and Orien.

"Stay here." She eased herself off her stool and made a show of stumbling a little, heading towards the privy pits. She caught the third man snap a glance her way and then straighten to watch for her long enough to be sure of where she was going.

The door to the outside flew open. Cold air smacked her in the face as a drunk staggered in, mumbling an apology as he brushed against her. Myla swayed and almost fell and glanced back as she caught herself. Their third shadow was following her. Good. As soon as she was outside, she ran down the path of filthy packed snow to the wooden shelter of the privies and on, towards the river and the jetties and the moored barges. The snow was piled waist-high on either side of the path; she jumped into one of the drifts and crouched, watching, waiting and shivering as her shadow followed her outside. By the time he reached the privies, he had a knife in his hand. He stopped by each door, listening. He pushed one open. Myla heard an indignant shout. He tried another door and then the third, then the last. He looked around, swore, then went back inside.

Go to the stables. Run.

Instinct said to take Orien's horse and ride, right now, but five minutes out in the cold and she was already shaking so much she couldn't stop herself. She'd freeze, simple as that, and so would the horse, and so she followed back inside, making sure to sway like she was drunk. She crashed onto the seat beside Orien, swung an arm around him and rested her head on his shoulders, and yes, partly it was façade, but partly it was because he was warm and she wanted to trust him. She already did. Sort of. In as much as he hadn't lied to her…

Yet.

"There are at least three," she murmured. "One followed me outside. He came with a knife."

"Where?"

"Uh-uh. Don't look. Do you have a private room?"

"No. I'm in the commons."

"Rich mage like you?"

"Rich? Ha!"

"Go get us a room. Off you go."

"What?"

She turned his head and kissed him, making sure her shadows saw, and offered a quick prayer to whoever might be listening that Orien understood this was still an act so she didn't have to stab him later, and rather afraid that he probably didn't.

"Oh, I see. *I* have to ask…?"

"Yes, you do. Now shut up and buy us somewhere where we won't be disturbed. With a lock, or at least a latch." She thought of her room in the Pig. "Preferably both."

Orien hurried away. Myla let herself sprawl across the table, toying with the half-empty glasses. Sword-monks weren't supposed to drink. Mistress Tasahre would have been horrified at how well Myla could play at being too drunk to stand. It was almost like she'd practiced…

After a bit, Orien returned with a key. Myla draped herself around him, and let him lead the way, up the stairs and around a small maze of corridors to a tiny little room piled with furs and blankets. As he locked the door behind them, she stepped away and rested a hand on the hilt of a knife.

"I know, I know," he said. "I'm not even going to ask." He looked a little crestfallen. Myla tried not to notice how a part of her was pleased about that.

No. Nope, nope, no. Not *happening.*

"They're going to follow us tomorrow when we leave," she said. "I thought we could give them the slip, but I don't think we can stop them from picking up our trail. If it was summer…" She shrugged, because it *wasn't* summer, and so forcing their way across country would leave a trail obvious to even an idiot and, unless Orien was a much better fire-mage than he'd let her see, the cold would kill them.

"Who are they?"

"*You're* asking *me*?" She laughed, and wondered briefly whether she should have made a deal with the Guild Mages instead, then found herself glad she hadn't. "Last chance, mage: *are* they with you? Because if you lie to me now and it turns out they are, I *will* kill you."

Orien shook his head, his expression contorting between annoyed and a little bit scared, but mostly disappointed. "They *could* be with the Guild, I suppose," he said. "If they are, there'll be a mage somewhere."

"Can you find out?"

Orien closed his eyes. "I can try."

He turned to go but she caught his arm. "Wait…" And it was probably more than he needed to know and an honesty she'd come to regret, but she told him about the night after Fings had stolen the Emperor's crown, about the fight in the woods and the betrayal. Most of all, she told him about the mage who'd tried to kill them. "Be careful."

"I will." Orien nodded. "Can I ask you something?"

"Of course."

"That night we met… I was downstairs when the Guild Mages spoke to you."

"I know. I saw you."

"The Moonsteel talisman you had. May I see it?"

Myla tugged the leather thong and pulled out the little Moonsteel trinket that Blackhand had given her. "They said it was spent. Does it mean something?"

Orien held it between his fingers. He shook his head.

"It's just a piece of Moonsteel. I don't think it was ever anything more." He let it go and stood there, right in front of her, looking into her eyes, close enough that she could feel his warmth. "Why are you doing this?"

"Doing what?"

"You could have taken that crown to Torpreah. You could have sold it there and lived like kings."

It was just as well that Fings had never thought of that, but then Fings did tend to forget there was more to the world than Varr. "Because whoever sent us knew where that barge was going to be, and when, and they knew all that long before the Emperor was dead. Which means they were the ones who killed him, you see? It's the only way it works." She met Orien's stare and saw the flare in his eyes as he realised what she was saying.

"Oh…"

"I'm from Deephaven, Orien. I wasn't alive for the siege but… You can't understand unless you grew up there. A quarter of the city died. I won't be a part of causing a war." She patted his arm. "We leave at dawn. As early as we can. I'll take you to what you want. We stay together until it's back where it belongs. After that… what happens is up to you. I already made one mistake that can't be put right. One is enough."

"If we live through all this, I'd like to hear about that." An uncertain smile flickered at the corners of Orien's mouth.

"If I tell you, I'll have a favour to ask. One that won't be easy." *Could* he help her with House Hawat? Probably not. But it couldn't hurt to ask…

Careful there. Hope is a dangerous thing…

They looked at each other, a moment of awkward silence.

"I'll go see if there's a mage hiding about the place, shall I?" Orien said.

"Probably best."

He slipped out while Myla sat in a corner to wait. And she must have fallen asleep because the next thing she knew, the door was opening again, and Orien was slipping back, closing it and turning the key in the lock as quietly has he could manage. He came over to her, and she didn't move, not quite sure why, almost as though she couldn't, but all he did was pick up one of the furs and lay it over her like blanket.

"No mages," he whispered, and went to sleep beside her.

29

WRAİTH

On the night after Fings took him into the catacombs, Seth lay in his bed in his cell and dreamed he drifted high into the sky. Mountains lay spread beneath him. A single red star burned overhead – the Baleful Eye, the Revealer, the Exposer of Truth, the Unraveller of Mysteries. Blankets of cloud wrapped him, warm against the winter air. A single pinprick of light appeared below, a pyre piled high and burning fiercely. Black shadows flickered, melting into formless shapes. Another figure flew beside him. White hair streaming from white skin. Red eyes that matched the star above. A wraith, the faded relic of one of the half-gods of the Shining Age. In his dream, Seth had tried to twist away, but the wraith had plucked him from the sky and hurled him across continents in a spin and a blur until only the Eye above remained. In the morning, when he woke, he tried to write it all down before the memories dissolved. He was training to be a priest, so he knew a vision when he saw one, and he knew that in such dreams lay shreds of truth. But when he'd looked at what he'd written, he knew there had been more that he couldn't remember.

He remembered now, as Fings hauled him from the vault with its restless bones. He was alone and cold and falling. Varr lay spread beneath him, vast and sprawling, pricked with the light of a million torches. He saw the rivers, the great Arr and the Thort, and a barge toiling against the currents into the heart of the city, and he *knew*, as he knew the stains and scars on his fingers, that inside it was something to flay his flesh and split his bones and shred his soul.

The wraith.

He felt its icy fingers touch his heart; yet when he looked again, the wraith wasn't a wraith at all. The face that stared at him was half his own, the other half ruined by scars and with one eye milky and blind.

He hardly felt Fings drag him away. A new epiphany gripped him, a revelation twisting the world on its axis. He'd been wrong about why they'd exiled him, why they'd denied him the light and treated him as though he was an abomination. It wasn't what he'd read or where he'd gone or even what he'd done. It wasn't even that he knew the truth about Sivingathm's sigils, because he hadn't discovered it back then, not really.

It wasn't what he knew. It was what he *was*.

A doorway.

He just didn't quite know what was trying to come through. The truth? Or was it something else?

30

FİNGS' GAMBİT

Fings woke the next morning to discover the city in the midst of a blizzard. Another foot of fresh snow had fallen overnight, curling dunes under a howling gale and everything white and frozen. Wrapped in all the clothes he could salvage from the sacking of the Pig, he fought his way to the Spice Market, all gritted teeth and clenched fists into the biting wind, only to find it almost empty. When he got back, Seth was in the kitchens with the fires going, something already smelling good enough to have Fings' stomach rumbling.

"You find what you were looking for last night?" Fings asked.

Seth gave a noncommittal sort of shrug and sat beside him in front of the fire. "Maybe. I found something to offer the Bithwar woman, at least."

"You were weird on the way back."

"I'm thinking... maybe you're right. Maybe that stuff down there is best left alone."

Fings didn't say anything. Didn't want to jinx it. Was always difficult with Seth. He was like a moth around a flame. Kept dancing in close, getting burned, flitting away again but never quite letting it go.

"So... Myla's gone off to fetch all the loot you stole from that barge so she can trade it for Blackhand?"

"Sort of."

"And you're going along with that?"

"Yeah." Fings couldn't meet Seth's eye.

There was a long silence. Then: "Really?"

"I suppose." Fings stared at his feet. "Don't suppose I'm going to get much choice."

"But?"

"But it's *so much money*! You could buy... a whole city with something like that...! And live like kings and... stuff!" The thought of *giving* it back, for *free*, without so much as a single half-bit in return, it made him sick.

"Yeah. So... You really want to trade all that for Blackhand?"

"No!" Fings froze. There it was, the sordid truth. No, he didn't want to trade it for Blackhand. Didn't want to trade it for *anyone*, only for what it was worth in delicious silver so that he and Ma Fings and all his sisters could trek off to Deephaven on some fancy barge and find Levvi and all be together again, living like royalty.

"You could just keep the silver and trade the crown to Bithwar. Don't know if she'd touch it and you wouldn't get a tenth of what it was worth but... that would still be a lot." Seth peered at the kitchen window. The snow in the alley outside was almost up to the sill and still falling. He shrugged and went to the ovens and pulled out a tray of something that smelled delicious. Then he grinned. "Pastries! Pastries! Lovely fresh pastries! Get your pastries, fresh as the day they were made." His grin widened he as took one, juggled it between his hands to slough off the heat and took a large bite. "Nice for that to actually be true, for once."

Two days later, when the snow stopped and they managed to dig themselves out, they found Dox and Arjay at the front door. Arjay was in a bad way and Dox was almost carrying her.

"Saw the smoke last night," Dox said. "We need a place." He looked Fings up and down. "Surprised to see *you* here. Thought you were long gone."

Fings shook his head, feeling a bit awkward and waiting for questions along the lines of *So where were you when the Spicers came* followed very shortly by *So was it you who let them in?*

"I keep saying," said Seth from behind him. "Those Guild Mages aren't going to stop looking." He looked Dox straight in the eye, then looked at Arjay. "Spicers?"

Dox nodded.

"They went after Fings' family that night, too."

"Speaking of mages, you seen Myla?"

Fings shook his head.

"She fucking left us."

Seth helped Arjay into the Pig. "Way she told it, it was her they were after and she didn't have much choice."

"Said that, did she?"

"How'd *you* get out?"

"Window. Jumped." Dox glowered. "She tell you about the mage she was with?"

Fings froze. *Mage*

"No," said Seth carefully. "She didn't." He helped Arjay to the kitchen and sat her close to the fire, then started poking at her.

"Can you help her?" Dox asked.

"It's a moon-priestess you want, but I can try. Get her warm, for now."

"What was that you were saying?" asked Fings, trying to sound as casual as he could manage. "About Myla and a mage?"

Dox told them as Seth fussed around Arjay, trying to get her warm and feeding her a little of Blackhand's brandy that the Spicers had somehow missed. Dox hadn't seen much, just heard lots of shouting. He and Arjay had thrown on some clothes and grabbed their knives and gone to see what all the fuss was about, only to run straight into half a dozen Spicers dragging Blackhand and Wil down the stairs, all staring at some scrawny-looking fellow with a pointy beard. Dox hadn't recognised him, but he remembered because it looked like he was throwing candles down the stairs at whatever ruckus was going on in the commons, and Dox hadn't been able to work out why at first, but the Spicers had all just stopped and stared, at least until Arjay stabbed one of them, which sort of focussed their attention, and that was about when he worked out that the scrawny fellow wasn't throwing candles, he was conjuring fire out of thin air.

Seth frowned. "Scrawny. Pointy beard. Wasn't he in the Pig earlier that night?"

Dox didn't know. "Myla came running up," he said. "One of the Spicers got Arjay. Myla dragged the scrawny fellow into one of the rooms looking over Threadneedle Street. They went out the window. We did the same."

Fings nodded, trying to act like it was all only slightly interesting, which was easy enough with Dox and Seth tutting over Arjay. It was sort of funny, watching Seth act like he had any idea what he was doing. Was a nasty stab in the side, Arjay had. The wound had closed and she wasn't bleeding, but the skin around it was an angry red and swollen and she was running a fever.

Seth shook his head. "Beyond my skills. Best thing is probably to leave it alone. Keep her warm and pray, unless you happen to have a few silvers stashed away for a moon-priestess."

Turned out that Dox *did* have a few silvers stashed away, hidden under a floorboard. Fings offered to go to the moon-temple on Spice Market Square while Seth and Dox looked after Arjay, and it said something about Dox that he said yes, and let Fings walk off with a whole silver half-moon.

There *was* a moon-temple on Spice Market Square, but Fings took himself to the chapel on the edge of Bonecarvers instead, Bonecarvers being a place where people largely saved their veneration for the Moon on the grounds that the priestesses didn't cause as much trouble when bodies mysteriously disappeared from corpse-carts. He handed over Dox's silver – enough to get a novice to head off out to the Pig – and then carried on into Bonecarvers until he fetched up at the Bithwar house. Tarran Bithwar wasn't at home, her servant told him, but Fings was happy enough to leave a message.

"Tell her that ring she's interested in is hers if she sets up a meet between me and whoever's got Blackhand."

Myla and a mage she somehow hadn't mentioned? Making deals behind his back, was she?

Oh no you don't!

And to think he'd almost felt bad, letting her head off on her own in the middle of winter, knowing it was a waste of time.

31

GOBLInS

There were three choices, Myla decided, for dealing with the men following her. The first was to carry on as though they didn't exist and be ready for them make their move; but only a fool let their enemy choose the time and place of a fight. The second was to immediately face them down. It was the sword-monk way of doing things: turn and walk straight at the biggest danger and dare it to cause trouble. Thing was, they *would* cause trouble. She'd had a chance to watch them now: six veteran soldiers, all mounted, against a half-trained sword-monk and a scarecrow in an orange robe? No, they wouldn't back down, and she'd seen how much use Orien was when it came to a fight; she couldn't take all six on her own, not at once.

Which was why she'd gone for the third option, leading Orien right past where she'd buried the Emperor's crown and on for another mile, and then leaving the road and doubling back. It had been snowing almost constantly since she left Varr. The roads were verging on impassable, the visibility was poor, and she'd done what she could to hide their tracks. The rest was down to fate. Hunkered down in a snowdrift, she watched the riders on the road as they passed. She was buying herself a head start, that was all.

The other riders vanished into the haze of falling snow.

"We may only be a few hands ahead of them." Myla looked up at the sun, low and bloated on the horizon.

"Is it far, now?"

"No." Maybe she and Orien could hide under the bridge again when the riders discovered they'd been tricked. She could tell Fings when she got back to Varr and they'd both laugh. A part of her wished he was here. He'd have found a better way to throw these sell-swords off his trail.

I can't fight six men.

By the time they got back to the bridge, the snow was falling more heavily. Myla reined in her horse and dismounted. "Do something for me," she said. "Ride on until you can't see me through the snow. Then come back."

Orien rode across the bridge. By the time he reached the other side, he was a hazy dark shape almost lost in the falling snow. He'd gone about fifty feet, so that was how far off the road they had to be to stay hidden. Or, put another way, that was how close the men hunting her could get before she'd see them.

He came back. "Is it here?"

"Bring the horses down."

The snow under the bridge was uneven lumps and drifts where their old tracks had been partially covered.

"Stay here. Keep out of sight and keep the horses warm."

Orien cocked his head.

"We buried it a little way towards the river. Far enough that no one will see me from the road." She half expected him to insist he come with her but he didn't. Then again, where else was she going to go?

She forced a furrow through the snow, following the path she and Wil had ploughed before. It was hard, almost like swimming, up to her waist in places so that every step was an effort. Winters in Deephaven were rain and wind, storms blowing in off the Gulf of Feyr, waterlogged cellars and ships lost at sea. They might have a sprinkle of snow once or twice if they were lucky, but mostly it was rain. This? This endless white freezing stifling suffocating silence?

She reached the stand of trees and walked between them to the depression where her dead branch should have been poking up out of the snow, her marker for where she'd buried the crown. She started closer, wondering why she couldn't see it, and then stopped. She could see the contours of the trail she'd left with Wil, now little more than creases in the snow. But there was another trail too, equally old and filled with snow, one that hadn't been there last time.

Someone had come here, not long after she and Wil had left.

Fings' goblins?

The tracks didn't lead from the bridge. They came from the river.

She looked back. She couldn't see Orien or the horses or the bridge or he road. She followed the trail another hundred yards towards the river. It led to the second road, the River Road, and veered off.

How?

She went back and found the marker she'd left, lying beside a hollow in the snow. She paced around it, digging, kicking holes, but her heart wasn't in it. There was no treasure hidden here, not any more. Someone else had come days ago. Someone who'd known exactly where to go and what they were looking for.

Sulfane?

But Sulfane was dead, and Wil hadn't left her side.

Could the soldiers searching the road have found it? But there was only one track. One man on his own, maybe with a horse, but certainly not a company of soldiers.

Fings.

Fings, who'd stayed behind in Varr and left her to come back here on her own. It had surprised her that he'd do that. But not if he'd known from the start that it was a fool's errand…

Fings.

Fings and his fucking goblins.

She heard a scream from the road.

32

GLASSMAKERS

Within the hazy boundaries of Haberdashers and Seamstresses and Bonecarvers and Glassmakers, which made up the more respectable half of the Craftsmans' Quarter between the Spice Market and the river, Tarran Bithwar was a Lady of Significance, as much as anything because she owned a carriage. It wasn't much of a one – battered and scraped around the edges, the repairs verging on shoddy, the paintwork touched up rather than re-done. Seth, if he'd been asked and had felt like being honest, would have guessed that it had once belonged to somebody else, possibly somebody who was still wondering where it had gone. He *wasn't* being asked, however, and he'd never ridden in a carriage before, and it *did* make him feel like he was somehow important. So he kept his thoughts to himself.

Another thought he kept to himself was that it might have been quicker to walk. By now, even some of the Longcoat Roads were blocked with snow.

"It's about making the right impression." Tarran's smile was all teeth and no eyes, the sort of smile that came from a lot of practice rather than from actually liking things. "You're right that Blackhand is in Tombland, but I'm a little hazy as to who's got him."

"The Spicers," said Seth.

"Yes, but someone else is pulling their strings." Tarran smiled, one of those *I'm-so-clever-I-know-so-much* smiles that reminded

Seth of Lightbringer Suaresh and made him want to stab things. He didn't much like Tarran Bithwar, he decided, even if Blackhand reckoned she could shift absolutely anything. Too clever and too well-informed. Too aware of herself. Truth was, he wasn't keen on being here at all. All it took was for the wrong Spicer to see his face and remember him from his last little visit and there was a good chance he'd be fucked.

He *did* rather like the whole riding around in a carriage thing, though. He reckoned a person could get used to that.

"Who?" he asked.

"I'm not entirely sure. Someone who's taken over the Constable's Castle."

"That's where the Mage lived."

"Yes. Someone appears to have taken on his mantle. Someone new. There's also a connection to Deephaven, someone with money and influence. Why are they after your sword-monk? What did she do?"

"I never asked." Seth wasn't sure he cared, either, but Bithwar clearly had wind of something.

"Deephaven to Varr." There was that toothy smile again. "A long way to run. A long way to chase after someone, too."

The carriage stopped. A moment later, the driver was tapping on the door. "I'm sorry, Lady Bithwar, but the Way of Kings is snowed in." *Lady* Bithwar, like she was some sort of royalty and not the daughter of a common-or-garden thief.

"Take the Avenue of Last Arguments," said Tarran. She smiled her *I-know-things* smile as they started to move. "Do you know why the Circus of Dead Emperors has its name?"

"You mean aside from being large and round and full of statues of dead emperors?" Seth smirked right back at her. "Yes, of course I do. Because once upon a time, when an Emperor died, the body was taken there for an official proclamation by the Constable before being handed over to the Path of the Sun. That happened quite a lot in the years shortly before the office of Constable was abolished, so I imagine it was fresh in people's minds. What's any of that got to do with Blackhand?"

Tarran beamed. "What I *do* find interesting in current circumstances is what happened to the Constable's House after Emperor Jahingar dissolved the office. It was sold to some minor scion of the twelfth House. The one that no longer exists?"

"And?" Listen to Fings and you'd think the whole of Tombland was so full of sprites and goblins and ghosts and spirits that it was a wonder there was room for anyone else. But maybe there *were* ghosts, just not the ones Fings meant, because there it was: the connection to Tombland and the mage and the mark Fings said he'd seen carved into Wil's dead skin.

They'd never gone back after Blackhand murdered the mage. Any of them. Until Seth, a few days ago.

"Interesting coincidence, I thought," said Tarran. "What with that ring Fings has."

The carriage stopped outside the Alchemists' Gate. Tarran jumped out into a bustle of people pushing and barging past one another towards the ramshackle Glass Market building. Seth had no idea what the Glass Market had started as, but these days it looked like half an unwanted temple tacked on to an over-ambitious rookery, the bits in between cobbled together from leftovers by an architect who was either confused, senile, or else drank far too much fermented Demonleaf.

"Here?" Seth caught Tarran's arm. She didn't much like that; nor did the brute of a bodyguard who'd followed them down from the carriage, but Seth didn't care. This end of the Glass Market was a haven for alchemists where you tried not to breathe more than strictly necessary. Another feature was its tendency to occasionally explode.

"No," said Tarran. "The Bridge of Questions."

She pushed on, leading the way into a shockwave of noise and heat and acrid smoke, through mind-boggling apparatus and bubbling liquids, garish colours, pops and bangs and clouds of smoke and now-and-then shouts of alarm. Beyond the Alchemists' Market, the rest of Glassmakers spread into old falling-down slums and yet held some of the most beautiful objects in the city, priceless, displayed in a ramshackle labyrinthine maze that only the locals could navigate.

From the back of the Alchemists' Market, the entrance to Tombland and the Bridge of Questions was through a diligent imitation of an old mausoleum. Four sarcophagi lay flat on the floor while skeletons hung in the corners with candles huddled in clusters around their feet. Tarran shot him another one of those smiles. "Did you ever wonder if this might have been a *real* tomb, once?"

"You don't think the temple sword-monks would suffer this to exist if it *was*, do you?"

Tarran gave him an odd look. "But it *doesn't* exist. I told you. After the twelfth House was destroyed by Khrozus, all their lands officially ceased to be. None of this exists any more. Any of it. The whole of Tombland."

Seth harrumphed. Lightbringers and Dawncallers and Sunbrights might worry about things like that, but he'd met enough sword-monks to know they gave precisely no shits for such nonsense when it came to Dead Men and warlocks and their ilk. They went where their work called them, and didn't care for such trivia as whether or not places happened to exist.

An arch on the far side of the fake tomb opened onto a narrow, covered bridge, faced with gaudy carvings of beasts and man-beasts alternately copulating with or consuming helpless peasant folk. At the far end of the bridge, guarding the true entrance to Tombland, stood a crude over-sized statue of an executioner, bare-chested and masked and clasping a sword big enough to behead an ox. Seth rolled his eyes: that was Tombland all over, where everything proudly set itself in opposition to the world outside.

The Mage was dead. Seth had seen it happen. So why had someone left his mark on Wil's face? Wil, who was one of the last survivors of the Mage's murder…

"Hard to believe there's a canal running under here, isn't it?" Tarran followed him though the arch. "Or that people used to cross this bridge without even realising what they'd done or where they were. Did you know that Tombland is an island? Canals along all sides? There were a few other stone bridges once but the Mage had them pulled down and replaced them with wooden drawbridges. The whole place is a fortress in disguise."

Except in the winter, of course, when the canals froze and anyone could walk wherever they liked, if they didn't mind wading through six feet of snow and a treasure trove of frozen shit, piss and anything else the locals had no further use for.

"A bit awkward, isn't it, having a place that doesn't exist that people can simply walk into by accident."

Water runs under the ice, even in winter. Which is all that matters for keeping ghosts where they belong.

Seth pinched himself. There were no ghosts in Tombland. No ghosts, no goblins, no sprites, and no more Dead Men here than anywhere else in Varr. The place had an open-air theatre, for Kelm's sake...

No wraiths...

The alleys on the far side of the bridge were packed with snow. The high overhanging houses plunged them into perpetual oppressive twilight. Seth stood in the middle of the bridge and shivered.

Walking dead, rogue mages, Blackhand bringing down a curse on the lot of us... "This is where the Spicers said to meet, is it?"

"Yes." Tarran was already pacing, impatient.

"They going to be long?"

Tarran shrugged. "Not long," she said. "I doubt they'll keep us waiting."

33

THE PİG

The moon-priestess was called Safaya and she came each afternoon to treat Arjay. Fings didn't really know why – Dox's silver half-moon should have been enough for one visit but not more. From what the priestess said, they had Myla to thank, and Fings had no idea why but he wasn't going to question it. Arjay was on the mend, that was the main thing.

Other Unrulys drifted in and out, men like Brick and Topher who hadn't been in the Pig on the night the Spicers came. They had a bit of a gathering one evening, lots of drinking and chest-beating and swearing how they'd break Blackhand out and smash the Spicers. In the morning, they drifted away again, tails between their legs once they knew Blackhand was in Tombland and heard Arjay talk about the men from Deephaven. Would have been different if Myla had been there, Fings thought, Myla with her swords. Then he remembered how she was betraying them all with a mage.

To begin with, the moon-priestess refused to come into the Pig while Seth was there. Later, she settled on refusing to be in the same room, which made it easier. She wouldn't say why, Seth acted like he didn't have a clue, and Fings didn't have one either. When Tarran sent a messenger, half frozen and covered in snow, saying the Spicers were ready to talk, they all agreed it should be Seth who went. Seth was better at talking. Fings – the one who knew where the treasure was *actually* hidden – would stay safely in the Pig.

Which was why Seth wasn't there when the Spicers came. Fings, upstairs with Dox and Arjay and the priestess when he heard a window smash, almost made it to the kitchens and the pantry tunnel but not quite: two Spicers were already inside. He ran back, yelling for Dox, although there was only so much Dox could do.

It all seemed to happen so slowly. Dox came out swinging a cleaver, such a rage on his face that even Fings almost faltered, and then something hit Fings in the back of the head. He stumbled and fell. From the floor, he saw Dox bury his cleaver in the side of a Spicer's face. Then another Spicer stuck him in the gut, and Dox staggered back, roaring and waving his cleaver and bleeding everywhere. Fings touched his head. His hair was sticky with blood. He forced himself to struggle back to his feet. Everything felt like he was moving through treacle.

The priestess came out of Arjay's room.

"Stop," she said, quiet like a whisper and yet clear as a bell. And for a moment, everybody did actually stop, even Fings. Then Dox looked at himself and noticed that someone had probably killed him, and swayed and took a couple of steps back, and then staggered past the priestess to be with Arjay, and the world started moving again. Fings ran, bolting for the stairs up to Blackhand's old rooms and the roof. He cast a last glance over his shoulder. The priestess was still standing there. She was young and small and unarmed. A gang of angry Spicers would have gone through her like fire though paper. It was a miracle they didn't really, if only to finish murdering Dox and Arjay.

But they didn't, and then he was round the corner and taking the steps two at a time, and he could hear the Spicers coming after him. His head pounded and throbbed. He raced into Blackhand's study and threw open the window and climbed out onto the ledge – wide enough for Blackhand himself – and up onto the roof of the Pig. He scrabbled over the roof, sending great swathes of snow sliding down the tiles and crashing into the street below, until he reached the alley between the stables and the rest of Haberdashers. He dug out the plank of wood that Blackhand kept for times like this and used it as a bridge from the roof of the Pig to the rooftops on the other side of the alley. When he was over, he kicked it away and watched it fall. A few Spicers were on the roof of the Pig now, coming after him, but they were cautious and wary of slipping in the snow and tumbling down to the alley below. They obviously weren't going to catch him, so he flipped them a few rude gestures, and then ran off across the rooftops when they answered by throwing more rocks.

He made his way across a few rooftops in Haberdashers and then dropped to the ground – although frankly it wasn't much easier to get about down on the ground than it was up on the rooftops, what with all the snow piled about the place – and wondered what to do.

His head still hurt.

Was luck he hadn't been in the Pig on the first night they came. Was luck Myla had come to Locusteater Yard that night, too. But now Myla wasn't here, and he'd given up his chicken's foot charm to keep her protected from mages – fat lot of use *that* was since apparently she was hanging out with one – and yes, he'd escaped the Spicers a third time, but they were going to keep on coming, and sooner or later, luck always ran dry.

He knew where they were hiding out. In Tombland, in the old Constable's Castle. Which was definitely a place he didn't want to go, but sometimes…

He sighed.

If you want something done, do it yourself. That was what Ma Fings always said.

VI

INTERLUDE

On the morning after Fings took him into the catacombs, after his dream of the wraith and the Revealer, after he tried to write it all down, Seth decided he was hungry and went to the kitchens. There was still an hour to go before dawn and almost no one was up, but there were always a few novices and priests whose duties kept them awake after twilight, or had them up before dawn so that some turned entirely nocturnal during the long days of summer.

He wasn't supposed to be there, but preparing food to follow dawn prayers was a chore for novices, so he could always claim he'd traded his place on the roster. He helped himself to a hunk of bread and went into the pantries in case there was some cheese that no one would miss. When he saw the rat, he did what every novice who ever worked in the kitchen would have done, grabbed the nearest broom and jabbed at it. He didn't expect to hit it because no one ever did, but when he looked, the rat was still there, lying on its side, twitching. After a few seconds, it stopped.

Seth stared at it. His first thought was to run around shouting about how he'd finally got one of the little bastards, but that would have to wait until he had a suitable audience. His next thought was to wonder who was on kitchen duty this morning and whether there was some fun to be had.

His third thought was to reach into his pocket and pull out his strips of paper and his charcoal stick and draw a sigil. Not the usual sigil for setting the Restless Dead to peace, but one of the sigils he'd seen in the catacombs, the one he remembered most clearly. He drew it and knew, without quite knowing how he could be so certain, that he'd done it right, and that it was something to do with the dead. On a whim, he touched the paper to the rat to see what would happen. Of course, nothing *did* happen, and he was about to head back to his cell, but then the paper was somehow stuck to the rat, which made him wonder if the rat wasn't quite dead after all and had bitten it, except it hadn't, and then the paper snatched itself from his fingers and...

There was a slight smell of burning fur as the sigil ignited and flashed to ash. Seth scratched his chin. If he'd found a sigil for setting things on fire, well, *that* could be useful.

The rat twitched. Seth jumped back and took a couple of hurried steps out of the pantry. The rat kicked helplessly for a few seconds and then righted itself and lurched towards him. Seth backed further but the rat kept coming. When he stopped, the rat stopped too, settling a few feet away, watching him with dead eyes.

There were marks on it now, he saw. The sigil he'd drawn was burned into its fur.

"What, in the unholy name of Shadow, is *that*?"

Sunbright Jakeda. Seth almost jumped out of his skin. "A... A rat, mistress," he said.

A Lightbringer came to him after dawn prayers and told him his duties had changed. He spent the rest of the day in the company of two sword-monks, ostensibly to help them if they needed help with anything, which they clearly didn't. That evening, they locked him into his cell. Two days later, the Sunherald Martial cut him off from the light and the Sunguard threw him out of the Temple. He didn't know if they ever caught the rat, but they'd all felt something that morning when the sigil had burned, like the slamming shut of some distant door. At least, that was what the other novices had said, before they stopped talking to him.

34

ORİEП

Myla ran back through the snow and then stopped. She couldn't see the bridge but the scream hadn't sounded like Orien, which meant someone had found them, which meant her trick hadn't worked. She plunged into the drifts, pulled her hood down to her eyes, scooped snow over herself and hunkered down to watch. She didn't have to wait long before she saw two men following her trail towards the river. The falling snow blurred them into hazy shapes but they were the same men who'd been following all morning.

Now what?

Could she take two of them at once? Yes, probably, in a sparring circle or an open field. Out here, in this? Anything could happen.

If I fight them, I have to kill them.

The crown wasn't here.

All we have to do is get away.

They'd keep following, of course. But maybe at the next waystation, surrounded by people, she could confront them. Convince them that she and Orien had come away empty-handed...

Two men here meant four back at the bridge. She let this pair pass and pushed on for the road, trying to keep low, eyes peeled for any sign of Orien, but it was the smell that came to her first, a stink of burning hair or fur. She fought her way up the slope from the frozen stream until she was level with the road, then crept closer, head down low. The snow wasn't as deep here, only up to her thighs. She counted the horses beside the road by the bridge. Three at first... four, five... six, the last with a rider on its back.

One up here, two heading for the river left three under the bridge with Orien?

Why leave someone on the road? As a lookout? A lookout for what?

He was watching the bridge towards Varr. She came up on him from behind through the falling snow, ducked low under his mare, undid his girth, then grabbed him and pulled hard, toppling him off his horse to crash at her feet in a flurry of snow. She was on him before he knew what had happened, a steel edge pressed against his throat.

"Shhh..."

His eyes turned wild as he understood who she was.

"Who's paying you?" she asked.

He shook his head.

"Jeffa?" she asked. "Jeffa Hawat?"

He looked blank.

"From Deephaven?"

A frown of incomprehension.

"Someone from the south, then? Torpreah?"

A slight shrug. Myla pressed her edge a little harder against his skin.

"Give me something or I cut your throat."

He gulped, and then nodded a little. She eased back. "A priest," he whispered. "He works for the priest."

Myla nodded, then straddled him, pinning his arms. She pressed her fingers into either side of his neck, under his jaw until she felt his blood pulse, then pushed hard and fell on top of him, smothering him. He thrashed and tried to cry out as she dug her fingers deeper; but after a dozen heartbeats, he fell still. She rolled him on his front and used the strap of his satchel to tie his hands and one of his feet, then tore the hood off his cloak and rolled him back and stuffed it in his mouth. By the time she was done, he was already waking up. She gave him a few seconds until his eyes focussed and he saw her squatting over him, the point of her sword hovering between his eyes.

"We both know I should have killed you," she said. "Make a sound before I come back and I will." Short of slitting his throat, it was the best she had.

She stepped away.

I could go now. Take one of these horses and run. The crown isn't here. Fings took it.

Did she owe Orien anything? Not really.

She crept through the churned snow leading down under the bridge until she could hear two of them muttering together.

"They ought to be back by now..."

"Maybe she was stranding this jackass."

"Her horse is here, though. Where's she going to go?"

She eased close enough to see figures through the snow, sheltering under the bridge with Orien's two horses. To see Orien on his knees, hands on his head, facing away. One soldier stood guard with his back to her, cradling a loaded crossbow. The other two were shuffling their feet, impatient and cold. They hadn't seen her yet, but there was no way she could sneak up on all three at once.

Knives?

The first to go had to be the one with the crossbow, before he could put a bolt through Orien. Her strike had to be fatal. Through all the leather and furs they were wearing, that meant swords, not knives.

And then what?

And then the other two would fight.

She steeled herself. Ran through the forms in her head as she eased closer, until one of the soldiers saw her.

"Yori?"

Through the falling snow, they'd mistaken her for the man they'd left keeping watch. She covered the last few yards in an ungainly spray of snow and flying limbs, swords whipping out of their sheathes. The soldier with the crossbow started to turn, and Myla was grateful because it gave her a choice. One blade snapped at his hand, hitting the crossbow where he held it and cutting off most of his fingers. As he screamed and arced back, she flicked the other low at his ankle. She felt the edge bite deep, slicing through the thick leather of his boot just above the heel. He shrieked and fell. He'd be a one-handed man who could barely walk but that was better than being dead, wasn't it?

She rounded on the other two as they faced her, as they shouted out, calling names she didn't recognise. *She's here! She's here! Get back!* The man she'd crippled clawed at the snow, screaming and bleeding, trying to get to his feet, not understanding why one of his legs didn't work, bewildered by the ruin of his hand.

Did she *really* need to fight these men?

"Orien! Let's go!"

Orien started to his feet. "Have you got–"

"It isn't here." She locked eyes with the two soldiers still standing. "You hear me? It isn't here. Some else already came and took it. Ask your two friends when they get back. Then ask yourselves whether it's worth your trouble to follow us. I'll put every one of you down if I have to."

"It's not here?" Orien looked at her, bewildered. The soldiers didn't believe her. Didn't *want* to believe her. They started to move apart, sidestepping away from one another, preparing to come at her from two directions at once.

"Orien!" The mage was on his feet, at least. "Go up to the bridge, get on a horse and go." She backed away. *Don't make me fight you.*

The two soldiers were barely watching Orien. Then, as he started to move, one of them lunged, and Myla realised it had been a trick. He stabbed out but the mage was quicker than he looked, and the thrust only caught in his coat, tangling the soldier's sword. For a moment, it was Myla and the last soldier alone.

"I don't want to kill you," she said. The man she'd crippled was still screaming. *I don't want to kill* anyone.

Orien and the other soldier fell, locked together, rolling in the snow, all incoherent grunts and growls, struggling over a knife. The soldier in front of her held his ground, watching.

"It's not *here*!" hissed Myla. "You really want to die for *nothing*?"

They didn't believe her.

DO something!

The bellowing from the soldier wrestling with Orien changed to a howl of pain. He dropped his knife and screamed, and Orien was still holding his wrist, and now it looked like the other soldier was trying to get away and Orien wouldn't let him, and then Orien had his other hand pressed against the soldier's face and Myla couldn't see–

They burst into flames. Both of them, right there in the falling snow. The soldier screamed again and finally tore free, clutching at himself. His hand and his face were burning, smoking, sizzling. Orien faltered his way to his feet, fire wreathing both his hands, flames leaping from his ripped coat, shaking so badly he could barely stand, never mind defend himself. The burning soldier grabbed a hatchet and hurled himself at the mage. Myla sprang and lunged. Her sword ripped out his throat. He took another step and then dropped like a felled tree. The second soldier threw a hatchet of his own. She saw it leave his hand and fly at her face. She jerked aside and felt the air of its passing brush her cheek.

The screams from the soldier she'd crippled subsided to a stream of animal grunts and moans. He'd managed to get to his knees. She could hear the other two men, the ones she'd passed in the gully, calling out, heading back as fast as though could through the drifting snow. They were close.

"Go!" she hissed at Orien. "Go!" She backed away as he stumbled past her, keeping her eyes on the three soldiers under the bridge. One alive, one crippled, one dead.

He was on fire. It was a mercy. Like the Spicer Fings stabbed.

But not on fire enough to have killed him.

This is what you are. This what you made yourself to be.

Sword-monks hunted Dead Men, but that hadn't always been their purpose.

The last soldier was bawling at her, bellowing how they'd hunt her to the end of the world and all the things they'd do when they caught her, how slow they'd make her end. His accent wasn't from Deephaven. These weren't Jeffa's men. He sounded southern, and they were all pale-skinned.

Torpreahns?

A priest. He works for the priest. What priest?

She took their horses to make sure they couldn't follow. Orien wanted to go back and take the two from under the bridge as well, but with the weather as it was, she might as well have killed the rest of the soldiers while she was at it. It would have been kinder.

"We *should* have killed them," he said, and he was probably right, but she'd go back to Varr and she wouldn't run and she wouldn't hide, and if they came after her... She'd face it when it happened.

They'll have to join the queue.

"It really wasn't there?" asked Orien a little later. He was fading by then, sinking into himself as though falling into a fever.

"It really wasn't."

"Someone got there before us?"

She thought for a long time about what to say, whether to explain how the tracks had looked, how someone had come not yesterday or the day before but not long after she'd left, and taken the crown and Fings' bags of silver. She might even have told him who she thought had done it, but by then Orien was gone, nodding gently on the back of his stolen horse.

Fings. Fings and his fucking goblins.

35

THE MAGE OF TOMBLAND

Fings trotted through Haberdashers and Seamstresses and Bonecarvers all the way to the Circus of Dead Emperors, mumbling to himself as he went. His first thought was to go after Blackhand right now, while most of the Spicers were scouring Haberdashers looking for him. His second thought was to wait until dark, because the sort of things he did were always best done under the cover of darkness, with Fickle Lord Moon looking down and not the Sanctimonious Sun. Not having made up his mind as he reached the Circus of Dead Emperors, he crossed it and lost himself in the chaos of the Glass Markets. He still hadn't made up his mind when he reached the back a window looking out over the frozen canal that separated Glassmakers from the Constable's Castle.

If he was in and out quick, he could be done before the Spicers got back from the Pig. He had his lockpicks. And sure as shit, they wouldn't be expecting him…

Fine.

He'd been to the Constable's Castle the night Blackhand had murdered the Mage of Tombland. He and Seth had roamed as much as they were allowed, looking for secret tunnels and passages and crypts. They hadn't found any but Fings still remembered where they'd gone. The castle had a dungeon. That, presumably, was where the Spicers were holding Blackhand.

He made his way a little further through the Glass Markets, stuck a feather between his teeth and then hopped out a window and ploughed his way across the canal. The ivy clinging to the castle walls was no trouble to climb, although it felt weird doing it in broad daylight, where anyone who looked out a window might see him.

He sucked on his feather. Anyone *did* see him, what were they going to do? Come out onto the canal and yell at him?

He reached the roof and tramped through the snow until he was looking down onto the castle's central yard, dropped to a balcony outside a window that didn't even have a shutter on it, and eased inside. The room beyond was thick with dust, like no one had used it since the murder of the Mage or even before, which maybe they hadn't.

So much the better.

He crossed to the door and stepped out into a narrow hall and listened. Nothing; but he felt a waft of warm air from somewhere, which meant the place wasn't as abandoned as it looked.

The Mage had been murdered in the Great Hall. By then, he and Seth had managed to explore the kitchens and find the tunnel down to the cellars. They'd gone up the Great Stair, too, where the Mage had his rooms, but they hadn't had the courage to climb to the top.

His memory flashed to the mark cut into Wil's cheek. *Best not go that way.*

Instead, he went back outside, back onto the rooftops, and dropped down to a window overlooking the canal. He forced the shutters, carefully avoiding a wire set across the inside that was attached to a bell. The wire was slack. Old. He crouched on the sill, looking down at an old rug with nails through its corners and sagging a little in the middle where there obviously wasn't a floor underneath. The rest of the room looked like the other: abandoned, untouched for almost ten years. He jumped carefully past the trapped rug. That was the Mage of Tombland for you. Mad as a barrel of bats, traps everywhere, always looking over his shoulder, convinced someone was going to murder him.

Wasn't wrong though.

The door to the rest of the castle was locked. Fings took a moment to pick it and then left it unlocked, reckoning this was probably how he was going to come back out with Blackhand, since the window was low enough over the canal that Blackhand would be able to jump and the drifts of snow would break his fall. He followed an abandoned passage until he reached a narrow stair and made his way down, stopping now and then to sniff the air and test for any hint of a breeze. By the time he got to bottom, the place was showing signs of being lived in: footprints in the dust, that sort of thing. The closer he got to the Great Hall, the more he saw. That, he reckoned, was where the Spicers were making their nest. The Great Hall and the Great Stair; but he didn't have to go that way to get to the dungeon...

He heard men coming, two of them, creaking and clanking with bits of leather and metal so loud they might as well have sent a herald ahead of them. He ducked into what turned out to be an old map room, left the door ajar and watched them pass. They weren't Spicers. They looked more like soldiers. Didn't look like they were from Varr, either.

Myla's Deephaven sell-swords? But how were the Spicers paying for them?

He let them pass and pushed on, flitting from one doorway to the next until he reached another stair going down. He'd seen a couple more soldiers by then. They looked bored.

There was no one watching the passage to the dungeons. Fings tiptoed along, not much liking this part because there was no other way out. It stopped at an iron door. There wasn't any light so he had to feel his way around it, which told him it had a lock and three solid-feeling bolts to keep it shut from the outside. Right now, the bars were thrown open and so was the lock, neither of which he much liked.

Yeah. But if someone was down there, they'd have a light, right?

He wasn't sure. Instinct said to turn back.

On the other hand, he'd come this far. It was black as pitch down here. They couldn't be *expecting* him, could they?

He eased open the door, feeling with his feet for whatever lay beyond.

Steps.

The air at the bottom stank of fresh shit and piss, which meant he was in the right place. A small dark hole in the ground, the sort of damp stone cell he'd always imagined for himself, albeit in the cliffs of the Kaveneth rather than the waterlogged cellars of Tombland. Blackhand was here. He could feel it.

Couldn't see a thing.

"Blackhand?" In the darkness, even a whisper sounded loud.

No answer. He found a barred door but it swung open at his touch. Couldn't be that one then.

Follow your nose.

Sounded about right. The stink was getting stronger.

He reached another cell. Someone was on the other side of the door. He could feel it.

"Blackhand?"

This one wasn't locked either. He pushed the door open.

This ain't right.

Couldn't see a thing, it was that dark, but he had the strong sense of someone sitting right in front of him, staring right back at him.

This ain't right! "Blackhand?"

A light flared in front of him. Quick as a snake, Fings turned, but still not quick enough. All he saw was a glimpse of three men coming at him with a sack to wrap over his head and then something stabbed him in the leg, and then the men were on him, wrestling him down, bundling him up and kicking and punching, and all he could think was how did they know he was coming, and how hadn't he seen them, and why did his leg hurt so much?

"Been waiting for you, Fings," said a voice that sounded horribly familiar, and then someone hit him on the head and he stopped thinking anything much at all.

Much later, when he *could* think again, he realised that his leg hurt because whoever had been waiting in the cell had stabbed him.

Also, his hands and feet were tied to a chair.

Also, he still had a sack over his head.

Shit. SHIT!

He had a go at wriggling free, and then at picking at the ropes with his fingers, but whoever had tied him knew their business. He was stuck there.

Another long time passed, long enough for Fings to have a good long think about that, and about how Seth had gone to the Bridge of Questions without him for a very good reason, and about how Myla would be finding out about now, maybe today or maybe tomorrow, maybe yesterday, that the Emperor's crown wasn't where she'd left it. He was fairly sure she was going to be quite cross about that. Although maybe that wasn't his biggest problem right now.

Eventually, the cell door opened. Men came in and picked him up and dragged him, chair and all, down a rough-stone passage to a room that felt bigger but smelled worse. Someone pulled the sack off his head and brought a candle near his face, dazzling him. Fings screwed his eyes shut.

"Hello, Fings."

That voice again. Except it couldn't be, because the Murdering Bastard was dead.

"Who are you? What do you want?"

"Who *am* I?"

"You ain't Sulfane because he's dead. So, who are you?"

The candle shifted. Fings heard a snap of fingers and then some shouting, Blackhand, no mistaking that roar of outrage and *How fucking dare you do you know who I am*! Someone lit a lamp and then three men carried Blackhand in, tied to a chair of his own, and set him across from Fings.

"What the fuck is this?" snapped Blackhand, as though somehow all of this was Fings' fault.

"Someone shut him up."

Blackhand roared and shouted and struggled as two Spicers stuffed a dirty ball of cloth in his mouth, but there wasn't much he could do about it.

"Fings is here because of you, Blackhand," said the impossible voice; and then voice moved into the light and it *was* Sulfane. The Murdering Bastard looked older than Fings remembered, the smug smile gone from his face and one arm in a sling. He rested a hand on the top of Blackhand's head. "Fings here came to rescue you. Can you believe that? After all the shit you've given him, after the way you treat his brother, he still came for you. Got all the way down here, right to where you should have been. If I hadn't been waiting, he might even have got you out. All on his own." Sulfane leered at Fings and tapped his nose. "But I *know* you, thief. I knew you'd come."

"You're dead!" Fings was faintly outraged.

"No." Sulfane had a knife in his good hand. He tossed it in the air, let it spin a couple of times and caught it. "No, I wasn't. But Fings... Wil told me, before I cut his throat, that *you* told *him* that I tried to kill *you*. That's not how *I* remember it."

"I..."

"How *I* remember it is that *you* tried to kill *me*."

"I saved your life back in the woods! From that mage! Remember? You'd be dead if it wasn't for me."

"And then you tried to kill me and left me there to freeze."

"I saw soldiers! I saw them take you!"

Sulfane shifted to stand behind Blackhand. He sank his fingers into Blackhand's hair, tipping back his head, exposing his neck. Blackhand started to struggle again, howling through the balled-up cloth in his mouth.

"Sort of mistake anyone could have made, I suppose," said Sulfane. "But they weren't soldiers. They were with me. To clean up. Except you fucked *that* up, too."

He slit Blackhand's throat, then. It happened almost in slow motion. One moment they were all glowering at each other, Blackhand wide-eyed and tense as iron like he knew exactly what was coming. And then Sulfane brought down the knife, and that one exquisite moment flash-burned into Fings' memory: seeing Blackhand's face right before the edge bit, the change in it, the shock, the sudden realisation that this was really happening, that look of wild, mad fury and fear and then everywhere was blood.

Fings gagged. Blackhand thrashed in his chair as the blood poured out of him. Finally, he slumped still. Sulfane brought the knife to Fings' throat.

"Where's my crown, thief?'

36

THE SPEAKER FOR THE DEAD

Seth wondered, sometimes, whether anyone had felt it when he'd given the dead Spicer in Locusteater Yard a tongue. Had the priests all suddenly woken as one in temples around the city, filled with a deep sense of dread? Had someone in the cathedral rolled their eyes and thought: *There he is, that Seth fellow, at it again, menace that he is*? He pondered asking the moon-priestess as she went about her business with Arjay. He saw the subtle glances sent his way and couldn't work them out. Was she planning to seduce him? Fat chance of that. Murder him, then? But moon-priestesses abhorred violence.

He didn't know. Did it matter? Maybe she knew who he was and it was simply the idle gawking of a young priestess faced by someone who'd managed to commit the worst heresy imaginable.

Probably that.

She was there when he got back from wasting his time in Tombland. He could feel her presence as soon as he entered the Pig, a vaguely uncomfortable itch that he could never pin down. Perhaps it was the same for her and that was why she kept looking at him, and he thought maybe he *should* ask; and then it dawned on him that something was very wrong because the inside of the Pig was colder than usual, and there was a breeze even though he'd closed the door behind him.

One of the windows had been smashed.

He ran upstairs. A Spicer lay dead on the hall floor with a cleaver from the kitchen buried in his head.

"Fings? Fings! Dox! Arjay?"

He stopped, stilled by a sense of movement. The priestess was standing in the hall outside Arjay's room. She hadn't been there a second ago.

"I know what you're going to do," she said.

Dox, white as a sheet and clutching his side and gritting his teeth, shoved her out of the way. He looked Seth up and down and shook his head.

"Where's Fings?" asked Seth.

"They came for him. He ran. Don't know if he got away."

"They? Who?"

"Spicers."

"And you don't know what happened to him?"

Dox only shook his head and limped back to Arjay's room.

The priestess was still there, still staring.

"*What?*"

"I know what you're going to do," she said again. And then she followed Dox and closed the door behind her, and Seth was left alone in the hall with a dead man.

Fine.

Be like that.

He wasn't a brave man. He knew that. He wasn't strong and he wasn't fast and he wasn't nimble. Most of the Unrulys, if anyone had bothered to ask, would probably have said he was a coward, but he liked to think they were wrong about that. He grabbed the dead Spicer by an ankle and hauled him down the stairs, listening to the *bump bump bump* of the dead man's head on the steps.

No fear for consequence. He'd read that somewhere. Something to do with a war and some famous general, or some hero like Kelm the Magnificent. He had a vague notion of a story that had had dragons in it.

He drew out the same sigil he'd used all those years ago on the rat, and slapped it onto the dead Spicer's face.

"You're going to tell me where you took my friend," he said to the Dead Man, "and then you and I are going to get him back.'

Nothing brings bad luck like a mage.
– Fings

37

THE SWORD-MONKS

Orien was still shaking when they reached the next waystation. Myla sold their stolen horses for a fraction of what they were worth and bartered for a boatman to take them down the river through the night, hoping the soldiers from the bridge wouldn't expect her to double back towards Deephaven and the City of Spires. Around midnight, they reached the waystation where Fings had stolen the Emperor's crown. Orien, by then, was sound asleep and she had to carry him to bed. In the morning, she looked for a barge to take them to Varr, only to find they were snowed in and no one was heading upriver until the roads were clear. So they waited, staying close, sitting outside in the cold if they had to, always one of them watching the river in case the soldiers from under the bridge came after them, but they never did.

"Why would they, when we don't have what they want?" asked Orien. A solid day of sleep and the mage was himself again.

Revenge for the one she'd crippled and the one she'd killed? Maybe it would be as simple as that. That and they probably didn't believe her that the crown had already gone.

"Did someone really did get there before us?" Orien asked again, much later.

"You think I came out here for the fun of it?"

"I think you just like having me around."

"Well… I *do* enjoy watching you suffer." Myla sighed. "When we get back to Varr, I have an idea who took it. I'll find him and you'll get what you want. Then you can go your way and I'll go mine."

And what way was that? The same old question: stay in Varr, a hired sword for Blackhand or some other man just like him? But no. Jeffa Hawat knew she was alive. She couldn't ignore that.

It took two days of clear sky and bitter cold before the roads were cleared and the river traffic resumed. At the dockside in Varr, she and Orien went their separate ways, Orien to light lamps in the palace or whatever it was he did in his spare time, Myla to find Fings and wring his bloody neck. By the time she reached the Teahouse, she was so lost in thoughts of what she was going to say to him that she never saw Seth step out of the alley until he'd grabbed her arm and started to drag her into the shadows. Instantly, her hand had a knife in it. She shook herself free, angry.

"I might have taken your head off!"

Seth snorted. "It's getting to be a daily hazard."

"Where's Fings? I need to talk to him. Now!"

"You were supposed to be back days ago." Something in Seth had changed. He had a grit to him she didn't remember. Whenever his eyes met hers, usually they shied away, but not today.

"Weather. Where's Fings?"

"He fucked up."

"Yes, he certainly did!" Myla forced herself to pause, to regain her balance and centre. She took a long look at Seth's face. Something was different.

"Why, what do *you* think he's done?" Seth asked.

"You know where I've been and why?"

He nodded.

"Well it's not there."

"And you think Fings took it?" Seth pursed his lips, giving it some thought. He didn't seem surprised. "It *would* be a Fings thing to do. Right. Well. It gets worse."

He told her then how he and Fings had discovered Blackhand was in Tombland, how Seth had gone to meet the Spicers and how the Spicers had come for Fings while Seth had been standing on the Bridge of Questions, freezing his nuts. No one had seen Fings since, and Seth had been busy, it turned out, because he knew where the Spicers were hiding, who they were with and how many they were. All the time as he talked, he dragged her through the streets; and when he was done with Fings' tale of woe, he showered her with stories of underground tunnels and buried chambers and unburned corpses, and of some ancient Sunbright who'd been buried for heresy; and then the history of Tombland and the story of the Mage who once lived there, and how Blackhand had murdered him. It was a lot to take in.

"There's someone in Tombland who hasn't forgotten what Blackhand did," he said as they crossed Spice Market Square. "They seem to have joined with this lot from Deephaven, fuck knows why. I don't know what the crown has to do with any of this." He shrugged. "Maybe it doesn't."

He dragged her through the bustle of the Spice Market and paid for two cups of hot, spiced wine, and *that* was something new, too, because the Seth she remembered never had two half-bits to rub together and never paid for anything if he could help it.

Myla looked at him askance. "Something on your mind?" she asked.

Seth nodded, and then looked her in the eye. "You can do that sword-monk thing, right? Where you know when someone is lying?"

Myla cocked her head.

"I'm glad you're here. I fucked up and I wish I hadn't done it."

"I don't know what you mean."

He kept looking straight at her. When she didn't say anything more, he pulled something out of his coat. The papers from the barge.

Myla gripped his arm. "I told you to burn those!"

"Do you know what they are?"

"I barely looked."

Seth pushed the papers back inside his coat. It was a nice coat. Nicer than the rags he usually wore, anyway, if a little big for him. "Path stuff. I thought you might have recognised it."

"I was a sword-monk, not a theologian."

"Yes." She could almost see his thoughts labouring up a steep incline. "But I'm thinking they taught you more than all those clever sword tricks, because they certainly taught us novices more than how to read and write, and one thing I started to notice before they threw me out was that on *some* things, priests and sword-monks don't seem to quite agree."

Myla tried to remember ever seeing something like that and found she couldn't. She said so, and then Seth told her about the sigils that even the novices learned for setting Dead Men to rest.

"Did *you* ever learn any sigils?"

"No." She thought about that. "But... the senior sword-monks have symbols tattooed on their skin. Some have many. I don't know if they are the same thing."

She hesitated, remembering. She'd grown up knowing the Dead Men were real, of course, not like Fings' goblins... but they'd never been a part of her world until she was six years old, and then the Dead Men suddenly came to Deephaven. For a long time there simply hadn't been any at all, and now they'd started to appear again. She'd lost a friend. It was a part of why she'd become who she was.

"We had a warlock in Deephaven once," she said. "A rogue mage who could make the dead speak. My mistress fought him. I was a child when it happened but she was famous for it. I... I think there was some dispute between her and the priests because of something he did. The warlock, I mean. She accused a Sunbright of conspiring with him. Or something like that. Other than that..." But it *was* odd, now she thought about it, because the year Tasahre had fought the warlock was the year the Dead Men had returned.

Seth was watching her intently. "I was thinking differences in doctrine," he said. "But... This warlock who could make the dead speak? You're sure about that?"

"I'm sure it's what I heard. What do you mean by differences in doctrine?"

"Other than the sigils? I don't know. I was hoping *you* could tell *me*." A series of expressions flashed over his face: curiosity, bewilderment, wonder, suspicion, distaste, fear, hope, ending with a grimace of something unpalatable. "Have you ever had anything to do with the sword-monks in Varr?"

"No. I thought there were only a handful here, all north of the river." History firmly placed the sword-monks alongside the Torpreahns as people viewed with great suspicion by the Emperor's court. There had been rumours for as long as she could remember that it had been a band of sword-monks in disguise who'd ambushed the Sad Empress on the road and murdered her.

"You don't see them much but they're here. I was..." Seth grunted, then let out a long sigh. "I have a favour to ask." He tapped his coat. "I need to talk to a sword-monk about what Fings found in that barge. That crown... It's not what matters. There's something else going on. I don't know if the Temple might be involved but... And I'd go to a priest, but the last one had two of the Sunguard hold me down while he pissed in my face. A monk might listen or a monk might simply kill me. I thought... I thought you might make sure they opted for listening rather than stabbing."

"But Fings–"

"Are we good?" he asked, suddenly.

Myla tried to imagine why he'd even ask something like that. "You're not the one who sent me running off into the snow and ice with soldiers on my tail chasing after something you knew wasn't even there."

Seth pursed his lips.

"I'm not about to chop you up, if that's what's bothering you."

"Was a bit, if I'm honest."

"Kelm's Teeth! What do you think I am?"

Seth shrugged. "I don't really know. I suppose that's partly the problem."

Myla had no idea what to say to that, so she waited. Eventually, Seth turned away.

"Fings went after Blackhand and got caught. They're holding him in Tombland. I can show you exactly where. There are men from Deephaven. Sell-swords and someone with a lot of money. I'm guessing you know more about that than I do."

Myla nodded.

"Fings says you want to give it all back." He laughed, and Myla realised she'd never seen Seth laugh until now, not without a self-mocking twist. "You should have seen his face! But I agree. I want to give the crown to the sword-monks. These papers, too. Something is rotten under all this. *Is* it true that a sword-monk can smell a lie?"

Myla smiled at that. "That depends on the sword-monk, and on the lie, and on the liar."

"Imagine Blackhand's face if you could..." They both laughed. "Will you come with me? To the temple?"

"Now?"

"I won't get through the doors without you. Do this and then we can worry about Fings."

Myla wasn't sure that she was *worrying* about Fings. He'd sent her on a wild goose chase. She'd killed a man because of it, and made another into a cripple. Maybe she'd killed all six, if they hadn't been able to get back to shelter before nightfall. So if she was *worrying*, it was mostly about whether he'd stay alive long enough for her to throttle him.

We left a horse for the cripple. It wasn't too far to walk. It's not like they could get lost. And why should she even care? They'd chosen their path, and they certainly would have killed her and Orien without thinking twice, and without the slightest worry about whether they'd done the right thing...

But she *did* care.

She turned to face the temple steps. The two Sunguard sentries were already watching. She started towards them and drew her swords, the two Sunsteel blades of a sword-monk. That got their full attention.

"I need to speak with my brothers and sisters."

They'd know who she was, of course, the crazy sword-monk who'd taken up with the Unruly Pig, which made her about as holy as dog shit, and no surprise she was standing next to a heretic. But Sunsteel swords weren't given lightly. They had an authority of their own. A true sword-monk could draw her blades and know that their mere presence would always be enough.

One of the Sunguard pointed at Seth. "Enter freely. But not him."

"I need him." There was a voice to being a sword-monk, too. An authority. She'd almost forgotten but here it was, coming out of her.

The Sunguard shifted and exchanged some unhappy glances, then one of them ran into the temple. A few minutes later, he returned, two sword-monks following behind.

"I'm here for my brothers and sisters of the blade and no one else," snapped Myla. "If your Dawncaller is here, she may listen to what I have to say. Otherwise leave." No one ever said sword-monks were good at making friends. Diplomacy was for priests. Monks were for when priests failed.

The Sunguard bristled, then stalked reluctantly back into the temple. Myla sheathed her swords and bowed to the two monks.

"I am Shirish of Deephaven," she said. "My mistress was Tasahre the Scarred." There was a good chance they'd heard of Tasahre. It was *also* possible, mind, that they'd heard of Shirish of Deephaven, which could be a good or bad thing, depending on whether what they'd heard included the whole business of her stabbing the Hawat heir in the testicles and then allegedly dying in a fire.

The monks started towards her. They came slowly, like stalking cats.

"I'm... not so sure about this," murmured Seth.

"You wanted monks," hissed Myla, also not liking the way this was going. "Tell them whatever you need to tell them, and do it quickly."

Seth pulled one of the sheets from the barge out of his coat, put it on the temple steps, weighted it with a stone and then backed away. He cleared his throat and then started talking, loud and fast. "A few weeks ago, a thief from Varr stole something," he said.

"Something so valuable that I think you might know what I'm talking about. I had nothing to do with that theft, but the thief took this, too. Idiot can't even read but he thought it might be worth something, and it is, and I think you need to see it. I think *you* need to see it. Not the Lightbringers or the Sunbrights or even the Dawncaller. You'll know what it is. It's where it was found that matters." He stepped back and took Myla's arm and tugged her gently away. "That'll do it. Time to go."

Myla didn't move. "I thought you wanted their help to get Fings."

"Nothing I'd like more than taking a pair of sword-monks into Tombland but it's not going to happen." Seth kept tugging and this time Myla let him pull her. With each step back, the monks advanced, holding their distance. "Are you sure you didn't look at them before you dropped them in my lap?"

"I *told* you!" Something in his voice sounded urgent but she didn't dare take her eyes off the monks.

"They're sigils, Myla. Like the sign we used to still the Dead Men, only different." Step. "They do different things." Step. "What happened to that warlock you mentioned?" Step.

"He was driven away." Step.

"Any idea where he went?" Step.

"No." The first monk reached the sheet Seth had left on the steps. She crouched, feeling for it, never taking her eyes off Myla until she had it.

"The sigil she's looking at now tells you how to make a dead man talk."

"You *what*?"

"Scribble it out, slap it down on a fresh corpse and they'll talk to you. That's fucking what."

Myla felt the blood drain out of her. Mistress Tasahre had always been very, *very* clear. A monk might tolerate many things, but a monk could not suffer a warlock to live.

"And how do you know that?"

The monk looked at the paper. Her eyes snapped back, this time to Seth, hand already at her belt and flinging something at him. Myla pushed him hard, lurching the other way. The knife flew between them. Behind, in the market, someone screamed.

"*Run!*"

The other monk was already in the air, leaping for Seth, swords drawn, and no one outran a sword-monk. Myla threw herself in the way and barged into the monk, knocking him sideways; then she had her own swords drawn, and lunged and almost caught him. He leaped and rolled and almost lost his balance before he sprang to his feet. She'd surprised him: no one ever fought back against a sword-monk.

Seth had gone, vanished into the crowd. The monks both had their swords drawn now. Myla backed away. She bowed. "He's not worth–"

The first came at her, weaving his swords in the familiar Sky Strikes the Earth form. Myla countered with the Leaping Horse but he was stronger than her and at least as fast and his form was better, and it was like fighting her old teacher, only *this* monk meant to kill her. Then the other came at her too, another pattern she knew, the Divided Kingdom. She blocked and dodged a flurry of blows and then a Wind of Heaven sent one sword flying, and the next thing she knew she was crashing to the ground, flat on her back, a sword coming at her throat and–

The blade stopped an inch from her skin.

The monk leaned over Myla, holding her blade steady. "Is your Mistress truly Tasahre the Scarred?"

Myla nodded.

"Speak so I know the truth of you."

"Yes. Tasahre of Deephaven."

"And are you here in our city on her purpose?"

Myla closed her eyes. "No."

"Then we will take your swords and return them to her. They are not yours. You know this. Such steel is only ever borrowed for our holy purpose." The monk's sword point hovered an inch from Myla's eye. "Is it true, what the Lightbringers say of you? That you consort with criminals as well as this heretic. That you are a killer and a murderer?"

Myla took a deep breath. "I've killed men, yes. But I'm not a murderer."

Wasn't she? What was the right word then, when you took a man's head from his shoulders when he was already beaten? When you left five others, one of them crippled, to freeze to death with only two horses between them to take them to safety?

"I am not a murderer," she said again, mostly to try and make herself believe it.

"The apostate. Were all his words true?"

"As far as I can know, yes."

The monk nodded, straightened and sheathed her sword. "You are not one of us, Shirish of Deephaven, not in this city. Return to your Mistress. Your fate will be for her to decide. Or don't, and be nothing."

38

SULFANE

"It's a pity," said Sulfane, when Fings' screaming died away to whimpers. "I always sort of liked you. Out of all of them, you were the most honest of the lot."

The man who'd been pushing slivers of glass under Fings' toenails took a deep breath and stepped away. The glass stayed where it was.

"Blackhand? Lying, murdering traitor. Would sell you into slavery without so much as blinking if there was money to be made. All-round dishonest pig-fucker. Not that you didn't already know that." Sulfane dragged his chair closer, close enough to grab Fings' face and force him to meet his eye. "Come on, Fings. Give me what I want and it'll all be over. I might even let you go."

"I don't—"

"Ah-ah! Don't say it. You *know* what happens when you tell lies. Give yourself a break, eh? If not for yourself, think of my poor man with his bits of glass. You've worn him out, Fings." Sulfane leaned close, whispering right into Fings' ear. "Who's going to come for you? Your friend Seth? Not really the sort, is he? Myla? Oh, but you sent her off into a proper winter storm, and I happened to notice six Torpreahn mercenaries follow her. I mean, thank you for getting them off my back and all that, and I *do* hope she properly fucks them up after their mage-friend tried to kill me, but is she *that* good, Fings? Six against one? And if she *is*, and she *does* come back, do you think she's going to *help* you after what you've done? We both know the crown isn't there."

He backed away.

"Where is it, Fings?"

"I don't–"

"Do you remember the last time you came into Tombland? You and Seth and Wil and Sand and Rev and Blackhand?"

Fings didn't say anything. Of course he remembered. The day Blackhand betrayed the Mage.

"You ever hear of a place called Valladrune, Fings?"

When Fings nodded, Sulfane cocked his head in surprise.

"You have? Now *there's* a thing. Was it Seth? I bet *he* knows, but why would he be talking to *you* about Valladrune?" The Murdering Bastard seemed to struggle with this for a few seconds and then gave up. "Did he tell you what happened there?"

Fings nodded.

"*Some* of us got away. I say *us*, but of course I wasn't born yet. Seth told you what they did, did he? But did he tell you why? Maybe he doesn't know?"

Fings shook his head.

"Because there were mages in Valladrune. Only a handful, but they had power. And Khrozus spent time there with them before the war. *Right* before the war, if you catch my drift. They did something for him, something he needed to keep secret so badly that he decided to make an entire city disappear. That's what this is about, Fings. Revenge for something that happened before either of us was ever even born."

"Why…" It was hard to concentrate. The pain from his toes was a screaming thing in his ears, blinding knives in his head.

"Why you? Why Blackhand? Because *some*one needed to take the blame, Fings, and it sure as fuck wasn't going to be me!" Sulfane stared into him and then shook his head. "You're still not seeing it, are you? The Mage of Tombland. He was from Valladrune. He was the one that got away."

"The mage is dead…" Wasn't he? Maybe he wasn't. Fings didn't know for sure. He didn't know *any*thing for sure, or that's what he kept telling himself, and Sulfane as well whenever the questions started. Maybe the Mage of Tombland *wasn't* dead. *Some*one had killed Sand and Rev, after all.

"You were there that night they murdered him," said Sulfane. "So was I. He'd fathered a good few bastards by the time Blackhand cut him down, but I'm the closest thing that fucker ever had to an heir."

"I... didn't have no part in it!"

"No. That you didn't."

"So this is all... revenge?"

"What?" Sulfane snorted with derision. "Fuck's sake! Don't be dim, Fings. All that effort when I could have murdered Blackhand whenever I fancied? But setting him up to take the fall... You have to admit, it would have been sweet if those Torpreahn fuckers hadn't doublecrossed me. They get their crown, I get rich, and the only thread left to pull leads the Guild of Mages and the Imperial Guard straight to Blackhand." He let out a long sigh, shifted his chair back to lean against the wall and beckoned to the torturer with his slivers of glass. "Ah, well. Wasn't to be. Fings, where's my fucking crown?"

39

LIGHTBRINGER

Back when he'd been a novice, Seth had asked Fings how he managed to sneak into the temple. Fings had tapped the side of his nose and smirked something about professional secrets; but years later, when Seth wasn't a novice anymore and the two of them had been planning to sneak in and steal everything that wasn't nailed down, Fings had shown him how it was done. An alley ran behind the temple. On the other side was a warehouse with a broken door that no one ever used. From there you could get to the roof, which was just the right level for the tiny shuttered windows along the back of the temple where the servants lived. Fings had showed Seth how to tell which rooms were empty and how the shutters on the windows didn't fit properly, so you could slide a thin blade between them and lift the latch on the inside, and *that* was how he used to get in and out without anyone ever knowing.

They never did burgle the temple. Fings had been all up for it, revenge for kicking Seth out, but Seth had baulked. The Path was his home, his friends, his family. He didn't really understand it then, what they'd ripped out of him. He'd still thought they might relent and take him back.

And how fucking stupid was that?

He watched as the monks took Myla's swords. He'd gone to the temple to show them how someone at the heart of the Empire was following the path of the heretic Sivingathm. He'd been trying to do the right thing. They'd stripped him of everything and yet here he was, still was trying to be a good servant of the path, and for that, two monks had tried to kill him.

Myla had stopped them. Myla whom he'd betrayed to the Spicers and the man from Deephaven. Now the Path was taking away who she was, just as it had once done to him.

He watched them carry Myla's swords into the temple. He watched Myla walk away and not look back. He should go after her, he knew, thank her, tell her how grateful he was, tell her he knew how it felt to be stripped naked and have everything taken away, but he couldn't. How could he? It was *his* fault, after all.

At least she can't chop your head off now for selling her to the Spicers.

Fuck off.

He was never going back. Months and months and it had never truly sunk in. All this time and some stupid part of him had never given up hope of forgiveness.

Did they smell it on him? Making the dead talk? There'd be money in that, good money, but that wasn't why he'd done it. In Locusteater Yard it had been to know whether the only decent person he'd ever met already knew he'd betrayed her. In the Pig it had been because the Spicers had taken Fings, and Fings was his brother, the last shred of anything that felt like family.

My fault.

All. My. Fault.

They'd taken Myla's swords. Myla, who'd never looked at him like the others did, with all their scorn and pity. She hardly knew him and yet she'd stood for him when he'd asked her for help, and how much of a hypocrite was he for *that* when he was the one who'd sold her out to that sneering oaf from Deephaven. Yes, he could tell himself all he liked that Blackhand had had it coming, that the rest of them were just unfortunate collateral damage, but the candle in Myla's window...?

Go on, justify that, you fucking insect.

She'd stood beside him when he'd tried for once in his life to do the right thing, and what had that got her?

He was never going back. Not even if they begged.

He stood in the crowds of the Spice Market for a long time, staring at the temple, and then he went home. Not to the Pig in case the sword-monks came looking for him, because they must know that was where to find him. Not to Locusteater Yard, which was the first home where he'd ever felt welcome. No, he went under the ground, to where the dead Spicer with a cleaver stuck in his head was waiting, full of everything he knew about Tombland and how Sulfane was still alive. He hid like a fucking coward and read the other sheets Myla had given him over and over, not because he hadn't already memorised them days ago but because it was something to fill the hours; except it didn't, and all he could do was stare at the pit of ash and piss that was his life until something finally broke inside, until suddenly he'd had enough, until in the depths-of-the-night dark, he went back to the Spice Market with his dead Spicer trailing along like an obedient dog, went to the alley behind the temple, into the warehouse with its broken door, climbed the roof and did what Fings had said, looking for the shutters that didn't show a glow of candlelight.

Never. Going. Back.

"I'll just borrow this," he said, and pulled the cleaver out the dead Spicer's head. It was a good enough blade for Fings' shutter-opening trick. He knew where they'd keep Myla's swords. The monks would give them to the duty Sunbright to be returned to Myla's temple in Deephaven. The duty Sunbright would keep them in his office until a courier was available.

He padded through the temple halls and stopped outside the office door. He listened for a moment to the stillness of the temple, then knocked. The Sunbright had a room of his own up high. Down here, at night, a Lightbringer slept in the office.

No answer.

He tried a little louder.

He pressed his ear to the door and heard movement. A muttering. A creak of boards.

He knocked again. "Lightbringer!"

"Who is it?"

He knew that voice. Lightbringer Suaresh. For one wild moment, Seth almost answered with the honest truth, if only to see what would happen. *It's me, Seth the heretic, with a Dead Man I brought back with a forbidden sigil. Would you like to see?*

"There's a Dead Man, Lightbringer," he said instead. He hadn't thought this through at all. In his head, there was going to be some sort of scuffle, a Lightbringer and the dead Spicer, and Seth would slip in without being seen and steal the swords and slip away again and no one would be any the wiser. Except that that very obviously wasn't going to work, now that he was here.

So that then?

Footsteps towards the door. "Who's there?"

Fuck. Fuck, fuck!

Seth slipped out of sight as the door opened. Suaresh stepped out, looked to his right and saw the dead Spicer, standing there, the silhouette of a man in the dark.

Can't you sense a Dead Man when he's right in front of you, Lightbringer? I'm told the sword-monks can.

"Lightbringer," he whispered. *Fuck!*

Suaresh spun around. Seth let him have a moment of recognition, then grabbed his hand and slapped a sigil onto it. Suaresh stared at him, eyes wide, then at the sigil, then at his hand as the paper burned away and the sigil became a mark on his skin.

"Be quiet and stay very still," whispered Seth. *What have I done?*

Lightbringer Suaresh stayed quiet and stood very still. Seth pushed past into the office beyond. *Fuck! Fuck! What have I done?*

Myla's swords were on the table by the window, gleaming in the moonlight. He took a moment to admire them, then wrapped them in a blanket, the picked them up, surprised at how light they were.

At least it was someone who deserved it.

Outside in the hall, Suaresh hadn't moved. Seth took a long hard look at him. Lightbringer Suaresh. The man who'd taken a piss on his face while the Sunguard held him to the ground. Maybe he *did* deserve it.

"What I left for the monks was one page out of six, Lightbringer. That one was a sigil to end the silence of the dead. The one burned onto your hand ends the will of the living. Best I can tell, sigils last until the light of the Sun burns away the mark. So come dawn, you'll be fine. You'll remember all this, of course. And then I suppose you'll be angry and send some sword-monks to come after me."

He stood in the dark, locked in the memory of crawling on his hands and knees in the middle of Spice Market Square, soaked in piss. Of the first stone hitting him.

"These sigils?" He lifted two other pieces of paper. "This sigil ends life, and this one ends the stillness of the dead. Somewhere out there, if the heretic Sivingathm is correct, is a whole Book of Endings, with a sigil for anything you care to mention, provided it will end something. Someone has been collecting them. I came to warn you all. But..."

No.

"I didn't come here to hurt anyone."

Never. Coming. Back.

"If it had been anyone else, Lightbringer. Anyone at all... But here you are. And I can't have you coming after me. Not now. Not with everything else. I really can't."

He lifted the first sigil and touched it to Lightbringer Suaresh's cheek.

"End, Lightbringer. End for me."

He watched the sigil burn into skin. He watched Suaresh's eyes until he saw the light go out, then touched the next sigil to Suaresh's other cheek and kissed him on the forehead.

"I promise you this, Suaresh: you're going to be a lot more useful in death than you ever were in life."

40

SACRİFİCE

The moon-priestess was upstairs with Dox, a slight roll of the eyes her only recognition that she'd just about finished fixing Arjay and now here was another idiot with a hole in them. Arjay was in the commons, setting things straight. Myla sat in the kitchens, thoughts wandering from Sarwatta to Blackhand to the men she'd killed. To Soraya, and to Lucius, the only one who seemed to understand what a terrible mistake it had been, how angry she'd felt, how she'd never meant it to happen. To the loss of her swords, the good she'd done with them and the harm. To the day Tasahre had given them to her because of what she'd done, the *other* thing, before Sarwatta. There had been pride in Tasahre's face that day. Myla didn't suppose there would be much pride there now.

They are symbols, no more. It is we who give them meaning by our actions.

And what meaning had *she* given them? Perhaps it was right that she didn't carry them anymore.

She reached for the Sun-mantras that the monks had taught her and let them blow through like a wind, emptying herself of thoughts and feelings. She closed her eyes until she could hear her heartbeat and smell the smoke and the spices trapped in the wooden walls. She and Tasahre would sit together in silence like this at the end of a day sometimes, watching the sunset. Tasahre would tell her to find a stillness and seek within it a perfect balance, and for a while neither of them would move, and then they would fight one last time until speed and strength failed. Myla imagined those fights to be beautiful, more graceful than any dance, more powerful than any drama. She felt herself flying, watching herself and the sword-mistress below moving in the perfect harmony of a single being.

Was Tasahre still in Deephaven? Myla hadn't been to see her before she'd fled; but even towards the end, she'd felt her mistress pushing her away. *Your technique is excellent. Your feet are swift and educated to perfection but your mind is always busy. Let the forms choose themselves and mingle as they wish. With the mind comes thought. With thoughts come questions. With questions comes hesitation, and with hesitation comes failure. Once blades are drawn, the time for thought is past. Place your mind elsewhere and leave only the spirit, or you will die.*

She hadn't done much thinking before she'd stabbed Sarwatta, but that probably wasn't what Tasahre had meant, and so it probably *was* for the best that the monks had taken her swords. Not that they'd ever been *her* swords in the first place, for a sword-monk's blades were never owned, only borrowed. They would find their way to someone better.

In the distance, she heard thumping on a door. She ignored it and took herself back to sitting cross-legged, eyes closed, to the fighting-room in Deephaven, bare walls, bare floor, bare sky...

"There's a priest here for you." Arjay was at the kitchen door.

Myla went out to see what more they wanted from her, but it was only Orien, dressed in his orange robes.

"Priest?" She raised an eyebrow. Arjay looked dubious. A hand rested on her club.

"Of the Divine Fire," smiled Orien, barging past. "Blessings upon you, child of the Light."

"Divine Fire? Divine Wind, more like," said Myla. She caught the look on Arjay's face and added quickly: "But he's a friend."

She led Orien upstairs to Blackhand's study, away from prying ears. She told him that if anyone knew where the crown was hidden, it would be Fings, and then what Seth had told her about who was holding him and where. The cold certainty she'd felt out in the snow under the bridge had gone. Fings and his goblins? Maybe, but maybe Wil and Blackhand had conspired and sent someone else, or maybe Sulfane had had friends, or maybe some complete stranger had watched them bury something in the snow and gone to see what it was...

It didn't matter. In a way, the loss of her swords sealed her decision, that and the knowledge Seth had given her that the Spicers and Jeffa were somehow allied. She'd help Fings. She'd do what she could to undo what they'd done. If she were somehow still alive by the end, she'd go back to Deephaven and face the punishment she deserved.

And because of all those things, she listened to Orien talk for a while, and then shut him up by kissing him, and let him stay the night, in part because she didn't want to be alone, in part because she wasn't sure she'd still be alive come Midwinter, in part because he was there and because she had no illusions about what would happen when she went back to Deephaven, and in part because the Pig was very cold, and he *was* a fire-mage.

He grinned when she told him that, but there was no grinning from him on the next morning when she told him what she wanted from him. She listened to his protests and then ignored them: he'd either do what she asked or he wouldn't, and if he didn't, well, then she'd probably die. When she'd had enough of him railing and protesting, she walked away and let him follow, if he could be bothered. Turned out that he could, across half of Varr at that, shouting that she was stupid and stubborn and pig-headed, the last two of which she had to agree were true. It was flattering, in its way, how hard he tried. Eventually he stormed off, telling her that she was on her own and to expect no help if *this* was how she was going to be. The more she thought about it, the more she smiled. She *was* stubborn and pig-headed, and had there ever been a sword-monk who wasn't? And Orien would get angry and make a huge fuss, do what she'd asked and then get angry again when it was done, because what else could you expect from a fire-mage?

In Locusteater Yard, no one had seen Fings' family since that night when two Spicers had been found dead in the snow. She went back to the Pig and bothered Arjay into finding a set of lockpicks. Lucky, maybe, that Arjay happened to know where to find something like that, but Fings had always been lucky.

Until now.

She touched her throat. The charm he'd given her was still there. Either she'd grown used to the smell, or it wasn't as pungent as when he'd given it to her.

Not that it did me much good.

It was a simple plan, really: she was going to Tombland. She was going to hand herself over to the Spicers, let them hold her hostage while Fings went to get the crown from wherever he'd hidden it and bring it back. The Spicers might not much like the idea but Jeffa Hawat wouldn't be able to resist having her in his power. As soon as the crown, the Spicers and Jeffa Hawat were all in the same place, Orien would see to it that the Guild of Mages fell on Tombland like a hammer. The picks and the blade were in case anything went wrong. She'd slip them to Fings either way. Fings being Fings, he'd find a way out.

She went to her room and hid what possessions she had left under a board. Her last few ties to her old life in Deephaven. The Spicers would strip her of everything worth more than a half-bit when they took her. No point losing more than she had to.

And when it was all over and done, after the dust settled and if she was still alive, she *was* going back to Deephaven, however it ended. She'd go back and she'd face Lucius and Soraya and Sarwatta and face whatever was coming. She wasn't quite sure what had finally tipped her mind that way. She'd been *thinking* about it ever since that night with the Dead Men, but somehow it had changed from an idea into an inevitability. And while losing her swords had given her an unexpected clarity, the real reason lay somewhere between Fings and Seth, somewhere between their hopes and their desperation and their casual betrayals. They had an air to them, she thought, an air of inevitable disappointment, as though they knew that, no matter how hard they strived, no matter how far they climbed, they would always find a way to undo themselves.

She needed to be better than that. The Hawats knew she wasn't dead. If they couldn't punish *her*, Jeffa had made it clear they'd punish her family instead. *Someone* had to suffer for what she'd done; and she could hardly pass that burden to another, no matter how it scared her to carry it herself. And it *did* scare her.

The Longcoat Roads were mostly clear now, the alleys and sidestreets more pot-luck. She told Dox and Arjay to stay away and thought they probably would – Dox was in no state to start any trouble and Arjay still had a moon-priestess's stitches in her. Seth… She had no idea where he was, but Seth would stay away because there really wasn't anything he could do. She had a last look around in case someone had left a bottle of wine lying around that she could drink on the way, but they hadn't. Pity. There probably wasn't going to be any wine after today.

Arjay caught her on the way out.

"Thank you," she said.

Myla wasn't sure what she'd ever done for Arjay – or any of them, for that matter – except bring trouble.

"The moon-priestess," said Arjay. "We don't have any money but she keeps coming back. She says it's because of you."

"Why?" Myla asked, bewildered. "What did I ever do?"

It was Arjay's turn to shrug. "I don't know. Whatever it was, thank you."

There was the thing in Deephaven that had earned her her swords, but they couldn't possibly have heard of that here. Probably some other sword-monk. Some debt to the Path of the Sun Myla would never know about, its repayment hopelessly misplaced.

She walked out, heading with eyes wide open to the sharp end of a knife.

41

DEAD MEN

Seth teetered on the brink of an icy ridge, sheer drops falling away on both sides into murky depths. Lightning burst back and forth across a sky turned dark by churning cloud, errant bolts striking the ice, blasting chunks into the abyss below. The winds tore at his clothes, almost lifting him off his feet. As he watched, the clouds twisted into faces: one jagged and inhuman, the other a mockery of a woman.

He ought to be terrified, he thought, but he wasn't. Quite the opposite. In his hands, he held a book. He touched it and the book responded, opening to pages as though it knew his thoughts. The pages glowed in his hands, the sigils offering themselves to him.

Sigils for ending gods.

When Seth opened his eyes, he didn't much like what they told him. He closed them again and counted to five in case they could be convinced to tell him something else, but the view steadfastly refused to go away. He was standing by the south shore of the Arr, at the far eastern edge of the city, staring across the freezing waters at the Imperial Gate. The sun was creeping over the horizon and priests would be gathering for dawn prayers. Right about now, someone in the Spice Market temple would be scratching their head and wondering: *Where's Lightbringer Suaresh? Not like him to miss dawn prayer…*

It wasn't that he had anything *against* being by the river shore. Nice place, sometimes, especially in winter when the river didn't stink. No, it was more that he had no idea how he'd gotten there or what had happened for the last few hours of the night.

He looked around. Footprints led back into the snow, so at least he hadn't appeared out of thin air. They led back into an alley he didn't recognise. To his left, Lightbringer Suaresh stood patiently beside him. The Lightbringer's expression was empty.

It occurred to him that he was a murderer, now. He hadn't thought about it at the time, how turning Suaresh into a shambling mindless zombie-thing had included, as its first step, actually killing him. Last night, he'd just done it. This morning, he found he didn't feel as comfortable about that as he'd hoped.

Well. They certainly won't take me back now.

He decided to stop looking at Suaresh and looked the other way instead, and then rather wished he hadn't. The Spicer with the cleaver stuck in his head grinned back at him. Seth didn't remember returning the cleaver and couldn't imagine why the dead Spicer had decided to put it back where it came from, but that really wasn't the biggest issue right now, because next to the dead Spicer was a skeleton. It was standing up, stiff and straight and looking bored, insofar as skeletons could look anything at all.

Oh. Right. That.

Now he thought about it, he *did* remember going back to the catacombs and the three dead skeletons, two of which weren't anything more than dust and old bones from the last time he'd been there, but the third... He'd only put two of the three to rest and so he'd summoned the last one back, mostly to see what happened. If he was honest, he hadn't really expected much, not with bones that were older than the city. Certainly not for the skeleton to suddenly move and get up and wave its arms and legs and walk around and start following him everywhere.

He had a moment of panic then, but they were a good way from the docks and no one was staring and pointing and yelling. Which was just as well: panicked citizens jabbering about walking skeletons would probably summon every sword-monk in Varr quicker than you could snap your fingers.

It *was* going to be a problem if this thing decided to keep following him.

"I think you'd best go back," he said, tempting as it was to send Lightbringer Suaresh home to his temple with an animated skeleton in tow just to see what happened.

Thing was, he *did* remember going back to the vault but not how he'd ended up *here*. He remembered the skeleton had moved and... *looked* at him, insofar as a pair of empty eye-sockets could look at anything. It had cocked its head, as if asking what Seth wanted and why was he bothering it. He'd used the speaking sigil but it had turned out that he was right and it didn't work on something without lips and all the other usual apparatus: all he got was some clicking and a soft hiss whenever the skeleton gritted its teeth.

I could give it a charcoal stick. Maybe it can write.

He hadn't thought of that in the catacombs. What he *had* thought was that the skeleton was giving him the eye, like it was annoyed, so he'd pointed at the nearest sigil-covered arch that went absolutely nowhere and told the skeleton to open it. And then...

And then he didn't know, and here they were, and it was all a bit disconcerting.

He still had Myla's swords, wrapped in their blanket. In his other hand, he was carrying a sack. Quite a bulky one. He no idea what was in it, which was...

His thoughts blurred. Never mind how he'd ended up by the river, what he needed to do was get back to the Pig, find Myla, return her swords and then help her rescue Fings. As a sword-monk, chances were high that Myla would take a very dim view of him traipsing around with a couple of pet Dead Men, so whatever had happened last night, they had to go.

He studied Lightbringer Suaresh. Suaresh was dead, but he *looked* perfectly alive and healthy, apart from staring into space like an idiot. The dead Spicer – Seth decided then and there to call him Cleaver – was a bit more borderline. He didn't look *too* bad, but there was dried blood all over his shirt and the cleaver sticking out of his head was a bit of a giveaway. And he'd already told Seth everything he knew about where the Spicers were keeping Fings.

The skeleton... Yes, walking across the city with an animated skeleton *was* likely to attract some notice.

"Go back where I found you," he said the skeleton. "Wait for me there."

The skull turned and drooped as if giving Seth a long sceptical look. Seth sighed and rolled his eyes.

"The moment anyone sees you, there's going to be screaming and wailing and shouting and running and more screaming and all sorts, until a gaggle of sword-monks show up and send you on your way and then properly murders me. Is that what you want?" *What am I doing? It's a skeleton. It can't think.*

Can it?

He wasn't sure he wanted to know.

The skeleton's expression didn't change, mostly because it didn't have one in the first place. It took a step sideways and tapped Cleaver on the shoulder for some reason – not that Cleaver noticed – then trudged through the snow, back the way they'd come. Seth supressed an urge to follow it so he could find out where that actually was. Despite being nothing but bones, it managed to move with a disturbing air of annoyance.

"You. Spicer. Take that cleaver out of your head."

Cleaver did as he was told, though Seth thought he looked a bit sulky about it.

I'm imagining this. All of it. I'm going mad. He took the sash from around Lightbringer Suaresh's waist and handed it to Cleaver. "Wrap that round your head. No one wants to see what's left of your brains leaking out the side of your skull."

With a bit of silk wrapped around him, Cleaver didn't look too bad. Suaresh was in his night clothes and had stockings on his feet, but he had his priestly robes on too, and the Longcoats would never bother a priest. He'd still have to set both of them free before he got to the Pig, but he wasn't going to say no to a free pass walking the Longcoat Roads.

Right then. Off we go.

He trudged southwards, navigating by guesswork between the deep artificial tributaries of the river Arr, the boat-building yards and an endless noise of smithies. He passed row upon row of silos, mirrors of the ones across the river and dwarfing everything around them, brimming with grain shipped in on the eternal parade of barges converging on the city. He passed clusters of bored Imperial soldiers but they didn't bother him. Beyond the boat-builders and the silos, he found himself in a huge fish market he hadn't known even existed. The market was crowded and full of hustle and bustle, but everyone seemed in too much of a hurry to wonder why a priest was wandering through when he should be at dawn prayer.

The smell of the fish market stayed with him after the shouts of the sellers faded. He passed a row of shops selling nothing but nails and finally found himself in more familiar territory. Clothiers. The stink of the Tanners' District drew him to Ox-Rope Square, one of the bigger city markets, where bolts of cloth, piles of furs and leather bent and sewn into all conceivable forms were thrust in the faces of anyone who looked like they might have a quarter-moon or two. He avoided that, tried not to breathe through as much of Tanners as possible, until finally he reached Seamstresses, Haberdashers and Threadneedle Street. Back in the Teahouse, he sent Suaresh and Cleaver to hide in Blackhand's old room, reasoning that that was the one place Dox and Arjay wouldn't nose about more than they already had, paid enough attention to discover that Myla had spent the night in the Pig but had already left again, then went up to Blackhand's room himself, slumped into a chair, dropped his sack on the floor, and fell–

Hang on a minute. Sack?

Oh.

Apparently, as well as Myla's swords wrapped in a blanket, he was carrying a sack. He dimly remembered noticing, back at the river. Then, apparently, he'd forgotten all about it and carried it all the way here without even realising, despite how bulky it was. Was that more or less disturbing than finding himself at the edge of the river with no memory of how he got there? He couldn't decide.

Not particularly heavy, though.

He opened the sack to see what he'd decided was worth carrying all this way. Two skulls looked back at him. Two skulls which were almost certainly the two other skulls from the catacombs.

All…right…

And I brought them with me because… Because…

Not having an answer to a question like that was, he decided, not a good sign. Along with not remembering how he'd left the catacombs, and waking up with a skeleton standing beside him, looking at him in a funny way, and forgetting that he was carrying the things. Yes. All in all, he'd racked up quite a collection of things that weren't good signs, unless your idea of a good sign was a strong indication that some old long-dead sorcerer was having a go at a spot of possession.

No, no, no, we're not having this. You can fuck right off with that nonsense.

He might not remember everything he'd done down in the catacombs, but he knew exactly what he could do *now*. He carried the sack down to the kitchen, put the skulls on the table and had at them with a mallet until they were smashed into little pieces.

There.

"What in Kelm's name are you doing?"

Seth almost hit the roof. He spun around. Arjay was in the doorway, rubbing her eyes.

"Seth? What *are* you doing?"

He thought about how to answer that. He *could*, he supposed, go with the truth? *I'm smashing two ancient skulls that I dragged all the way across the city from an ancient crypt because I don't remember taking them or why I wanted them and half the time I don't even remember I'm carrying them around.*

Or maybe not. Maybe some reason that sounded a bit less deranged.

"Priest stuff," he said. "Where's Myla? I've got her swords. I need her to help Fings."

Arjay pursed her lips. "She's already gone."

"Gone?"

"To the Spicers. Didn't have that priest with her this time."

"Priest?"

"Priest, mage, whatever... Scrawny fellow with the pointy beard from the night the Spicers took Blackhand. The one who was throwing fire about the place? He came back with her from wherever it was they went." Arjay shrugged. "Not my business, but he was in her room all last night."

"From when the Spicers took Blackhand?" asked Seth.

Arjay shrugged again. "Are we going to talk about that?"

Shit.

A horrible thought wrapped itself around him like quicksand. "She doesn't know, does she?"

"Know what?"

"Sulfane! He's not dead! He's working with the Spicers."

"He's... *What?*"

Shit! He hadn't told anyone because he didn't know how to explain how he knew. *Shit, shit, shit!* "She's walking into a trap! We have to stop her! How long ago did she leave?"

"Hours."

"Fuck! We need her!"

Arjay made a face, sort of sad and confused both at once. "You know, I think she *did* know."

"About Sulfane?"

"About it being a trap."

Seth clenched his fists. "We need another plan." How the fuck was he supposed to rescue Fings from Tombland all on his own? Did he have to rescue Myla now, as well?

But he *wasn't* on his own...

"You good to walk as far as Bonecarvers?" Arjay nodded. "Good, because we're going to need that Bithwar woman again. Go get her. Quick as you can." He fumbled around until he found the bronze dagger from the catacombs. "Give her this. Tell her it's hers if she helps."

Dox and Arjay might not be fit to fight but they didn't need to be. He had Cleaver and Lightbringer Suaresh.

And as big an army of Dead Men as I want.

Yes, there would be fun times in Tombland tonight.

42

TWILIGHT

Fings woke in a dark room, cold and damp. His head was pounding. For some reason, his feet hurt like they were on fire.

Oh. Right.

The rest of the memories came back like a reluctant child called away from something far more interesting. The Pig. The Spicers. Sulfane murdering Blackhand. He had an idea someone had hit him on the head again after that. When he tried to feel for the lump, he remembered his hands were tied.

How long ago was that? Minutes? Hours? Days?

When they ran out of toes, they'd start on his fingers. He wasn't sure if he could take that, but he was never going to tell Sulfane what the Murdering Bastard wanted to hear.

A heavy door opened and then closed in the distance, echoing between the stone walls. He heard footsteps and then voices, calm and measured. They were talking about him. What they'd done. As the footsteps came closer, Fings counted at least three sets. They were bringing something new. He could feel it.

Something worse than glass?

A thought smacked him in the face, hurled him upright and would have carried on hurling him right out of his cell and through the door if he hadn't been tied down. *A mage.* Was that what it was? They were bringing a mage?

A pair of Spicers stomped in. He could hear others right outside. He wanted to scream. A mage could rip what he knew right out of his head.

But it was Myla, not a mage, missing her swords and dressed in some rough collection of furs and rags that made it look like she'd been looting bodies. Fings gulped for air. What in Kelm's name was *she* doing here? It made sense that Sulfane might go after her, but Myla wasn't in chains. True, she didn't have her swords, but with Myla, Fings wasn't entirely sure how much that mattered. She looked angry, too, not scared. Was she with the Spicers, now? But that didn't make any sense at all!

He watched as she circled from one corner of the room to the next to the next, looking at him.

"Myla?" he rasped. "What's going on?"

She jumped at him then, hands gripping his head like claws, and thrust her face into his until they were nose to nose. "You *stupid* bastard! What were you thinking? Leave them under the bridge, that's what we agreed. You, me, Wil and Sulfane! Leave them under the bridge until we know what to do with them. Imperial Guard swarming up and down the road but you just couldn't leave it alone. Why, Fings? *Why?*"

Her anger sounded real enough but for a moment her eyes flicked downward. Fings' eyes did the same, all on their own. The tunic she was wearing was loose at the throat. She had something around her neck on a leather thong, but the leather disappeared under her clothes and he couldn't see what it was.

She pulled away. Tossed her head and threw back her hair and ran her hands through it in frustration as she walked in another circle around him.

"You stupid…" The words stumbled out of her mouth, clogged with fury. "Stupid, lying *thief!*"

Well… yeah…

She circled him a third time, clenching and unclenching her fists like she had no idea what she was going to do, then lunged at him again. This time, the thing around her neck hung down between them. It was his lucky chicken's foot.

"I *was* going to tell you!" Fings protested. *Why are you here?*

"But you didn't!"

"Yeah, well, there was a sort of problem about that. Like when we–"

"I don't care!" For a fleeting flashing moment, Fings saw a red haze of rage glaring down at him. She clutched his face again. "I ought to break your neck! There were sell-swords. They followed me. Torpreahns. I had to kill one of them. And for what? For *nothing*! What were you *thinking*?"

Fings cracked. "I was thinking it was all just *there*, and all these soldiers looking for it, and it was so much money, and they were going to *find* it! *That's* what I was thinking! And there were going to be mages and... *Someone* was going to do it. Someone was *always* going to do it!" He was shaking.

Myla gripped him by the chin, held his face and drew back her other hand, fingers balled into a fist ready to punch him, then clutched at the back of her neck instead. "Sounds to me like you found a buyer and decided to help yourself," she said. As she did, the lucky chicken's foot dropped onto the chair between his legs.

"No! Who? *How*?" Fings shook his head. "Sulfane... I *had* to do it! I was going to tell you, I really was." It was true, too, although he supposed Myla might wonder that he'd taken so long about it. "Sulfane wasn't going to wait! *Some*one had to do it."

"Bollocks!" He saw the pain in her face as she leaned into him again. Was that for Wil or for Blackhand, or for him, or was it for all of them?

"Myla! Why are you here?"

"I'm here to make you tell them where it is."

"No!"

"Yes!"

"No!"

"Yes!"

"Why? Why would I?"

"Because this is the only way you get to live, you stupid fuck."

"No!"

313

"*Yes*! I'm trading me for you. You'll trade me for the crown. That's the way it's going to be."

"No!" He heard how pathetic he sounded. "Myla... After all this, the Murdering Bastard wins?"

"Dead is hardly winning."

"He's not dead!"

Myla almost froze. "*What?*"

"He's not dead."

She stared at him. "That's not what you said at the time."

"Well... I *thought* he was. I was wrong, wasn't I!"

He saw the panic in her eyes then, and knew they were doomed. She leaned in close and whispered in his ear: "It doesn't matter. Tell them. Trust me."

A hand grabbed her from behind. One of the Spicers. Myla spun and punched him in the gut. He doubled over... and there was the Murdering Bastard in flesh, standing in the door, his arm in a sling across his chest, and for one wild moment, Fings thought maybe this was it, maybe Myla was going to save him...

Sulfane snapped his fingers. "He's not going to tell her. Hold her down."

Myla kicked him in the knee. He yelped as his leg buckled. The two Spicers by the door lunged. Myla dodged and punched one in the side of the head but the other caught her as two more came charging in. She kicked one in the groin and then the last two Spicers wrestled her down, pinning her to the ground no matter how hard she struggled.

Sulfane hauled himself upright. He slid a knife from his belt and showed it to Fings.

"Last chance. Tell me where it is or she goes the same way as Blackhand." Fings twisted his head, trying to see, but they were behind him, and all he could hear apart from Sulfane was Myla snarling and growling as she struggled to break free.

"You're not going to let either of us go."

"No, Fings, I'm not. But if you tell me, I'll sell Myla to her friends from Deephaven. Not the best outcome, but she won't be dead, so who knows, eh? More to the point, I won't have any reason to go after your family. But if you *don't* tell me... If you don't, then I'm going to cut her until either she stops bleeding because she's dead or until you change your mind, and then I'm going to go after your sisters and bring them back here and do the same to them, one by one, right in front of you. So take your time. As long as you like." He started to walk around behind Fings to where the Spicers were holding Myla down. "How about we start big and lose an eye?"

"No!" yelped Fings.

Sulfane paused, knife poised.

"I'm sorry, Myla. I did what I did. Had to be done, was all."

"Fings! No one cares! Where's my crown?"

Fings bowed his head.

"The catacombs. There's an entrance behind the Sun Chapel incinerators on the Circus of Dead Emperors. It's down there. There's a vault. You'll need some rope."

43

THE FIRST DAY OF MIDWINTER

Seth crossed the Bridge of Questions. The sun was high and bright, and Tombland was crowded with streetsellers offering everything from pornographic lithographs to steaming grass soup to broken glass from the Glass Market, swept up and strung into lacerating bracelets. Anything even vaguely solid was piled in mounds and offered as an aromatic alternative to firewood. Five more days and the sun would set forever on the year, and for the few hours before the next dawn, chaos would reign. Lords would sit with common men in taverns. Affairs and seductions, feuds and friendships would begin and end. Sword-monks and priests would wander drunk in the streets and crowd into whorehouses. In Tombland, people would swear they'd seen Dead Men join the revelry as everyone drank enough to fill the river all the way to Deephaven.

Through the hubbub, criers rang their bells and yelled the new Emperor's name to all and sundry. Which was a bit of a cheek, Seth thought, since the coronation wouldn't happen until the day *after* the festival, which still left plenty of time for a carelessly wielded dagger, a clumsy crossbow incident, an accidentally misplaced phial of poison, or all manner of unfortunate trips and falls onto the wrong end of any number of sharp and pointy things.

Ah well. Not my problem.

He made his way to where Arjay was dressed like an alchemist in a battered and singed leather apron covered in pockets over thick rough clothes, standing across the street from a tiny shop which sold bowls of winter stew. They stood around, pretending not to know each other until a gang of six Spicers crossed the street. As the Spicers went into the shop, Arjay signalled and then slipped in behind them. Seth stayed where he was, watching.

The Spicers emerged back onto the street. Four carried large bowls that steamed gently in the cold; the other two held loaves of bread piled against their chests. As they did, a small commotion broke out further up the road. A young man in rough clothes was ducking and weaving between the hustle and bustle. Tarran Bithwar hurtled after him.

"Come back here!" she shouted. "How dare you run away from me!"

The young man bounced off a woman carrying a tower of baskets on her head, ricocheted into a handcart full of mangy rabbit pelts, pinged off into a crowd of bearded men clustered around something small, furry and terrified, and emerged full tilt towards the Spicers with their steaming bowls. They saw him coming and stopped. The young man veered to go around them; but as he did, a large man who looked suspiciously like Dox in a bad disguise stepped out in front of him and they collided. Dox staggered away while the young man flew straight into the Spicers, arms flailing. Bowls, loaves, Spicers and stew landed in an ungainly mess on the street.

Seth watched, wondering if any of these Spicers were the ones who'd beaten him half to death. If they were, he had some sigils waiting for them.

Tarran caught up to the tangle before any of them managed to right themselves. She skittered to a stop as one of the Spicers reached for a hatchet.

"Hey!" she snapped. "That's *my* servant."

The Spicer with the hatchet looked at her long and hard. He saw the rich clothes and his hand slipped back to his side. Everyone who ever sold stuff that wasn't strictly theirs eventually came to know Tarran Bithwar.

"Thank you," said Tarran primly.

The Spicers brushed the remains of whatever had been in the bowls from their coats. What they *really* wanted was to kick the shit out of someone; but they knew who Tarran was, and that she wasn't someone to cross, and so they stood politely as she kicked her manservant towards the shop. He staggered in, mumbling a stream of apologies until he was sure no one outside was paying attention, then spat on the floor. Seth followed him inside while Tarran took the opportunity for a quiet word with six brave strong men of dubious morals about some nefarious business that most people would probably have called smuggling. It kept them from paying attention to what was happening inside the shop.

The nice thing about looking like an alchemist, Seth thought, was that no one questioned why you were carrying odd-looking bottles. Right now, Arjay had two, which she was tipping liberally into six large bowls of Midwinter stew. She passed them one at a time to Seth, who passed them on in turn to Tarran's servant.

None of the others would have thought of this.

Midwinter stew, even at its best, tended to be leftovers topped up with passing vermin. No one was going to look too carefully or be all that surprised if a touch of the flux followed, that was what mattered.

Tarran's manservant carried the bowls back out to the street and passed them around. Tarran and the Spicers seemed to be getting on well, some scheme already hovering between them, and they talked for a few minutes more. When they were done, Tarran slapped her man round the head and dragged him away, and that was that.

"I think that actually worked," said Arjay.

Seth watched the Spicers vanish into the crowd. "I think it actually did."

The rest of Seth's plan was rather more straightforward: creep in at night with some Dead Men to scare the crap out of any Spicers still able to put up a fight, then let Arjay and Brick and Topher in with lots of knives and sticks and shouting and other things Seth didn't do, all assuming Myla didn't simply hack her way out with Fings tagging along behind, and never mind that she didn't have her swords.

But that was for later, and it would take while for his stew work its charms, and until it did, he had other things to do.

He took one last look at Tombland over his shoulder as he left, made a little bow, and stole away.

44

THE THİEF

After Fings told Sulfane what he wanted to know, the Spicers dragged Myla to another cell and left her there. She sat quietly, waiting. It was down to Orien, now. The mage wouldn't be able to resist the opportunity to prove himself, and so she was giving him the chance. He'd followed her to the Constable's Castle and now he was keeping watch, waiting for the Spicers to make their move. Grab the treasure, rescue the girl. She wasn't sure she *wanted* to be rescued – certainly hadn't been expecting to *need* it – but the crown was more important than pandering to her own ego.

There was no chance Sulfane would let either of them go. That part of the plan had always been risky, which was why she'd smuggled Fings his picks. He was Fings. He was a lying shit-rag, but he was a *patient* lying shit-rag who knew how to do things right. It would have been nice if someone had bothered to mention that Sulfane was alive… But in the end, what did it matter? Orien simply had to follow some Spicers instead of following Fings.

You use the tools you have. That was the merchant's daughter showing herself. Was it fair? She was taking advantage of Orien but… he *was* easy on the eye and he had a nice smile and he was clever. And so far, at least, he'd been honest with her.

You like him.

She did, and she wasn't ashamed of it either; and yes, if her only way out was Orien storming in at the head of a company of Imperial soldiers, so be it.

What if he doesn't come?

She could almost feel Sarwatta looking up from whatever he was doing in far-off Deephaven, staring across the thousand miles between them, grinning and laughing and whispering about all the things he was going to do to her before he had her hanged.

Tasahre was there with her too, her voice iron. *If he doesn't come, you fight until you can't.*

If that's what it took.

"We merchant-daughters learn to look after ourselves," she muttered. And then, without warning, there were tears in her eyes. *I made such a mess of everything.*

We all make mistakes. What matters is what we do next. How we make amends.

Tasahre usually had nothing but scorn for self-pity. Usually, but she'd been in a strange mood the day she'd said that. As though she was talking about herself.

A sound at the door of her cell. "Myla?"

"Fings?"

She heard the scrape of metal on metal as he worked the lock and then the door swung open.

"You took your time."

Fings stood in the doorway, uncertain, a black silhouette against near-black darkness. "Got any weapons?"

"Do I *look* like I have any weapons?" She took two quick steps towards him. Fings made a startled noise and backed away.

"The thing is–"

"You said Sulfane was *dead*!"

"He *was*, I swear!" Fings backed away some more. "Well, I mean, I thought he–"

"No! That's the problem. You *don't* think!"

Myla stalked closer, a simmering cauldron of righteous ire and things that needed to be said if they were ever going to get out of this. Fings backed into the torture room with its chair, holding out his hands in placation.

"I *told* you I didn't want to go with him!" The only light was a single candle in a censer at the far end of the passage, by the foot of the stairway leading out. "Murdering Bastard did exactly what I said, waited until we'd gone far enough that you couldn't see and then turned around and went back. I mean, he *said* he was going for a piss but it was obvious he was going back to see where you and Wil buried it so he could take it for himself."

"And you didn't try to stop him?"

"What was I going to do? Tell him I was coming to watch? He would have killed me."

"He was in no state–"

"Says *you* with them swords!"

She stopped. Her swords. The ones she no longer owned. "The crown," she said, as softly as she could, and then watched him squirm, which was good enough as an answer.

"I had to do it," he said at last.

As they stared at each other through the darkness, Myla felt her fury fall away. Something was gnawing at the edges of her mind, something that didn't belong. She turned and followed the passage to the stair and up to the door at the top. It was a heavy thing made of iron. It looked old.

"What is this place?" she asked.

"Some old palace. Used to be for the city Overlord, back when there wasn't anything but fishing villages on the north bank of the Arr." Fings shrugged. "At least, that's what Seth says. Although I don't think anyone proper has lived in it for ages. Used to be where the Mage of Tombland held court, but was a beggars' palace even then, run down and falling apart at the seams." He joined her at the top of the stair and poked at the lock.

"Can you open this?"

"The lock? Course I can." He pushed at the door and then rattled it a bit. "Problem is, it's bolted from the other side." He let out a long sigh and sat down a few steps from the top. "Came here a couple of times back when the Mage was still around. Years ago. Last time I was here... was me and Seth. We weren't supposed to come but I wanted Seth to see this place. Blackhand was coming to meet the Mage. I didn't think much of it, one way or the other. Didn't know..." He trailed off. "That was the night Blackhand murdered the Mage. Him and Wil and Wil's brothers, Sand and Rev. A few days later, Sand and Rev were both dead. Blackhand and Wil ran off. Didn't come back for two whole years. Way I'm putting it together, Sulfane, he's... I don't know. The Mage's bastard or something. Might have been him that did for Rev, at least. It's all about some old grudge he's holding. He murdered Blackhand right there in front of me. I *knew* there was something wrong about him. It was all supposed to fall on us, this whole thing with that barge. He just disappears while we get to spend the rest of our lives being tortured by Mages." Fings suddenly went wide-eyed. "That's it! He was going to take everything and we'd all think he was dead! We'd go back and there'd be nothing there and all start blaming each other, and then the mages would come! Just as well I–"

Myla had a hand round Fings' throat before she even knew what she was doing. She took a moment, squashing the rage back in its box before she let him go. "I think you'd better shut up about that for a while."

Fings rubbed his throat, eyeing her warily. "He was going to sell it to the Torpreahns who were going to give it to one of their own and claim he was the new emperor. Something like that. It was them that doublecrossed us in the woods."

Like the Torpreahns who'd come after her and Orien.

"He *looked* dead, alright."

Even from this close, Fings was only a shape in the darkness. She couldn't make out his face, couldn't read his expression. "When I left Varr, you already knew it was gone. That's why you let me go on my own. You knew and you didn't tell me."

Fings shifted a little.

"I killed a man, Fings. Maybe two. Maybe more. For something that wasn't even there."

"What about that mage, then?" Fings' voice was rich with accusation. "The one that came that night when the Spicers took Blackhand. Didn't mention *that*, did you? Found out from Dox and Arjay, some bloke throwing fire from his hands, they said. Said you knew him. Said you got him out of there. Didn't say nothing about that to me or to Seth, though, did you? You were going to give it to him. Behind my back and without even asking. All that work. All that money. One of them Guild Mages, is it?"

Myla took a deep breath and closed her eyes. "His name is Orien and he's not a Guild Mage, and if you can't open that door, there's a good chance he's going to save your life." She sighed. "I did *tell* you it was going back where it belonged. Yes, he came with me. Yes, I'm helping him. We're helping each other."

"Yeah, and I don't remember ever agreeing to *any* of that." Fings let out a long hiss. "So now what?"

"When the Spicers go to fetch the crown, Orien will follow them. When they bring it back here, he'll bring in the Emperor's soldiers. We probably all end up in the Kaveneth. The Spicers, Sulfane, you, me. Unless we can get out of here on our own."

"Yeah." Fings sounded resigned. "It's always the way. There's always some pillock decides to do things by themselves."

"Like you did?"

Fings shrugged. "Like you're doing, too."

"Did you let the Spicers into the Pig?"

"What? No!"

"Don't lie to a sword-monk, Fings." But he wasn't lying, even if he knew something he wasn't saying, and Blackhand was dead, and so maybe it was best to let that one go, at least for now. Although Dox and Arjay certainly wouldn't. "*Is* there any way out of here before the Emperor's soldiers arrive?"

Fings snorted. "When they open that door, we jump them and fight."

"*You're* going to fight?"

"Got no choice, have I?" Fings stretched.

"You're going to fight the Imperial Guard?"

"No, I'm going to fight the Spicers. Your plan ain't going to work. I lied about where I hid the crown. They ain't going to find it."

"You lied?" He'd sounded so broken when Sulfane had been threatening to cut her. She'd thought he'd told the truth. A part of her had even thought that he'd done it for her.

"Ain't nothing else keeping that Murdering Bastard from slitting my throat. Yours either, for that matter. Course I lied. What, you thought I somehow got it all the way to Varr right under your nose? No. I'd get some rest if I were you. We got time. Don't know how long it'll take Sulfane to figure a way into the catacombs, but it's dark outside and there's no way they'll go down until morning. Then they got to search the place. *Then* they'll come back, and they're going to be angry."

"Fings... It's not dark outside! When I got here... It wasn't even the middle of the day."

There was a long heavy silence.

"Oh," said Fings after a bit. "Shit. Guess they'll be back a bit sooner then."

"Do you have any idea of their numbers? I saw maybe a dozen?"

"Spicers? More like twenty, I reckon. I saw a few of them soldiers you were on about, too. Six. But that's only what I saw. Doesn't mean there aren't more."

Jeffa's sell-swords. But if Jeffa was here, she'd have known about it by now. He wouldn't be able to resist coming to see her to have a good gloat. If he *wasn't* here and then he came... take Fings' count and double it?

Twelve Deephaven mercenaries and twenty-odd Spicers?

They snuffed the candle and sat at the top of the stairs in the dark after that. Voices and footsteps and a light creeping in around the edges of the door, that would be their warning that the Spicers were coming; and so they waited in silence because surprise was the only weapon they had. Whether that was enough would depend on who came, and how many. She'd have to cripple at least one Spicer before they knew what was happening. She'd have to take his knife. After that? In a doorway where they couldn't surround her? Maybe she could fight her way out, maybe she couldn't, but probably not.

It was what it was.

She heard their voices first, when they came. Four, at least. Then the bolts on the door sliding back, one, two, three... As soon as the door opened, she threw herself at them. The nearest Spicer had one hand stretched towards her, a burning brand in the other and a look of paralysed shock on his face. She grabbed the hand and pulled hard, yanking him through the door and pulling herself the other way at the same time, taking his legs from under him as she shoved him tumbling down the stair for Fings to finish. She punched the next Spicer in the nose and stamped on the ankle of the one beside him, made a grab for the knife in his belt and missed, and it was about then that she realised there weren't *four* Spicers, there were seven, and that was too many. She punched the Spicer in front of her a second time, this time in the throat, and kicked him into the men behind.

"Grab her!" Sulfane was pushing forward, pulling a man out of the way to try to reach her. "Just get hold of her and don't let go!"

The Spicer she'd stamped grabbed at her arm. She caught his wrist and twisted and turned him, spun him around and took his knife. She didn't want to kill him but...

I'm not going to die here!

She slashed his neck and pushed him into others. He threw his arms up in horror, spraying blood and getting in the way as Sulfane tried to barge past. *Three down, four to go.* All of them armed.

I am not *going to die here!*

"You and me, Sulfane!"

"I don't think so." Sulfane pushed the dying Spicer at her, forcing her back into the doorway. The one she'd throat-punched stood between them, clawing at his neck and trying to breathe. Sulfane rammed into the back of him, the weight of them both crashing into her, knocking her back onto the stair. He kicked the Spicer and she had to take another step back to find her balance. The Spicer staggered past and lost his footing and fell, tumbling towards Fings, but Sulfane had what he wanted. He grabbed the door and, before she could stop him, pulled it shut. She heard the bolts slide. One, two, three.

And that was that. No way out.

"Fings, you fuck!" Sulfane called from the other side. "I will search the Empire from top to fucking bottom until I find your sisters and you *will* watch them bleed until you give me what I want. And as for you Myla... your friend Jeffa will be on his way by now. Open your wrists before he gets here, that's my advice."

"You know what you can do with your advice!" Myla raged, but Sulfane had gone.

At the bottom of the stair, one of the Spicers had a broken neck.

"Nearly bloody landed on top of me." The other one was still moving. Fings kicked him and then squealed in pain, hopping around clutching at his foot. Myla dragged the two Spicers into one of the cells, searched them, locked the door and took stock. Three knives and one burning brand, still alight. At least they could re-light their candle.

And, Sun be praised, a half-empty skin of cheap watered wine. She took a long swallow and thanked the Gods for small mercies.

Three knives; and the next time the door opened, the men on the other side would be Jeffa and his Deephaven sell-swords. Proper fighting men, armoured and ready.

No chance.

No, no, no, you don't get to give up. Look around you and think. Think!

"Where is it, Fings?"

"Where's what?"

"The crown."

There was a long pause. "Deephaven," said Fings eventually. "Or on its way."

"*Deephaven*?"

"I didn't *take* it, exactly. I moved it. Then I told Ma Fings to get it. I *had* to! Like I had to get them out of Varr..." He sounded so penitent that Myla almost believed him. "I told her where it was and to take it to Deephaven and keep it safe."

Almost believed him. "You told Sulfane it was in the catacombs." She'd believed him when he'd said that, too. He'd sounded defeated.

"I had to tell him *something*, didn't I? I thought it was dark, and there ain't no way anyone was going down there at night. I was buying us time, that's all. Fat lot of use, as it turned out."

"Where is it?"

"I *told* you!" Outrage again, and it made her sick. "Deephaven! But I couldn't tell Sulfane *that*! Not when it's my family on the line."

Myla grabbed Fings and shoved him against the nearest wall. "I've had a very difficult few days, Fings, and sword-monks can smell lies, and I just don't believe, after all the fuss you made, that you left it behind. So, what I need, Fings, right now, is for you to tell me exactly what happened after you and Sulfane left us at the bridge."

vii

İΠTERLUDE

The snow was getting worse as Fings followed Sulfane up from under the bridge, leaving Myla and Wil to bury the crown in its box, along with his three sacks of silver. *His* three sacks of silver, because no one else had told him to steal them. *Get the box. Don't look inside. Help yourself to whatever else takes your fancy.* Simple instructions. No one had said anything about crowns or mages or meetings in the woods with strange men who tried to kill you.

Leave it all buried in the snow? No. One of them would come back and take it because that was what always happened. Sulfane would do it first chance he got. Wil, too, except he'd do it for Blackhand, and then they'd both be all *oh, sorry, Fings, someone else got to it first so there's no money after all.* Myla... It was a good act she was putting on, not wanting anything to do with it. He wasn't sure he believed her.

No. Wasn't having it. They could have that crown-thing. More trouble than it was worth, probably. But the silver... that was *his.* That was for him and Ma Fings and his sisters. That was for finding Levvi. That was for none of them being cold or hungry ever again.

They continued along the road a little way, Sulfane on his horse, Fings striding beside him.

"Who were those idiots in the woods, then?" Fings asked.

"Never you mind." Sulfane was slurring his words. Fings brightened a little, thinking maybe there was still a chance Sulfane was going to die after all. Still couldn't quite get over the fact that he'd saved the Murdering Bastard's life.

They carried on in silence long enough for Wil and Myla to dig a hole in the snow and bury everything. The further they went, the surer Fings became that he was making a mistake. What if Wil and Myla were thinking the same? What if they simply took the lot and buggered off in the other direction? Or... Burying it had been Myla's idea. She had a horse and she knew how to ride it, not like Wil. She'd eat Wil for breakfast in a fight. Could be that Wil was already lying dead under the bridge and Myla was on her way to Deephaven...

"I need a piss." Sulfane wheeled his horse and headed off the road towards a small stand of trees, barely visible through the falling snow. "Stay here and keep your eyes open."

Fings watched him go and reckoned the Murdering Bastard was a liar. He was going back. Only question was whether he was going back to see what was taking so long, or whether he was going back to help himself to some buried treasure. Fings reckoned he ought to do something either way, but what? Sulfane might be knocking on death's door but he still had a horse. Still had his bow, too, if he had the strength to use it.

Didn't make much sense, mind you, Sulfane going back. Myla and Wil would show up at any moment. If Sulfane legged it, Myla would go after him.

Myla decapitating the Murdering Bastard? Now *there* was a happy thought...

After a bit more thinking, when Sulfane didn't come back and there was still no sign of Wil or Myla, Fings decided he'd best have a look after all. The thought struck him that maybe they could make a deal, just the two of them. Sulfane wanted the Moonsteel circlet in its box. Fings wanted the silver. That worked out, didn't it? They could each take what they wanted and go their separate ways...

Make a deal with the Murdering Bastard?

Maybe not.

He hefted his stick, the same stick he'd used on the mage in the woods because any stick that could take down a mage was clearly lucky. He followed Sulfane's trail around the trees, and there was Sulfane's horse, Sulfane's bow and coat thrown across its rump, and there was Sulfane, taking a piss like he'd said, standing with his back to Fings.

Fings crept closer. There *had* to be something else to this. This was Sulfane. The Murdering Bastard. There had to be some sort of trick he was playing. *Had* to be.

Somehow, Sulfane didn't hear him, even when he got right up close.

Had to be a trick, didn't it? And he couldn't see it.

And still Sulfane didn't turn and see him. He was finishing up.

Never going to get a better chance than this.

He swung the stick and lamped Sulfane on the back of his head. Then he jumped back, ready to run, but the Murdering Bastard went down like he'd been hit by an axe, face first into the snow.

Oh shit! What you do that *for?*

He gave Sulfane a poke.

You killed him!

"You dead?" It was hard to tell, what with all the mess from where Sulfane had already been shot and stabbed. He still had blood leaking out of him. Leaking out the back of his head now, as well.

He *looked* dead.

It crossed Fings' mind, then, that maybe *looking* dead should be enough. If he poked and prodded and it turned out that Sulfane was only *nearly* dead, well, then he'd have to do something about that, which meant either finishing the Murdering Bastard off or else trying to come up with some sort of reasonable excuse for having crept up behind him and lamped him with a log, neither of which, if he was honest, he much fancied.

Sulfane twitched and let out a quiet groan. Fings jumped and skittered back.

You really ought to finish him.

He wasn't sure about that. Yes, it made sense but... He wasn't sure he could.

Or...

The first thing Myla and Wil would ask was *Where's Sulfane*, and Fings would have to tell them, and then Myla would insist on coming back to see for herself, so he'd be coming back for another look anyway, he reckoned. He could make out like this was the first he knew of it. Sulfane hadn't ever *seen* him, after all...

Yeah.

They'd come back later, the three of them, and find Sulfane rubbing his head and all cross, and Fings could give him back his horse and say he'd found it wandering, and it had led them there.

Yeah. That would work.

He led Sulfane's horse back around the trees. With the snow coming down as it was, he wasn't sure he'd see Myla and Wil unless he stayed on the road, so that's where he went, and then started back towards the bridge, thinking more and more how he didn't want to be doing this with all these soldiers about, and how maybe this was a mistake and he should have stayed, and how the Murdering Bastard was going to get angry about Fings swiping his coat and his horse...

The snow grew heavier.

He reached the bridge and he still hadn't seen Wil and Myla. Which didn't make any sense, and all he could think was that one of them had murdered the other and run off.

The best thing, he reckoned, was to go down to have a look.

They weren't there, dead or otherwise. What *was* there was a trail leading further down the stream towards the river. When he followed it, it didn't take long to work out what had happened. They'd settled on doing their burying a little bit away from the bridge, and then had kept on towards the river, switching to the other road, the one that ran right beside the river for the barges and the animals that dragged them upriver against the current. *That* was why he'd missed them.

He looked around. Even through the falling snow, it was obvious what they'd done.

He looked up at the sky but that was just lots of white. No way to know how much more snow would come before it stopped. Would take *hours* to hide all this mess, though. Hours and hours and even then, anyone who could read a trail would be able to see that someone had carved a path off the road and where it went. He could even see where they'd buried it. They'd tried to cover their tracks but they hadn't done much of a job of it. Some idiot had even marked the spot with a branch...

Some things were best left to the experts. At the very least, he could do a better job of covering it all up.

Or...

He'd almost forgotten Sulfane, but now he made up his mind to go straight back and get the Murdering Bastard on his feet. Then he'd find Wil and Myla and tell them what had happened – minus the part about it being *him* that had lamped Sulfane – and how burying everything the way they had was a terrible idea, and how they needed to think of something else. And that was still what he was telling himself, how he was doing the right thing by everyone, as he dug up the crown in its box and stuffed it into the saddlebags on Sulfane's horse, and the silver too, packed in tight so it didn't jingle.

Yeah. Take it all back. Tell them what you did and try again somewhere else. Just do a better job of it.

Yeah. That's right.

He got back to where he'd left Sulfane only to find four horsemen clustered by the trees nearby, and then he didn't know what to do. They hadn't seen him, not yet, and even if he couldn't make out much through the snow, one of the riders definitely had what looked like a body slung over the back of his horse, and Fings was buggered if he was getting any closer, but that body *had* to be Sulfane, surely, and who could these riders be except some of the soldiers he'd seen going up and down the road all morning?

And it *did* solve a lot of problems, things working out this way. Could even call it lucky.

Later, when he found Myla and Wil wandering the road in the falling snow, he told them what had happened. He wasn't quite sure why he made up the bit about the Murdering Bastard trying to shoot him, but he had to admit it *did* sound better that way. After he'd said that, the whole bit about him going back and swiping everything from where Myla had buried it was something that could wait, he reckoned. So he kept quiet, waiting to see how things turned out, and Wil took Sulfane's horse while Fings rode with Myla, and no one ever looked in Sulfane's saddlebags. When they reached the next waystation, Fings hid the crown and the bags of silver again, and frankly did a much better job of it. And after that, somehow, the moment never seemed right for telling anyone what he'd done.

45

DON'T PUSH IT

"They weren't soldiers," said Myla, when he was done.

"Yeah." Fings understood that now. They were the men Sulfane had hired to murder him and Wil and Myla after he'd made the trade for the crown. The men who were supposed to make sure the bodies were found by the Emperor's soldiers and would lead them back to Varr and Blackhand and the Unruly Pig, while Sulfane vanished like a ghost. "I was right, wasn't I? He *was* going to murder us."

"He was going to try."

"So... All of this is about who gets to be in charge? Some knob from Torpreah thinks he fancies being Emperor? Not because he thinks he can do it better but because he thinks he's got a right to it because some other knob from the City of Spires decades ago kicked yet another knob off the throne and paraded his head on a spike?"

"That's about right."

"And somehow, our Murdering Bastard gets wind, and he's all up for it because of what happened in some place a thousand miles away before he was even born?" Fings shook his head. "I sort of get the bit about laying it on Blackhand. I was there when they murdered the Mage. I suppose Sulfane has a point about Blackhand being a bit of a wanker. He weren't *all* bad, though."

Myla snorted. "Any man who seeks power over others to further his own ambition is already long down the road of becoming a monster."

"Sulfane was going to murder us all but he didn't. He must have gone back to look and found it wasn't there." Fings shuffled his feet. "I *was* going to tell you. You and Wil. Not straight away, because then you'd just have gone back. Was going to tell you when we got to Varr. Except… Well… You know what happened. Was all a bit…" Then he grinned. "But I actually saved everyone, right? Shifting it all?"

"Don't push it." Myla gave him a hard look. Fings settled back to wait.

"This ain't going to work, is it?" he said, after a bit.

"What?"

"Fighting our way out."

Myla made a gesture like she didn't much care. "Probably not. There's too many."

"But we *are* going to fight, right?"

She nodded, and Fings could see that she was content with that, and wondered why. Was a shame, because he hadn't *planned* on dying, but that was how it was looking.

Still, he'd kept his promise to Levvi. The Emperor's silver was somewhere safe, and Ma Fings and his sisters would never be hungry again.

"I just wish I knew what Jeffa Hawat had to do with any of this," said Myla.

"Nothing," said Fings. "I mean… you'd have to ask Sulfane, but the way I see it, you stick out like a sore thumb. Anyone looking for you, they *were* going to find you sooner or later." He shrugged. "Maybe Sulfane started asking questions. Reckoned you might be a fly in his soup when it came to taking on Blackhand. The word spreads. Gets to the wrong ears. Someone puts things together. Just bad luck, is all."

They waited a bit longer, then Fings said: "You're actually alright with this, are you?"

"What do you mean?"

"Going down fighting."

Myla gave a snort. "Solves a lot of problems."

"Hmmm." Fings screwed up his face. "Maybe. But what if there was a way to get Sulfane's lot and your Deephaven lot to turn on each other? How would you feel about *that*?"

46

SCRAWNY FELLOW WITH A POINTY BEARD

The lifeblood of Tombland was the road that ran from the Glass Market and the Bridge of Questions on one side to the Old Gatehouse on the other. It was, to Seth's mind, a proper road: respectable and cleared of snow and crowded full of people trying to sell things, a paradise of pocket-picking opportunities. A Longcoat Road, in other words, if Tombland had had Longcoats.

The *rest* of Tombland was a bewildering mess without any proper streets at all. Any space wide enough for a generously proportioned man to pass had long ago been given a front door, a roof, usually three or four extra floors, and was now home to an entire mountain village from a place no one could pronounce. From the looks of things, residents of Tombland occasionally woke to discover their door to the outside world now opened onto a secluded private courtyard instead of an alley, or, in some cases, someone else's living room. Seth found himself leading Cleaver and Lightbringer Suaresh through a labyrinth of ladders and stairs and tiny passages and narrow halls, of shops and homes. Even when he found a few dozen yards of unexpected alleyway, scattered planks still bridged the sky overhead.

There was a brief ruckus when Cleaver's hood came down, and Seth discovered that the Dead Man had put his blade back into the side of his head again, much to the alarm of everyone nearby. Seth hurried them on, blathering about being performers for the theatre. As soon as they were alone, Seth snatched it out of the Dead Man's head. Cleaver started lagging behind after that, shuffling like he was sulking, even though Dead Men didn't have feelings on account of being... well, dead. In the end, Seth gave it back.

"You keep it out of sight, mind," Seth told him, "until we get to where we're going. You can stick it wherever you like once we start scaring people." Cleaver seemed to perk up after that.

Seth led them up some crude steps to the open window of what had once been a warehouse, now partitioned by ropes and blankets. He waded through in a roughly straight line, weaving past pots and babies and screaming children and wafts of strange smells and, at one point, the most remarkable collection of beards he'd ever seen gathered in one place. On the other side of the warehouse, he opened a shutter and jumped down into what resembled a normal backstreet, not that it went anywhere.

"That leads towards the canal and the Glass Market." He pointed to the only actual door he could see, although he counted over a dozen windows – as far as Tombland was concerned, there didn't seem to be much distinction. "If something happens, don't go that way." He wasn't sure why he was talking to the Dead Men. As far as he understood it, they were supposed to be blank automata like Lightbringer Suaresh. Cleaver, on the other hand, showed signs of having opinions on things, even if most of his opinions were on where to put his cleaver.

The two windows directly across the alley were shuttered tight. The next opened into the back of a Moongrass house. You could ride a horse through there and no one would notice, so that was going to be his way out if things went sideways. And on the *other* side of the alley... *Those* led into the back of what had once been the Servant's Quarters of the old Constable's Castle.

He gestured to a pile of barrels stacked at the far end of the street. "Move those so we can reach that window."

Suaresh and Cleaver obediently walked to the pile of barrels and tried to pick them up, only to find they were too heavy. The dead Lightbringer kept trying, but Cleaver managed to push one of the barrels over on its side and roll it into place. Seth couldn't decide whether Suaresh was being difficult for some arcane reason Seth didn't understand – his two Dead Men having been made in different ways – or whether it was simply down to him being Suaresh.

Eventually, Seth and Cleaver managed to roll a barrel into place and get it back on its end and climb up to the window. Seth tried the shutters and then made a face. The air inside was foul. Which was good – if he'd judged his poisons right, half the Spicers should have shat themselves into exhaustion by now.

He waved Cleaver over. "Give me that. You can have it back when I'm done."

Cleaver shuffled over and handed up his blade, freshly sticky from whatever was still inside his head. Seth tried not to think about that. He slipped the edge between the shutters and lifted the latch.

One day someone's going to get wise to this.

"Come on Suaresh, you can go first. If anyone's getting stabbed, it might as well be you." Here came the hard part, the getting inside without being seen, catching the first Spicer or two with his sigils before they knew what was happening. Once he had half a dozen Dead Men loose in there, he reckoned he could largely sit back and watch.

"Hey! Seth, isn't it?" called a voice from behind. Seth looked back, ready for a fight, but it wasn't a Spicer, only some idiot in a ridiculous orange robe.

Although...

He peered at the face looking up at him. He'd seen it before, on the night the Guild Mages had come to the Pig. Scrawny fellow with a pointy beard...

Shit. Myla's mage. He stilled Suaresh while his hand slipped into the pocket where he kept his sigils, already drawn.

"You *are* Seth," said the mage. "I saw you in the Unruly Pig." Fire sprang from his fingertips. "Name's Orien. Myla probably mentioned me."

"Nope." Seth whispered to Cleaver to follow and climbed down from the stack of barrels. He watched the flames flickering from the mage's fingers.

Awkward. Fire and Dead Men didn't mix.

"She really didn't?" Orien looked somewhere between baffled and hurt. Seth rolled his eyes.

"Kind of busy here. What do you want?"

The mage was eyeing Cleaver now, evidently starting to catch on that something was wrong with him. "What's going on here?"

"Probably best for everyone if you turn around and fuck off, is what." Seth raised his hands, a sigil in one and the cleaver in the other, but the mage was still staring at the Dead Man.

"What's wrong with him?"

"Show him, Cleaver." Seth tossed the blade to the Dead Man. Cleaver caught it, grinned, pushed back his hood and stuck it into his head. The mage gawped. As he did, Seth took a few quick steps, and then at the last minute changed his mind about using a sigil and punched Orien in the face instead.

"Ow! Fuck!" Seth clutched his hand. It felt like he'd probably broken several bones. The mage staggered back, momentarily dazed. "Cleaver! Punch him! Knock him out!"

Cleaver did as he was told, clearly a lot less bothered by breaking a knuckle or two. The mage went down like a sack of cabbages.

Good enough.

It *was* tempting to try a sigil – the opportunity to experiment on a mage wouldn't come again in a hurry. He stood there for a moment, nursing his hand. And the mage had seen what Cleaver really was. If Seth let him live, he was going to have questions. Difficult ones.

You're not a fucking murderer!

But he *was* a murderer. Lightbringer Suaresh was right there. Unliving proof.

Cleaver squatted by the unconscious mage, apparently ready to take a bite out of him.

"No!"

No, he wasn't ready to start randomly murdering people just because they were inconvenient. There had to be *some* line you didn't cross, right? Besides, Myla would probably notice...

Cleaver gave Seth a baleful look but did as he was told. Seth let out a long unhappy sigh. Was going to be trouble, leaving this mage alive.

He borrowed the cleaver again, climbed back to where Lightbringer Suaresh hadn't moved, and threw open the shutters. There were two Spicers on the other side. One was squatting over a bowl, head in his hands, breeches round his ankles, while the other one was leaning against a wall with a glassy expression, sweat streaming off his face. They looked up and stared at him with blank eyes. Seth poked Suaresh. "Go on then. In you go. Do your thing."

The Spicers gawped as the dead Lightbringer slipped inside with all the grace of a dying horse and then disappeared with some ripping sounds and a muffled crash. Seth peered inside. Underneath the window, someone had helpfully cut a large hole in the floor and then nailed a cheap rug across it. Seth stared at this for a moment.

Seriously? Why does this crap never happen to Fings?

For a moment, he thought about giving up and going home, but by then, Cleaver was already climbing past him. He seemed disturbingly enthusiastic.

47

FİGHT UNTİL YOU CAN'T

By the time the door to the Spicer dungeon opened again, Myla had gone through anger, frustration, boredom and fear, and had settled on hungry – and yes, sword-monks had fast-and-prayer days now and then, but she'd generally skipped those and stayed at home. She was hungry and disappointed and annoyed, and fully expected to die.

At the top of the stair, Jeffa's sell-swords were all packed together with heavy leather coats and wearing helmets, with their short stabbing swords already drawn. Flattering, in a way – Jeffa clearly wasn't taking any chances. All she had were a couple of knives, and *they* were the ones who were scared?

"I wouldn't come any further than that," she said.

They stayed where they were.

"Shirish!" called Jeffa. She couldn't see him but he had to be close, right behind the men blocking the doorway.

"Jeffa."

"No windows for you to jump from this time, Shirish."

"How much is it costing you to buy me? Come on down and save yourself some money. You and me. As we are. Loser dies, winner walks free."

"I don't think so."

"I'm a woman dressed in a glorified sack and armed with a knife, Jeffa. You're a man in armour carrying a sword. Are you *that* scared?" Two knives, actually, one of them tied to the end of a piece of thread around her wrist, but Jeffa didn't need to know that.

"That's not going to work, Shirish. I know what you are."

"Do your men? Because the first one to set foot on those steps, dies. Do they understand that? Have you decided which one it's going to be?"

Sulfane answered. "Myla, Myla, give it up, girl. Either you surrender right now or I close this door until you're so weak from hunger that you can't even move, and then they take you anyway. Your choice. I really don't care what happens once you and these monkeys are out of here."

Myla approached the bottom of the stair and there he was, standing behind the two swordsmen blocking the door. He had a crossbow levelled at her.

She squinted. "It's a bit dark down here, Sulfane. Is that Jeffa beside you?"

"Right here, Shirish." She still couldn't see him even though his voice was clear. Lurking at the back, then, like the coward he was. "You should listen to your friend. I want you strong enough to suffer for what you did to my brother but I'll take what I can get."

"You need to see something, Sulfane." Myla retreated from the stair and came back dragging Fings by his feet. His head lolled and he was covered in blood. She pulled him to the foot of the steps. "I didn't want to do this but you didn't leave me much choice, and he *did* doublecross both of us. Fings told me where it's hidden. I don't know what Jeffa is paying you, Sulfane, but you have to choose, because you can't have both. Does he know, by the way, what you stole? I don't suppose he does. You should be careful about making new friends, Jeffa. Never know what you'll get caught up in."

There was a long uneasy silence from the top of the stair, and then Sulfane started to laugh.

"Nice try." He raised the crossbow. "If he's dead, it won't matter if I shoot his corpse, will it? Get up, Fings."

Myla stepped in front of Fings. "Shoot *me*," she said. "See what happens."

Sulfane waggled his head. "Alright."

He pulled the trigger.

Seth followed Cleaver through the window and just about managed not to fall through the hole in the floor. If the two Spicers had understood what was happening, they could have grabbed him as easily as snatching a child; but as it was, neither of them seemed to know what to do. They were both staring at Cleaver. Admittedly, he *was* a bit of a sight, what with a sixteen-inch blade sticking out of his head.

"Sorry," said Seth. "You probably know each other, don't you?"

They kept staring as Seth pulled a sigil from his pocket and walked up to the Spicer by the wall. "Can I show you something?" He slapped the sigil onto the man's face and pointed to the one squatting over the bowl. "Cleaver!"

Cleaver launched himself. There was a squawk and a gurgle and then some crunching sounds. Seth took a moment to assess where he was. He thought he might dimly remember this place from the night he'd come with Fings and Blackhand, all those years ago. It had been a trophy room then. From the array of chairs, the table covered in half-eaten loaves and empty stew bowls, he guessed this was some sort of refectory now, but it wasn't where the Mage had hosted his banquet. *That* had been a proper fancy hall, which was where he needed to go in order to find his way to Fings.

A shout of alarm echoed from somewhere below. Either someone had found Suaresh, or Arjay, Brick and Topher hadn't waited. Seth turned to see what was happening behind him and wished he hadn't – Cleaver was a messy eater. He waited until it was over, then brought the two dead Spicers back with his sigils.

Two more Dead Men. The more, the merrier.

He mulled over whether four Dead Men might be enough and that maybe he should leave, but then the door burst open and a staggering Spicer half-entered, stopped as he saw Cleaver grinning with his face covered in blood, then stumbled the rest of the way in because of the two other men pushing behind him. All three looked pasty and sweaty. They weren't armed.

"Last time you're eating from *that* place, eh lads?" said Seth.

One of them even nodded as Seth waved his Dead Men forwards. "Kill this lot. When you're done, make your way down the stairs and wait for me in the hall at the bottom. You see anyone too stupid to run away, you can kill them, too. Apart from me, obviously."

He stepped back to watch.

Myla was already moving as the bolt flew. It ricocheted off the stone floor somewhere behind her.

"Very good." Sulfane set about reloading. "How often can you do that, do you think?"

"If you kill that man beside you," called Myla, "I'll tell you what you want to know."

"You don't *know* what I want to know. *Fings* does. And he didn't tell you, and you didn't murder him. Neither of you would do that." He pointed the crossbow back down the stair. "Get up, Fings. Last chance before I shoot you in the kneecap."

Myla sighed and backed away. "Get up," she hissed. It had been worth a try. She hadn't expected it to work, not really.

Fings hauled himself upright; and then, when he was on his feet, he pushed in front of Myla and put a knife to his own throat. "*Fuck* you, Sulfane. Going to kill me anyway, aren't you, you murdering bastard?"

"Fings! Don't be–"

Fings slashed the knife across his skin. Blood sprayed as he convulsed and fell back into the gloom and kicked and writhed. Myla stared aghast and then screamed and ran at the stairs, at the soldiers braced to meet her.

"Don't–" Sulfane looked stunned, wide-eyed and wild, like he didn't quite know whether or not to believe what he'd just seen.

Good. Two steps from the top, Myla threw the knife concealed up her sleeve straight at the face of the nearest swordsman. It flew badly and hit him sideways, but it was enough to draw blood and make him lurch back. Her hand flicked, snapping taut the thread tied to the knife, whipping it back to her.

The other soldier tensed to lunge.

"No! I need her alive!" Sulfane tried to grab at the soldier's arm but the crossbow made him clumsy. Didn't matter. Myla saw it coming, blocked the thrust with her other knife, stepped in close and rammed the first knife into the soldier's neck. Blood sprayed into her face. He twisted, dragging her with him, pulling her away from the swordsman with the bleeding face, putting space between them, leaving her exposed.

"Don't!"

She saw the thrust coming and knew she couldn't avoid it.

Ah well. Worth a try. And it was a shame, because there was Jeffa, right there, standing behind the man about to kill her. One lunge and she could have reached him...

The thrust never came. The soldier jerked and staggered and for a moment she didn't understand... And then she did: Sulfane had shot him.

"*Fuck's sake*! I need her *alive*!"

She saw Jeffa stare in disbelief. She saw the Spicers and the sell-swords behind him turning on one another. She pulled free and lunged. Jeffa skipped back, crashing into two of his men grappling with two Spicers. He grabbed Sulfane, pushing him into her, knocking her back. For a moment, their eyes locked, her and Sulfane. She saw the madness in him, naked at last, pleading with her.

"Fine!" he hissed. "Tell me where it is and I'll help you."

"But I don't need your help," she said, and stabbed him.

Six Dead Men was definitely enough. Seth sent them out to wreak havoc, reckoned on leaving them to it, and went back to the hole in the floor that had swallowed Lightbringer Suaresh. The drop wasn't *too* bad – only down to the floor below – and Suaresh wasn't lying there crippled. He was probably wandering around somewhere doing his Dead Man thing and generally causing mayhem.

Yes, Seth knew he *ought* to turn and leave now, but instead, he followed in the wake of his Dead Men until he found the grand flight of stairs that would take him to the Mage's banqueting hall. He watched from the shadows as two Spicers ran past, heading down, faces awash with panic. One was holding up his breeches and they both looked waxy and pale. From below, he heard shouts and screams. He wondered why, when all the Spicers had to do was run away and call a priest. Dead Men weren't all *that* dangerous, even when one of them had a cleaver and an unusually bad attitude...

Not my fault if more of them die.

He closed his eyes then, and smiled, and oozed out onto the stair and soaked himself in the air of the place. The size of it. A proper palace, if you looked past the ruin of it.

I could cope with living in a place like this.

The thought made him laugh. Him as the new Mage of Tombland? Wouldn't last five seconds.

And yet.

It crossed his mind that whoever was in charge these days – Sulfane or whoever was pulling his strings – they probably had the old Mage's rooms. He ducked into a doorway as another Spicer came running down, then trotted up the stairs. The whole top floor of the Constable's Castle had once been the Mage of Tombland's private preserve.

That smell... He recognised it as soon as he arrived, from all those years ago. The smell the Mage had carried with him.

The first rooms were discouraging. Old, empty and abandoned. Then he found himself in a bedroom; it was plush with expensive wool blankets, a chest, some drawers and a fancy glass lantern. He sniffed at the air again. Someone lived here. In fact, he knew *that* smell, too. It was different. It was someone... familiar.

He saw the bow. Sulfane.

Well then…

He went to the chest, a heavy old lump of wood covered in ornate carvings of some battle. The quality of the work was excellent. The battle of the Lasot when Kelm defeated the Sorcerer-king? Thandra seizing the river crossing at Varr…?

Time to find out who you really are, archer.

He frowned. A closer look revealed that what he'd taken for a scene of battle looked more like a city set ablaze. Not a battle but a massacre.

The chest wasn't locked. Seth opened it a crack, instinct driving him to stand to one side, and peered in. He couldn't see any thread attached to the lid and there didn't seem to be anything moving in there that might have fangs and so he ducked behind the bed, threw the lid open and stayed very still, waiting to see whether anything would happen. When it didn't, he went back to have a proper look.

At the bottom of the chest was a wooden box that turned out to be a book, bound in wood and faced in leather, with a lock to keep it shut. A quick hack with a knife and the book fell open. A seal was engraved into the wood on the inside: a winged serpent rampant wearing a solar halo wrapped around a sword. The same seal as on Fings' ring. The sign of the Mage of Tombland.

The sign of Valladrune and the Twelfth House, apparently.

He knew books. Religious books had pictures and fancy lettering. Books of proclamations and laws and such had fancy lettering but no pictures. Journals and histories had sketches and sometimes pictures but not much going on with the lettering. But this… *this* was nothing but strings of letters grouped into words that made no sense, and why would you…?

He supressed a giggle. A cypher. The whole book was written in a cypher. Why in the name of Khrozus the Bloody did Sulfane have a book written in a cypher from a place that had been wiped from existence?

You could always ask him.

Like that's going to work.

He felt his inner voice giving him a very long, hard stare, as if waiting for him to work out something that should have been obvious.

Oh. Right. Kill him first and then *ask him.*

He snapped the book shut, tutting and shaking his head. It really was going to take some work, getting used to that way of thinking.

"You did this," she said. "All of this."

Myla stabbed Sulfane a second time. He grunted and staggered. Then Jeffa lunged at her with his sword and she had to dance back. There were two corpses between them, as well as Sulfane sinking slowly against the wall. Jeffa swung again, trying to keep her off-balance as she stepped between the bodies. She ducked and snatched up a sword from the man Sulfane had shot. As Jeffa swung for a third time, she parried, twisted, turned him and kicked him in the side. He howled and staggered away. Behind him, his remaining two sell-swords turned to face her. The last of Sulfane's Spicers were either dead or running away.

"Myla…" Sulfane was staring up at her, teeth gritted against the pain. "It's not what–"

"Shut up." She bent down, never taking her eyes off Jeffa, and picked up a second sword from the floor. They weren't made of Sunsteel, and they weren't as light or as well balanced as her hook-swords, but they were good enough.

"Let it end, Jeffa. Go home. Leave my family alone and you never need hear of me again." The hall was wide enough for two men to fight side by side. Two, but not three.

Jeffa shook his head, sliding between his two swordsmen as they took up their guard.

"I don't particularly want to hurt you," Myla said. "But I will."

"Is that what you said to my brother before you mutilated him?"

"Do you *want* to know what I said to your brother?" She shivered, a flash of the old anger coursing through her. Three of them, one of her. "Your brother made a promise. All he had to do was keep it."

Jeffa rolled his eyes. "You can't have expected–"

"Can't have expected him to marry down so far?" Myla shook her head. "Sarwatta said the same. Do you want to hear my answer?"

"I don't give a–"

Myla lunged, so fast that the swordsman in front of her didn't even move. Her point caught him square in the midriff. His hard leather held but it was enough that he doubled over, gagging for air. The other sell-sword stabbed at her. She caught the thrust with her second sword, knocked it aside and swept his legs out from under him. Myla stamped his ankle as he hit the ground and heard the bone snap. He screamed. The first sell-sword flailed at her and then Myla had her sword-tip to his throat.

"Drop it."

He dropped it. He was still gasping.

"Now go." She jabbed a little, pricking his skin. "Go!"

He backed away.

"*Run*, fuckhead!"

He ran. Myla turned to Jeffa. Just the two of them, and Sulfane behind her, slumped against the wall and slowly dying.

"Go back to Deephaven," she said. "Go back to your brother. Live your life."

He swung at her. She dodged around his blade, kicked him to the ground and trod on his hand, crushing his fingers until he dropped his sword.

"Go home, Jeffa."

"Myla!" Sulfane was slumped against the wall where she'd left him, eyes pleading with her. "The crown. You can't give it back."

She backed away, eyes flicking between Sulfane and Jeffa. "If you had anything worth saying, Sulfane, you should have said it a long time ago."

"Myla… You can't… You don't know what it means… If she has it, they *will* come for her. It will be a war like… nothing you can image. A war of mages…"

Myla turned her back on them both and walked away.

"Myla."

No.

"Myla!"

No.

"*Myla!*"

Some edge to his last call made her half-turn, just enough to see Jeffa back on his feet, running at her, sword raised, face twisted in rage and yet silent. She met him head on, steel ringing as their swords met, as she turned away one lunge and then another.

"I'll tell you how I answered your brother."

He hammered at her, gasping and panting, more enraged with every attack she blocked.

"I told him that all he had to do was say that he was sorry."

The blows rained harder. Jeffa had lost all his technique. It was wild fury, now.

"All he had to do was say one little word and I wouldn't hurt him."

Jeffa threw himself at her. Skewering him would have been easy but she wanted him to at least have a chance to save himself. He tried to grapple with her, wrapping his arms around her, head low, bulling into her. She brought the hilts of her swords down hard on his spine, one behind the other. He arched and screamed and let go and dropped his steel.

"Stay down, Jeffa. Stay down."

Jeffa snatched up his sword. Spittle flecked his mouth.

"Jeffa! Stay down!"

Jeffa snarled. "I'm going to *kill* you!" He dragged himself to his feet. Myla settled into guard.

"One little apology, Jeffa. That's all. Do you know what he did?"

Jeffa threw himself at her. She made a turning step forward, right sword swinging low, snapping a cut to his groin. She felt it bite. She swept at his legs, making him jump, then dropped low. A flick of the wrist for extra speed, a rising cut from the right-hand blade while the left sliced down...

For a moment, they were both still. Jeffa stared at the severed stump where his hand used to be.

"He told me that people like him didn't need to apologise to people like me," said Myla. "And then he laughed and dared me to do my worst."

A half-step forward, both swords in wild converging arcs. A moment of pure focus as the form completed into a low deep stance, swords spread wide to the stars; and then she rose and turned.

She was already walking away as Jeffa's head hit the floor.

On his way down to the old dungeons, Seth passed a couple of Spicers dead from wounds that looked suspiciously like they'd come from a cleaver. He caught up with his Dead Men one by one and told them to follow. When he had them all together, he walked them down to the old banquet hall. It was all still there, all the way he remembered it from that night almost a decade ago. The tables, the throne, the chairs… like it was only yesterday.

He had his Dead Men sit where Blackhand and the Mage had sat that night: Cleaver got to be the Mage on his throne while the four Spicer Dead Men got to be Blackhand and Wil and Sand and Rev. When he had them arranged just so, he drew sigils, one after another, and set his Dead Men free, letting them have their peace, off to be with the Sun or the Moon or the Hungry Goddess or whoever would have them. He saved Cleaver for last. A part of him didn't want to let Cleaver go, but then again, even if he could hide the Dead Man from the daylight, a sword-monk or a priest would find him, sooner or later, and that would mean no end of trouble.

As he hesitated, Cleaver grinned, tapped his nose, and ran off. Seth looked on in complete bafflement.

"Stop?" he tried. Cleaver ignored him. Which wasn't supposed to be possible, assuming he understood the sigils right, which very probably he didn't.

He stood, wondering what to do with himself, then remembered he was supposed to be opening the door for Brick and Arjay and Topher, and looking for Fings. Except when he turned to go, the door was already open and he wasn't alone. Orien stood across the room watching him, a big ugly bruise on one cheek.

Slap a sigil on him!

It *was* tempting.

And maybe Orien read his mind, because the fire-mage stopped, and flames flared from his fingers.

"We need to talk, you and I."

Fuck. Fuck, fuck, fuck! Seth held up his hands to show they were empty. "I don't know about you, but I'm just here to help my friends."

Orien eyed him suspiciously.

So what does *happen if I turn a mage into a Dead Man?*

Shut up!

You have to admit, it would *be interesting.*

"I was a priest," said Seth. "We learn a bit more about Dead Men than we generally let on." Would he fall for that? How much did he know about priests?

"Is that so?"

If he talks to Myla, you're fucked. "You know it wasn't only the Emperor's crown that went missing, right?" Seth cocked his head.

"What do you mean?" Orien's guard didn't waver.

"There were papers. But you already knew that."

There. A flicker. A moment of hesitation. Seth wasn't sure how to read it. Did the mage know exactly what he was talking about, or was it something else, some inkling of a suspicion now confirmed?

Just sigil the fucker and get out of here.

"I'll show you, if you like."

Very slowly, very carefully, Seth reached into his pocket and pulled out a strip of paper. He offered it to Orien.

Go on. Take it.

The mage reached and took it, and then jumped back.

Seth waited for the look of horror to seep into Orien's face as the sigil took hold. As it burned itself into the skin of Orien's fingers.

Too fucking easy. "Put the fire away."

The fire disappeared from Orien's other hand.

"You here to help Myla?" Seth asked.

Orien nodded.

"I'm going to leave now," said Seth. "I'm going to send some friends of mine to join you. They're called Brick and Arjay and Topher. You're going to help them get Myla out of here, and my friend Fings, too." Seth shrugged. "Better job you'll do of it than I could at this point. Anyway. You're also going to forget you ever saw me tonight. Not here, not in the alley outside. You're going to forget anything you think you know about me except that I'm Myla's friend. And you can be fucking grateful that's all I'm going to do to you."

With that, Seth walked out the door.

Should have turned him into a Dead Man.

Come dawn, the light of the sun would burn away the mark on Orien's hand and the power of the sigil would fade. When that happened, Seth didn't know how much the mage would remember.

Come dawn, you'd better be gone.

Which was no great burden.

Outside the open gates to the castle, Seth waved to the shadows where Brick and Arjay and Topher were lurking. He told than about Orien – well, obviously not the bit about using heretical sigils to mess with the mage's head – and watched them run inside. When they were gone, he turned his back and walked away, heading for the river, for the entrance to the Undercity and whatever else was waiting for him there.

Be safe, Fings. But don't come looking for me.

When everything turned quiet, Fings picked himself up. He walked to the top of the stair. One of the Deephaven sell-swords was lying face down with a bolt from a crossbow sticking out the back of his head. Another was slumped against the wall, covered in blood. A third was splattered across the place a little bit further down. The one who'd been in charge. Jeffa, was it? Apparently, he'd misplaced his head.

Irritatingly, the Murdering Bastard was still alive. Sweaty and pale, breathing fast and shallow, clutching his side, but definitely not dead. He stared up as Fings looked down at him.

"You..." said Sulfane.

Fings nodded. "How you doing down there?"

"I saw... You... I saw... you..."

"Cut my own throat?" Fings shook his head, then opened his shirt and showed the Sulfane the empty wineskin tied to his arm. "Present from one of your lads who fell down the stairs." He untied the skin and upended it. A few drops dribbled out. "Was mostly piss. Figured it was too dark for you to see the difference."

"Myla...?"

"That one was all me. Got the idea from you, actually." Fings frowned. "So... Are you actually dying for real this time?"

Sulfane looked at him. "Where... Where's... my... crown?"

Fings squatted against the opposite wall, carefully keeping his distance. "I *did* tell you about the goblins. I *did* say not to leave it all behind like that. One of you pillocks was always going to go back on your own and try to take it all for yourselves. That's what always happens." He shrugged. "In the end, we all did. You, me, even Myla."

"You'd... you'd better... you'd better finish me this time... If you don't... I'll find you."

"Way I hear it, there's mages on their way. So I leave that up to you."

Fings pushed himself back to his feet. He gave Sulfane a last look as he walked away, and almost felt sorry for him.

Almost.

48

THE MOONSTEEL CROWN

Myla got it out of Fings once they were all back at the Unruly Pig. The crown was on its way to Varr. That and the three bags of silver.

"We give it back," she said.

"You and your mage?" Fings asked.

"That's right."

"And then?"

Myla shrugged. "You can keep the silver."

"You going back to Deephaven?"

"Don't see I have much other choice. Jeffa's brother knows I'm alive. I can't walk away from that. You?"

Fings shrugged. Sometimes, with Fings, it was like getting blood out of a stone.

"Maybe I'll see you there," she said.

"There's a bridge that no one ever uses over a canal in Bonecarvers," she told Orien later. "We'll do it there." She took him to see it, since Bonecarvers wasn't the sort of place that someone like Orien would ever go on his own. He looked around and nodded and went away.

"Midwinter's night." He said, when he came back the next morning. "Two hours after sunset." He handed her a bundle that turned out to be a set of pristine sword-monk robes. "Don't ask. As far as anyone else is concerned, you're simply doing your duty to the throne."

"And you take the credit?" Myla raised an eyebrow.

"Yes." Orien grinned. "Although most of it will go to my mistress."

They went their separate ways, Orien to wherever it was that he lived, Myla to the Pig where she packed what little she had, dressed in the robes Orien had given her, and went to see Arjay. The Pig felt like a haunted house these days, so still and quiet. Somehow her swords had made it back to her room and were hiding under her bed. Fings, she supposed.

"I'm leaving," she told Arjay. "I'll be in the Angry Man on Spice Market Square for a few days if anyone needs to find me."

Arjay nodded. They both knew she meant Fings.

"What about you?"

Arjay cracked a smile. She spread her arms and gestured at the room around her. "This. The Unrulys are done but the Pig lives on. Going to open it up again."

"I'd like to see that," said Myla.

Arjay looked her up and down, taking in the robes and the swords. "That who are you now, is it?"

"I don't know." Myla met her eye. "I hope so."

"You could stay, if you want. I could do with someone to help run this place."

"One day, maybe."

A young woman showed up at the Angry Man on the afternoon of Midwinter. It took Myla a moment to recognise her as Fings' sister, the one she'd saved that night in Locusteater Yard. She came with a box, handed it over and left without a word. It was the box from the barge. Myla found herself some salt and some iron and checked – this *was* Fings, after all – but the crown was still inside. She met Orien at sunset and they walked together into Bonecarvers. He kept looking at her, and she didn't know whether it was the crown that drew his eye or whether it was something else.

"It *is* in there," she said as they crossed Haberdashers. "I can show you, if you like." After that, he didn't look at her as much, but he didn't stop either. For some reason, that pleased her.

They stopped in a small crowded square near Samir's Folly and shared a cup of spiced wine to pass the time and keep warm. The air buzzed with noise and that wild edge that came with Midwinter night.

"Anything goes tonight," said Orien. He obviously wanted to kiss her again.

"And means nothing come sunrise," she answered.

"If we make it that far," he said.

"We will."

He blinked and looked at her for long time, and then it seemed that he understood, and his expression shifted to something softer.

The last sunlight of the year faded from the sky. Deep night settled on the city and its revels. Stars shone bright. The Baleful Eye gazed down, and the moon, full and ripe. Two hours after sunset, Myla and Orien stood at the middle of the Folly watching four figures on horseback approach from the other side, their breath steaming in the night. Three wore black armour from head to foot. The fourth was a woman in orange robes, a match for Orien's except that the woman's robes were richer and finer by far.

"That's your mistress?"

Orien nodded.

They walked to the middle of the bridge. Orien's mistress dismounted and came to meet them. Orien bowed.

"Sun help you if you're mistaken about any of this," said the woman in orange.

"I feel them," said Orien.

"We *all* feel *some*thing. But that doesn't make it what you say it is." She sounded annoyed and… nervous? "Where is it?"

Orien gave Myla a nod. Myla pulled the crown in its box out of the satchel across her back and offered it.

The woman in orange looked at her for a long time. "Don't sword-monks answer to the Autarch of Torpreah?"

Myla nodded.

"And will the Autarch of Torpreah recognise his Highness Emperor Ashahn the Second as the rightful ruler of the Empire?"

Myla met her eye. You didn't have to be a sword-monk to know that the Path of the Sun had never accepted Khrozus seizing the throne. "You want to know, go and ask him." She held out the box. "Do you want this or not?"

Flames flickered in the woman's eyes. She took the box and opened it. The Moonsteel Crown gleamed bright and eager under the night sky. Myla could almost hear it whispering, calling to the darkness.

The sorceress in orange turned to leave, but then one of the horsemen in black dismounted, stepped onto the bridge and lifted her helmet. Orien immediately dropped to his knees and pressed his head to the snow. Myla wondered why, because all she saw was a dark-skinned woman with long black hair tied in a plait that reached to the small of her back. Her glittering black armour was Moonsteel mail. Her soul-stealing eyes were emerald green. She wore a golden circlet across her brow that shone with a soft silver light...

The golden Circlet of the Moon.

Oh.

The sorceress princess. The Imperial regent.

A power radiated from her; but mostly Myla's impression was that the Princess-Regent was surprisingly short. The regent came up to her, looked at Orien, and then looked back, as if asking why Myla wasn't on her knees as well.

"I'm told it was one of your kind who killed my mother," she said. Her voice was soft and measured.

They studied each other, both as if searching for something.

"I wouldn't know," said Myla.

"There's a storm coming. From the sea. Can you feel it?"

Myla bowed her head. She had a reckoning of her own coming, that much she knew. "My teacher would say that it is we who must be the storm."

The regent touched a finger to Myla's cheek. "Your teacher is right. Thank you for this, sword-monk. I will remember."

* * *

"What's a fire-mage then?" asked Fings. They'd walked the length of Threadneedle Street together, Fings setting a brisk pace to get this over with as fast as possible, Orien striding comfortably behind. So far, Fings had learned exactly two things about the mage. The first was that he carried a sword openly on the street, the second was that people were more than happy to get out of his way. Quite possibly these were related.

He didn't *want* to know, of course. What he *really* wanted was for the mage to vanish down an alley and for their paths never to cross again. Trouble was, Orien didn't look like he planned on doing any vanishing any time soon, and Fings feared that knowing only two things about the man might be construed as a lack of effort. He didn't know what fire-mages did with people who didn't pay them the proper degree of attention, but he strongly suspected that some sort of burning might be involved.

"We specialise in fire sorcery," said Orien, with a note of pride.

"You mean you burn stuff?" *See!*

"And we put fires out. It will be one of the tenets of the new guild that we'll be responsible for extinguishing city fires."

Fings was briefly impressed. Every summer, some part of the city caught fire. Often as not, an entire district burned to ash. Mostly, the Longcoats – and eventually the residents – sat around by the surrounding canals making sure the fire didn't get uppity and have a go at crossing the water. Trying to put the fires out once they were too big for a couple of frantic men with buckets never seemed to occur to anyone.

"What new guild's that then?"

"The Fire-mages' Guild, obviously." Which was all the answer Fings wanted, but Orien had clearly found his favourite topic of conversation. "It's about time there was something new. The old guild is far too introspective and serves little useful purpose to the Empire at large."

"Er... right."

"Now that her Highness has been declared regent of the Empire, she has promised to honour what my mistress did for her by granting a guild charter to the fire-mages. I should tell you…" Orien's voice dropped to a very loud conspiratorial whisper, "that Lady Novashi is now one of the Princess-Regent's closest confidantes. Especially now we've returned her father's crown."

"Er… That's… good." Fings marvelled at the way that even the crowds in the Spice Market – perilously busy now that the snow had been cleared – parted for Orien. He couldn't help wondering, though: if all this was true and Orien was about to be hobnobbing with royalty, what the bloody Khrozus was he doing hanging around a place like the Unruly Pig?

"When it comes to the Torpreahns, the four main northern houses can be counted on…"

Fings' attention wandered to the stalls and the people and the occasional carelessly dangled purse or unguarded handful of coins. The new year had started with vigour and purpose and an unexpected break in the weather. Usually, he'd be out in the market every evening while it lasted, his pockets full of half-bits by the time he went home, and then Seth would be up before dawn with the other scavengers, looking for scraps and leftovers – and occasional frozen bodies – left lying in the snow. Everything was going back to normal.

Almost normal. It occurred to him that he hadn't seen Seth since Tombland. Although he did have a fairly shrewd idea where to look.

He sighed, not much liking the idea, and then it also occurred to him than that he didn't actually *need* to be cutting purses any more either, not with three bags of the Emperor's silver carefully stashed away. Just didn't know what else to do with himself.

There's always Levvi, I suppose. About time someone went looking…

Orien carried on talking politics. The word *gold* briefly caught Fings' attention – something about a mine.

"So, er… with all this going on and everything, why are you…?" *Why are you still here bothering us* was what Fings wanted to ask, just couldn't think of a way to say it that wasn't rude and might cause an unfortunate outburst of things getting set on fire.

Orien turned on him. "Would *you* trust a Guild Mage?"

Fings shuffled from one foot to the other. Fortunately, they'd reached where they were going, so he pointed at the entrance to the Angry Man. They walked together through the door and Fings left Orien to do the talking, because on the whole people looked at Orien and his swanky robes and thought *Here's someone I don't want to annoy*, whereas when they looked at Fings, they mostly started to check whether they still had all their belongings.

"We're looking for Myla," said Orien, stopping one of the serving boys, but the boy only looked confused. He called an older man.

"Myla?" The older man shook his head. "Don't know any–"

"You can't miss her! Sword-monk. You know, robe, pair of swords, a bit prickly–"

"Oh! You mean Shirish." The older man was nodding now, smiling a knowing smile.

"Who?" started Orien.

Fings caught his arm. "That's what them Deephaven lot called her."

Orien stared. "Yes! Wait... Shirish? *The* Shirish?"

"She here?" asked Fings. He shot Orien a sideways glance but the mage seemed to be in some sort of state of shock.

The older man shook his head. "Paid up and left yesterday."

"She say where she was going?" asked Fings, although he was fairly sure he knew.

"No, sorry."

"Did she leave a message?" asked Orien. "For me? My name is Orien!"

The man shook his head. "No. Just said to say to anyone who asked that she wouldn't be coming back."

ACKNOWLEDGMENTS

Once upon a time in a galaxy far, far away, there was a roleplaying campaign. The characters of Myla, Seth, Fings, Orien, Wil and Tarran were born there, as was this story. A lot has changed since but I think those involved will still recognise their bastardised chronicle. I know quite a of things were different and some things were a wrench to cut – Fings' on-going obsession with chairs as the optimal weapon against the Dead Men, for example, thanks to one lucky roll.

Thanks especially to Michaela (Myla), who read every word of the first draft of this story as I laid it down years ago. Thanks to Eleanor and Sam at Angry Robot and Margo-Lee Hurwicz for bending the story into a better shape.

A special thanks to KJ Parker, without whose encouragement, long ago, none of this would ever have existed.

Myla, Fings, Seth and Orien will return in *The Book of Endings*. For those who want more and don't want to wait, a certain Swordmistress Tasahre features in *The Warlock's Shadow*, volume two of my *Thief-Taker* series.

And for any of you out there who read the *Memory of Flames* series from start to finish and were left wondering what happened to Red Lin Feyn in chapter 18 of *The Silver Kings*, well, you've now met the witches of fire and ice. It's coming, gods of sales-numbers permitting…

Fancy some more heist-like highjinks? Why not try Steal the Sky by Megan E. O'Keefe

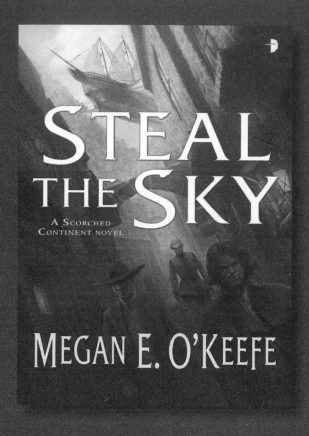

Read the first chapter here!

CHAPTER 1

It was a pretty nice burlap sack. Not the best he'd had the pleasure of inhabiting, not by a long shot, but it wasn't bad either. The jute was smooth and woven tight, not letting in an inkling of light or location. It didn't chafe his cheeks either, which was a small comfort.

The chair he was tied to was of considerably lesser quality. Each time Detan shifted his weight to keep the ropes from cutting off his circulation little splinters worked their way into his exposed arms and itched something fierce. Despite the unfinished wood, the chair's joints were solid, and the knots on his ropes well tied, which was a shame.

Detan strained his ears, imagining that if he tried hard enough he could work out just where he was. No use, that. Walls muted the bustle of Aransa's streets, and the bitter-char aromas of local delicacies were blotted by the tight weave of the sack over his head. At least the burlap didn't stink of the fear sweat of those who'd worn it before him.

Someone yanked the bag off and that was surprising, because he hadn't heard anyone in the room for the last half-mark. Truth be told, he was starting to think they'd forgotten about him, which was a mighty blow to his pride.

As he blinked in the light, the blurry face of his visitor resolved into an assemblage of hard, almond-brown planes with sandy hair scraped back into a tight, professional plait. Ripka. Funny, she looked taller than the last time he'd seen her. He gave her a stupid grin, because he knew she hated it.

"Detan Honding." He liked the way she said his name, dropping each syllable in place as if she were discarding rotten fruit. "Thought I told you to stay well clear of Aransa."

"I think you'll find I've been doing my very best to honor your request, watch captain. I am a paragon of lawfulness, a beacon for the truthful, a–"

"Really? Then why did my men find you card-sharking in Blasted Rock Inn?"

"Card sharking?" he asked in the most incredulous voice he could muster. "I don't even know what that *is*. What's a sha-ark? Sounds dangerous!"

Ripka shook her head like a disappointed proctor and took a step back, tossing the bag to the ground. Detan was sorry to see such a fine sack abused so, but he took the chance to take in his surroundings. The room was simple, not a stick of furniture in it aside from his own chair and the corner of a desk peeking out from around the eclipsing curve of the watch captain.

By the color of the warm light, he guessed there weren't any windows hiding behind him, just clean oil lamps. The floor was hard-packed dirt, the walls unyielding yellowstone. It was construction he recognized all too well, though he'd never had the pleasure of seeing this particular room before. He was in the Watch's station house, halfway up the levels of the stepped city of Aransa. Could be worse. Could have been a cell.

Ripka sat behind what he supposed must be her desk. No books, no trinkets. Not the slightest hint of personality. Just a neat stack of papers with a polished pen laid beside it. Definitely Ripka's.

Keeping one stern eye on him, she pulled a folder from the stack of papers and splayed it open against the desk. Before it flipped open, Detan saw his family crest scribbled on the front in basic, hasty lines. He'd seen that folder only once before, the first time he'd blown through Aransa, and it hadn't had anything nice to say about him then. He fought down a grimace, waiting while her eyes skimmed over all the details she'd collected of his life. She sighed, drumming her fingers on the desk as she spoke.

"Let's see now. Last time you were here, Honding, you and your little friend Tibal unlawfully imprisoned Watcher Banch, distributed false payment, stole personal property from the family Erst, and disrupted the peace of the entire fourth level."

"All a terrible misunderstanding, I assure–"

She held up a fist to silence him.

"I can't hold you on any of this. Banch and the Ersts have withdrawn their complaints and your fake grains have long since disappeared. But none of that means I can't kick your sorry hide out of my city, understand? You're the last person I need around here right now. I don't know why you washed up on my sands, but I'll give you until the night to shove off again."

"I'd be happy to oblige, captain, but my flier's busted and it'll be a good few turns before she's airworthy again. But don't you worry, Tibs's working on getting it fixed up right."

"Still dragging around Tibal? Should have known, you've got that poor sod worshipping your shadow, and it's going to get him killed someday. What's wrong with the flier? And stop trying to work your ropes loose."

He froze and mustered up what he thought was a contrite grin. Judging by the way Ripka glowered at him he was pretty sure she didn't take it right. No fault of his if she didn't have a sense of humor.

"Punctured a buoyancy sack somewhere over the Fireline Ridge, lucky for us I'm a mighty fine captain myself, otherwise we'd be tits-up in the Black Wash right about now."

Her fingers stopped drumming. "Really. Fireline. Nothing but a bunch of uppercrusts taking tours of the selium mines and dipping in at the Salt Baths over there. So just what in the sweet skies were *you* doing up there?"

A chill worked its way into his spine at her pointed glare, her pursed lips. Old instincts to flee burbled up in him, and for just a moment his senses reached out. There was a small source of selium – the gas that elevated airships – just behind Ripka's desk.

A tempting amount. Just small enough to cause a distraction, if he chose to use it. He gritted his teeth and pushed the urge aside. If he were caught out for being a sel-sensitive, it'd be back to the selium mines with him – or worse, into the hands of the whitecoats.

He forced a cheery grin. "Certainly not impersonating a steward and selling false excursion tickets to the baths. That would be beneath me."

She groaned and dragged her fingers through her hair, mussing her plait. "I want you out of my city, Honding, and a busted buoyancy sack shouldn't take more'n a day to patch up. Can you do that?"

"That would be no trouble at all."

"Wonderful."

"If it were *just* the buoyancy sack."

Her fingers gripped the edge of her desk, knuckles going white. "I could throw you in the Smokestack and no one in the whole of the Scorched would lift a finger to find out why."

"But you wouldn't. You're a good woman, Ripka Leshe. It's your biggest flaw."

"Could be I make you my first step on a downward spiral."

"Who put sand in your trousers, anyway? Everyone's wound up around here like the Smokestack is rearing to blow. Pits below, Ripka, your thugs didn't even take my bribe."

"Watch Captain Leshe," she corrected, but it was an automatic answer, lacking any real snap. "You remember Warden Faud?"

"'Course I do, that fellow is straight as a mast post. Told me if he ever saw my sorry hide here again he'd tan it and use the leather for a new sail. Reminds me of you, come to think on it."

"Well, he's dead. Found him ballooned up on selium gas floating around the ceiling of his sitting room. Good thing the shutters were pulled, otherwise I think he would have blown halfway to the Darkling Sea by now."

Detan snorted. He bit his lip and closed his eyes, struggling to hold down a rising tide of laughter. Even Ripka had a bit of a curl to her mouth as she told the story. But still, she had admired the crazy old warden, and Detan suspected she might just consider carrying out the man's wish of turning him into leather if he let loose with the laugh he was swallowing.

He risked opening his eyes. "How in the pits did it all stay in there?"

Her face was a mask of professional decorum. "The late warden had been sealed with guar sap. On all ends."

"Still got him? ... I could use a new buoyancy sack."

Detan was too busy laughing until the tears flowed to see her coming. She swept the leg of his chair away and he went down with a grunt, but he didn't care. It was just too much for him to let go. When he had subsided into burbling chuckles, Ripka cleared her throat. He felt a little triumphant to see a bit of wet shining at the corner of her eye.

"Are you quite finished?" she asked.

"For now."

She produced a short blade of bone-blacked Valathean steel. It probably had a poncy name, but all Detan cared about was the fresh glint along the cutting edge. It was a good knife, and that was usually bad news for him. Good women with good knives had a habit of making use of them in his general direction. He swallowed, tried to scoot away and only dug his splinters deeper.

"Now, there's no need for–"

"Oh, shut up."

She knelt beside him and cut the ropes around his wrists and ankles. He knew better than to pop right up. Irritable people were prone to making rash decisions, and he'd discovered there were a surprisingly large number of irritable people in the world. When she stepped away he wormed himself to his feet and made a show of rubbing his wrists.

"Some higher quality rope wouldn't be too much to ask for, I think."

"No one cares what you think, Honding." She jerked the chair back to its feet and pointed with the blade. "Now sit."

He eyed the rickety structure and shuffled his feet toward the door. "Wouldn't want to take up any more of your time, watch captain…"

"Did I say you could leave?" Her knuckles went bloodless on the handle of the blade, her already thin lips squeezed together in a hard line. Detan glanced at the chair, then back at Ripka. A few traitorous beads of sweat crested his brow. He thought about the selium, looming somewhere behind her desk, but shunted the idea aside. She pointed again.

He obliged. He had a life philosophy of never saying no to a lady with a knife if he could help it. And anyway, something had her wound up crankier than a rockcat in a cold bath. She needed something, and needful people often played loose with their gold.

"Thought you wanted me gone yesterday," he ventured.

"Then it's too bad you're here today. I want a timeline from you, understand?"

"Oh, well. Let's see. In the beginning, the firemounts broke free from the sea–"

"Stop. Just. Stop."

He shut up. He didn't often know when he was pushing it, but he knew it now.

"Thratia is making a grab for the warden's seat, understand? I can't have you in my hair when I've got her in my shadow."

"Oh."

"Yeah, *oh*."

He grimaced. Detan had been all over the Scorched Continent a half dozen times easy and he had yet to run into a woman more ruthless than ex-Commodore Thratia Ganal. Sure, she was Valathean bred and all sweetness and light to anyone with gold in their pockets. But it had to be the right amount of gold, backed by the right intentions.

Poor as a smokefish? Better work for her. Enough gold to buy a proper uppercrust house? Best pay your fire taxes, Aransa was a dangerous place, after all. More gold than her? Better invest in whatever she wants and then sod right off to wherever you came from.

A pleasant conversationalist, though, so that was something.

Rumor had it Thratia didn't appreciate the spidery arm of Valathean law meddling with the Scorched settlements, which meant Ripka was in the shit if Thratia took over. Even with the whole of the Darkling Sea between Valathea's island empire and the Scorched, the empire's control over its frontier cities was absolute through its selium-lifted airships and its watchers. The watchers held to imperial law, and kept the Scorched's selium mines producing to fill Valathean needs and Valathean coffers.

And Thratia didn't much care for Valathean needs, now that they'd kicked her loose.

He stifled another *oh*, watching the honorable watch captain through enlightened eyes. The way she kept glancing at the door, as if she were worried someone would barge in. The way she held her knife, point-out and ready to dance. She was scared senseless.

And scared people were easy to play. Detan leaned forward, hands clasped with interest, brow drawn in grave understanding.

"You think she was behind the warden's death?" he asked, just to keep Ripka talking while he worked through the possibilities.

"That crow? I doubt it. It's not her style, wasting something as valuable as selium to make a point. The favorite theory going around right now is it was a doppel." She snorted. "Caught one a few days back, impersonating some dead mercer. City's been seeing them in every shadow ever since. Might as well be a ghost or a bogeyman, but I can't ignore the possibility. Your mouth is open, Honding."

He shut it. "Are you serious? A *doppel*?"

He'd heard of the creatures – every little Scorched lad grew up with stories of scary doppels replacing your loved ones – but he'd never seen one before. The amount of skill and strength it'd take to use a thin layer of prismatic selium to cover your own face, changing hues and sculpting features, was so far beyond his ken the thought left him speechless. He was all brute strength when it came to his sel-sensitivity. He even had trouble shaping a simple ball out of the lighter-than-air gas.

"They're not pets, rockbrain," Ripka said. "They're extremely dangerous and if they're geared up to attack the settlements then we're going to have to send word to Valathea."

Detan's mouth felt coated in ash. Valathea liked its sel-sensitives just fine, but as Detan had found out to his own personal horror it liked them weak, fit for little more than moving the gas out of mines and into the buoyant bellies of ships. Anytime the sensitives got too strong, or their abilities deviated from the accepted standard, Valathean steel came out ringing.

"That'd mean a purge," he said.

She tipped her chin down, and her gaze snagged on the knife in her hand as if seeing it for the first time. For just a moment, her mask slipped. Detan squinted, trying to read the fine lines of her face. Was that sadness? Or indigestion? Ripka rolled her shoulders to loosen them and retightened her grip.

"I can't have half this city's sel-sensitives wiped out because they might be breeding too strongly. The Smokestack is an active mine, we need the sensitives to keep it moving. I'll find the murderer before Valathea needs to get involved."

He shook off the thought of a purge and focused on what mattered: Thratia was filthy rich. And, even as an ex-commodore, the owner of a rather fine airship.

Even trolling around the smaller, ramshackle steadings of the Scorched, Detan had heard of Thratia's latest prize. The *Larkspur*, she was called, and rumor had it she was as sleek as an oiled rockcat. Being both fast and large, that ship was making Thratia mighty rich as mercers across the empire paid a premium to have her ferry their goods to the most lucrative ports long before slower, competing vessels could catch up. Detan had no need for the *Larkspur*'s goods-delivery services, but he rather fancied the idea of ripping the rug out from under Thratia's quickly growing mercer collective. And anyway, he thought he'd probably cut a pretty handsome figure standing on the deck of a ship like that. Although he'd have to upgrade to a nicer hat.

"Well, watch captain, maybe we can help each other out."

She looked like she'd drunk sour milk. "You're kidding. Only way you can help me is by getting gone, Honding. You understand?" Ripka turned away from him and sat behind her desk once more, her thigh bumping the side with a light clunk as she did so. Detan allowed himself a little smile; so the brave watch captain wore body armor while in his presence.

"Oh, pah. You and I both know that if Thratia wants the wardenship she's going to take it. People fear her too damned much to risk not voting her in. And you'll be too busy chasing your boogeyman to do anything about it."

"Fear? You got it wrong. They respect her, and that's the trouble of it. She'll get voted in, nice and legal. No need for a coup," she said.

"So what if I could… undermine that respect? Make a public fool of her?"

"The only public fool around here is you."

"Well, you want me gone, don't you?"

"Yes."

"And I don't have a flier to get gone with, do I?"

She just frowned at him.

"And you want Thratia undermined, right?"

"I suppose…"

"So I'll steal her airship!"

"You're out of your sandbagged mind, Honding."

"No, no – listen up, captain." He leaned forward and held his hand out, ticking off the fingers with each point he made. "Thratia's got power here because she's got respect, right?"

"And money."

"Right, and money. So we can get rid of her respect, and a substantial chunk of her money, in one big blow." He made a fist and raised it up.

"You only made one point there, and you've got five fingers."

"Er, well. That doesn't matter. It makes sense, Ripka."

"Watch captain."

"Watch captain." He gave her a smile bright as the midday sun and leaned back in his chair with his fingers laced behind his head. "It's brilliant. She'll look like a doddering fool and you can swoop in and save the day. Then let me go, of course."

She snorted. "Why in the blue skies would I want to do that?"

"Because I'd tell Thratia it was your idea if you didn't, obviously."

"And then I look the fool for letting you escape."

"No, we let it sit for a while. I'll slip away after you've got the wardenship secured. Tell everyone you shipped me off to serve hard labor on the Remnant Isles."

She started, eyes narrowing. "You think I want to be warden?"

Had he misjudged? Detan held his hands up to either side, palms facing the sweet skies to indicate he would defer to her better judgment. "Well, you must. Or you've got someone in mind, surely?"

She pressed her fingers together above the desk, the arc of her hands outlining the mouth of a cave, and leaned forward as she thought. It was odd she seemed to be thinking so hard about this. He'd thought she'd have someone in mind worth the promotion, but he still couldn't help but grin. Her body language was open, interested. There was a little furrow between her brows, deep and contemplative. He'd got her.

"Mine Master Galtro would be a good candidate," she said, and he chose to ignore the hesitance in her voice. Didn't matter to him who she picked. He planned on being long gone by the time that particular seat was being warmed.

He leapt to his feet and clapped once. "Good! Marvelous! Hurrah! We have a warden! Now you just need to let me do my–"

"Whoa now. What's in this for you?"

"The thrill of adventure!"

"Try again."

"Fine." He huffed. "Say, perhaps, the ship has a little accident in all that excitement. Say, just for example, that some convincing wreckage is found made of the right materials, with the right name emblazoned on the heap. Say *that* to all the citizens, and let me keep the blasted thing."

She drummed her fingers on the desk. "Thratia's compound is

the most secure in the whole city. Just how do you think you're going to get anywhere near her ship?"

"That's my worry, partner."

"I am not–"

"Watch captain."

She scowled at him, but quieted.

"Look, don't worry over it all too much and don't count on it yet either, understand? I'm going to have a look around, see if it's even doable, and then I'll contact you again with our options."

"You get snagged, and I'll swear I sent you packing this day."

"Wouldn't expect it any other way."

"And if you can't find a way to work it?"

"Tibal will have the flier fixed up by then, nice and smooth."

Ripka eyed him, hard and heavy, and he thanked the stable sands that he had a whole lot of practice at keeping his face open and charming. She grunted and dragged open the top drawer of her desk.

"Here." She tossed him a thin cloth pouch and he rolled it over in his hands, guessing at the weight of the grains of precious metal within. "You'll need to stay upcrust if you want any chance of getting eyes on Thratia, and I'm guessing ole Auntie Honding hasn't provided you with an allowance fit for something like that."

Detan winced at the mention of his auntie, the stern-faced warden of Hond Steading, a mental tally of guilt piling up for every day of the calendar he hadn't bothered to visit her. Forcing a smile back into place, he vanished the pouch into his pocket and half-bowed over upraised palms. "You are as wise as you are generous."

"Get gone, Honding, and don't contact me again until you've got a plan situated."

Detan Honding prided himself on being a man who knew not to overstay his welcome. He made himself scarce in a hurry.

Liked what you read? Good news!
You can read the whole Scorched
Continent series...

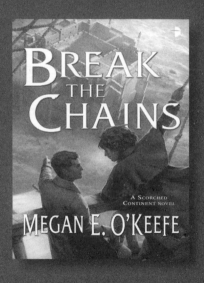

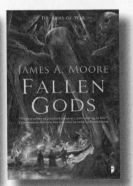
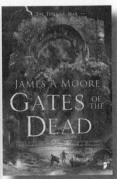

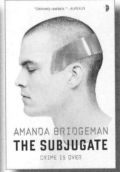

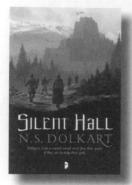

We are Angry Robot

angryrobotbooks.com

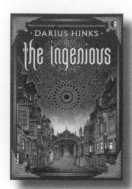
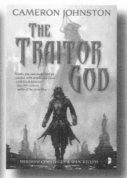

Science Fiction, Fantasy and WTF?!

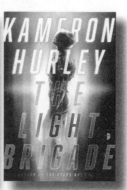

@angryrobotbooks

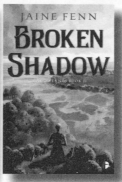
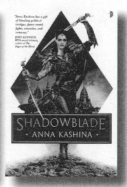

angryrobotbooks.com

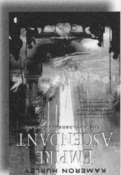

We are Angry Robot